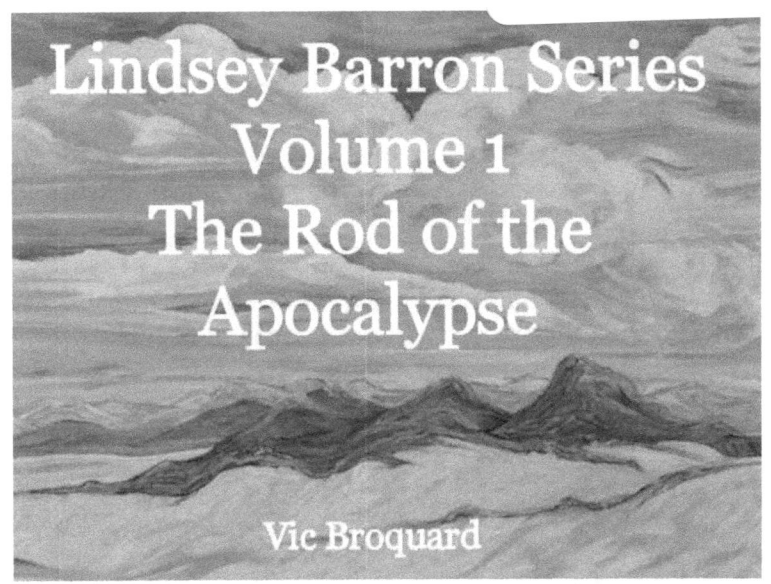

Lindsey Barron Series
Volume 1
The Rod of the
Apocalypse

Vic Broquard

Artwork by Crooked Willow Studios.

Published by:
Broquard eBooks
http://Broquard-eBooks.com
author@Broquard-eBooks.com
103 Timberlane
East Peoria, IL 61611

For Morgan and L. Ron Hubbard

Table of Contents

Chapter 1 — The Scholarship

The hot late-afternoon sun bore down on Lindsey Barron as she raced along the gravel road toward home. She had passed sixth grade and the school had locked its doors for the summer, a fact filling her with both immense relief and happiness. No longer would she have to trudge into Plano and the one room schoolhouse. Plano, population 500, spread out on the high plains of Colorado, some hundred miles east of Colorado Springs. Off all major roads, Plano had the school, a grocery store, rundown gas station, hardware store, but very little else, except the Dairy Queen run by her aunt Leona.

Commercial cattle ranches surrounded her tiny town for dozens of miles. Cradled in a ravine lay her mother's tiny ranch. Isolated, their nearest neighbors resided in Plano, other ranch homes even farther away. One of the last actions her father had done before he died was gravel the mile long road that led from Plano to their home.

Ahead of her, the Barron ranch, nearly fifty acres of useless gully land, snaked along the Nike Creek, dry most of the year. Perhaps tomorrow, she'd hike its length, collecting arrowheads and spear points. Her growing collection now boasted over a hundred, carefully arranged in the display case her father had made for her.

Lindsey sprinted swiftly along the arrow-straight road. Running had become her passion, ever since that first day of school, six years ago. Sweat streamed down both sides of her face, her long, brown hair and heavy backpack bouncing with each stride. Six minutes usually separated home from school, though she walked to school to avoid arriving soaked with sweat. Only when she was heading home could she pour on the speed. Home was her sanctuary, relief from the snide whisperings, the gooey sympathy, and the endless taunting and teasing from a number of her classmates.

Lindsey had no hands.

She was born with a perfect body, just without hands. In school, Lindsey had finally discovered why. Thalidomide.

1

When she asked her mother about it, her mom cried and explained that a chemical company had illegally disposed of the chemical up the creek from their ranch. Over time, the storage barrels rusted out, leaking into their shallow well. Lena had drunk the tainted water.

Her mom explained how fortunate Lindsey was to be perfectly healthy in all other ways, and when Lindsey finally saw images of other Thalidomide children on the school's computer, she counted herself very lucky that all she was missing were her hands.

As she ran along the road, she remembered her father, how he had loved and doted on her. She was only five when she discovered the accident, finding her father crushed beneath the overturned tractor. She'd just stood there, helplessly screaming. "I miss you daddy," she whispered to the tumbleweed beside the road as she raced past. Her breath caught as she ran.

Lindsey's feet kicked up dust onto her homemade clothes. "Poor, but proud," her mother reminded her often. Though Lena could have applied for welfare and food stamps, she flatly refused. "We may be poor, Lindsey, but we're thankful for what we have and what we earn for ourselves." Still, Lindsey would have loved to have a "real" dress like all the other girls at school, even jeans or a plaid skirt.

She remembered vividly that first day of first grade, six years ago. Her mother had walked her to school. Lindsey had shuffled into the room with twenty children ranging in ages from six to fifteen. All the other children had hands, new fashionable clothes, fine shoes, even good backpacks, and cell phones.

Terrified, she froze that first day. The kindly Mrs. Higgens had helped her with countless little things, including the total embarrassment of feeding her at lunchtime. All day long, other children teased her, taunted her, made silly rhymes about Little Miss No Hands, or stared at her as if she was somehow poisonous or full of cooties, whatever those were.

When that first day was finally over, Lindsey ran the mile home. She hadn't shown one tear at school, but now she was free and cried all the way home. "Please don't make me go back there ever again, mommy!"

She flicked a dribble of sweat from her forehead and smiled, recalling how her mother comforted her. "There, there, Lindsey. Remember: be proud of what and who you are. I'm very proud of you, my dear, and your father would be too. I'll make you a promise. When the snows come, the drifts will be too deep for you to walk to school. So while snow covers the road, you can stay home and I'll be your teacher. How's that?" That was perfect. At least half of the school year, Lindsey wouldn't have to suffer the endless teasing or the sickening sympathy of others.

She glanced at the ends of her arms and sighed. Writing caused her major problems in terms of speed. She'd insisted on learning how to write with her arms, yet she was very slow at it. At home during the winter, no one saw that she took an hour to do what her classmates did in five minutes.

Life on their ranch was difficult, too. If Lena and Lindsey worked hard, they were able to make ends meet. There was no money left over for a TV, computer, or cell phones. Their only outside contact with the rest of the world was through the radio that her father had bought her for her fifth birthday. Even without hands, she could easily operate her radio.

This hot early summer day, Lindsey raced on down the gravel road towards home and freedom from her classmates. She had a whole summer to herself and her mother. Freedom!

Ahead, she saw their barn, the corral with her small quarter horse, Betsy, looking up at her. Mom would be out in the gullies with the cattle, since it was nearly noon. As she reached the log rail fence that her father had built around the outer edge of their homestead, she spied a calico cat sitting on one of the wooden, split-rail fence logs. Breathing deeply, she stopped to look at this new arrival.

"Hello, cat. Are you lost? This is the Barron ranch. I haven't seen you around here before. It's pretty hot sitting out on the fence. I bet you're thirsty. Are you thirsty, little cat? I sure am. Come on. I'll get you a cold drink of water." She gently picked up the cat, cradling it in her arms, and walked on up to the front of her home, where she gently lowered the calico onto her porch. With effort, she took off her book bag and sat it by the door.

"I'd pet you, kitty, but—oh well." She stroked it gently with her forearms. It purred. "Okay, let's get you and me a drink and then I'll show you to Betsy. She's my horse over there. If you need a home, this is a fine place. We have lots of mice in the barn." The cat tagged Lindsey to the water trough. Years ago, she operated the pump handle by using both of her arms, rather clumsily. Now however, the handle went up and down, worked by invisible hands. Her invisible hands lifted up the tin cup from its metal hanger at the side of the pump and soon it filled with cold, clear water.

The cat sat up straight and blinked at her as if surprised. Lindsey laughed. "I bet you've never seen anything like that before, cat. It started in the spring, just after my seventh birthday when the spring thunderstorms hit. You see, I love to sit on our large porch and watch the sky show. That year, when the lightning arced from cloud to cloud, I felt energy flow at the ends of my arms, strange tingling sensations. Then, I found little arcs, like miniature lightning bolts, reaching from the ends of my arms to wherever I pointed." Using her arms, she took a drink, showing the cat that it was safe to drink and then floated the cup down to the ground. She didn't trust lowering it with her arms and doing it this way wouldn't startle the cat, she thought.

While the cat graciously accepted the drink, Lindsey sat on the porch step. "I didn't know what to make of it at first. Slowly I discovered that I could make things happen around the ranch. One day, when I was milking the cows, I began using imaginary hands instead of my arms. Next, I discovered that I could somehow levitate and move the silver milk pails. I spent hours seeing if I could make a pencil move and write for me, and one night, the pencil began moving at my command!" The cat looked up from the cup amazed and Lindsey giggled.

"When I showed my mother what I could do, she said, 'Lindsey! That's fabulous! You must have a bit of magical powers in you!' Did you know, cat, that the world was full of wizards and witches? I listen to the news on my radio every night to gather information on the magical happenings. I'll bet you didn't know that at least ten percent of the people in the US were wizards or witches, living in harmony for the last hundred years."

When the cat had its fill, it sat primly down and began licking its paws, head bowing up and down as if nodding to her. It was a scorcher day, already in the high nineties and Lindsey didn't mind sitting a little longer before chores.

"I heard marvelous reports of how a wizard rescued a small boy who'd fallen down a deep mineshaft, levitating him up some hundred feet to safety. One girl had been thrown from a horse and broken her back. The healing witches in Denver completely healed her. Then, there was the big fiasco at the New Stapleton International Airport. The new mechanical baggage handling system was a total failure with passenger's baggage routinely damaged or put on wrong flights. A wizard volunteered to repair the system. One day later, the baggage system worked."

Lindsey paused and looked down at the ends of her arms as she thought of another magical miracle, one that hit close to home. The cat stopped bathing as if waiting for her to continue. "Last year, a child's hand got caught in a corn picker and was so mangled it had to be removed. His parents took him to the Denver Department of Magical Healing and a week later, he'd grown a new hand!" She sighed as the cat rubbed against her legs. "I know my mother would give anything to do the same for me, but I didn't ask her about it. We'd never be able to afford it."

She reached down and patted the cat's soft coat, cheering up a little with the company. "Of course, at school, when I made the pencils do the writing for me, the other kids teased me even harder, calling me a witch. I realized my classmates were slightly afraid of me, worried I'd turn them into toads or snakes. As much as their taunting hurts me, cat, I've no desire to turn them into toads—or worse!"

Lindsey laughed and picked the cat up again. "Miss Calico—that's what I'm calling you until I can think of a proper name—this here is Betsy, my mare. She's a quarter horse, you know, but I expect you see her as a really big animal, don't you? Why don't I show you the barn? I should do some chores so mom doesn't have to do them later, and you can watch me. Maybe you'll see a mouse. Come on, follow me." She let the calico walk along behind her.

Feeling free from school, Lindsey tore through the chores. In the mornings, she fed the chickens, gathered up eggs, and milked their two cows. Afternoons, she cared for Betsy, a gift from her mother when she was seven. At twelve, she was quite the horsewoman and assisted her mother with the cattle on their ranch.

The calico cat hopped up onto a horizontal support beam and sat there while Lindsey went about her tasks, as if interested in what the human was doing. Several times, Lindsey stopped to pet her new friend. Then, she heard hoof beats approaching. "That'll be mom. Come on, Miss Calico. You can meet mom and she'll fix us both something to eat. How about a slice of cheese or a saucer of cold milk? It's fresh from the cows this morning, the real deal. Come on."

Outside the barn, Lena rode up and dismounted. She was thirty-seven with blue eyes and long, brown hair tied back in a ponytail. She wore homespun clothing identical to Lindsey's, made herself during the long, cold winters. "Hi Lindsey. School's out. Did you pass? In seventh grade next fall?"

"Yep, I passed. Look what I found sitting on our fence when I got home! Miss Calico. I think she's lost. Could she have walked a whole mile from Plano mom? I bet she's hungry. Can I give her a bit of cheese and milk? She won't each much."

"Sure, dear. Next, you'll be asking if you can keep her. We already have three barn cats, so what's one more, eh? She's rather pretty, isn't she? Come on inside."

Lindsey picked up Miss Calico and followed her mother, opening the door with her illusionary hands. By now, her mom was quite comfortable with her unusual skills. They often wondered aloud where Lindsey could have inherited them. Neither her mom nor dad had any trace of magical skill.

Her mother poured a small pudding dish with milk and Lindsey carefully carried it to the table in her arms. While Lena made sandwiches, Lindsey asked, "Mom, tell me again how you met dad." Her mother had told her the story countless times before, and she loved hearing it again as much as her mom loved telling it. Miss Calico licked the milk while Lindsey sat at the table, awaiting her lunch.

Lena brought a plate of liver sausage sandwiches to the table along with two glasses of milk. "If you feed yourself, I'll tell you again," her mother teased her. Ever since she discovered that she could make her invisible hands work, she'd been able to feed herself, relieving Lena from this awkward task.

"Fourteen years ago now—golly how time has flown. I was struggling to make a go of the ranch, and one summer's day, this young man in his middle twenties came walking down the dirt road up toward the house. He was tall and handsome, black moustache and the most enchanting green eyes. You have his eyes, you know. Anyway, he said he was looking for work and heard I might need a ranch hand. I was desperate in those days so I took him on. He carried nothing but a carpetbag with some clothes and personal things in it. I figured he was down on his luck as well."

"Right away, I could tell he'd never worked on a ranch, but he worked hard and was a very fast learner. You take after him, Lindsey. Anyway, he was so charming, so kind, and so romantic. Do you know he used to pick wild flowers each day for me?"

"Yes, I remember too, mom. He'd always bring in a fresh bunch as we sat down to breakfast, didn't he?"

Lena sighed. "Yes, Sam was the finest man I've ever known. He'd be so proud of you, Lindsey, seventh grade this fall!" Lindsey smiled; she longed for one more hug from her father, knowing it would never come.

Just then, Lindsey dropped her sandwich and her mom gasped. Miss Calico began growing in size right before their eyes! Lindsey blinked and saw the cat was looking more like a person, and then a woman appeared where the cat had been sitting! She wore a fashionable calico-colored print dress, her blonde hair tied in a bun, and she had pale, blue eyes.

"Forgive my sudden appearance. I'm Loretta Lasgrove, a Magic School Seeker from the Arthur Bradbury School of

Magic. You can call me Lottie, though, everyone does. Lindsey, thank you for your kindness today. I was quite thirsty. It was a long trip here. Am I correct in assuming that you're Mrs. Lena Barron and this is Lindsey Barron?" She held out her hand to Lena.

Lena gaped and mechanically shook Lottie's hand. Lindsey exclaimed, "Wow! A real wizard, mom, right here in our house!" Lindsey didn't offer her arm, no one but her dad had ever dared shake her handless arm. Lottie, however, took hold of her right arm with both her hands and shook Lindsey's arm, surprising her.

"Yes, I'm Lena. I don't understand. Why should a wizard come here? Are you lost?"

"Witch, if you please. Men are wizards; we women are called witches. As I said, I'm a School Seeker." She must have seen the confusion in our eyes because she hastily explained, "A School Seeker is responsible for finding new fall-term students for our magic school, Bradbury's in this case. I traipse all over eastern Colorado. Most candidates are easily found in the large towns and cities. So very few are out here on the high plains. Had a devil of a time finding Plano; it's not on many maps. No matter. Anyway, Lena, by now you've probably realized that your daughter, Lindsey, displays quite a bit of magical talent."

"No, not unless, well, yes. I don't know what I think," Lena stammered. "I thought so, but then I wondered if her 'special' skills were a result of her birth defect. I suppose that doesn't make any sense, does it?"

"I've been watching her for an hour now and believe me, Lindsey is most remarkable. She has an amazing command of magic already, simply amazing. For whatever reason, Lindsey is very blessed with magical skills, which should be nurtured and trained. In six years, she should be a most powerful witch. I'd like to offer her a chance. It's my hope that Lindsey will come to Arthur Bradbury's School of Magic this fall. This is one of the best magic schools in the country. We have top instructors and excellent facilities."

Lindsey's eyes popped open, while Lena sighed, and said, "I guess I've suspected she had magical talent, and I want to give her every opportunity she deserves, but I have no money to pay for this special school. It's all that I can do to keep us both alive. We don't have anything of value and the ranch is pretty much worthless too."

"I understand, Lena, but money isn't a problem. Each year, we grant a full six-year scholarship to the most deserving young students who could not otherwise afford Bradbury's. It gives me the greatest of pleasure to announce to both of you that Lindsey Barron is this year's recipient of the Bradbury Scholarship for Apprentice Wizards and Witches!"

"We don't take charity," Lena protested with a glance at Lindsey. She bit her lip.

"I'm sorry, this isn't charity. This is an *academic* full scholarship. Lindsey has *earned* this scholarship by her performance in her school and the skills she's already learned on her own. We are most proud to reward her scholastic achievements, Lena."

"Oh, well, then that *is* different." Lena nodded thoughtfully. "Still, we can't afford it. We've no money for her clothes, books, food, and whatever else a witch might need. I can barely afford to send her to our simple Plano school."

"Oh dear me, no, no, no. You misunderstand me. I said a *full* scholarship. This includes her room and board, her books, supplies, a clothing allowance, even a small personal expense allowance for her to spend as she sees fit. Oh yes, even transportation is provided to and from your ranch. She'll need absolutely no dollars while at Bradbury's, as long as she keeps her grades up, mind you." She smiled and arched her eyebrow at Lindsey. "You see, this will even save you some money, since you won't need to provide anything for her for the next six years. Once she graduates, she'll be a top quality witch, capable of earning quite a lot of money for her services."

"You mean it will cost us nothing at all?" asked Lena in complete disbelief.

"Well, not exactly. She'll have to live nine months of the year on the Bradbury campus in our dorms, but we allow our students to return home for Christmas break. She'll also be returning home for the summer months as well."

Lena seemed to look at Lindsey in a new light, but then

another dark cloud came over her face. "But she, well, she, ah, Lindsey has no hands. She needs so much special care. Surely this is going to cause her immense, if not insurmountable problems. She came home from her first day at school in Plano in complete tears. I know she endures so much teasing that she dreads going there at all. Who will look after her needs, like brushing her hair, the simple things that require hands?" Lindsey could tell that her mother was trying not to embarrass her, but they both well knew how much help she required.

Lottie replied happily, "Well, were we not all teased at one time in school? I was called Miss Ugly Wart all through my first six grades. I had this ugly wart right on the tip of my nose in those days—most embarrassing. Yet, Lindsey has managed to perform very well in school in spite of the taunts. As far as her needs go, the Board of Governors took that into consideration. Her special needs will be met by very caring, loving people. I assure you that her scholarship wasn't awarded in haste or without proper thought."

She continued, "Now with that settled, the real question falls to Lindsey."

The School Seeker waited as Lena drew a deep breath and faced Lindsey. "Dear, would you like to go to Bradbury's School of Magic?"

"Wow! Yes, yes!" she replied. After a moment, she held up her arms, her eyes wide. "So that's what I'm doing when I use my invisible hands?"

Lottie smiled. "Yes, dear child. You have an impressive magical talent within you. At Bradbury's you will learn so many more fabulous things."

"Wow! Like turning into a cat? Like you did?"

"Yes, even so, if you choose to learn that bit of magic. Now then, school begins on the first day of September. However, new students are obliged to attend Orientation Week. You'll report to Bradbury's on August 24. The term ends on the last day of May. On June 1, she'll return here."

"Okay, but where is this school? How does she get there?" Lena asked.

"The school is not on any map. We take the safety and security of our students *seriously*. There are many enchantments on the school so that no one can easily find it. Lindsey will be safer at Bradbury's than she is here, though she is quite safe here. Now, there is a free Magical Bus that will come directly to your door to pick you up on August 23. Let me enter you into the bus route." Lottie waved her wand and a handheld computer appeared in her hands. She punched several buttons in rapid succession.

"But I can't hold a wand, Miss Lottie." Lindsey suddenly recognized a horrible problem.

"Don't worry, Lindsey, something will be worked out for you, I'm sure. Now, it looks like you will be the second passenger picked up that day. The bus should arrive here at ten o'clock sharp. Be ready, we can't hold the bus up. There are twenty other students that we must also pick up on this trip."

Lena wrote the information down and asked, "What should she bring with her? What should I pack?"

"Oh, just little personal items, nothing bigger than will fit in a backpack—hairbrush, photos, that sort of thing." She waved her wand. A stylish plaid dress materialized, along with undergarments, socks, and a pair of nice, black shoes, slip-ons, without aces. "Here are your traveling clothes. During Orientation Week, you will receive more clothing and your official robes. You see, you need not worry, my dear. It's all taken care of in your full scholarship."

Lindsey gasped! She'd never owned a real dress before. "It's so beautiful!" she exclaimed, tears filling her eyes. Even her mother's eyes watered.

"Well, a beautiful dress for a beautiful young woman, I always say," Lottie replied.

"Now then," she switched to a more serious tone. "We must determine which of Bradbury's five dorm halls will be best for you, Lindsey. We group like-minded, like-personalities together—makes for a better living arrangement. To help us, I have this little survey for you to take." She waved her wand and a four-page test booklet appeared along with a marking stylus.

"You just mark your choice for each question. Answer each question honestly. Your mother and I will be outside so you can have peace and quiet in which to take the survey.

Come on, Lena, how about showing me around your ranch?"
Lena and Lottie went outside, leaving Lindsey to take the
survey.

At first, Lindsey tried to open the booklet with her arms
but found that was too difficult, so she used her invisible
hands. Holding the marker in her arms, she began. *What is
your favorite color? Yellow, red, brown, blue, black?* She
marked "yellow." *Are you cheerful? Yes or No?* Lindsey
marked "yes." *Are you an important person? Yes or No?* She
marked "no." On she went, answering one hundred questions
about herself.

At the precise time Lindsey finished marking the last
question, Lena and Lottie re-entered the home. Lindsey
wondered if Lottie somehow knew she'd just finished. "Now
we will compute the results," Lottie explained, again waving
her wand. The test booklet disappeared in a flash and a small
piece of paper floated back down to the table. Lottie picked it
up. "Ah, just as I suspected. Lindsey, you will be staying in the
Yellow Hall."

Lindsey and her mom shared a blank look, so Lottie
explained, "The Yellow Hall is for those wizards and witches
who are brave and fearless, prefer thought as a means of
solving a problem, are cheerful and like light and air. In
contrast, the Blue Hall is for those who love water, who are
compassionate and caring and believe that emotions should be
used to solve problems. Many in the Blue Hall are healers,
succoring those in need. Now the Red Hall is fiery for those
who believe passions and love is what rules, that hot emotions
should be used to solve problems." Lottie counted the halls off
on her fingers as she went through her recitation. "The Brown
Hall represents the earth. Here are those who love to grow
things, both plants and animals. They are stalwart and
dependable to a fault. They believe honest efforts solve life's
problems. Those in the Black Hall stand for pure logic. They
see themselves as all-important, though some are foolhardy
and take risks to solve problems. Might and strength—effort,
in other words—is their hallmark." Lottie nodded at them
both. "I suspected that Lindsey would be in the Yellow Hall.
Myself, I was in the Blue Hall.

"Well that's good. I sure wouldn't want her staying with those foolhardy, might-makes-right, children," Lena commented.

Lottie smiled. "Now, I really must be getting along. I've three other young people to visit yet today. I'm sure that Lindsey has a million questions. That's what Orientation Week is for—to get all those answered." She waved her wand and conjured up a glossy folder. "In the meantime, here's an information packet for you to peruse over the summer. Once again, let me congratulate you, Lindsey! You should be proud of your academic achievements, and I look forward to hearing how well you do during your next six years at Bradbury's.

Lottie rose to leave. "It's been a pleasure meeting both of you." She shook Lena's hand and then Lindsey's arm. Lena showed her to the door, and once outside, Lottie waved her wand and said something. Poof. She disappeared.

Once the shock of Lottie's sudden magical departure wore off, Lindsey jumped up and down! "Mom! I get to go to magic school! Wow!"

Lena gave her daughter a long, loving hug. "If anyone deserves to learn more about magic, it's you," she said. "This scholarship will give you what I couldn't."

"You spent hours with me, mom." Lindsey hugged her back. "All those hours you patiently helped me with homework paid off."

"I'm going to miss you something terrible come fall. I never expected you to leave the nest so soon. If only Sam were still here. Now let's see what you look like in your new school clothes, Lindsey," her mother suggested, just as excited over the "real" clothes.

"Mom, I'll never manage getting myself dressed in these," Lindsey admitted when Lena finished.

"I suppose they also know that and will have someone there to help you, dear," her mother answered. Lindsey pirouetted around a bit. Lena, holding her hands to her face and wiping a tear, added, "You look like a little princess, Lindsey. I'm so proud of you. Your dad would be too. Just look at you!" Lindsey beamed; she felt like a real person just now— well, dressed like one anyway.

Chapter 2—The Bradbury Magical Bus Ride

August 23 finally arrived, hot and dry as usual, here on the high plains. "Is it ten o'clock yet?" asked Lindsey for the tenth time. She was very nervous; she couldn't sit still. Dressed in her new plaid dress with the Yellow Hall patch on her white blouse prominently displayed, she paced the living room once more. Lena had her school backpack filled and ready to go, though it was nearly empty. Lindsey had insisted on bringing her radio and her favorite family photo, showing all three of them, taken on her fifth birthday.

"Not yet. Do you have to go to the bathroom, Lindsey? You don't know how long you'll be on the bus or whether there's a restroom on it or who might help you if there is," Lena fretted, more worried than anything else. Her little girl was about to leave for some distant school, not even on the Colorado maps. She was so helpless, so dear, and so cute in her new dress. Multitudes of conflicting feelings and emotions raced through her mother's mind.

"No. I'm so nervous mom. What if they don't like me there? What if I'm too dumb to learn? What if. . ."

"Dear, you just do your very best. That's all your father and I would want. Hold your head up proudly and do your very best. If it's not good enough, then so be it. I don't know anything about this magic stuff and I don't think your father did either. If it's too hard for you, just ask them to return you home to me. I love you so much, Lindsey. I'm going to miss you terribly." She hugged her daughter tightly, but could not stop her tears from wetting her face yet again.

"Come, it's nearly time," Lena finally said. "Let's go sit on the porch and wait for the bus to come, shall we?" The two went outside into the baking heat and sat on the porch swing that her father had built for them.

At precisely ten o'clock, as both were looking down the long, straight gravel road that led here from Plano, they heard a soft popping sound and saw the Bradbury School Bus suddenly appear in front of them. Neither had seen it coming down the road to their ranch home. Both were startled by its sudden appearance. "Cool!" exclaimed Lindsey, when she realized this was her bus. It was hard to miss. Across the front banner scrolled "To Bradbury's School of Magic." The school logo was also plastered across both sides of the yellow school bus as well as above the rear emergency door.

Yet this was not your ordinary school bus, rather it looked more like a double decker Greyhound bus, a mixture of a London two-decker and a Greyhound coach. A large cargo bay below held the students' gear. Two stories of seats meant this bus could carry at least a hundred passengers. While the two stared at the yellow bus, a young man in his twenties stepped out to greet them.

He had long blonde hair, tied back in a ponytail, and blue eyes with a small blonde moustache. As he smiled at the two, Lindsey saw that he was missing his two front teeth. "Bradbury School of Magic. You mus' be Lindsey Barron. Los' 'em in a rodeo," he winked. "Jimmy Jones, a' your service." He bowed to Lindsey and shook Lena's hand. "I'll pu' your bag below, ma'am. You can hop aboard. 'Ake any sea' you like. Only one o'her is aboard. Plen'y 'o pick up 'oday."

To Lena, he said, "I'll 'ake good care of her. Be 'here before noon, jus' in 'ime for lunch." He smiled reassuringly to Lena, who waved farewell to Lindsey, as her young daughter climbed up the steps into the huge bus. She saw another young girl her own age sitting near the rear and walked back towards her.

She was also dressed in a similar plaid dress with a Yellow Hall symbol on her blouse as well. Lindsey figured she must be in her dorm as well. "Hi, I'm Amanda, Amanda Whitewater," the girl said, offering her hand. "Oh my!" Amanda noticed that Lindsey had no hands at all and felt ashamed that she had not noticed it sooner before she made a fool of herself. To Amanda's surprise, Lindsey extended her right arm for a handshake, which a flushing Amanda shook ever so gently, as if afraid she might somehow hurt Lindsey.

Amanda had very brownish skin, thick, long black hair,

heavy black eyebrows, and thick lips. Lindsey knew that she must be a Native American. "Hi, I'm Lindsey Barron." She sat beside Amanda, but noticed that Amanda had her seat belt fastened. "Can you possibly fix my seat belt, Amanda? I don't know how they work. I've never seen them before."

"Sure, it pulls across you like so and this metal end goes in here," she explained. "Do they hurt? I mean your hands, er, your arms there?" Amanda asked, extremely curious. "What happened to you?"

"No, not at all. I was born this way. Are you an Indian?" asked Lindsey, just as curious about her new companion.

"All ready 'o go?" asked Jimmy, who had climbed back into the driver's seat and closed the door. "Sea' bel' fas'ened?"

"Yes, sir," Lindsey called out.

"Righ'o, I'll jus' punch in the nex' s'op in the Geosa' Loca'er and we'll be off," he explained.

"Wow! Cool!" exclaimed Lindsey, as the bus began to move.

"Full blooded Apache," Amanda explained. "I've got two older brothers who are also in Yellow Hall. Jim is third year and Tom is fourth year; they will be coming along next week. We are from Arapahoe. It's right by the Kansas border, so we are always picked up first. Was that your ranch?" asked Amanda in mild interest.

"Yes, just mom and me. My dad died when I was five. Did you see my horse, Betsy?"

"Yes, quarter horse mare, right? You mean you can ride, er, like with no hands?"

"Oh yes, I can even get the hackamore on her myself, but mom's got to put her saddle on for me. I can't manage that, though I often ride bareback when mom is off riding the herd. Do you have a horse too?"

"Oh yes. We've many horses. We're Indians, you know. Cool! Look at the country flying by! Tom said this would be cool! He's right!" Indeed, the countryside flew by them at a terrific speed.

Amanda explained, "Tom told me all about the bus. They have a GPS locator up front and the driver has the coordinates for each stop all programmed into the bus system.

It goes automatically from stop to stop. That way, Jimmy can't forget to pick up someone. He's kind'a hard to understand though. Without his front teeth, he can't say his 't's properly. He ought to get someone to fix them magically, you know. Tom is always telling me that. Now I agree, don't you?"

"I suppose so. We must be going terribly fast!" Lindsey commented as the hills flashed by the window.

"Yes, Tom says that the bus is running in something called magical twisted space. That way, we can't run into anything, like those cars and trucks. We sort of pass right through them somehow." After a pause, Amanda asked, "Are you going to Bradbury's on a scholarship? Tom said that we would have a full scholarship student starting this fall."

"Yes, I am. It's just mom and me and we couldn't afford any of this ourselves. This is the first real dress I've ever owned! Mom has always woven and made my dresses before now. Say, are you nervous? I'm really nervous."

"Yes, a little, though for years Tom and Jim have been telling me all about Bradbury's. Oh look, we're stopping again." The tall water tower said "Aroya;" it was another very small, high plains town. One twelve year old, curly haired blonde girl climbed aboard. She wore a Blue Hall patch and came back to join Lindsey and Amanda, sitting in the seat next to theirs.

"Hi, I'm Jennifer Toggs, Blue Hall. I see you are both Yellow Hall. Oh dear me! You, you have no hands! Oh how absolutely dreadful!"

"Hi, I'm Lindsey Barron from Plano, and this is Amanda Whitewater from Arapahoe. I know, birth defect, born without them," Lindsey explained with a sigh. She figured she'd be explaining this repeatedly for the next few days. While she felt awful about having to "explain" her predicament when she first went to school in Plano, she had not had to explain this to others for the last five years. Suddenly, here she was having to meet all these new kids and to explain it all again. She wished she could just say it once and be done with it, but she knew that she was facing this little embarrassment at least a hundred more times, maybe more. She sighed again.

"Well, you should go to the Department of Magical Healing in Denver and see if they can grow new hands for you, at least that is what I think should be done. I'm only a first year Blue Hall student. I'll ask around for you and see if it's possible. It must just be so horrible to, well, not have any. I'll help you as much as possible," Jennifer declared flatly. "You can just call me Jen, by the way, everyone does, you know."

"Thanks Jen, but there's only mom and me, and we can't possibly afford to do it. We don't have very much money you see. I've managed to get by twelve years now, but I sure don't know how I'm supposed to hold a wand. We'll be getting wands, I assume. The School Seeker who came to me had one."

"Oh yes, we'll be getting our first wands—during Orientation Week when we get our first year supplies and books. My older brother, Henry, he's a third year Blue Hall student now; he told me that's when we get them. Golly, Lindsey, how are you going to hold your wand? This is just awful. A witch has to be able to use her wand somehow. I'll talk to our House Mother about it for you."

Lindsey noticed that the bus was now scooting along US 40 heading northwest. Yet in a matter of minutes, it stopped once more—Limon, the water tower announced. Another twelve year old girl with short curly brown hair climbed onboard. She had a Yellow Hall patch on her blouse as well. Amanda saw the patch and called out, "We Yellow Halls are back here." She smiled and joined the small group at the rear. "I'm Amanda Whitewater. This is Jen Toggs, Lindsey Barron."

"Hi, I'm Kathy Townsend. Pleased to meet you." She shook hands with Amanda and Jen, however, her eyes opened wide when she reached for Lindsey's hand.

Lindsey stuck her arm out for a shake anyway and bypassed Kathy's surprise. "Hi, birth defect. Pleased to meet you Kathy." Gently, Kathy shook her arm and sat near by the small group.

"So you were born without any hands, Lindsey? That's a tough one. Still, you must be qualified if you were chosen to come to Bradbury's. A Seeker is not known for making mistakes in recruitment, at least that's what I've heard. Say, you must be attending on the full scholarship. Loretta

18

Lasgrove said that there would be one in the Yellow Hall this year."

"Yes, but how did you know that? Just because I don't have hands?" Lindsey asked, slightly annoyed.

"I didn't mean to offend you, Lindsey. It is just logical that's all. If your family had money, surely they would have taken you to the Department of Magical Healing in Denver and had new hands grown for you. Ergo, your family must not be able to afford it, so the scholarship follows."

"Yes, I see. It does make sense, though does everyone know that the Department of Magical Healing can grow new hands?"

"Well, at least in magical families they do. I don't know about norms though," Kathy replied conservatively. "Norm is the term we use for people who have no magical abilities. I'm sure that you will do just fine, Lindsey, really."

Jen spoke up, "Well, I'm going to check into whether it's possible for the Department of Magical Healing actually to grow her some hands. It is just awful, having no hands. I couldn't live that way."

Lindsey wanted perhaps just to disappear for a while; she squirmed in her seat. Fortunately, the bus stopped again, and all attention shifted to outside. "Colorado Springs," Jen announced. Lindsey had never seen such a large city before and stared at the sights.

A large number of students clambered aboard. First onboard were two much older students. Amanda giggled. "That's my brother, Tom, and his girlfriend, Sandy Rains. They are fourth year Yellow Halls and are our Floor Monitors." Sandy had long, straight, mousy brown hair, a dark complexion, and deep brown eyes. Tom looked like his younger sister with his long black hair tied in a ponytail. Both came back to join the Yellow Hall first year students.

"Hi there. We are your Floor Monitors this year. Tom Whitewater," he said in a quiet voice.

"I'm Sandy Rains, Arapaho full blood. I'm here to help you first year girls learn about Bradbury's, while Tom does the same with the boys. I hope you have some, Tom," she winked at him. So far, there was none for him. Sandy shook hands with her charges, checking each off her list. "Ah, you must be Lindsey. Well, you're my special needs charge, that's obvious. I was told to expect one. Well, Lindsey, you must be good to be chosen for Bradbury's, so you can count on me for help. You need anything, just give a holler. Excuse me a minute, I need to make sure everyone is accounted for at this stop." Sandy went toward the front, checking off names on a list.

Now Lindsey could see some of the others climbing aboard. One was Janis Smelter, a first year Red Hall student. She had a very pretty face and wore bright red lipstick. Her long nails were painted in a matching shade. She sat by herself a couple rows in front of the Yellow Hall group. Now four very noisy first year students climbed onboard; three were boys. The taller boy was the leader. As they took their seats at the very front of the bus, the taller boy stood and said, "Hi everyone. Deiter Cross here, Black Hall. We're the best. Any Black Hall's back there? No, I didn't think so. Anyone seen our 'special needs' student? We heard that we have one this year, rotten luck."

"She's back there, Yellow Hall, Deiter," Sandy replied. Lindsey again wanted just to disappear, and she sat a little lower in her seat.

"Oh yeah? Let's see her," Deiter swaggered and walked back towards the rear group. His three companions followed at his heels.

"Hi, I'm Lindsey Barron," she said politely, but didn't offer her arm; she had an instant dislike of Deiter.

"Oh brother, Yellow Hall has a real winner here—no hands! Well, Lindsey, don't go asking us in the Black Hall for any help. Wizards and witches have to be able to do everything for themselves. Obviously, you can't. Some witch you will make!"

"Peaches Colt," his girl companion announced. "Yeu, no hands. How awful. Well, you won't make much of a witch at all. Silly wasting all that scholarship money on the likes of you." She tossed her shoulder length black hair and returned to the front of the bus.

The second boy angrily said, "Loyd Armstrong, just stay the heck away from me." He followed Peaches to the front.

"Bill, Bill Bracken. Spooky, that's what I say. No hands. Spooky!" he followed after Loyd. Deiter just glared at Lindsey and followed Bill.

Lindsey suppressed a tear, wiping her right eye with her shoulder. "Don't listen to those Black Hall creeps! Black Hall's are the most self-centered idiots in the school. I don't know why they are even allowed into Bradbury's," Sandy said sympathetically. She had to buckle her seat belt in a rush; the bus began moving once more.

Tom deftly changed the subject. "Next stop is Pueblo. One of my new charges is getting on there." Soon, the bus stopped in the quaint town.

An older boy of Mexican descent climbed on first. He had well-oiled black hair and eyes. "Hey, hi Tom! Got my younger brother with me. Come on, Emilio; here's your Floor Monitor. Tom, Emilio."

Emilio also had very black hair and eyes and a darkish skin color. He looked somewhat bored, Lindsey thought. "Hola, Emilio Lopez," he said in a monotone. Quickly, Tom introduced his fellow Yellow Hall first years.

One by one, Emilio shook hands with his fellow students. When he got to Lindsey, he stopped. For an instant, his boredom left him. "Well, that must be a bit of a bother for you, Lindsey. Downright annoying. Ah well, such is life you know. If you need some help, just ask, Senorita. My brother, Francisco, is the fourth year Brown Hall Floor Monitor. Way too much work, if you ask me."

"See you around, Tom," said Francisco, "I've got to see to my new first years. Rodrigo Hermez there—he looks utterly lost." The two boys chuckled. Indeed, Rodrigo just stood in the middle of the bus looking around. Francisco made him take a seat and buckle up. The bus rolled off once more.

Both Sandy and Tom began counting heads. Evidently, their counts agreed, Sandy announced, "Only one more to go. Must be the Canon City girl, Peggy West." She rolled up her paper list.

Tom concurred. "I bet you she will be wearing that gaudy red lipstick too."

Sandy giggled. "No bet. It's a sure thing." Looking at the

bewildered faces of the four first year Yellow Halls, she added, "Oh, the Red Hall girls have this thing going where they all insist on wearing the brightest, gaudiest red lipstick they can find. Looks garish, if you ask me. Besides, when I was twelve, I sure didn't want to mess around wearing lipstick."

Tom teased her, "Yes, but you do now, Sandy." Her face flushed slightly.

"Well, I'm older now, fifteen, Tom. I think twelve is just too young." Shortly, the bus stopped in Canon City. A young girl with short blonde hair climbed on board. She wore a deep blue eye shadow, very overdone, and cherry red lipstick. Yet, Lindsey thought that at any moment she would begin to cry. Peggy hastily moved on past the Black Hall crowd. Janis called out to her, and Peggy joined her Red Hall fellow student.

"Now comes the long haul, first years," Tom explained. "We've picked up all you first years on our route and will be making a bee line to Bradbury's, but it's nearly half a state away. We've got an hour to kill, but the scenery is gorgeous."

He and Sandy settled down beside each other, their arms around each other's shoulders. She leaned her head on his shoulder and the two whispered away.

The mountains and valleys were splendid. Lindsey had never been to the mountains before. She stared at the scenery in wonderment.

Meanwhile up front, Deiter began chanting a rhyme.

"There once was a girl named Lindsey,
She had no hands you see,
What kind of a witch will she be,
If she cannot hold her wand you see."

Now his three companions joined in. Sandy jumped up, her wand at the ready. "Deiter, that's quite enough. One more word and you all will spend Orientation Week in detention!"

"Whoa, you scare me!" Deiter taunted Sandy, but quickly sat down, careful not to press his luck too far. He knew about detentions and certainly didn't want to spend this week doing such mundane chores, so utterly beneath his dignity.

Lindsey was in tears, however. "Don't listen to that idiot Deiter," said Emilio.

"Yes, he's full of his own, well, I won't say a dirty word,"

Kathy added. Amanda merely wiped Lindsey's eyes for her.

Lindsey sniffed. "I got teased and taunted every day in Plano. You'd think I'd be used to it by now, but I'm not."

"Well, look at the mountains," suggested Amanda. Lindsey did so and soon forgot about the taunts.

The hour passed too quickly. Jimmy called out, "Bradbury's School of Magic." The bus stopped before a pair of massive wooden gates set in a twenty-foot tall stone wall, reminiscent of an ancient castle wall.

Sandy spoke loudly for the benefit of all the first years. "Bradbury's outer walls are heavily enchanted to protect all of us inside. There is no way to fly over the walls or climb them. This is the main gate, which leads to the parking lot, where you will see many of the professor's cars. The shape of these outer walls is that of a pentagram. Inside, the buildings also form an enormous pentagram. In the very center is the pentagram dorm building where we students all live. Each side is a different hall color. Black Hall is at the bottom of the dorm pentagram. Blue Hall is on its right, while Brown Hall lies to the left. Above Blue Hall is Yellow Hall and above Brown Hall is Red Hall. Yellow Hall and Red Hall adjoin each other. In the center of the dorm pentagram is the courtyard and the large dining hall, where we all meet and eat our meals."

The gates had already opened and the bus moved just inside. Jimmy opened the door and stepped out to begin unloading the student's bags. Tom added, "First, find your backpack from home and then find your Floor Monitor. Blue, Red, and Black Hall students, your Floor Monitors will be outside awaiting you. First, we will take you to your new dorm rooms."

Everyone began disembarking. Amanda commented to Lindsey, "Another reason to sit way back here is that the Blacks will have already gotten off, found their packs, and be on their way by the time we get off." Lindsey smiled; she'd had enough Black Hall students for one day.

Indeed, only the Yellow Hall students were still around when Lindsey finally stepped off the bus. Emilio said, "Senorita Lindsey, I suppose that you will want me to carry your pack for you?" He was still rather bored, even though he had never been here before. Lindsey wondered how he could be so detached. She was thrilled and excited beyond words.

"Oh no, see, I can manage my own pack." Lindsey slipped her arms into the pack straps and hoisted it up onto her back. With some effort, she began to get her hair out from under the pack. Without saying a word, Amanda helped her free her hair, Lindsey gave her a big smile, thankful that she had not had to ask openly for her help.

"We're standing in the parking lot. Right next to us is the Administration Hall. Normally, you will not need to visit there," Sandy explained to her first year group. "It's where the professors meet and such. None of us really knows what all goes on in that building. Please note this is the bottom left corner of the pentagrams of buildings. Straight on across this bottom in the middle of the bottom is the Infirmary. If you get sick or injured, you will be brought here. Let's hope that never happens. Now follow me; we're going to go to your dorm pentagram building first; that's where you'll be living."

Sandy and Tom led the small group; they walked past the Administration Hall and turned north or left between this two story modern looking building and the single story brick Infirmary building, which looked the least inviting of all the buildings. Lindsey thought perhaps that was meant to encourage students not to get sick or hurt.

"Here is our heated swimming pool. No swimming unless there's a lifeguard on duty. There will be a posted schedule in the dorm so you can know when you can go for a swim. Just north of the pool is our dorm pentagram building," Tom pointed out the two story, five sided building. Each side looked much like any other modern college campus dormitory, however. Each fifth was painted a different color. Lindsey saw that there would be no way she could not find the Yellow Hall, on the northwest side of this huge building.

"What's that huge thing just beyond our dorms?" asked Lindsey. The unusual open aired structure caught her eye.

"Ah, that is our stadium," Tom cheerfully replied. "It has a running track and a huge soccer field. It's where all the soccer matches are played. Each of the Halls fields a soccer team and we play each other during the year. If you are interested in trying out for the Yellow Hall soccer team, let Sandy or me know this week sometime. Honestly, Yellow Hall has not won the Bradbury Cup for the last six years straight."

"Actually, we've been in last place, Tom," Sandy grinned. "You ought to tell them that, you know."

"Who has been winning it?" asked Emilio.

"Black Hall, five years in a row now," Tom said dejectedly. "No matter. Now, you can enter the dorm at any of these doors. Just inside is a hallway that leads all around the pentagram. When it's raining, we usually head for the nearest door and walk to our hall." Today, they walked around the dorm to the northwestern side, which was canary yellow. Sandy opened the door and Tom held it for the others.

"Wow! Cool!" exclaimed Amanda as she entered the commons room. Yellow tapestries hung from the walls. Great sofas and overstuffed chairs lined the room. A stone fireplace occupied the southern wall and there were several tables and chairs.

"Here's where you can chat and play games and such. Others from the other halls are allowed in here, as long as they don't create any problems. You can visit your friends in their commons rooms as well," Sandy went on with her description. "Now the second half of this floor is the study area. In here, as you can see, we have many tables and chairs, very comfortable ones I might add. Yes, if you want to study with some friends from another hall, they are welcome in here as well. Just no noise, but whispering is allowed."

Tom walked to the doors at the far end of the study. "Pay attention to the doors. There are four sets of doors, two in here, two out there in the commons. They lead up to the sleeping quarters and down to the bathrooms. Only Yellow Hall students are allowed to pass these doors. They're magically enchanted to reject any other hall's student, so don't try to sneak them past these doors."

"Neat!" exclaimed Kathy.

"Now I'm not yet done. As you go up the doors, you'll notice the universal signs for men and women," he pointed them out rather didactically. "There's a girl's only bathroom and showers and a girl's only sleeping quarters. Likewise for

25

the guys. Kathy, you try to walk past the guy's door on your right. Go ahead; it will not hurt you, be brave."

"Do you suppose it's all right for me to try? After all, it clearly shows a guy on it," she replied rather conservatively.

"Sure, go ahead. This is just a demonstration," Tom encouraged her. Kathy walked up to the door, but nothing happened. Cautiously, she tried to open the door.

At once a loud voice bellowed, "Boy's dorm. Girls are not allowed past these doors." It continued repeating itself until she let go of the door handle and the door closed.

Everyone giggled. "So you see, boys can't enter your private areas nor can you girls sneak into the boys' area. The magical enchantments will not let your body pass." The girls continued to giggle over this. Lindsey felt she was really going to like this place.

"Okay we split up now. Girls, you follow me," Sandy said, motioning them to her. Tom led Emilio to their door.

The girls climbed up a circular stairs, which opened to a long, narrow hall. Dim gaslights provided the illumination. Along the walls were portraits. "These are former Yellow Hall wizards and witches who have become famous. There're certainly a lot of them," Sandy pointed out.

"Notice each room has a number on it. This first room here, Number One, is where I live. Anytime you need anything, especially you, Lindsey, just come and find me here. Now because you are first years, you three are in Number Two, close to me. The fourth girl is due in later this afternoon. I think she is coming from Sterling, Pam Betts. The sixth year students are all down at the far end. Lindsey, because of your needs, your door here has been enchanted for you. Just say, 'Open Please' and the door will open. The rest of you can also say it or just use the doorknob. Go ahead, Lindsey, say it."

"Oh this is so neat! Open please," Lindsey spoke with confidence. The door opened slowly for her.

"That's what I call a neat piece of magic," Sandy stated authoritatively. "Now let's go inside." All four entered the rather spacious bedroom. Two bunk beds with curtains for privacy lined two of the walls. Four dressers with mirrors and two tables with four chairs occupied the other walls. "Each of you has your own dresser. Now I'm told that Lindsey must have a bottom bunk and this dresser here."

Lindsey chuckled, "I can see why this one is mine! I can open the drawers!" Indeed, where normally small rings or knobs would be placed to open them, on hers, large, wooden bars came out four inches and then curved down four more inches. Lindsey could easily put the ends of her arms in them and pull out the drawers. She tried it and found them smooth and easy to do. "This is fantastic," she beamed, knowing that this was one less thing that she would have to depend upon others to do for her.

"Okay, deposit your packs on the bed of your choice and let's go down to the bathrooms next," Sandy explained. Presently, they entered the girl's bathroom. Such luxury Lindsey could not imagine! There were three huge bathtubs and seven shower stalls, in addition to a dozen toilets, not to mention the floor to ceiling mirrors and washbasins.

Sandy suddenly looked a little embarrassed. She just remembered something she was ordered to ask. "Lindsey, I don't mean to embarrass you, but I have to ask you this. Can you manage the baths, showers, and toilets by yourself or are you going to need help with them?"

Lindsey smiled; she knew this topic would eventually make its appearance. "If someone can help me dress and undress, I can shower or bathe myself. I just can't handle my clothes. As far as the toilet, if I'm wearing this dress and no panties, I can pee by myself, but not the other. I know; it's an awful thing to have to ask for help with, please; I'm sorry I need that kind of help." Her eyes began watering of their own accord.

Sandy heaved a sigh of relief, "Whew, that is excellent, Lindsey. I thought at first that you would need help with it all. I'm sure I won't mind helping you, Lindsey."

"I solemnly promise to help you any time you need it here," Amanda spoke up.

"Me too," Kathy added.

"Thanks, all of you. I think one of you will have to help me right now, at least pull my panties down. I need to," Lindsey didn't get to finish her sentence, all three moved to assist her. In the end, Amanda won out.

After all four finished and washed up, Sandy said, "Okay, I'm starving. It's time for lunch. Follow me and I'll show you where and how we all eat here. There is an amazing variety of choices, better than a buffet actually. Come on." She led them up to the first floor and then out into the charming courtyard, where tall plants were interspersed with wrought iron tables and chairs, rather like dozens of private bungalows. Already, several Red Hall students were eating their lunch out here in the courtyard.

They entered a set of swinging doors and Lindsey gasped at the huge dining hall, which would seat nearly six hundred at one time. "How can this be? It doesn't look this large from outside."

"Magically enchanted, it's rather huge isn't it," Sandy replied. "Up there is where the Governor and the professors dine, on that one long set of tables. As you can see, there are ten long color-coded rows for us." Already Emilio and Tom were seated at the head of the first of the yellow tables. Just behind all the tables was the buffet line. "Come on, usually there is a long line to get to the food, but this week it will be very short. Grab a tray. As we walk through the line, help yourself to what appeals to you. You can always come back for seconds and thirds; they never run out of food." She took a tray and picked up several napkins and silverware.

Lindsey went next, surprising everyone by using her magical hands to pick up the tray and the silverware as well. All three gaped at her. "I didn't know that you could do advanced, non-verbal magic and without a wand even!" exclaimed Sandy.

"Way cool!" said Amanda.

"Fantastic!" added Kathy.

"What? Am I not supposed to do this myself?" asked Lindsey, rather embarrassed with the sudden attention.

"No, that's fine, only you are using magic that we are normally taught in our sixth year here. Some never do learn it, even with their wands," Sandy answered her. "Pretty incredible, Lindsey, go for it. Just let me know when you need help, please. It's my job to help you this week and all that."

Lindsey agreed and the four walked through the buffet line. Lindsey had never seen so many different dishes laid out before her, such variety! She was used to liver sausage sandwiches. Some of the names of the dishes she could not even pronounce, let alone knew what they were. She finally settled on chicken, rice, a large helping of peas, and a bowl of applesauce. With each, she used her invisible hands to help fill her plate and pick up the bowl. When she came to the beverage line, she decided to ask Sandy to fill up a milk glass for her, the motions were slightly too tricky for her simple invisible hands and she definitely did not want to spill her milk or even worse, drop and break the glass.

Finally, she had Sandy place her tray in her arms and followed them to the yellow table. Again, she waited for Sandy to take her tray from her and sit it on the table. Sandy sat by Tom, naturally, and Lindsey sat next to her. Amanda sat across from them, beside Emilio, Kathy across from Lindsey.

Lindsey now used her invisible hands to begin eating this luxurious meal, but soon noticed all eyes were watching her. Her face reddened. "That's amazing, Lindsey!" exclaimed Tom.

"Wow! You sure do know a whole lot of magic already, Senorita Lindsey," Emilio added.

"Thanks, I do need someone to cut up my meat sometimes, but I try real hard to feed myself. I am a bit slow at it, as you can see. It is *so* embarrassing to have to have others feed me as if I was a baby. I had to, you know, for the first two years of school. I hated lunchtime. Now it is not so bad."

A little later, Sandy explained, "You can come down for breakfast anytime you want after six o'clock. Breakfasts and lunches are buffet style. Once school starts, dinners will be formal affairs—you know, all the professors will be dining with us as one huge group. It gets very noisy then. They will place all the food on our tables, and we help ourselves, passing everything around; but this week, dinners will be buffet style as well."

Once lunch was done, they took their trays to a conveyor belt and deposited them. Lindsey watched the long line of trays disappearing into the back of the room. She assumed that someone must be there doing up all the dirty dishes.

"Okay, everyone, this afternoon, we are going to get you your supplies and clothes. Follow Tom and me, the Bookstore is the next building due east of us." Again, they entered a modern looking building, normal clothing was in the basement, magical supplies were on the first floor, and specialty magical items, such as wands, were on the second floor. Tom and Sandy handed out a list of supplies that each girl needed to acquire. Lindsey held her list between her arms, rather awkwardly. Sandy noticed this and simply took charge of it for Lindsey.

The group went from station to station on the first floor, picking up quills, inkbottles, pens, pencils, and the many textbooks each would need. By the time that they had gotten every item on the list, Sandy held a huge pile for Lindsey. "All that is mine?" she asked incredulously.

"Lots to study," Sandy grinned and got out her wand. She waved it over Lindsey's pile and spoke clearly, "Lindsey's bed." Poof! The entire pile disappeared. She explained, "All of the stuff is now sitting on your bed waiting for you. Simple Move Object spell." Likewise, Tom and Sandy did the same for the other's large piles. "Of course, next year, you will have to do this for yourselves or carry them back to your room. Now, let's go up to the specialty areas. Each of you has to get a wand that is suited to your temperament. This way."

They climbed a spiral stairway and entered a musty smelling room. Boxes and boxes of wands lined the shelves. Unfortunately, Deiter Cross and his group were already here getting their first wands. "Look here comes handless Lindsey! Sir, she needs a wand that doesn't require any hands to hold it!" he said in a picking voice. Sandy glared at him; he glared back at her.

Herman Freeze, their Floor Monitor, cautioned Deiter, "Watch it. They are Floor Monitors, Deiter. You don't want to get them upset talking about handless Lindsey not being able to use a wand, which, of course, she can't. No good getting detention over handless Lindsey."

"Herman, that's enough from you too!" Sandy glared at

Herman, who sneered back at her. Lindsey realized that there must be a good deal of animosity between the Black Hall and the Yellow Hall, though she didn't know how bad it might be.

Soon the four Black Hall first years had their wands. As they left, following Herman, they waved their wands around, as if performing some magical incantation, just to show Lindsey what she was supposed to do with her wand.

There were several wand attendants. An elderly gentleman, Amos Fog, chose to assist Lindsey. "Ah my dear, Lindsey Barron I believe?"

"Yes sir. I'm not sure what I am to do though," she felt horribly self-conscious and stared at her wrists.

"Well, I've been expecting you. Now let's see what wand is best for you, such a charming Yellow Hall student. Now when you handle the right wand for you, you will feel a tingle of electricity between you and your wand. It will feel almost like it is a natural part of you. Don't worry, though. If what we choose here today should not work out properly for you, simply return it to me, and we will find another. Now then, I have a few questions for you that will assist me in refining the choices. Do you like to run and play or prefer to sit and read, my dear?"

"Oh run most definitely," Lindsey replied.

"Good, good. Now do you prefer dawns, mornings, afternoons, evenings, or nighttime? Which do you enjoy the most?"

"Oh early evenings. I get to do my chores and have fun doing them." On he went with what seemed awfully silly questions to Lindsey.

Finally, Amos said, "Ah, I have the perfect wand for you. Supple, yet with a strong inner strength, power, oh yes. Here is the wand for you," he presented her an opened box with a brown wand, about eight inches in length.

At first, she tried to pick it out of the box with her arms, but saw immediately that would never work. She had to use her invisible hands to pick it up. Immediately as she took it, she felt that electrical tingling, which she had often felt when she stood on her porch watching the lightning storms in the springtime. "Whoa, this feels really good! I've had this feeling lots of times," she declared. Amos merely smiled.

"Look at Lindsey; she is holding her wand just like us!" called out a very surprised Amanda. Lindsey beamed with happiness. She rather wished that Deiter were here to see her holding her very own wand, but quickly vanished the thought.

"Now girls, notice this slit in your skirts, this is where we ladies often store our wands when we don't need to hold them. It slips in like so. Guys, you have to carry yours; you don't have dresses like we do," Sandy teased both Tom and Emilio.

"Yea, yea, yea," Tom teased back. "Come on; down to the basement. Clothes and robes time." He led them down two flights of stairs.

The girls spent two hours picking out two more sets of dresses and blouses, two pants and blouse sets, various underwear, socks, shoes, one pair of heavier boots, and of course, a fancy witch's robe. Each also got a heavy cloak to wear when the weather got chillier. When winter came, they would also be issued parkas.

Again, when they finished, Sandy whisked their clothes back to their rooms. Now they returned to their quarters to sort out everything and put their new clothes in their dressers. Each also had two large duffle bags with which to carry their things home at the end of the school year. Each had a backpack in which to carry their books to their classes. They barely had time to put their clothes away when Sandy called them for dinner.

At dinner, Sandy and Tom handed out their class schedules for this year. All their schedules were the same, routine for all first year students:

```
 8:00 Math
 9:00 Science
10:00 English/Literature
11:00 Physical Education
12:00 lunch hour
 1:00 History of Magic
 2:00 Beginning Spell Casting—Grade 0 and
```
I
```
 3:00 Conjuration-Summoning Theory I
```

```
4:00 Enchantment-Charm Theory I
5:00 Dinner
```

"Now don't forget, when you finish your sixth year here, you have to take the Colorado State Exams to get your high school diploma. No goofing off on the morning's work," Tom carefully explained. "I know the afternoons are what you crave, but you must pass that state exam or there will be hell to pay."

"Is there a lot of homework each day?" Lindsey asked. "It takes me a lot longer to write out things than you all will take." She was very worried because for the first time she would have eight subjects, though she didn't expect any homework from PE. Still, seven major classes had her worried.

"The norm's classes usually give you time to work on the assignments at the end of the period. The magic classes dump tons of homework on you. Each year, it seems to grow and grow. You won't see many sixth year students playing around or goofing off. You can always play catch up on the weekends too, Lindsey. If you are too slow because of your situation, let the professors know. I'm sure that they will make some kind of allowances for you," Sandy tried to sound hopeful.

She went on, "Now after breakfast tomorrow, we will take you around the campus, going from class to class that is on your schedules. We will do it each day during Orientation Week so that when classes start next week and all six hundred of us are running from class to class, you will have confidence in where you are to go, that sort of thing. Oh yes, I almost forgot. Tomorrow we will meet your House Mother who will give you your own cell phones, special magical ones."

Tom added, "The rest of the evening here is your free time. You can do whatever you want. Probably you girls all want to chat up a storm in your rooms. However, Emilio and I are going to go for a run at the stadium. I'm on our soccer team. I need to get back into practice and Emilio wants to try out for the team. If any of you want to come for a bit of a run, you are welcome to join us."

"Great. Can I come too? I usually go for a run every day," Lindsey asked. She added, "Are girls allowed on your soccer team?"

"Great, go get changed into your pants, Lindsey. Sure girls are welcome. I think that overall about a quarter of the soccer players are girls, though you know it is rather a rough game."

"Come on, I'll help you change, Lindsey. Tom will be upset with me if I don't come and watch him run," Sandy teased her boyfriend. A half hour later, the two girls met up with Tom and Emilio on the stadium grounds.

"Golly the stands are really big," Lindsey commented, looking at the tall stands surrounding the field. A running track went around the circumference of the grassy field.

"Two times around is a mile," Tom called out. "Let's have at it. Show me your stuff, Emilio." The two began to run around the track. Not wanting to be left out, Lindsey raced to join them, keeping pace, slightly behind both of them. Running with the wind blowing her bobbing ponytail behind her made her feel totally alive. Indeed, for six years now, she always ran the mile from her Plano school to her home as fast as she could go.

After the first mile, both Tom and Emilio were showing signs of pooping out. "Come on, we've only started," Lindsey called out. After the second mile, both boys stopped and cooled down. However, both continued to watch Lindsey racing around the track. After four miles, she had a good sweat going and decided it was time for her to cool down as well.

"Say, you are an impressive runner!" Tom called out. "How long have you been a runner?"

"Six years, ever since I began going to school. I was always picked on so badly that I wanted to get home as fast as possible. You know, it hurts, sometimes—to be taunted about something I can't do anything about. Well, I live a mile from Plano, and I can get home in six minutes usually, sometimes faster," she replied, a hint of sorrow in her voice as well as a certain hesitancy. Yet, she felt like these were now her friends and she could say what she felt.

The four chatted all the way back to their rooms. Sandy volunteered to help Lindsey with her first shower, since she wanted one as well. When they were back in their rooms and Pam Betts had arrived while they were out running, Sandy explained to the four girls, "Now just place your dirty clothes here in these baskets by the door. The House Mother will see that they are washed and returned the next day. She uses magic on them, of course. Pam, tomorrow first thing in the morning, I'll take you to get your things." The new arrival grinned, showing the wide gap between her two overly large front teeth. Pam was a rather homely young girl, with short black hair and an oval face, which only exacerbated her appearance. Pam was also very shy and retiring, but had a sharp mind.

While she was talking to Pam, Lindsey tried to get the news. "Rats, I've missed the early news."

"You listen to the news?" asked Kathy, surprised that anyone would listen to anything but music.

"Well, yes, my dad got me started when I was very young. He says that they always exaggerate or outright lie in the stories so that the announcers can make it seem more horrible than it was to keep listeners tuned in and ratings up. He said don't believe what you hear, but realize that something happened that might be important," Lindsey explained what her father had told her when she was five.

"Oh, you are talking about norm news," Sandy interrupted, finally grasping what Lindsey was saying. "Around here, we get the Magical News on KMAG. Here, let me fix your radio so you can get KMAG." She waved her wand and said, "KMAG." At once, her radio tuned to the radio station of the magical community. "From now on, Lindsey, just say 'Tune to KMAG' and it will do it. If you turn the dial nob, it'll go back to norm stations. KMAG has news at the top of every hour, but the music they play the rest of the time is ghastly. There is a big screen TV down in the commons, which you can use to watch norm TV shows or KMAG, our local magical station. The news announcer, Hugo Whitefield, is really a handsome devil. Some of us watch the news just to see him. Well, I'm turning in, big day tomorrow. Night everyone."

"Thanks, Sandy, night," Lindsey returned, turning the volume on the radio down. Indeed the jazz music did not suit her. Sandy left the four, who continued arranging their room and chatting.

"Golly, Lindsey, you really don't have hands!" Pam said, her voice full of concern. "It must be so hard for you. I guess we can all help you when you need something. Did it hurt terribly, I mean when you lost them?"

"No, birth defect, never had any. I'm used to it now," Lindsey replied, dreading the next few days of having to explain it over and over and over again.

"Yes, but Lindsey can do all sorts of non-verbal magical spells, without a wand even!" Kathy explained, intending to bolster Lindsey's morale.

"What? Non-verbal and without a wand? Well, I can't see how you can even use a wand, but my dad says—oh, he's the Director of Magical Misuse for all the high plains of Colorado—he says, that learning how to do the non-verbal spells is the absolutely hardest thing to learn here. He can only do a couple such spells. Wow, Lindsey, that is really something! Where are you from?"

The girls chatted for a while, but at eight o'clock, Lindsey turned on the KMAG news for the first time. "Top of the evening you glorious wizards and witches out there in the big wild west, this is your favorite news anchorman, Hugo Whitefield, bringing you the latest. Remember, if Hugo didn't report it, it didn't happen."

"Golly, he sure has a big ego," whispered Amanda.

"Yes, but he's really cute!" Pam added. "Who cares what he says, it's how he says it. I usually watch him on TV."

"The big story today—and this is a grim story indeed—I recommend that you cast a Cheering Spell when I'm finished. Dominus Malefic is on the loose once more. I repeat, that master of black, evil magic, the ruthless murderer, Dominus Malefic has escaped from Denver Municipal Magical Prison today. Guards at the detention facility reported that, when they brought him his breakfast this morning, they found his cell completely empty! We cannot say just how badly this reflects upon the Department of Law, who oversees the Denver Magical Prison. Just between good old me and thee, expect some heads to roll over his escape. The question that everyone is asking now is: What will Dominus Malefic do next?"

"I put that question to Wizard Herman Melvil, Denver's

Department of Magical Misuse, earlier today. He, of course, refused to comment. This horrible news casts fear into all good people, including the norms. So tune in tomorrow when I, your faithful announcer, Hugo Whitefield, will give you a summary of what this powerful wizard has already done. I will also present Madam Penelope's Magical Predictions on what this wizard will do next. Tune in tomorrow for the latest; you'll not be disappointed." Lindsey turned her radio off.

"What's that all about?" she asked. Lindsey realized that she knew absolutely nothing about the entire world of witches and wizards, the entire magical world around the globe. She felt terribly stupid.

Amanda and Kathy mostly shrugged their shoulders, but Pam replied, "Well, my dad won't really tell me much about it—all hush, hush, secret stuff, he says, but he did tell me that some wizards go bad. Dominus has gone 'bader' than bad. He's used magic to murder people and used magic to cause big disasters, though no one knows why. Remember that big hurricane called Ben that hit New Orleans head on three years ago? It wiped out the city killing tens of thousands and leveled half the city, excepting the French Quarters. Well, I heard dad saying the Dominus caused it! While the Louisiana Department of Magical Defense worked like mad to force hurricane Ben to take a different route, Dominus overpowered them and forced it to hit head on."

"Wow. I didn't know that there are bad wizards," Lindsey said, "but there are bad norms, so I guess I shouldn't be surprised."

"How true," Pam replied, "that's why we have the Departments of Magical Misuse and Defense. They are supposed to protect us and the norms from those who turn bad. Well, I'm turning in; it was a long bus trip from Sterling to down here. Night all."

Chapter 3—The Bradbury Grand Tour

At breakfast, a matronly woman, whose hair was tied back in a tight brown bun, met them, along with her husband, a tall, just as stern looking man. Both were in their forties. "I'm your House Mother for you girls, Ann Bitterroot. You're to call me House Mother, got it? Now, then, my husband Fred, over there talking to the boys, is the Hall Father, though you will not normally see him." She spoke with a commanding and stern voice. Lindsey thought that she would tolerate absolutely no nonsense at all.

"Now then, if you have any problems, worries, concerns, anything at all, you are to come and see me. I live in the penthouse suite just above your floor. I know that the Floor Monitors did not show you the penthouse yesterday."

"First, the School Rules. No students are ever allowed on the campus grounds after midnight, ever. No excuses allowed. Instant detention. Second, all first and second year students must be in their own Halls at ten o'clock every night. I will be checking on each of you every night to be sure. All older students, curfew is midnight, no exceptions. Third, no boys are ever allowed in the girls quarters and vice versa. Instant detention for both parties."

"Forth, unless you have a written pass from the Hall Parent, no student is ever allowed to venture beyond the stone walls of Bradbury's, nor are they allowed onto the mountain to the east."

"Why all these severe rules? We are totally responsible for your safety while you are here at Bradbury's School of Magic. We want you to have a totally safe environment in which to learn. All we Hall Parents as well as all the faculty and staff here at Bradbury's take this responsibility for your safety quite seriously."

"Now then, first years, if you will follow me, I will present you with your magical cell phones. Please take extra care of them; they are expensive and valuable. Put your trays on the conveyor and line up, girls."

Hastily, the first year girls did as she asked. Lindsey felt a little funny walking in the single file line behind this rather portly old woman as they marched out of the dining room. She saw others from other halls watching them, several girls were giggling. Lindsey wondered if these others had more pleasant House Mothers. They marched across the courtyard and into Yellow Hall. Then, they walked up the circular stairs, but continued up past their floor. Lindsey noticed a sign that she had not seen yesterday, "Hall Parents—Penthouse."

Soon, she entered the luxurious suite at the very top of the Yellow Hall dorm building. They remained in line as they stood in her large living room. While she would have liked to look around at the many interesting items in the room, Lindsey listened carefully to Ann as she presented the others in front of her with their cell phones and instructions.

When she came to Lindsey, Ann's stern tone softened. "Ah, Lindsey Barron, our full scholarship recipient. I have a special cell phone for you, one that you ought to be able to operate, given your circumstances. Have you ever had a cell phone before, I mean a norm cell phone?"

"No House Mother. Mom and I never had any money to buy one," Lindsey replied softly, hoping that the others would not hear her.

"I thought as much. You can push buttons?"

"Yes, if they are not too small."

"Good. I have automated your cell phone just for you. Press '1' and it dials your mother. Are there any other numbers you wish me to preprogram right now? You can always program other numbers later on; get one of your roommates to assist you."

"No, House Mother."

"Good. Now then, pay attention. If you get lost, just press the 'L' button; the phone has a GPS locator in it, and it will display a map of where you are located. That way, you can see where you are at and where you need to go. Try it; press the 'L' button." Lindsey did and watched a map of Bradbury's appear on the screen. A dot flashed where she was standing, inside the Yellow Penthouse.

"Now then, if you need help, just press the 'H' button. It will signal us and the Administration. Someone will come at once to assist you. Finally, if you need to get a hold of me, press the 'M' button. It will instantly dial me. It also has the usual cell phone features; you can text message, take pictures and videos and send them to your mother—all the usual features the other children have on theirs. However, only yours has the speed dial along with the 'L' and 'H' and 'M' buttons. I'll put the full instructions on its use in your pocket, dear. Have one of your roommates help you with it."

"Let me welcome you, Lindsey, to Bradbury's. I'm sure you'll love it here. If you need anything, please let me know." Lindsey was surprised by the big hug that Ann gave her. She had not hugged any of the other girls before her. She heard several others giggling behind her and her face flushed slightly. At last, the big woman released her and she returned to the end of the line, while Amanda got her cell phone and instructions.

"Now that's that. You are to return to your rooms and await Sandy. She is going to take you on the grand tour this morning." The group of excited girls left and went down one flight to their rooms. Sandy was waiting on them in the hallway.

"Here, put your cell phones in this pocket in your dress," she explained. "Wands in the long, narrow one, phones in the short larger one. Now I have a map of Bradbury's for each of you. It is very durable and not easily damaged or destroyed. You should keep it with you at all times for the first few weeks, until you have everything down pat. Everyone ready?" Lindsey awkwardly held onto her map while the other girls held theirs open in their hands. She felt a bit ill at ease over this, but resigned herself to doing the best she could.

Outside their dorm at the north point of the pentagram building, Sandy pointed out, "To our right is the Book Store that we went to yesterday. If you need any supplies, clothes, or such, just go there and ask. Due north of us is the Stadium. Your PE classes will meet at the Stadium. Due west of us is the library. It looks small, but it is huge inside, magical expansion.

Due south of us is the swimming pool. Everyone got this?"

The group had and Sandy led them around the Stadium to the northern point of the Bradbury pentagram of buildings. "Here is the Math and Science Hall. Most of you will have your first classes of the day in this building. Math classrooms are on the third floor, the others are for science classes." Lindsey thought this building looked just like the pictures she had seen of college science buildings, lots of steel and glass windows, rather modern looking.

Sandy led them southwestward to the next building. "This is the Hall of Alteration Magic. As you can see, this building continually changes its appearance each day. Yesterday, it looked like a castle but today I'd say it looks like a rocket ship or something. Cool building to look at, anyway." She led them on southwestward to the next building in the line, which marked one of the five corners.

"This is the Hall of Illusional Magic. Each day, it changes its color scheme." The building looked like a grand old mansion, today constructed of red-brown bricks. Ivy grew up one side of it. Sandy led them along the southeast line to the next building.

"Here is the Humanities Hall. You all come here for your English and Literature classes." Lindsey thought that this stately building looked like an English manor house. Ivy completely covered all sides of the building. Sandy walked them further along this southeast line to the next building.

"Here is the Hall of Invocation-Evocation Magic. It looks like a dragon, so you can't mistake this building." Indeed, the main entrance was through the dragon's gaping mouth. Lindsey wondered what neat magic she could learn in this place. It certainly looked exciting to her!

Sandy led them on southeast. "Here is the bottom east corner of the pentagram of buildings, the Administration Hall. You probably will never have to go inside this one. I've never been inside it. Now let's go due east along the bottom of the pentagram of buildings. This way."

"Here is the Infirmary building. Yes, it looks like a norm hospital. Now let's continue going east to the bottom east corner building." Everyone followed her.

Lindsey immediately took a dislike to this next one. "This is the Hall of Necromancy, the dark arts." The building was entirely black. Stone serpents climbed up the walls on either side of the doors. Human skeletons were carved into the stone walls at periodic intervals. Lindsey hoped that she would not have to have any classes in this building; it gave her the creeps.

Sandy also didn't like this building and hurried them on northeastward. "Here is the Hall of Divination Magic. Kind of a strange looking building isn't it? It's supposed to be a crystal ball sitting in the ground." Indeed, a giant translucent sphere rose from the ground. Lindsey wondered what the rooms inside looked like.

Sandy led them on northeastward to the next building. "This is the Hall of Abjuration. It always looks like a miniature castle. Now let me point out the Dark Woods. See this dense patch of woods here? It stretches from here all the way to the mountainside and all the way down to the outer ramparts wall that surrounds Bradbury. First years are not allowed to go into the woods without a professor with them. It is dangerous, primarily because wild animals sometimes come down from the mountains around us."

"Now from here on northward and all the way to the eastern ramparts wall are the Formal Gardens. They are fabulous. One path we call 'Lover's lane,' but you will find out about that later on," Sandy teased the young girls. She then led them to the easternmost corner building.

This is the Hall of Charm and Enchantment Magic. You will have your theory class in here. I know it looks like a small English cottage, but that is only its enchantment. Inside it is really large. You will soon see what I mean. Okay, only one more building to go. This way." She led them northwest.

"Here is the Hall of Conjuring and Summoning, where you will also have a theory class. The building resembled a Greek building with many marble columns and arches. Part was out in the open, part was enclosed. Sandy explained, "If you summon something, it has to have someplace to stand, hence the big open areas." She led them back to the Math and Science Hall.

"On nice days like today, most of us walk to and from our classes, just like we are doing now. However, when it rains or snows, we all go a different way," Sandy added rather spookily.

She led them into the entrance doors of the Math and Science building. "Now let's go down the stairs," a teasing note in her voice. Soon the stairs opened into a long tunnel deep underground. Five could walk abreast in here. Periodic lamps provided good illumination, however.

"You see, there's a vast tunnel network connecting all the buildings on campus. When it's cold out or deep snow, we all go from place to place following the tunnels. Notice that at each entrance point, the signs are clearly marked." Lindsey noted that one direction arrow said "To Hall of Charm and Summoning," while another directional arrow said "To Hall of Alteration." A third tunnel arrow said, "To Stadium and Dorms."

Sandy explained further. "The outer line of tunnels goes from building to building in a giant pentagram of tunnels. However, there are numerous cross tunnels, the shortcuts, as we call them. Here is the shortcut tunnel that leads to the Stadium and then to our dorms. Let's say that you are here in the Math Hall and you need to get to, oh the Infirmary. You could walk the long way around either side of the giant perimeter pentagram tunnels. However, if you take the shortcut tunnels, here to the Stadium and the dorms and then the tunnel from the dorms south to the Infirmary, you can cut the walking distance nearly in half."

"Be careful, you can also get yourself messed up down here. Let's say you are here at the Math Hall and need to get to the Charm-Summoning Hall. The shortest way is along the outer perimeter tunnel, just follow that sign there; it leads directly to it. However, you could walk on down the shortcut to our dorms in the middle of the entire campus and then take the shortcut tunnel from there, which leads to the Charm Hall. If you went that route, you would walk nearly four times the distance you need to go!"

"Now follow me. We are going to the most confusing location on campus, the tunnel hub underneath our dorm!"

Part way along the tunnel, a sign pointed to a side stairs that led up to the Stadium. At last, they reached the huge hub below the dorm pentagram building.

"Wow!" exclaimed Lindsey; the others echoed her sentiments.

They stood in an underground room nearly as large as their dining hall above them. All around the perimeter of the room shortcut tunnels sprang; all twelve of them were clearly labeled. Hence, one could not get too lost down here. "See, in bad weather, you just go down here and find the right tunnel and off you go. Only problem is that there's going to be six hundred of us coming down here at the same time. It gets to be a big mess at certain times of the day, as you can imagine," Sandy stated from her three years of experience.

"Okay, time for lunch. Let's go up into the dining room and you can see where to go to get down here." They climbed up the stairs and found themselves at one end of the dining room. Lindsey noted a large sign over the door they had just exited, "To Tunnels."

During lunch, Lindsey observed that there were now about a hundred young students here, about evenly divided between the five halls. At her table, some twenty first years were eating and getting acquainted with each other. All the new students had arrived. It was a long lunch period, because all the new students wanted to meet each other and chat. Lindsey noted that now there were ten boys as well as ten girls, not just the one and four from yesterday.

Many of the new arrivals were talking about the extra security precautions that had been taken, due to the break out of this Dominus Malefic man. They were magical checked and searched as they entered the bus, as well as their small backpacks. Apparently, this prisoner escape was not being taken lightly, though Lindsey could not dream why this man would present any danger to the young students or the Bradbury school.

At last, Ann signaled Sandy, who interrupted the chatting. "First year new arrivals, I'm Sandy, your Floor Monitor for you girls. Tom here is Floor Monitor for you boys. We are now going to take you around and get you your things and so on. However, some of you who got here earlier, like Lindsey, you are to go to your rooms and await House Mother Ann and Hall Father Fred. They will be bringing you your laptop computers. Okay, new first years, gather around Tom and me, please."

Lindsey and her roommates headed up to their room. "I didn't know that we would get our own computers," said Lindsey very surprised. "I always had to use the ones at our one-room school, sharing it with twenty others."

Pam said very officially, "Oh yes, we are being given our very own laptops. They are ours to keep. State of the art and very fast. Good ones, my dad says so, but I guess we will see for ourselves very soon."

"You know a lot about them?" Kathy asked, curiously.

"Oh yes, I've played with them since I was a little girl. Oh, here comes House Mother Ann now," Pam replied.

Ann brought in four laptops, one for each of the girls. "We have a wireless network here at Bradbury's. You should be able to connect to the Net from anywhere inside the outer walls. Now these are yours to keep and use as you need, especially for research and reports. However, I will say this only once," Ann said in her sternest voice, "these computers are enchanted to allow absolutely no pornographic materials. If you attempt to download any porn, your computer will sound an alarm, loudly so that everyone can hear it." Four girls giggled; Lindsey had no interest in looking at naked men or women.

"Your email address has already been installed and is your full name, such as LindseyBarron. All are @Bradbury.magedu. Your email client program is called Agent, and it is already setup for you to send and receive. Your browser is called FoxFire500 and it automatically will open the Bradbury.magedu home page, where you can find out general information about the school and any special announcements. Please note that the Administration will often post announcements for students here on the home page, so do check it out daily. Have fun, girls." She left to deliver the next batch of computers.

"Way cool!" exclaimed Pam. "These are state of the art

laptops! Wow, 8G of memory and 8G CPU speed, quad-quad core even. These are screaming demons!"

Lindsey was impressed; she didn't understand half of what Pam had just said, but took her word for it—that these were good ones. Awkwardly, she began to fiddle with hers. Soon, she realized that either she had to use her magic invisible fingers to operate it or use the mouth stylus that Ann had given her. She was too embarrassed to poke keys with her head and stylus, so used her slow going, imaginary fingers.

"Now there, that's better," declared Pam. "Hey you three, get close together so I can get a picture of you three with my cell phone." They obliged. Pam pressed a few buttons and then fiddled with her computer. "Ah, perfect. Look at this gang," she proudly suggested.

There on Pam's computer was the picture of the trio. She had it installed as her desktop background. "It would be better if all four of us were in it," she sighed.

Of course, all three wanted to know how they could send pictures from their cell phones directly to their laptops. Pam went from computer to computer and phone to phone, setting them all up for her roommates. Lindsey also asked her to pre-program the other three's cell phone numbers for her, using numbers 2 through 4. Both Kathy and Amanda also wished that they had a picture of all four of them together, but Sandy was off with the new arrivals.

"I can do it, if you want," Lindsey said very quietly. She hated to bring attention onto herself this way.

"You can?" asked Pam. "That would be super! Come on; let's get a nice pose here. Lindsey, you sit front and center and we will crowd in close. How will you do it?" She suddenly realized how impossible this was going to be.

Using her invisible hands, Lindsey concentrated and lifted her cell phone up and moved it to the far end of the room. "Way cool!" declared Pam, thoroughly impressed. Amanda and Kathy cheered as well. Lindsey smiled. Soon, all four had this picture of the four of them as their desktop background image. Thus engaged, the afternoon past swiftly.

As the supper hour approached, Sandy stuck her head in, "Remember to wear your robes to supper tonight. It's meet the faculty night. They will all be there to meet you so look your best, please." Sandy looked very haggard. Lindsey realized that Sandy and Tom were working overtime, having to do everything they had done for Lindsey all over for the many late arrivals. She felt a bit sorry for her.

"Oh bother, I guess one of you will have to help me into my robes, I can't manage it," Lindsey sighed. Here was yet another thing she couldn't do for herself. Darn. Amanda quickly helped her into her dress robes and straightened out her hair nicely.

"There, you look great, have a peek," Amanda said with a smile. Lindsey looked at her appearance in the mirror and saw a reflection of a young witch. She was impressed and excited. Then, the four headed down to the dining room, a bit nervous to meet their teachers.

Soon well over a hundred first year students, their Floor Monitors, and the House Mothers and Hall Fathers gathered at the five different colored tables. Lindsey sat with her four roommates. Emilio, who had taken a fancy to them sat next to Amanda, who sat next to Lindsey. His three other roommates sat beside him. All eyes stared at the long table at the head of the dining room.

Sixteen adults sat at the professor's table, discussing things among themselves. All student eyes focused on the man in the middle, the oddly dressed man in his fifties. Whispered word had quickly spread that this was the school's top man, Governor Alister Broadwell. While everyone else wore their wizard robes, he was dressed in an out of style by several hundred years, black business suit complete with a top hat that a norm magician might use to pull a hare out of a hat.

Still, Lindsey thought he looked kindly enough, with his black moustache and goatee beard and long sideburns. At last, he rose and a complete silence fell in the dining room. Alister spoke clearly and slowly, as if each word held some kind of magical power behind it. "Fellow professors, House Mothers and Fathers, Floor Monitors, and first year students, welcome to Orientation Week at Arthur Bradbury's School of Magic. I'm the Governor, that's head man to you students. . ." That last was a sort of joke and the many adults present chuckled.

"I am Governor Alister Broadwell and it is my pleasure to welcome yet another class of first year students to Bradbury's, even if it is in these most difficult times. You must forgive my appearance; I have just come from an important meeting with the Department of Defense. All this talk of Dominus Malefic's escape has given everyone the willies." Again, many adults chuckled, and Lindsey thought it must be a joke or pun, but didn't understand it.

"I assure you all that you are all going to be quite safe here at Bradbury's. After all, what could Dominus possibly desire with beginning magic students?" This remark was intended for several of the professors, and he stared at several as he spoke these words. The tension appeared to ease somewhat among the teachers.

He grinned broadly and said, "Now Professor Elaine Mac Elroy, your English and Literature teacher, has accused me of not being romantic enough, so I dressed for this occasion. How is this, Elaine?" He looked at one of the older teachers, who grinned back and shook her greying head at him. "Oh, you mean I am several centuries off?" Now the whole group of teachers chuckled. Even Lindsey smiled; he did look terribly old fashioned.

"Ah, then how's this?" He waved his hand, and in a flash, he was wearing his wizard robes, looking much like the other teachers. Lindsey though this was a useful spell for her. With it, she could dress herself and be independent of others having to help her put her clothes on. She made a mental note to inquire about this spell.

Alister continued, "Ah, still not romantic enough for the professor, so try this." He waved his hand and thousands of small candles burst into flames high over the heads of everyone, while the normal lights turned off. The room took on a distinctive yellowish glow, a warm glow at that. Several students cheered and broke out into a clap.

"Allow me to introduce our faculty to you," Alister continued. "Starting here on my right is Professor Blake Smith, Conjuring-Summoning. Girls, you have no doubt noticed just how handsome Professor Blake is, but unfortunately he is married to Professor Janice Smith, sitting next to him. She is your Charm-Enchantment teacher. She also will be teaching you your Grade 0 and 1 level spells this year. She is in charge of the Red Hall." Lindsey looked at her. She was the most beautiful woman Lindsey had ever seen, a glamor queen or model. However, her smile appeared forced or faked.

"Next to her is Professor Jerry Thalmus, Abjuration. He also will be your History of Magic teacher and is the head of Blue Hall." He looked to be around fifty years old and was quite bored with this whole meeting. "Next to him is Professor Mary Ann Thornby, Divination." Her hair flew off in all directions as though she'd just had an electric shock or something. She seemed awfully nervous. Lindsey could see her trembling slightly.

"Next to her is Professor Delius Dogs, Necromancy and head of Black Hall." He had a dark complexion and an antagonistic stare. Lindsey didn't much care for him and was glad that she did not have a class with him. However, he received a round of applause from the twenty-some, Black Hall, first year students. He managed a smile. "Next to him is Professor Arthur Thornby, Alteration, and head of Brown Hall." Several Brown Hall students clapped for him, but Lindsey wondered why he was not sitting beside his wife.

"Now on my left is Professor Huan Su Sung, Invocation-Evocation, and beside him is Professor Cho Lin Sung, Illusions and head of Yellow Hall." Not to be outdone, those around Lindsey began clapping, and she clapped her arms together, mostly symbolically though. Cho Lin looked directly at Lindsey for a moment and smiled.

"Next to her is Professor Herbert Mac Elroy, your Math teacher. Students take note; he is not a wizard. He will tolerate no monkey business in his classroom." Lindsey thought this was interesting. A norm would be one of her teachers here in the school of magic. Interesting. "Next to him is Professor Elaine Mac Elroy, English-Literature; she is a witch, mind you." Several on the staff chuckled, but Lindsey wondered what was funny.

"Next to her is Professor Jasper Jones, Science. He is also not a wizard. Let me warn you all. Do not call either

Professor Jones or Mac Elroy a norm or you will find yourself in detention." This was a stern warning, Lindsey noted. So the school has two non-magical teachers here, she thought, how interesting!

"Next to him is our Librarian, Lillian Angel Jones, who will assist you in finding your research and study materials. She would like me to remind you that the library closes at ten p.m. Next to her is Doctor Frank Caterwall, our resident physician. Let us hope that none of you needs to visit him this term." He grinned and many chuckled, for who wanted to see a doctor?

"Finally, at the far end are Hank and Betsy Walls, your PE teachers. First years," Alister winked at them and leaned forward as though he was letting them in on a secret, "let me warn you in advance. Those two are fitness freaks! They are even trying to get me to lose some weight!" At that, the staff all chuckled.

"You see, Bradbury's has a very wide and talented set of professors, perhaps the best in the United States. I suspect that's because we are in the Rocky Mountains. After all, isn't this the vacation spot of the country?" Everyone chuckled. Even Lindsey knew that Colorado had huge revenues each year from tourism. In the wintertime, people flocked to the many ski slopes.

"Now let the feast begin." He waved his hands and piles of food suddenly appeared on the tables before the students and teachers. Lindsey carefully noted that he had not used his wand yet this evening, a fact she found encouraging. She still had no real idea how she would be able to use hers. Those thoughts quickly evaporated and everyone began picking dishes and eating.

After dinner, when Lindsey and her roommates got to the commons, they found that nearly everyone was sitting around the giant big screen TV waiting for the start of the KMAG newscast. "There he is!" exclaimed one young girl, who proceeded to sigh. Several others sighed as well. "Isn't Hugo just the handsomest man you ever saw?" Similar comments plus groans from Emilio and several other boys made it hard for Lindsey to hear what he was saying.

"Yes, it is safe to say that everyone is in a panic today. The Department of Defense has greatly increased security on all school buses taking our students to the magic schools, causing many delays in Orientation Week around the country. KMAG has had numerous anonymous tips concerning the whereabouts of Dominus Malefic. Some say he was sighted in San Francisco, Chicago, New York, and even Peoria today. Now, this reporter asks you, how can he be all across the country in one day, eh?" He winked at the audience, and the girls gathered around the TV all sighed loudly. Lindsey didn't however.

Hugo continued, "Today, I decided to look into the past and see just how this villain was captured. It was fourteen years ago that the combined efforts of the Department of Law and the Department of Defense joined their forces to apprehend this fiendish criminal and his cohorts known as the Death Stalkers."

Hugo leaned forward as if he was about to speak just to you privately on some vitally important secret. "I visited these departments today and asked who had actually apprehended these criminals fourteen years ago. Do you know what I found out? No one can remember! That's right!" He sat back now.

"No one in the Department of Law or the Department of Defense can remember just how these worst villains of all time were actually apprehended. Obviously someone did, but there is *no* record of who did it!" He paused so that the audience could gasp appropriately. Lindsey noticed that several around her did just that. Hugo was playing them perfectly.

"Now I found that terribly interesting, which is why I am putting off until tomorrow the recap of the evil deeds of Dominus Malefic that I promised you last night. I went to the World Wide Web. I found nothing about how he was finally apprehended, just the date that he was! I went to the Denver Public Library, the huge norm library, and searched there. Guess what I found? Nothing!"

"Now I ask you: doesn't this sound like a cover up of some kind? Has everyone in the Department of Law and the Department of Defense been Mind Wiped? Has someone erased all traces of just how these villains were finally captured? To this reporter, it *sure* seems so. I and KMAG would like to ask you for your help. If any out there in the big wide world remembers just how these nasty villains were actually apprehended, KMAG is offering a reward for your information. Yes, you heard me, a reward. You see, we at KMAG have discovered that someone has tampered with our own news video archive! All traces of our reports from fourteen years ago have been erased! Naturally, KMAG has filed a grievance with the Department of Magical Misuse and with the Department of Law. So if you recall just how Dominus Malefic and his Death Stalkers were finally apprehended some fourteen years ago, call KMAG at once. The number is on your screen."

"I will show you what video remains of the past deeds of these men on tomorrow night's news, assuming those video tapes have not been erased as well! So tighten up your security tonight, viewers out there in the world. Dominus Malefic is on the loose once more. This is your favorite news anchor, Hugo Whitefield, saying good night and stay secure."

"Wow, Mind Wipes!" declared Pam to Lindsey when the four had returned to their room.

"What's a Mind Wipe?" asked Lindsey, who had no idea what Hugo had been saying or Pam, just now.

"That's when powerful wizards go into your mind and erase certain memories that they have been ordered to remove. It is a very nasty thing to have done and falls under the Department of Magical Misuse, because it is a crime to do that to someone!" Pam stated authoritatively; she should know, since her father was the Director of Magical Misuse for all the high plains of Colorado.

The girls discussed the events of the day and their first impressions of their new teachers. Both Emilio and Amanda passed on what their brothers had told them about these teachers, when they had had them a few years back. Slowly, Lindsey began to worry about the large amount of homework she was facing.

At last, she called her mother to tell her all the wonderful things about her new school. She found that she had talked for nearly an hour before her mother finally suggested that she get to bed. Lindsey grinned and did just that; it was ten o'clock and her usual bedtime.

The next day, Sandy had them all walking to and from their classes, so that they would become better familiar with the campus layout. In the afternoon, Sandy and Tom presented their twenty new charges with a scavenger hunt. Lindsey and Amanda were partners. Each group had a list of small items to go and find. Tom had hidden them at various locations around the campus. The real idea of the hunt was to have the new students become more familiar with all the buildings and locations on the campus. When each team returned with all the items, Tom presented them with a Wizzle's Dark Chocolate candy bar.

The following morning, they took a stroll through the magnificent formal gardens. In the afternoon, they all went swimming. The pool was reserved for two hours for Yellow Hall's use. Lindsey had two problems with this. First, she had no swimming suit. Second, she did not know how to swim nor did she think she could, what with no hands. Hence, Amanda took her to the Book Store and helped her pick out a green bathing suit. Lindsey refused to wear a bikini style. For several hours, Lindsey enjoyed playing in the waters. Amanda began to teach her how to swim, but they had not gotten very far along. Lindsey was rather fearful of getting in water over her head.

Black Hall had the pool reserved just after Yellow Hall's two hours, and near the end of their swimming time, Lindsey took quite a lot of teasing and taunting from Deiter and his crowd. What had been fun now turned into an embarrassing time for Lindsey.

Starting that evening, many other buses began arriving with the older students, several days ahead of schedule. Security problems were cited as the main reason the administration had speeded up the arrival dates. Lindsey overhead many older students griping about how long it had taken them to be searched and get onto the buses. Many were quite upset about being searched. Lindsey wondered why students needed to be searched. This made no sense to her.

By the weekend and two days early, Yellow Hall was

filled with the returning students. Lindsey estimated that there were one hundred twenty in her hall. Many of the older students wanted to meet her, primarily to see for themselves that the administration had allowed a person with no hands to enter their magic school. She overheard considerable gossip about her "condition," which made her feel very uncomfortable again, just as she had been getting used to Yellow Hall. Amanda kept telling her to ignore them, but Lindsey never had been able to do that. Her only solace was heading for the Stadium track in the evening, where she ran as long as she could.

Of course, there were others out running, getting back into shape. Students from all age groups were on the track and field teams or on the various soccer teams. As soon as they saw that she could run well, these kids accepted her completely. One needed no hands to run well.

At last came the opening night dinner, where Governor Alister Broadwell gave his usual start of term speech. By now, Lindsey had heard all the key information, sometimes more than once. For her, it was anticlimactic. Still she was nervous, tomorrow was the big first day of classes.

Chapter 4—The First Day of School

September 1st dawned bright and sunny; the tail end of summer was still quite warm, though the evenings had a definite chill to them. Lindsey awoke at 6 o'clock, but none of her roommates was awake yet. She lay still and tried to calm her ever-rising nerves. For her, the first day of school had always been one of the most terrible of all days. She remembered each one of them from Plano's one room schoolhouse. It seemed that all of her classmates had been saving up a tease or taunt all summer just to try it out on her this first day. "Please don't let it be that bad here," she whispered to her pillow. So far, Lindsey felt that she was in heaven here at Bradbury's, well mostly. She knew that, unlike Plano, she could not run home at the end of classes. In fact, she didn't know that she could even go home until the vacation came.

By seven, the others were up, and Amanda helped her get dressed and get her backpack ready for the morning's classes. All four headed down to breakfast together, carrying their packs on their backs. They would head off to class straight from breakfast. Amanda and Pam both helped her with her tray and the foursome ate together. Lindsey still noticed quite a few others were covertly watching how she managed to eat. At least they aren't staring at me, she consoled herself. Soon, they were rushing off to math class along with some six hundred other students, fanning out to the various buildings.

The four arrived a few minutes early and took a seat near the front. A while later, Deiter and a half dozen other Black Hall students arrived, taking seats in the rear. Soon the taunts began, as Lindsey feared they would. Someone said, "Poor Lindsey cannot count; she has no fingers." Another corrected him, "No, she can count to two, two arms you see." Several others chuckled. Lindsey slumped as far down in her chair as she could, trying to be as invisible as possible.

Soon Professor Herbert Mac Elroy entered, his white

55

hair rather disheveled. He looked like he needed a shave, however, but he had a warm smile on his face. Lindsey remembered that he was a norm and had no magical abilities at all. "Good morning students. You can call me Professor Herbert. First thing, I want to call role. When I call your name, please raise your hand."

Deiter whispered overly loudly, "Lindsey hasn't got any to raise." Several others giggled. Lindsey was not prepared for what happened next. Suddenly the blackboard eraser flew straight at Deiter, knocking him in his head.

"That will be all of that, Deiter Cross is it? Learn to be civil. She can raise her arm as well as you can. Raise your hand is a figure of speech, Mr. Cross. It is not literal. You need to pay more attention in English class. Now then, roll call. Ashley Alms." One by one some thirty students raised their hands. Lindsey raised her arm, though she saw that some twenty others were staring at her as a result. It could have been worse, she thought to herself. At last, he finished roll call.

"I have what is called a photographic memory. One roll call and I now can remember each one of you, which is good since we don't have to call roll tomorrow. Now then, I will be your math teacher for the next six years, assuming that you do not flunk out of Bradbury's. Math is important. Yes, I know that you must pass your Colorado State Math Examinations at the end of your senior or sixth year or you will not get your high school diploma. Yet that is not what math is about, passing an exam. Math is highly useful in the business of living your lives. So put away your wands and get out your math text. There is no magic in math. By the way, do not think of using magical means to cheat on my tests. My wife, Professor Elaine has enchanted my tests so that if you cheat, large red letters spelling "Cheater" will appear across your exam papers. That results in an automatic flunk for that quarter."

"Now then, down to business. Our first problem as a class is one of diverse educational backgrounds. Some of you come from one-room schoolhouses, I'm told. I thought those ended centuries ago, but I guess not. Others come from very large schools. In math class, I don't care what kind of school you came from. What I care about is what do you know, and what can you do with math. Let me give you an example. This happened to my wife, a witch, shortly after we first met so many years ago now. She was in charge of filling the public swimming pool for opening day of summer. She waved her wand and presto water filled the pool. Isn't that what you all would prefer to do?"

Everyone nodded and grinned. While none here knew such a spell yet, they either had seen something similar or thought it possible or heard about a similar spell. "Well, I am sad to say that Professor Elaine was a bit weak in her math skills. She greatly underestimated the volume of water that she would need magically to create to fill the pool. After her sixth attempt, though the pool was filling, I told her how to make that simple calculation, and on her next wand wave, the pool was filled perfectly. Very often, class, as witches and wizards, a magical spell does require some estimation of size, quantity, area of effect, and such on your part. If your estimations, your calculations, are way off, so goes your spell. With people such as Dominus Malefic and his Death Stalkers now on the loose, this is more important than ever. Your very life may depend upon it. Now then, assuming that your pool is ten feet wide, ten feet deep, and ten feet long, how many cubic feet of water would you need to conjure? Raise your hand if you know?"

No one responded, so Lindsey raised her arm, resigned to hearing snickers. "Ah, Miss Barron?"

"One thousand cubic feet, Professor Herbert."

"Precisely correct, Miss Barron. Now I am not a mind reader, though I understand that Professor Mary Ann can do that. Some of you may have calculated the volume, but been too shy to raise your hands. Some may have gotten the wrong result; some may have no idea how to calculate it. Hence, before I can begin to teach you math, I have to know precisely where each one of you is at in your knowledge of math. The rest of this period, you will take this assessment test. It is not graded, but try to do your best. From it, I will know just at what level your current math skills lie. Tomorrow we will begin to improve those skills." He then handed out the booklets.

By the time that the bell rang, signaling the end of this

class, Lindsey had only gotten half way through the booklet. She felt horrible. On their way down the stairs to their Science class, she said, "I must be the class dummy!"

"Why?" asked Amanda.

"I only got to question one hundred. There were one hundred more to go!" Lindsey wailed.

"Wow! You got that many done? I only got to number eighty," Amanda confided.

"Hey, I only got to sixty-three," Emilio stated.

"Well, I got to ninety-nine," Pam replied.

"I got to eighty-three," Kathy added. "So you are ahead of all of us, Lindsey. I bet that Deiter fellow only got to fifty at most." Everyone chuckled at that.

"Darn, it looks like everyone who was in our Math class is also in our Science class," Amanda interrupted. Lindsey looked around; sure enough, she recognized every face, though she didn't know all their names yet.

Shortly, the forty-five year old norm man, walked in, saying, "I am Professor Jasper. Now put away your wands! There will be *no* magic used in this class, not *ever*!" He was loud and very antagonistic, and he pounded his fists together for emphasis. Lindsey certainly didn't have her wand out.

He glared at the class before him. "It is my responsibility to teach you about the basic Laws of Nature. You wizards and witches think magic is all, but I am here to tell you that it is not all! If you are alive, and I hope that you all are alive, then you are being subjected to the laws of this universe, period. Yes, you can use magic to bend them a little, to alter outcomes, and so on, but you are nevertheless subjected to them. Let me give you a little example of this. Miss Lindsey Barron, will you come up here and participate in a little demonstration for the class?"

Lindsey's face flushed. *Oh my god, no! Not in front of everyone!* Her feet unwillingly walked her up front. Naturally, all twenty-nine classmates were staring at her.

"Now I have picked on Miss Barron for a reason. You can all see that she has the misfortune to have had a birth defect, caused by a corrupt chemical company who dumped toxic waste near her family's water well. She is proof of what can happen when companies do illegal chemical dumping. Laws of Nature. Now then, here is the situation that Miss Barron is facing. Pay close attention, class!" He barked so sharply that even Lindsey jumped.

"I'm going to pretend that I'm this Dominus Malefic murderer. I have this small, nine mm Saturday night special handgun here. See?" He waved a real gun in front of the class. "Now I see Miss Barron coming toward me and I intend to shoot her with this very gun. I aim for her chest, her heart, assuming that you even know where it's located. Here's the most critical piece of data, Miss Barron is one thousand yards away from me when I fire the gun at her. Like this." He pulled the trigger. Bam! The gun echoed noisily in the classroom. Everyone jumped; several screamed. Amanda and Emilio already knew this was coming; their older brothers had told them that this was his favorite first day action.

"Now then class. The question I pose to you is this. I fired a blank, by the way. If it had been a real bullet that Dominus just fired at a thousand yards from Miss Barron, how many would say that Miss Barron is now quite dead? Show of hands, please, higher, let's see them. Miss Barron dead?" Nearly the entire class raised their hands. Professor Jasper turned to Lindsey.

"How about you? How do you vote?"

"I'm not dead, not even hit, Professor Jasper," Lindsey replied quietly.

Deiter gave a snickering laugh and several of his companions joined in as well. Professor Jasper then said, "Show of hands, how many agree with Miss Barron, that she was not even hit by the bullet?" Only Amanda and Emilio raised their hands. Deiter snickered once again, but Jasper ignored him completely.

Jasper smashed his fist hard onto his desk, startling everyone. Lindsey jumped nervously. "Three out of thirty of you are right! That means twenty-seven of you would be witches and wizards are complete dopes!" He punched the desk again.

"Miss Barron, would you explain why you are not hit by the bullet, please?"

"Professor Jasper, this little gun isn't very powerful. Its bullet comes out slowly and gravity will pull it into the ground long before it gets to me."

"Miss Amanda Whitewater? Anything to add to Miss Barron's explanation?"

"Muzzle velocity is low; she is right; gravity will pull it into the ground at one thousand yards. At ten feet, she's dead, but not at that distance," Amanda replied.

"Mr. Emilio Lopez? Anything to add?"

"At that distance, Dominus should have used a rifle, which has a far higher muzzle velocity. Then Lindsey would be dead, sir."

"Brilliant, brilliant, all three are precisely right. This is just a problem in simple physics! Thank you, Miss Barron for being a good sport. You may sit down now. Now you gentlemen have probably all played hours and hours of Doom 99, right?" Most of the boys nodded; this was one of the latest, hot, computer, first-person shooter games. "Let me ask you another question that you *might* get right. The giant demon is coming at you. Do you shoot with your shotgun, your pistol, or your Big Gun?" Everyone got that one right. Thankfully, he didn't ask the girls. Lindsey had no idea what he was talking about, never having played computer games before.

"Good. Now open your textbook to chapter one. This first term we are studying astronomy. Miss Whitewater, why do we on earth have days and nights?" She got that one correct and so went the rest of the class period. His assigned them to read chapter one for tomorrow. When the bell rang, Lindsey was very glad to leave the class. No doubt about it, Science class was going to be a tense and stressful one for her and many others as well.

The group dashed off towards the western end of the campus to the Humanities Hall for their English class with Professor Elaine Mac Elroy. The quiet, laid-back atmosphere of her class was refreshing, almost as if by design. The first term consisted of a complete review of all grammar rules along with elementary composition. Their first assignment due next Monday was a one-page essay on why magic was important. Yes, they could either write it out long hand or turn it in via computer. She had a Blackboard Version 20.1 Internet program setup for turning in papers. No one did it long hand, to Lindsey's great relief.

"I caution you all. When you upload your essays to me, a plagiarism program scans your work. If it finds that you have copied from someone else, that this is not your work, it is flagged as a copy, a forgery. You will lose all points for that assignment. Is that clear? You are here to learn, not to copy from others." When the bell rang, Lindsey felt a little better. At least with this first term, she felt confident in her grammar skills. The essays would be hard for her, time consuming, and she would have to use her invisible hands a whole lot.

The group headed east to the Stadium for PE class. As they arrived, the boys and girls were separated. Hank took the boys, while his wife, Betsy, took the girls. "Okay, take off your book bags and prepare for the change into your PE outfits, ladies." Lindsey had no idea what she was saying, but did as instructed.

"This is really cool magic," Amanda whispered to her.

When all the girls were lined up and ready, Betsy said, "I will change your clothes for you, one by one. You see, years ago, we wasted half of our PE period just dressing and undressing. Now I take care of it for you. Watch." She swished her wand, and said distinctly, "PE Clothes." Instantly, Lindsey found herself wearing shorts, gym shoes, and a yellow tank top. Everyone said either wow or cool! In two minutes, all the girls were ready.

"Now Hank and I believe that a strong, well-toned body is absolutely essential for any witch to have. So for you out of condition ladies, this period is going to be your worst nightmare come true! You are all out of shape, so this week, we run ladies. Around the track, forty minutes of running each day!" Everyone but Amanda and Lindsey groaned loudly. Shortly they heard the guys complaining as well.

Amanda and Lindsey took up positions side by side. Amanda whispered, "I'm an Apache; running is second nature to us. Follow my lead so you don't get too tired. Forty minutes is a bit long for you, I suspect." Lindsey had never run full out that long and agreed to follow Amanda's lead. Off they went, fifteen young girls running around the long track. The boys were sent running in the opposite direction and on the inner side of the track.

Five minutes later, Amanda and Lindsey had left the others way behind them. Lindsey noticed that Kathy and Pam were doing rather badly, near the end of the pack of girls, panting heavily. She also noticed that Deiter was having a great deal of difficulty keeping up. Emilio was far ahead of all the other boys. This pace was a good one for her, fast, yet not so tiring. Time flew by, Lindsey felt the frustrations of the day seep out of her, as if borne away on the swear pouring off her body.

As the period neared its end, they had lapped the others several times. "Come on; race you to the end," Amanda challenged Lindsey. Both poured it on as Betsy blew her whistle to end the running. She watched as these last two raced down the track, trying to beat the other. Amanda reached Betsy about four feet ahead of Lindsey. Gasping, she said, "You run like Apache." Lindsey grinned, taking that for a big compliment.

"Ladies, will you both see me after class? I wish a quick word with you two. Now then line up and I will re-dress you. No need for a shower; it will be part of the magical package." One by one, she worked her spell on each girl. To Lindsey, it felt like she just had a shower, though she was still catching her breath from the long run.

While the others headed off to grab lunch, Betsy said, "Amanda, Lindsey, that was terrific. I would like for each of you to try out for our track and field team and for our soccer team. It's Saturday morning, here on the field, nine o'clock sharp. You are the finest first year runners I have ever seen." Both girls grinned and promised that they would.

After lunch, they headed for the Hall of Abjuration, where Professor Jerry Thalmus would lecture them on the History of Magic. As the foursome walked into the building and began hunting for their classroom, Pam declared, "Now we get to the real courses." Once more, it was nearly the same bunch of kids in the class.

Again, Deiter took this opportunity to taunt Lindsey.

"In all the history of magic, has there ever been a witch with no hands? Hardly likely."

Unfortunately, Professor Thalmus had just walked in, wiping traces of lunch from his lips. He looked at Deiter and then at Lindsey and said in a rather bored manner, "So Mr. Cross, why is this such an important history detail? Some great lesson there that I have missed utterly? I think not, Mr. Cross. History of Magic has many lessons for us all, but this is not one of them. Oh yes, I must call roll, mustn't I. Now where did I leave my roster book?" He rummaged around and finally gave up. He waved his wand and the roster book, which was underneath his textbook, popped up for him.

Once roll call was done, he began lecturing in a droll monotone. Lindsey's stomach was full, which made for a dreadful combination. She soon found herself dozing off, but so did most of the class as well. When he got to one spot, however, he livened up and she woke up and did her best to take notes on her computer, along with everyone else.

"So in the Old Age, wizards and witches lived in secret, and many were burned at the stake, though usually the norms burned the wrong person." The class chuckled at his little joke. "The Wizard Board of Review then opened the New Age by casting down these four inviolate laws. You must have these memorized verbatim by Monday or spend next week in detention!" he wrote these out on the board.

1. Thou shalt not use magic to injure or harm another unjustly.

2. Thou shalt not use magic to kill another unjustly.

3. Thou shalt not use magic to steal from another that which is not yours.

4. Thou shalt not use magic to force another to do something against their will unjustly.

"Beginning wizards and witches, violate any one of these and the Department of Magical Misuse will arrest you and throw you into prison for a very long time. It is only our strict adherence to these laws that allows the norms to tolerate our open presence in society. After all, we possess extraordinary powers from their viewpoint. If we do not follow these laws to the letter, the norms will become terrified of us and seek our destruction, as was done all throughout the Old Age."

"Now you have all heard of the recent escape of Dominus Malefic. Why is this such a terrible thing? He does not follow these laws! He has killed unjustly thirty-six people, both norms and wizards and witches alike. He has stolen money and gold from the norm's banks. Worse, he has force many norms to do his bidding, raping, robbing, and he even caused one to murder another for him."

"Now he is loose on our society once more. Why is this so terrible? True, many witches and wizards and even norms may be murdered. No, the real terror may be the norm's backlash against all the rest of us. Yes, norms may once again seek to murder and destroy all of us! This is the real danger that Dominus Malefic poses: the annihilation of the entire New Age of cooperation. Let us hope that the Department of Law and the Department of Defense can stop him soon, before it is too late. It very nearly was last time, before he was captured. I want you to have these four laws memorized by Monday or else."

Then, he dropped back into his monotone lecture mode, putting nearly everyone to sleep once more. The bell startled most awake rather sharply. Lindsey and her group chatted about the impact of Dominus on their way to their next class. For Lindsey, the next class was extremely important; she was about to learn how to cast magical spells!

As they entered the classroom, several of the boys whistled. Professor Janice Smith was sitting on her desk, her long legs very visible below the hem of her robes. By any standard, Janice was exceptionally gorgeous, a fact not missed by even these young boys. Indeed, Lindsey thought that Professor Janice was exposing a bit too much of herself, for a teacher. Professor Janice smiled at the whistles—one of those "I know I am hot" kind of smiles.

"Welcome First Years. I am Professor Janice Smith. Please address me as Professor Janice." She gave a flirtatious wink toward the boys, who had taken most of the front seats, forcing Lindsey and her group more toward the rear of the classroom. "Today, you embark on a long journey of learning just how to cast marvelous magical spells, though some of you, I regret to tell you this, really I do, some of you, well there is no easy way to say this. Some of you are just not going to cut the mustard, as we say."

"Now then, as I call roll, please take out your wands and open your spell book to chapter 1." Lindsey immediately had some troubles. Getting her book out of her pack was difficult because the book was rather heavy. Holding it between her arms, it slipped and made a loud noise as it hit the floor. Amanda leaned over to pick it up for her and sat it on the desktop. Of course, the sound interrupted Professor Janice, who said with a grin on her very red lips, "Of course, some cannot even handle this simple task." Half of the class chuckled and snickered. Lindsey's face went red. She wanted to explain that it was almost too heavy for her to lift with her arms, but thought better of it. That would only provoke more taunts. Seeing her struggling to get her wand from her dress pocket, Amanda cleverly slid her arm over, pulled Lindsey's wand out, and sat it on her desk for her. Lindsey flashed her a smile and mouthed "thank you."

As their names were called, each student raised their hand. "Barron, Lindsey," called out Professor Janice. She had said her name with an extra emphasis, however. She raised her arm and half the class turned to look at her and it. "Yes, some of you are just not going to cut the mustard," Professor Janice repeated, and Lindsey flushed red once more.

"Now then, today we begin. For a spell to work properly, it must be done precisely correctly. This means that you must have the precise wordings, the precise intentions, the precise diction, and the precise wand motions, though some of you will most certainly have insurmountable hurdles with the precise wand motions." Lindsey felt that was a direct statement to her and flushed red once more. Several boys gave her a side glance as well, convincing her even more that it was being directed at her. Her eyes watered slightly, and she wiped them on her sleeve when no one was looking.

As if to drive this point home even further, Professor Janice asked, "Now can anyone tell me why a wand is so vitally important to spell casting?"

Deiter Cross's arm shot up. "Yes, Deiter?" she smiled and batted her overly long, heavily mascara-darkened eyelashes his way.

"Because you can't do magic without a wand," he said antagonistically, throwing a glance towards Lindsey. Several around him nodded their total agreement. Lindsey held her breath; surely, this wasn't so, because if it was, she felt doomed before she even began.

Smiling at him, she cut him to the quick with, "Oh, so many first year students believe just that. Anyone else wish to add to Mr. Cross's answer?"

"Wands provide the magical energies, Professor Janice," Emilio volunteered. Lindsey thought that was a good answer; so did Amanda, both nodded.

"Very astute, Mr. Lopez. I see that you have already learned something from your older brother, what was his name, oh yes, Francesco," she replied, smiling her magnificent grin, which only made the barb bite deeper into Emilio, whose face flushed slightly.

Pam shot her hand up, violently. She was not about to let this pass. "Yes, Miss Betts? Your father is the Director of the Department of Magical Misuse, is he not?"

"Yes, Professor Janice. Wands are not necessarily needed to cast spells. First, we will eventually learn how to cast the spells without saying any words. When we get very good, we will not even need a wand for some spells. We all saw Governor Broadwell doing just that last night at the feast. He waved his hands and said nothing. We all saw him do it."

She gave her a forced smile, "Well, it is to your dad's credit that he has at least taught you something. Yes, when you are in your fifth and sixth years, some of you, I dare say a very, *very* few of you will be able to cast a few of these spells without words. We call it non-verbal casting. However, perhaps one student out of this entire school of six hundred will be able to graduate and cast even the simplest spell without a wand. For all practical purposes, then, wands are required. Is this clear?"

Pam flushed, but she knew Professor Janice was right. Non-verbal spell casting was very tough and casting without a wand, well, very few wizards could do that. It was rumored that one of the reasons that Dominus Malefic was so feared was that he could cast many spells without using a wand. Pam now began to think this was just how he had managed to escape his prison cell. She made a mental note to ask her father about this.

"Now then, at the beginning of this first term, we're going to be learning many useful spells, little spells. None of these are even remotely difficult—no challenge in them at all. I expect that every one of you will have these down perfectly by the end of this month, that is, if you have any notions of continuing your magical education." Her words cut into all the students. Deiter squirmed in his chair, Lindsey noticed.

"Today, we are going to learn how to do three useful little spells—well some of you are, I should say. Now then, two of these are evocation oriented. The definition of evocation is: the action of calling or bringing forth. With evocation spells, you are then bringing forth something into existence. This means that you must *intend* for this to come forth. You must have firmly in mind that you wish this to *be*, to be real. If your intention is weak, it will not come forth into existence. Is this clear?" Everyone nodded, though by now, no one dared to speak otherwise.

"Now you may have wondered why the desks are so arranged as they are in this room." No one had particularly. The desks were arranged in close pairs with several feet separating each pair. "You will be pairing up with the person who is beside you. Lindsey, that means you and Amanda are pairs. Everyone find your partner. Yes, that's right. This first useful spell is called Chill. With it, you suddenly lower your target's temperature by some forty degrees, very useful on these hot summer days, I might add. The chill only lasts for a brief instant and you cannot harm your partner. The chill will never go below freezing, so don't try to chill off in the wintertime; nothing will happen at all when it is so cold outside."

"Pick up your wands. Here is the proper way to hold a wand. Everyone, look at the way Mr. Cross is holding his wand." Everyone pivoted to stare at Deiter. He had grasped his wand as if it was a bicycle's handle bar, a firm, solid grip. He smiled, but his presumed victory was short lived. "Mr. Cross is showing us precisely how *not* to hold a wand! Gently, like this, your index finger should be extended outward along the side of the wand, so that you can make tiny, subtle motions. Grasping it like it was an axe is a certain way to fail utterly." Hastily, Deiter and everyone else adjusted their grip, mirroring Professor Janice's hold.

All except Lindsey, who held hers awkwardly between the ends of her arms. She hoped and prayed that Professor Janice would give her some better ideas of how she might be able to do this. She didn't, but continued. "You make a slight downward push with your index finger, and as it is going down, you say very clearly and with the *full* intention that you will be bringing a temperature drop into existence, say Chill. That is all there is to it. Now, practice this on your partner, who will immediately know if it has worked since they will be able to feel the effects instantly. Of course, it doesn't last but a second so they will warm up rapidly. Now begin. I will be walking among you to provide any assistance you might need."

"I'll go first," Amanda suggested. Lindsey was more than willing to let her. Amanda pointed her wand at Lindsey and made a downward motion, but forgot to say the word. She tried again, but nothing happened.

"Well, the wand motion looked like hers," Lindsey suggested, "and you said the word. So it must be that you didn't intend for me to be chilled down a little. I think you have to really mean it." Amanda smiled and tried it again, twisting up her nose while trying to force Lindsey to become chilled.

Both saw the magical energy flash and Lindsey suddenly felt a strong chill over her body. "You did it! I got lots cooler!" Lindsey exclaimed. Amanda grinned broadly. She'd done her first spell. She practiced it a couple more times, gaining more and more confidence with each try.

Suddenly, Deiter let out a yell and everyone looked at him and his partner, Loyd. The class gasped, Loyd was entirely covered in a thick layer of frost! Professor Janice waved her wand and said, "Warm." Instantly the frost melted and Loyd recovered, shivering a little. "Mr. Cross, I can see that you will do well with cold based spells." He took that as a compliment. "However, today we only wish a chill. Continue practicing, Mr. Cross."

Now she moved beside Lindsey and Amanda. Amanda performed her first spell perfectly. "Well, done Amanda. Excellent. Now reverse rolls and let me see how Lindsey does." Quickly, Amanda's face changed from a satisfied, confident look to one of concern.

Lindsey looked very silly, she thought, holding the wand between the ends of her arms, sort of like a torch. She made a downward motion of the wand, intended to chill Amanda, imagining her sweating after a long run, and said "Chill." At once, Amanda called out, "Wow! You did it. I'm a whole lot colder. This is so cool! We can use it to cool down after our runs."

"Miss Barron," the covert voice of Professor Janice interrupted the two, "I'm well aware that Miss Whitewater was indeed chilled. However, are you trying to say that you are *beyond* the sixth year casting skills?"

Lindsey's face turned beet red. "What?" she squeaked, her voice sounded miles away. All the class stopped to listen. "Your wand did not activate. Were you not paying attention earlier when I said that the wand is supposed to activate and provide the magical energy for the spells? Are you trying to show off, Miss Barron? I will tolerate no grandstanding in my classes! Now do it again and get your wand to active properly."

"But she did it. I was chilled," Amanda protested.

"That's enough, Miss Whitewater. Lindsey, do it properly." She glared at Lindsey, who tried once more. Again, Amanda was chilled, but the wand did not activate. "You will not get a pass on this until that wand of yours activates, Miss Barron. Is that understood?" Lindsey nodded, tears swelling in her eyes. "Now continue to practice, Miss Barron." Thankfully, she walked over to another pair of students. Lindsey continued to try. She chilled Amanda another ten times, but the wand had not yet activated properly.

"Class, now that most of you have this spell mastered, we are going to work on the reverse of this, Warm. Again, it will just warm you up a few degrees, nothing more. You cannot harm your partner. In the cold Colorado winters, this can be a very useful spell indeed. You use the same wand motion, only this time speak distinctly and clearly the word Warm. Now go to it."

Again, Amanda went first and rapidly got the hang of this variation of the spell. After warming Lindsey up ten times, they reversed roles. Once more, Lindsey was successfully able to warm Amanda up routinely, but her wand still refused to activate. The class was interrupted by Deiter's screams and the smell of smoke.

Loyd had attempted to Warm Deiter, but something went wrong, and Deiter's robes burst into flames. Professor Janice rapidly waved her wand and the flames went out. She waved it again and the minor burns disappeared, much to Deiter's satisfaction. She waved it again, though none caught the words she spoke, and his clothes magically returned to normal. No trace of the fire remained. Finally, she waved her wand again and said, "Clear!" All traces of the smoke were gone. "Mr. Armstrong, I can see that you will excel with fire based spells. However, today you are only to warm up Mr. Cross, is that understood?" Loyd crimsoned and muttered that he was sorry.

A little later, Lindsey was again scolded for not having her wand activating. Still she was very nicely warming Amanda up repeatedly—it was just that her wand was not activating properly as it should. It was all she could do to keep from crying.

"Okay, most of you have this one mastered. The last spell for today is abjuration based. Since most of you do not know what this word means, I will define it for you as we use it. Abjure means that you are formally or solemnly renouncing a belief or claim. The spell is a most useful one, Clean. When you cast it, dirt, grime, food stuck to plates, dirty windows, all come spotlessly clean. Now this spell only affects a small area, two feet by two feet. One of your partners should come up here and pick up a box of dirt. Spread it on the floor, but do not spread it beyond a two foot square."

"The wand motion is a circular one, rather like washing a plate." She demonstrated the circular swing. "While the wand is in motion, you speak distinctly, Clean. However, this is an abjuration based spell. You must firmly and conclusively intend that there be no dirt left on the floor. You may even think 'I swear that there is no dirt left.' Sometimes, you may find that tip helpful. It is your *conviction* that makes this spell work. Is that clear? If you are not convinced, absolutely certain that the dirt will be gone, it won't be. That is the primary reason for the spell failing you: your abjuration is weak. Well, for some of you, it may well be wand action." She looked straight at Lindsey when she said this. Again, Lindsey felt embarrassed and wanted to become invisible again.

Amanda retrieved the box of dirt, and while Lindsey held it in her arms, sprinkled some dirt, being careful of the two-foot limit. After her third try, Amanda succeeded, all traces of the dirt vanished. Both cheered. Amanda practiced this four more times and had it down perfectly. Then, they switched roles.

The first few times Lindsey tried the spell, nothing happened. "I think you are not convinced that the dirt is going to go away," Amanda suggested, remembering Professor Janice's words. Lindsey concentrated even harder. At last, the dirt vanished completely. "You did it! Yes!" Amanda complimented her.

"Yes, but my wand is still not working. I'd better work on it again," Lindsey said, very glad that Professor Janice had not seen her wand failing again. Five more times Lindsey managed to clean up the dirt. However, on the very last time, her circular motion finally worked and the wand did activate! Lindsey thought, "Thank god for a small miracle!" Indeed, Professor Janice had been observing her on this try and saw the wand activate.

"Well, one activation in the entire hour is little to cheer about, Miss Barron. If you had not observed, your classmates have had their wands activating dozens of times. You had better practice much harder before tomorrow's lessons."

When she was out of earshot, Amanda whispered, "Darn it; at least she could have complimented you. You did get the wand to work once." Tears trickled down Lindsey's cheeks. She had given up trying to suppress them. If she were home in Plano, she would have just left the room and run all the way home. Worse, she knew that an hour from now she would have another magical theory class from Professor Janice. The bell rang finally, ending her torture. She ran out of the room to the bathroom where she could hide in a stall and let her tears flow. Amanda quietly picked up Lindsey's things and followed her.

A bit later, they walked into their next class. Lindsey's eyes were red, but she dutifully took notes on Conjuration-Summoning Theory I. Professor Blake Smith, the husband of Professor Janice, was their teacher. He was extremely handsome, and the other girls watched him constantly, just as the boys had done with Professor Janice.

"The definition of conjuration is not what the norms believe: tricks performed by rapid, quick, deceiving hand movements, sleight of hand. No, conjuration is the real deal." Several laughed at his pun. Actually, it is rather a complex subject, which is why you have this theory class. There are three spheres of conjuration, based upon the three different meanings of the word."

"First, conjuration can mean to cause to be or to happen. In a few weeks, my wife will be teaching you how to conjure up a blue light, so that you never are in the dark again. That's very useful. Later this winter, she will teach you how to conjure up a horse. Imagine you find that your car runs out of gas in the middle of the high plains. The nearest town is many miles away, as quite a few of you know firsthand." He winked at Amanda. "Think how useful it will be for you to be able to conjure up a horse for transportation. Another useful one that you will be learning very shortly is Unlock and Lock. Here you will be causing a lock in a door or chest to unlock itself or to lock itself, that is, to cause to happen."

"Second, conjuration can mean to affect or influence. Soon you will be learning the Annoy spell. Some of you will really enjoy this one, because when you cast it on a person, you are compelling them to do some little annoying thing, like scratching their nose, or itching their bottoms. Yes, in a few weeks, you will see many of your classmates running around being annoyed, but it's all in fun here, you see. Next year, you will learn how to influence a swarm of ants, bees, rats, even spiders to come and do your bidding for a short time. Imagine what your enemy will think when he sees a thousand rats running at him! Yet, if you get very, very good at spell casting you may be able to force your enemy into a mental maze, where he wanders around lost and helpless for a period of time. It is said that this is one of the spells that Dominus Malefic uses on his victims."

"However, the one spell that you must be very, very, very careful with is Mind Control! Yes, with this spell, you can totally control and influence another person. You can make them do whatever you wish. Remember the Four Laws you must follow. I call your attention to the fourth. 'Thou shalt not use magic to force another to do something against their will unjustly.' Yes, class, Dominus Malefic and his Death Stalkers use this spell all the time. With it, he could get our country's President to do what he so desires!" The whole class gasped, which was the professor's intention.

"Ah, but there is yet a third definition of conjuration: to cause a spirit, devil, demon, or monster to appear before you or to disappear and leave you alone. Of course, you will not be learning these spells for several years; they are most powerful indeed. Imagine you are out for a stroll in the mountains and run into a grizzly bear. Wouldn't it be nice to be able to make that vicious bear leave you alone and leave? Yet, I admit, these types of spells can also lean toward the darker side of magic, as those who study necromancy will attest."

"It's my task this year to get you completely familiar with these aspects of conjuration. Some of you may not be quite up to the task, I'm sorry to announce." He lectured on, but Lindsey drifted off into a worried fog. How was she ever going to be able to manage? She couldn't hold her wand; she was doomed to failure even on the very first day. Why had they even considered allowing her to come to this school in the first place? Were they all just looking for someone to make fun of, someone to ridicule relentlessly? Were they just being sympathetic to her plight and had no real intention of her being a successful witch? Was it a total sham that she was chosen?

The bell rang and soon she found herself back with Professor Janice once more. She noticed that she had touched up her lipstick. Her lips were fiery red once more. As expected, she sat on her desk, seductively displaying her long legs before the boys, who now all sat in the first rows. Lindsey and Amanda took seats in the very last row. Lindsey sank low in her chair, hoping to become invisible for an hour.

After calling roll, Professor Janice began, "Enchantments and Charms are my specialty, charms particularly so. Allow me to demonstrate." She waved her wand and spoke to Emilio. At once, he rushed up to her and began kissing her feet. Everyone began laughing, but Emilio took no notice, totally engrossed with kissing her feet. She broke the spell and a greatly embarrassed Emilio took his seat, sliding down, trying to disappear as Lindsey had.

Again, she waved her wand and said something to Deiter. He rose and got down on one knee and began spouting, "Ah Professor Janice, I am so in love with you. I long for your lips. I pine for you every minute of the day." She cancelled her spell, while the class roared with laughter. Even Deiter was embarrassed.

"What young woman would not find such spells useful, eh? Attracting your handsome beau? Yes, charms are very useful indeed. Likewise, enchanting is most important because you are imparting magical energies into someone or something. While Charming is easy to master, enchanting is much more challenging. I know some of you will have an awful time with this, especially those who cannot master their wands." She looked directly at Lindsey. By now, everyone in the class knew who she meant. Lindsey could not stop the tears from flowing, but thankfully, only Amanda could see them. How Lindsey longed for the bell to ring, though she was anything but hungry.

At last, it rang. She and Amanda were the first out of the room, making their way to the dining room for supper. Soon Pam, Kathy, and Emilio joined them. "Honestly, Professor Janice has no right to pick on Lindsey like that!" declared Emilio. "I swear she has no heart at all."

"Really, I would have thought that she would have given

you some guidelines, some help in how you might be able to use your wand," Pam stated flatly. "I will email my father about it tonight. Honestly, all she does is flirt with the boys!"

"I bet she makes a terrible enchantment teacher. All she knows how to do is charm people!" Kathy declared. "I wonder if she is really that pretty. I mean maybe she has just altered her appearance, making it just *look* like she is Miss USA."

"Gang, it wasn't as if Lindsey wasn't able to do those three spell," Amanda pointed out. "She did them really well and really fast! I was chilled and warmed, and she got all the dirt cleaned up quickly. It is just that her wand didn't work."

"But that means she is using very, very advanced magic," Pam pointed out. "It's beyond non-verbal—using magic without a wand. It takes very powerful wizards and witches to do that! Dad says that Dominus Malefic can do magic without wands. I should think that Professor Janice should have been praising Lindsey for what she was doing, not condemning her."

"She's flunking me," wailed Lindsey, allowing her tears to come even though she was in public. No one else paid much attention to her, as the tables filled up with supper dishes and everyone began clamoring for the food. "Maybe I should just leave and go back home."

"You can't do that, Lindsey! You are doing the spells just fine—it's just that your wand is not working," Pam stated. "Now what I think you should do is go and see our Hall Professor, Cho Lin Sung. Tell her what has happened and have her check out the wand. Perhaps the wand isn't working properly or perhaps they gave you the wrong wand. I remember them saying that can happen, when I was getting mine in the bookstore. Really, Lindsey, you should go see Professor Sung right after supper."

"I just can't! She'll tell me that I am no good as well. I should just quietly leave," Lindsey replied.

"No, you should eat something," Amanda insisted, putting a bunch of chicken nuggets onto her plate for her and then dumping a huge pile of peas on it as well. After sampling one nugget, she realized that her body was starving and Lindsey ate rapidly.

After Pam finished, she saw Professor Sung rising and ran to her. Shortly afterwards Pam returned and announced to Lindsey, "There it's settled. You are to go see Professor Cho Lin as soon as you are done eating. I made an appointment for you."

"But I can't face her," Lindsey protested, tears coming down once more.

"At least she can check out your wand. Beside, Lindsey, she is supposed to be looking out for us in Yellow Hall," Pam insisted. "You are to meet her in her office in the Hall of Illusions right away. Come on. I'll go with you."

"Me too," declared Amanda. "I can vouch for the fact that Lindsey's spells really did work without her wand working." The two forced Lindsey to go with them, and soon they were walking over to the Hall of Illusions. The building looked like a grand old mansion, today constructed of yellow-brown bricks. Ivy grew up one side of it. The building looked inviting, Lindsey thought. Pam led the way and Amanda followed behind Lindsey to make sure that she followed Pam. The three marched into Professor Cho Lin's office.

Dressed now in a Chinese long, yellow silk dress, Professor Cho Lin had also let her long, black hair down. She looked sympathetically at the three first years. Pam quickly related what had happened during the spell casting class, and Amanda enthusiastically explained just how well Lindsey's spells had worked. Lindsey just sat there, wishing she could run home and forget this horrible experience had ever happened.

"Thank you, Pam. You have done well to bring Lindsey to me. Both of you have shown the high qualities that make Yellow Hall so powerful. You may go now and allow Lindsey and me to work this out." It was said softly, but carried a powerful command value. Hastily, Pam and Amanda left the room, but decided to wait for Lindsey just outside the hall.

"May I see your wand, Lindsey?" Cho Lin said softly. Lindsey sat there morosely; it would be an effort to get the wand out from her pocket. To her amazement, Cho Lin said nothing but her wand slipped up and out of her pocket of its own accord. Cho Lin smiled at her as their eyes met. "You are not alone with your special skills," Cho Lin whispered. "Now let me check this wand out. It can happen that wands malfunction. One in five hundred students are mis-matched with their wands." She examined the wand thoroughly and performed a number of tests with it.

"The wand itself is perfect. Now let's check on the match with you. Please hold out your right arm like so. Don't feel ashamed that there is no hand there. I am going to touch the wand to your stump like so." She felt the wand touching her skin and saw Cho Lin shutting her eyes. Lindsey felt the magical energy tingles that she had felt the first time when she was seven observing the lightning storm. Cho Lin opened her eyes. "The wand is a perfect match to you, Lindsey. Thus, there must be something else preventing its activation."

"I want you to Chill me. Go ahead and do what you were doing with Amanda this afternoon. Yes, don't worry about the wand, just do the spell." Lindsey did as she was told. "Yes, I feel the chill." She spilled a bit of ink on her desk. "Now do the Clean spell, just as you did it this afternoon with Amanda, please." Lindsey, holding the wand awkwardly between her arms, tried to make the motion as she said Clean. As before, the ink disappeared, the desktop was spotless. Her wand sputtered slightly.

"Yes, I see the problem here. I am *not* surprised that Janice didn't see it. She is good with charms, mind you, but not much else. You have a remarkable gift, Lindsey, one that many a good wizard or witch would die to have. How do you manage to operate your computer?"

"Oh, I pretend that I have these invisible hands and have them press the keys," Lindsey replied. "Otherwise, I have to hold a stick in my mouth and use it to press them, but that's so horrible that I won't do it unless I have to," she replied sadly and a bit worried that she was doing something very wrong.

"I thought as much. Now I want you to use your invisible hands to pick up your wand and hold it as if you were casting a Chill spell. Can you do that?" Cho Lin asked.

Lindsey obeyed; the wand appeared in midair. "Now using your invisible hands to move your wand, I want you to cast your Chill spell on me, please." Lindsey obeyed. She saw the small flash of magic as the spell detonated. A large smile grew on her face, mirrored with a similar one on Cho Lin's.

"Yes, that is all that was wrong. In the future, while you can easily perform the spell without the wand, when you need to use the wand, first pick it up using your invisible hands just like you did just now. You should have no further problems with Professor Janice on this account. I know she demands that the wands activate. However, in your case, you have my permission to continue to experiment and see if each new spell will activate without using your wand, Lindsey."

"Wow, thanks, but isn't this a bit like cheating? I mean I'm using magic to get the magic out of the wand. Won't she hound me for that?" Lindsey asked.

"If the wand *activates*, she will be satisfied, but I think that it is time for me to teach you one little useful spell, perfect for your needs. Your classmates will likely be learning this one in the springtime. Yet, you are advanced enough that you can learn this one now, if we keep it simple enough." Lindsey's heart skipped a beat; she was about to learn a new spell, one that no one else yet knew.

"I want you to visualize what your hands might look like, if you had them there at the ends of your arms. Yes, that is a good image, just the right size and shape, very nice looking hands. Yes, I am seeing your mental image of them, Lindsey. Now with that image strong in your mind, think the words Phantasm Appear. Yes, just like that. Good girl. Now look down at your hands."

Lindsey jumped out of her chair. She had two perfectly normal looking hands at the ends of her arms! She moved them around just as if they were real, but when she touched her chair, they went right through the desk.

"They are an illusion, Lindsey. Use them now to pick up your wand. You control the illusionary hands. Very good. Now use your left hand to touch the desk, imagine how a real hand would touch it and do so. Yes, you have it. All you have to do is imagine what your hands should do, and the illusion will follow it. Now use the wand, make the motions Janice taught you today and Chill me."

Lindsey did so and the wand energized perfectly. She spilled more ink on the desk. Lindsey made the circular motion and said "Clean." The wand activated and the desk was once more spotless. Lindsey let out a shriek of joy! I can do it! I can do it!" She was so excited, so relieved that she began jumping up and down. Cho Lin smiled along with her.

"Now put your wand away. Good. Now retrieve your wand with your phantasm hands. Good. See how easily you manage this? From now on, when you need 'hands' to do something, first use this new Phantasm Appear spell to make your hands appear. Then use the 'hands' to do what you need them to do. I think this will work out extremely well for you, Lindsey."

"How can I ever thank you, Professor? I was ready to quit and go home when I came in here tonight."

"I know, dear. Yours will be a tough road ahead, but I know that you can do it. You would not have been chosen to attend Bradbury's unless you had great talent. I'll let you in on a little secret. Bradbury's only takes the *most* talented wizards and witches in Colorado. This is a *very* exclusive school, the *best* in the state, perhaps the best in many states. So remember this always, that you were selected to attend here is *no* accident. You have the potential to be a very great witch, Lindsey. Now I suggest you go tell your friends about this and practice this tonight so tomorrow will go better for you. In the future, if trouble comes your way, please come and see me right away."

"Thank you. Thank you ever so much, Professor. I will." Lindsey skipped out of the room. Outside, she found Pam and Amanda waiting for her; both looked very glum. When they saw the huge smile on Lindsey's face, they cheered up.

"Look at this!" Lindsey declared. Her phantasmal hands appeared. Both girls stared and gaped. They watched the hands retrieve the wand from her dress pocket. They watched as Lindsey's right hand made the dipping motion and she commanded, Chill." Both felt the chill and saw the wand activate.

"Wow! You can do it!" Amanda cheered.

"That's incredible! You had hands there. I saw them."

Pam stated, and then added, "Ah, those must be illusionary hands. Cool! Did she teach you a new spell?"

"Yes, I am using magic to produce magic!" The three headed back to the dorm, chatting all the way. For Lindsey, total disaster had somehow been completely averted.

During the evening, the foursome were Chilled and Warmed quite a few times, as they practiced their new spells. The Clean spell they put to use almost at once. Professor Janice was right about this spell. It was most useful indeed. Then, Lindsey set about the task of memorizing the four Laws. Well, she got a start on it anyway, before tackling her English paper. Now she continually used her new phantasmal hands as much as possible.

Chapter 5—The Track Meet

Indeed, the rest of the week went far better than the first day, though the homework continued to pile up. As expected, Professor Janice gave Lindsey a stern look, as her phantasmal hands waved the wand, which energized quite nicely. Yet, the professor said nothing to Lindsey. After all, she was getting what she had asked for: wand activation.

All over campus, the older students knew that the first years were into the beginning spells. They'd learned the Color spell and girls were going around with pink, orange, and red hair one day and purple, green, and blue the next. "Do I look better in purple or blue?" asked Pam, after she had changed her hair from orange.

Amanda chuckled, "Me thinks thee ought to leave well enough alone." The four laughed. They had learned how to dampen an area or to dry it out, useful when it rained, of course. The boys groaned about learning how to dust, but the girls loved this one too. By the end of the week, the first years were flavoring their food, freshening up their drinks, gathering their dirty clothes from the various piles in their rooms and putting them into the clothes hampers, polishing their desks, shining their dress shoes, and mending small tears in their clothing.

Professor Janice drilled into their heads the idea behind enchantment spells, that of endowing properties to other things, and alteration spells. This last was accomplished by clearly viewing the object to be altered and then holding steady an image of its new desired appearance, while switching the wand down sharply in a commanding manner.

All four had the Four Laws memorized by Friday. It was somewhat easy to do, because they all started with the same wording. As the week ended, the five of them—Emilio had now joined up with them, studying as a quintet each evening in the study hall behind the commons—began to know their weaknesses. With Lindsey, it was all about speed. She was slow using her phantasmal hands, because she had to control each individual motion that they made, making typing very slow indeed.

Both Emilio and Kathy were way behind in both science and math, while Amanda was weak in science. In Pueblo, science was not well taught, and Emilio had always disliked math. Kathy had an aversion to both subjects, and Amanda's original norm school almost had no science taught at all. Pam, while excelling in math and science above all her friends, was having an awful time with grammar and writing essays. By the end of the week, all five were helping each other out with their homework.

Friday evening while the five were studying away, an older boy named Glen came rushing into the study room, "Hey everyone, you got to come hear the news! It's bad, really bad news!" The dozen in the study room rushed out into the commons where nearly a hundred others were packed around the large screen TV, watching Hugo report the news.

"I repeat: KMAG has just received confirmation that Dominus Malefic has just brutally murdered Warden Herb Jones. Herb was the warden of the prison in which Malefic had been held these past fourteen years. Also slain were five of the guards who watched over his cell. The Department of Law has released this message found pinned to what remained of Warden Jones. I quote:

> Be it known to all that I, Dominus Malefic, have begun avenging my unlawful imprisonment. All those who had a hand in capturing my Death Stalkers and me will meet the same fate as this idiot warden, who made my life miserable for fourteen years.
>
> My demands are simple: it is time that **we** take over total control of earth. The norms have long held us at bay, forcing us to be less than we are. It is time to arise, all yea wizards and witches, reveal yourselves in the mighty glory that is rightfully ours. Cast out these inferior, weak, pathetic norms. Soon, I will reveal my foreseen Golden Path to all wizards and witches of earth!
>
> Dominus Malefic

"Wizards and witches everywhere: you heard it here on KMAG. Dominus has shown you his complete and undeniable guilt. He has broken the Four Laws! Now there is no question about his guilt or innocence!"

"Breaking news!" Hugo pretended to look at some papers being handed to him, but any astute observer could see that he was reading the tele-prompt.

"KMAG has just received even more bad news. Late this afternoon, Chicago Prison for Magical Misfits has been broken into and the Death Stalker, Rubius Hornby, has escaped. Three more guards perished during the escape. As you may recall, Rubius was one of the more violent Death Stalkers, with ten confirmed murders to his credit and another six unconfirmed."

"However, I bring you now this public service announcement from the Department of Defense and the Department of Law. This is Spokeswoman Elizabeth Shrew of the Department of Law."

A middle aged woman, with strawberry blonde hair, short and curly, dressed in a fine grey business suit, stood before the wall of microphones. "Good evening. At this time, I would like to inform you that you need not fear that the remaining nine Death Stalkers will be released. They have been moved to various, secret locations around the world. Dominus, if you are listening, none of these nine remain where they were this morning. I have one word for you from the Department of Law: Check! Further, the exact location of these very violent prisoners is not known to any one person in the Department of Law. The locations were written in a journal and that journal is at this minute being taken to an obscure location, out of your reach. No one person knows the location of these prisons and the precise location of this journal is known to only one person, the sender of the journal."

"Our advice to you, Dominus, is to surrender to the nearest Department of Law immediately, and you will avoid the death penalty. If you do not surrender, I'm authorized to state clearly that you will be executed. Your move, Dominus."

There were the usual flurry of questions thrown at her, but she merely turned and walked away from the podium. The

TV camera caught the magical flash as she teleported away from the news conference room.

The cameras returned to Hugo, who smiled, showing his brilliant white teeth and big smile. "There you have it. Check. Now tomorrow, I will have an exclusive interview with Colorado's own Director of the Department of Defense. I assure you that this will be a most informative interview, with emphasis on how you can protect yourself and your loved ones from these two madmen. Thanks for watching. Be safe." The TV switched to a commercial, and the five friends returned to the study room.

"Gosh, I never knew anything like this was ever going on," exclaimed Lindsey. "It's rather scary."

"We should be very safe here," Pam explained. "My dad says that Bradbury's has an enormous number of protective spells on it. I do hope dad's okay. I should email him tonight."

The news was upsetting to Lindsey, for it brought back the awful memories of that day when she found her father crushed underneath their tractor. By midnight, she still could not fall asleep. She heard the noises of her three roommates and knew that they were soundly asleep. She got up and opened the curtains of their window, which faced northeast. In the pale moonlight, she could see the formal gardens off to the northeast and to the southeast, the tall, twelve thousand foot tall mountain rose like a black, ominous specter.

Suddenly, she saw a light in the sky, moving from above the mountain downward towards the campus. It had to be flying. It moved too fast to be a car. Besides, a car could not drive on the steep, rocky mountain. One could barely climb it on foot. As she watched, it slowed and began hovering over the campus and moved slowly over the lower part of the walls and out of view. She estimated that it might have landed in the parking lot by the Administration Building. All this, Lindsey found most curious and wished that she could go for a walk and see what it was. However, no student was allowed out of the dorm this late at night. She sighed, closed the blinds, and made another attempt to fall asleep.

"Wake up, sleepy head! You have to hurry up and eat if you want to go to the tryouts!" Amanda giggled her awake.

Rubbing the sleep from her eyes with the ends of her arms, Lindsey got out of bed and allowed Amanda to dress her in her running clothes. The two headed down for an early breakfast, while Kathy and Pam slept in on Saturday morning. Emilio was already there and nearly done eating. "Hi ya. All ready for the tryouts, senoritas?" he said somewhat bored with the process. "Either I will make the team or I won't. Simple as that. If I don't, I can sleep in more. If I do, I will have even less time for my homework. Ah well. Guess I would rather run than do homework. How 'bout you, Amanda?"

"Yeh, me too. This science stuff is so darn hard. Do we really need to pass some exam? I wonder what happens to us if we don't?" she replied, sleepily.

"Dunno. Probably nothing much. I think Francisco said something about it being harder to get a job without the high school degree."

Lindsey interrupted them. "Say did you see that light in the sky around midnight last night?" Neither had. She described the weird sight that she had witnessed.

"I don't think planes can fly like that, Lindsey," Emilio answered. "Maybe it was a UFO."

"Don't be silly, Emilio," Amanda teased. "They don't exist. It's just a wizard messing around with enchanting strange things, like making cars fly. Come on you two, or we'll be late."

A few minutes later, the trio joined a large number of other students warming up around the track. The students were in groups according to their hall colors, and the trio quickly went over to the Yellow Hall group. They were the only first years trying out for the Yellow Hall teams.

"Hi, I am Bill Ferney, Captain of Yellow Hall Track and Field and Captain of Yellow Hall Soccer Team. Good to see all of you back this year. You are all on the team. We have three new first years here who want to try out for the teams." He was a tall, thin young man, rather handsome, Lindsey thought.

"I'll introduce the others here. This is Sally Ridgeway, fifth year." Sally was a black young woman with curly hair and a big smile, but she was also well-muscled in her legs. Lindsey knew she was a force to be reckoned with on the field. "This is

Becky Salinos, fifth year." She was also of Mexican descent. "Our two fourth years, Jake Rattlebeam and Tom Whitewater. Finally, our returning third year, Jim Whitewater." At last, Lindsey officially met Amanda's two older brothers. They definitely looked like her brothers, Apache through and through.

"I know two of our new first year tryouts," Bill continued. "Who doesn't know Lindsey Barron at this point?"

"Bill! That's not being very nice," Becky chided him.

"Well, it's true. How many handless students do we have on campus? In fact, has Bradbury's ever had a handless student, eh? No offense, meant, Lindsey." He smiled.

She returned his, "None taken."

Bill continued, "Of course we all knew their sister would be trying out, Amanda Whitewater."

"Emilio Lopez," Emilio volunteered. "My brother is on Brown Hall's team."

"Excellent, glad you all want to try out. I won't keep this from you, because you are bound to hear it soon enough anyway. We are short team members. If you can run, you are on the team; but that is not saying much. We've lost all track meets for the last six years, and we haven't won a soccer cup in well over seven years now. You'll probably take some ribbing about it all, though. Just wanted you to be prepared. Now let's see what you three can do."

Amanda spoke up, "Tom, Lindsey is at my running level." His eyes opened wide, as did Jim's. Bill looked at her questioningly, so she added, "She runs like an Apache." His face broke out into the largest grin Lindsey had seen.

"Well, I'll be. Maybe we do have a chance this year! Okay, I want to see this. Tom, Jim, you set the pace; let's see if these three can keep up. The rest of you act as spotters; see if there is anything that we can suggest to improve their speeds."

Tom said, "You three try to keep pace with us. When Bill blows his whistle, that's the signal that you are coming down the home stretch. You should pour it on and try to beat us all across the finish line. Sally and Becky will hold a finish line tape for you to see. Good luck."

The five began running around the large oval track.

Indeed, the two Apache boys set a stiff pace, but Lindsey took her guide from Amanda and kept pace with her. Emilio, wise to what was going on, stayed with the two girls. As they passed Bill on the first lap, Lindsey noticed he had a stopwatch and was making notes on his clipboard. She wondered if they were going fast enough.

After the fifth lap, Emilio had to pull out; he was winded and pooped. Yet he had done two and a half miles at nearly a mile per six minute speed. Bill told him, "Good job, Emilio, I have just the place on the team for you. I can see you are a shorter distance runner. We need you too." Emilio grinned; he went from a feeling of failure to one of success. He leaned over catching his breath, while watching the other four continue to run. "Coming up on four and a half miles now," Bill called out. "This is incredible!"

"You bet, Bill!" yelled Sally. "We got a good chance this year! I know it!" After the four passed them, Sally and Becky stretched a yellow paper tape, waist high, across the track, simulating the finish line. Bill blew his whistle. "Now we will see," Sally said to Becky. Both watched the four runners intently.

Tom and Jim rapidly pulled out in front of Amanda and Lindsey—their longer legs taking as big a stride as possible. Amanda shook her head "no" and Lindsey continued to maintain pace with her. She knew her brothers and their running styles all too well. As they got to the last quarter of the track, Amanda yelled "now," and put on every ounce of effort she could muster. Her brothers had now exhausted their reserves, and Amanda began closing on both of them. Lindsey was right behind her, but knew she could not catch this fleet-footed Apache.

As the four raced to the finish line, Bill, Sally, Becky, and Emilio began cheering them on—such speed this team had never had! Amanda broke the finish line one head ahead of Tom and two heads ahead of Jim. Lindsey was four heads behind her, about two feet. It was that close of a finish of a five mile run. All eight jumped, yelled, and cheered. Only when the four had caught their breaths did Bill finally make the last stopwatch reading.

"Darn it! Amanda, you beat both of them! Incredible. Boys, you let your little sister beat you?" he teased them. Both smiled and hugged Amanda, who beamed. "Lindsey, you are amazing. We all know that it is next to impossible to beat an Apache in long distance running, but do you realize that you were only two feet behind? Unbelievable! With you four in the long distance team relay run, we are sure to win this year. The rest of us are short distance runners. Sally's won the 100 meter run the last three years straight. So Becky, Jake, Emilio, and I will do the one mile relay race, and you four take the twenty mile relay race. We might actually win this year!"

"How about the soccer team?" asked Sally. She was far more into soccer than mere running.

"I'm sorry. I don't know the first thing about soccer," Lindsey volunteered. Neither did Amanda and Emilio, so she felt better about her ignorance.

"It's really a modified soccer game, altered from what the norm's play," Bill explained. "First, I should say that when you are doing the running, the relays and such, there is no magic allowed. As the teams race, the referee is constantly alert for magical use. If you are caught using any magic at all during the race, the whole team is disqualified and loses. In other words, the track events are a test of your abilities not magically altered abilities."

"The soccer games are very different. Magic is allowed there. Some people call it Wizard Soccer, but most of us think that is being sexist. Why not call it Witches Soccer, eh?" The older girls laughed.

"Let's go out on the field here and I'll show you. Each team has a side and its own goal area with nets. When we play, our side will be all in yellow, naturally. The other team will be trying every way imaginable to get the ball past the metal frame and into the net. The goalkeeper's job is to stay within the marked goal area rectangle here around the net. Sally is our goalkeeper and a good one. Her job is to block the opponent's attempts to get the ball into our net. She can't leave this marked area, and no other players on either side can enter this goalkeeper rectangle."

"Now our game is played with nine players, so you are

all on the team. Two players are stationed back here on our side of the field, to help defend our goal. Their positions are called the left and right fullbacks. Becky is our RFB and Jake is our LFB. They should never, ever go beyond the middle of the playing field, and normally never beyond halfway there. They must protect our net."

"Now Emilio and I will be playing the middle fielder positions, left and right. I play LMF, and Emilio, you will be the RMF. We play around the very middle of the field, our job is to coordinate our attacks on the other team and to help defend our net when they come after us. He and I will move around from about halfway along the field from the center line. We can retreat halfway to our goal or attack about halfway to the enemy's goal, but no farther."

"Our attackers, the ones who are trying to score goals for us, are called the forwards. Tom is our LF and Jim is our RF. Amanda, we are going to try you out at the CF, center forward position. The forwards can go anywhere in the enemy half of the field, but you can also retreat into our half if you need to. The forward's job is somehow to get the ball past their goalkeeper and into the net. Now you are all wondering where Lindsey is going to play. She's going to be our secret weapon. You see the forwards do an awful lot of running, long distances. Yes, they get a big workout during the game. Lindsey will be simply designated as a forward, with no defined location. That means, you, Lindsey, can move all over the place at will, trying to get into a good position for a goal shot."

"Now compared to the norm's version, there are not too many rules we must follow. First, you cannot carry the ball around in your hands. You can catch it, but you must throw it before you move your feet. You can bounce it off your head, kick it with your feet, throw it, just don't move your feet if you are holding onto the ball with your hands. When you want to move the ball forward, usually you give it small successive little kicks."

"You can use all the magic you desire, but the ball is magically altered so that no magical spell at all will affect it, so don't even try. I know, we've tried it a couple times." Sally laughed.

"With your magic, you cannot *ever* cast a spell that affects an opponent player. If you do so, it will be a foul and that person gets a free goal kick attempt. Don't try to Trip another player, for example. You can use all the magic you want on yourself, with one exception. You cannot make your body invisible. Yes, we even tried that one last year, got called for a foul." Sally laughed again.

"It does get very physical out there. However, you cannot *ever* directly hit another player. Yes, you can bump into them while trying to steal the ball from them, but no direct hitting is ever allowed. Man, the refs watch that like a hawk! I even got called for spitting on a player last year. You cannot tackle another player, even if they have the ball. However, in trying to steal the ball, sometimes feet are tangled up and both get thrown to the ground. It does get a bit rough out there."

"Now about stealing the ball. You can snatch it with your hands, kick at it with your feet, and so on, but be careful. If you kick, make darn sure you hit the ball and not the player or the ref will immediately call a foul on you for hurting an opponent."

"Now when someone passes the ball, kicks the ball, or is throwing the ball, even if it's headed for the goal net, you are allowed to block it with any part of your body anyway you can. I've seen players throw their bodies just to block a shot. Ground comes up mighty hard though."

"Above all, stay in your assigned areas. This is a lightning fast game. One second the ball is way down there, the next instant, after a kick, the ball is way up here! You have to stay alert and focused at all times."

"Tell them about what magic to expect," Sally suggested.

"Okay. Some players will grab the ball and levitate into the air, then pass it way down field, knowing that their pass cannot easily be blocked. Some will try to throw you off by making illusions of themselves doing other things. Sometimes, they will make you think that they have suddenly grown ten feet or have shrunk to a foot tall. I always say, just be prepared to have them make you think you see anything at all, don't worry about whether or not it's real. Most of the time, it's just illusions anyway. So don't even wonder if what you are seeing is real or illusionary, just assume it is an illusion and focus only on the ball."

"Oh yes, you cannot pick up the ball, hold it, and then fly around; that is the same as moving your feet with the ball being held. You can hold it and levitate straight upwards, just don't have any horizontal movement. Okay, let's spend the rest of the morning teaching our new three how to move the ball. Tom, Jim, you two work with Amanda and Lindsey; you are all the forwards. I'll work with Emilio. The rest of you, just practice; see if you can devise some new clever strategies. I think that we might have a shot at winning a game or two this year!"

The rest of the morning, the three worked on moving the ball along with their feet while running. For a short while, they practiced kicking goals, while Sally blocked them. Lindsey realized that getting a ball by Sally would be quite a challenge. At lunchtime, as they headed for the showers, Bill told them, "Same time next Saturday. Our first track meet will be in two weeks on Saturday afternoon, so we need to spend our next practice getting everyone ready for the meet."

"Who do we race against?" asked Sally.

Bill sighed, "Black Hall. I know, I know, they are the champions seven years running. I couldn't help it; that's the way the matches came up."

"Fat chance we have of beating them," she muttered. Lindsey thought that this could only mean Black Hall must be really a good team.

"Well, we get a break on the soccer side. Our first match is not until mid-October, so Lindsey will get a chance to see Black Hall versus Brown Hall. We will be playing Red Hall first," Bill replied. Lindsey was grateful for this, since she would be able to see a game before she actually had to play one.

As they entered the dorm, Bill asked, "Say, did anyone see those weird lights over the mountain there last night, must have been around midnight?"

"You saw them too?" Lindsey asked. "Yes, I did too.

What was it?"

"No idea. Could have been a plane, but there is no landing strip anywhere around here. I didn't hear any propellers, not a helicopter either. I'll ask around and let you know if I find out anything."

After lunch, the group hit their books again, crowding around a round table. Emilio doodled with his pen, "I just can't concentrate well. These figures make my head spin."

"Well, let me check what you've got done so far," Pam offered, and immediately found three errors in the four problems he had worked. Emilio sighed and looked out the window; he'd much rather be outside on this sunny afternoon. Meanwhile, Lindsey looked over Pam's essay and made five corrections to her grammar. By supper, they had most of their homework finished. To celebrate, they all went for a walk in the formal gardens.

The next week passed rapidly. Between her excitement over learning the new spells each day and all the assignments, she had little spare time. However, Bill came by each evening to talk about how the races would be conducted, strategies to follow, but most of all just how the baton would be passed to and from Lindsey. He finally admitted, "Lindsey, I've never been around someone like you, I mean with no hands. I really don't know what is possible or what is the best way. I feel like I am letting you down. I'm supposed to be your captain. It would be so much easier if we were allowed some small magic for the hand-offs."

"I cannot run while holding my arms together around the baton, that's for sure. Maybe I can hold it in my mouth and still run well enough," she suggested. "If only I could use my phantasmal hands, I could take and give the baton with them."

"Well, if you can run with it—no, you can't run well with it in your mouth. I've just had an idea. There is nothing in the rulebook about having to hold the baton in your hands while running. It says," he waved his wand and a rulebook appeared, opened to the right page, "the baton is passed from one runner to the next runner. Ah ha, it doesn't say how it must be passed. What if we made a pocket on the side of your pants big enough to hold the baton? Then when it is time to pass the baton to say Jim, he can pull it out of your pocket."

"That will work with me," Lindsey sighed with relief; she could run after all!

September 21 came, a sunny, but chilly first day of fall. Already the aspens on the grounds had turned to gold. The Yellow Track team waited nervously in the small waiting room, conjured by Professor Cho Lin for them. Nearby, the Black Hall team waited as well. Nearly six hundred students and teachers packed the stands around the Stadium awaiting the start of this first track meet of the year. Lindsey heard Professor Blake Smith announcing the rules, emphasizing that magic use of any kind would mean instant elimination.

Since the twenty-mile relay race took so long, the dual lengthy competitions took place at the same time, only the two event participants ran the track in opposite directions from each other. Today it would be Blue Hall versus Brown Hall and Black Hall versus Yellow Hall.

"And now let's have a big welcome for the Black Hall track team, winners for the last seven years, the unbeatable Blacks!" The crowd gave them a hearty welcome, cheering, whistling, and yelling.

"Now let's give a warm welcome to Yellow Hall. Perhaps they will be better this year." The applause was significantly smaller.

"Okay, let's do it!" Bill exclaimed and led the group out onto the field. They took their positions at one end. Lindsey noticed the crowd and became very nervous, so many were watching them. Worse, she felt that every student in the school had their eyes staring at her!

The first event was the 100-meter run, Sally's specialty. "On your mark. Get set. Go," yelled Professor Blake. Very quickly, he added, "And that's another victory for Black Hall. Five points to Black Hall. Score is five to zero." The crowd roared and cheered. Sally returned looking rather dejected.

"You did your best, Sally, that's all we can ask. You nearly beat him," Bill consoled her. She nodded and sat down to watch the remainder of the contest.

"Next, we have the one-mile relay race. Now we've heard rumors that Yellow Hall has been practicing on this all summer, so let's see how it has paid off. Runners, assume your starting positions." He announced the four runners for Black Hall, and then with the Yellow Hall runners in their starting positions, evenly spaced around the track, he said, "Becky Salinos will begin the run, handing off at the quarter mile point to Jake Rattlebeam, who hands off to the newcomer to this event, Emilio Lopez, the little brother to Brown Hall's speed demon, Francesco Lopez. Emilio hands off to the Yellow Hall captain himself, Bill Ferny. Let's give them all a big round of applause." Indeed, the crowd yelled and cheered, probably, Lindsey thought, to cheer on Black Hall, not Yellow Hall.

The race began. Professor Blake announced, "Look at this, Becky sure has improved; it's a virtual tie at the first handoff!" The noise of the crowd almost made it impossible to hear his amplified voice. Lindsey found herself cheering wildly, as Jake remained neck and neck, handing off to Emilio.

"Come on, Emilio! You can do it!" she yelled loudly, but her noise merely joined the cacophony echoing around the Stadium.

"Will you look at that? This new Emilio has kept pace with Armstrong, neck and neck. Now it all comes down to the speed of the two team captains. They are running neck and neck, coming down the finish line. Well I'll be, Yellow Hall actually won the race! Bill was one foot ahead of Henry! What a photo-finish race that was. Ten points to Yellow Hall. The score stands: Yellow Hall, ten; Black Hall, five. If memory serves me right, isn't this the first time that Black Hall has been behind in the scoring in years now? Wow!"

Next, Brown Hall and Blue Hall competed in these same two events. Lindsey was so worried about her race she paid no attention to these shorter competitions, concentrating on getting warmed up and ready to go. Soon, she could not ignore Professor Blake and his announcing.

"Well, it all comes down to the really big race, ladies and gentlemen. The race you have all been waiting for, the twenty mile relay race, testing man's and woman's endurance to the limit. Each racer must run five miles before handing off the baton to their next racer. That's five grueling miles, ladies and gentlemen. How many of you can race five miles, eh? See your PE teachers if you cannot. That's a commercial, by the way." It was Professor Blake's lame attempt at humor.

While Professor announced the runners for Black Hall, Tom put the baton into Lindsey's leg pocket on her right side. "Now remember, don't look at your opponent at first, try to set the pace that we've been training with, you can do it. Just find that pace. He will blow the whistle when you are entering your last lap around the field, that's when you make your speed move. Just remember to get in synch with Jim so he can take the baton from your pocket. You can do it I know it, Lindsey. You must have Apache blood in you. No one else can keep up with us." She smiled, but didn't think that was so, unless her father's side had some Indian blood in it somewhere.

"And now for Yellow Hall, first year Lindsey Barron will take the lead off position. Our hearts go out for this *poor*, young student, who gives it her all. She will pass off to the Apache trio, yes, trio. Jim Whitewater runs next, passing to his brother, Tom, and surprise, surprise, the finish runner is none other than their sister, first year Amanda! Incredible. Let's hear it for these Apaches and Yellow Hall. Remember, this contest can now go either way, with the twenty points available to the winner. This race will determine the winner of the entire match. Runners, take your positions."

Lindsey had so many butterflies in her stomach that she lost count. "Focus, focus," she told herself. Then, she was off and running. She resisted the strong temptation to look over at her competitor. Instead, she concentrated on finding the pace that Jim and Tom always set for her and Amanda. At last, she found it and just ran. All thoughts left her mind; the crowd dissolved into nothingness. It was just her, the smooth track, and the wind blowing against her face, a cool wind at that, not the scorching summer heat.

She knew that she had to make ten trips around the entire stadium track. Already, her Black Hall opponent, whose name she had forgotten, had passed her by putting on a burst of speed. From long experience, she knew this was either a taunt by him or a very dumb move on his part, because there were nine long trips around the track yet ahead of them.

As she finished her first pass and went by Tom, Jim,

and Amanda, all three were nodding their heads, so she knew that she had the right pace—the pace that they wanted her to use. She concentrated on breathing and maintaining that pace. On the third circuit, her opponent fell back behind her, unable to keep up his original pace. Again, Lindsey did not know if this was because she had not taken the bait and broken her pace or if he really was tiring because of a foolish move on his part. Only when the last lap came would she know which one it was.

Lindsey did not know that the pace the Apaches had set for her was continuous six-minute miles! Five of them in a row. She had never really been interested in sports; she just loved to run, run home to escape the cruel teasing at school in Plano. Run home. She continued to run home around the track.

Around her, the crowd went wild, yelling, cheering, and whistling. She couldn't see that she was close to lapping her opponent! She didn't know that if all four ran as she did, six-minute miles, that they would be breaking the Bradbury school record time for this relay race. Lindsey just ran home.

At last, the whistle blew, signaling to her that this would be her last lap. Now she poured it on, gave it everything she had held back in reserve. Lindsey flew down the track, approaching nearly a 5:30 mile. As she neared the last long straight stretch, she couldn't see her opponent; she was close to lapping him twice! She watched as Jim began to run, getting up to her speed. Once he was matching her, he would be reaching for the baton in her pocket. The crowd went wild with enthusiasm.

Wham! From the corner of her eye, Lindsey saw a flash of magical energy; she felt her feet lock up, the ground came flying at her face. She put out her arms instinctively and they hit the ground hard. Crack. Pain! Shooting pain arced up both of her arms. She screamed and blacked out.

It was dark. Her eyes opened, but it was dark. Her arms throbbed. She screamed. A soft voice said, "There, there, you will be just fine." She'd never heard that voice before. She struggled to sit up, but couldn't move either arm for some reason. A dim light turned on.

She was lying in a hospital bed. Both of her arms were wrapped in big bandages and securely held in place above her waist so that she couldn't move them at all. "I'm Doctor Frank Caterwall. You took a very nasty fall there, Lindsey Barron. You've broken both arms in several places, but you will be just fine in a few days, all healed up. Trust me," he winked at her and gave her a kiss on her forehead. "I want you to take a sip of this; it will help you sleep and allow my magic to work even better."

Lindsey did as he asked, but began crying. "It hurts so badly," she whimpered.

"I know, I know, but it will feel better each day. Tonight is the worst. Now lie back and sleep; it is the middle of the night." She heard no more of his words; his brew worked on her at once; she fell sound asleep.

Light. She saw light. Lindsey opened her eyes. The room smelled like a doctor's office, all sterile, but the blinds were open, allowing in the morning light. "Hello? Anyone here?" she said timidly, looking at her heavy bandages and wondering how she could go to the bathroom or even eat. At once, a nurse came and helped her to use the bedpan.

"Are you up to eating and having visitors, Lindsey?" she asked.

"Yes, I am very hungry, but I can't move my arms." The nurse smiled and left. She returned shortly with a tray of steaming, hot food. The entire Yellow Hall track team followed her, along with Pam and Kathy. Even Professor Cho Lin and Governor Alister followed them to her side.

"We all came to feed you," Amanda said sympathetically. "How are you doing? Gosh, it looks so bad. We heard that you broke both arms in three places."

"It doesn't hurt so badly just now, sort of throbbing, and they feel funny. What happened to me? My legs just stopped working. I saw a magical energy flash."

Bill spoke up, "You are right. Governor Alister found traces of the spell someone cast against you, even before the doctor got to you. That man is a genius, I swear! He traced the magical energy back to a specific wand! It was the Black Hall boy, Lyle Armstrong. He cast a Trip spell on you. You will be glad to know that Lyle will be spending the next month in detention. It's the longest detention on record here at Bradbury's!"

"Besides, we won the race! After Governor Alister discovered what had happened, he awarded Yellow Hall the victory. Of course, he also threatened expulsion for anyone who tries anything like this again. He was really mad!"

"He's right," Amanda added. "His face was bright red! I thought he might just beat up Lyle on the spot!"

"Oh dear, was it that noticeable?" the voice of Governor Alister spoke up from behind the group. Bill's face turned red as he turned to see who spoke. Governor Alister's smile melted his embarrassment.

"Okay, I think Lindsey has had enough company for a little while," Doctor Caterwall said, as he came to check up on his patient. "One of you may come back at lunch if you wish to help feed Lindsey. I know that she will appreciate it." Amanda promised first, but so did Kathy and Pam.

With her classmates gone, Governor Alister said kindly, "Well, Miss Barron, Bill tended to exaggerate a bit there, I'm sure. The essence is true. Your team was on pace to set a new school record, I believe, but soon you four will have another shot at that. What Lyle did, no one can condone, a terrible misuse of magic. I can only chalk it up to his extreme youth and desire to see his team win. I had a decision to make, Miss Barron. By now, you know the Four Laws of Magic Use. It would seem that Lyle did violate them, wouldn't you say?"

"Well, yes. Thou shalt not use magic to injure or harm another unjustly," Lindsey remembered and said, just as she memorized it two weeks ago.

"You see, I had to make a choice with Lyle. Send him to prison, expel him from school seeing to it that no other school would accept him, or give him a long detention. I chose detention. Does that seem fair enough to you, Miss Barron?"

"Well, yes, sir. We are only just learning how to do magic. I know he has been often angry towards me, but I think Deiter Cross has been egging him on. I'm glad that you didn't expel him. Can people change? I mean so many seem to dislike me here."

"Who can say? Perhaps detention will. I'm glad that you agree with my choice. Doctor Caterwall has assured me that you will make a full and complete recovery, Miss Barron. I for one will be anxiously awaiting Yellow Hall's next track meet. I do hope you four can set a new school record. We haven't set new track records for many years now. I'll let you in on a little secret that Bill hasn't told you yet."

He leaned over and whispered, "If you set a new record, Yellow Hall will be going to the National Track Meet in Des Moines, Iowa, in the spring. Bradbury's has not been to Nationals in many years. I'm rooting for you." He smiled and had a twinkle in his eye. Lindsey managed to return his smile. He then left, leaving Professor Cho Lin with her.

"Well, Lindsey, I'm very proud of the way you handled yourself on the track, true to Yellow Hall standards of bravery and fearlessness. You beat out a fourth year track runner, well done. Are you sure that you don't have some Apache blood in you? Just teasing, dear. Don't worry about missing spell-casting classes. When you are well, I will assist you in catching back up in no time, if you need it."

"Thank you, Professor, I was really worried about missing so much."

"Ahem, Professor Cho Lin, I really do need to examine my patient now," Doctor Caterwall interrupted. She nodded, gave Lindsey a kiss on her forehead and left.

"There now, how's my patient doing today? Feeling better?" he asked, his voice full of sympathy.

"Well, it doesn't hurt so, only throbbing and it feels awfully funny like," Lindsey answered.

"Ah, that is good. Now I want you to listen to me very carefully, Lindsey. This is terribly important. I want you to drink ten glasses of milk each day, ten. More if you can. I will have the nurses keep your glass here filled. You can use these tubes I've fixed up for you. Suck, and the milk will flow. Ten glasses, promise me."

"Yes, sir. Is that because my bones need to heal? Will they be stiff and sore forever now?"

"Yes, milk for your bones. Actually, Lindsey, it isn't exactly milk. I've added a lot of calcium from green vegetables to it, since it's so hard to get you children to eat your veggies. That's why its color is a bit odd. As for your second question, I expect you will be fitter than fit in a week's time, yes indeed, fitter than when you came in here, yes indeed." He had a mysterious twinkle in his eyes.

The day passed very slowly for Lindsey, who was used to an active lifestyle. She drank as much milk as she possibly could and kept the two nurses busy with the chamber pot. Amanda came to feed her lunch, while Pam came for dinner.

That evening, Doctor Caterwall returned with an armload of new bandages. "Now then, are you feeling up to watching me change the bandages, Lindsey? It might be a trifle painful. If not, I can give you a sleep potion first."

"Will it hurt badly?" she asked. "What would you recommend?"

"I'd recommend the sleeping potion for tonight, Lindsey, unless you can tolerate some pain. I'd prefer it if you didn't move your arms while I am working on them." She agreed and sipped some more of his potion, the same stuff she remembered sipping earlier. Before she could comment on it, she fell into a peaceful, deep sleep. Doctor Caterwall went about his business, unwrapping her arms.

"Ah, indeed, very, very good. By golly, I expect I'll be able to get a paper in the Magical Physician's Journal out of all this." An hour later, he had her all wrapped up once more. After checking on the magical milk supply, noting on her chart the quantity that she had consumed this day, he kissed her forehead and left.

The next morning, Kathy came to feed her breakfast. "We have all agreed that we will be taking notes today in all our classes for you. Pam is fixing it up so that all our notes will be sent to your computer. Then, tonight we will all come by and do our studying here with you, going over everything, though I suppose you will have to just pretend doing the new spells, until you are well again."

"Thank you, Kathy. Tell the others thanks for me will you?"

"Sure. You'd have done as much for one of us. Pam will be by to feed you lunch. Emilio is coming to feed you supper and have you look over his math papers. Honestly, he is worse than I am at math and I thought I was bad!"

After Kathy left, Lindsey finally learned what utter, true boredom was like! She could only lie in bed and do absolutely nothing but sip on milk all day! She relished the brief visit by Pam, who fed her lunch, and she counted the minutes until suppertime, when Emilio would come.

She welcomed him with open arms, figuratively, since hers were fixed securely in an open position. While he fed her supper, she looked over his math papers and suggested ten changes, which he dutifully made. "I don't know what I would do without you, Lindsey."

"You'd be flunking math, that's what," she teased him. He grinned. Soon, the other three joined him, bringing in all their computers. Emilio carried in a table and Pam fixed up Lindsey's computer screen so that she could see it. Rapidly, the group went over Monday's math and science lectures.

"Golly, if I am in here a week, I will be so far behind that I can never catch up," Lindsey complained.

"I've thought of that today," Pam declared, "and being the techno-geek that I am, I have come up with a solution for you." She plugged in a phone jack. "This used to be one of those handless phones, which you put in your ear and the mouth microphone swings down like so. I've rigged it up to your computer and installed dad's VR software, that's Voice Recognition. You can speak and give the computer orders to follow. Try saying 'Open new document.'" Lindsey did so and watched her word processor open up a new document.

"Wow!" she exclaimed. Immediately, the word 'Wow!' appeared on the screen.

"You can dictate your essays and answers to the math and science assignments. I have already gotten permission from the two professors to allow you to complete them this way. At least, you won't be much behind on these. I'll talk with Professor Elaine about your doing your grammar and essays for her this way as well. Hopefully, you will only be behind in what is really important, spell casting."

Amanda interrupted, "Yes, but we've decided to spend much of each evening going over them with you. We can practice them with you. Maybe you will be able to catch up quickly, once you have your arms back."

For Lindsey, the evening passed altogether far too quickly. When they finally had to leave near ten that evening, she thanked them repeatedly.

Shortly after that, Doctor Caterwall made his nightly round. "And how's my only patient doing this evening? How's those arms feel?"

"They still throb some, but they feel even funnier than last night. I think that they are very itchy somehow. Is that all right?" Lindsey was a little concerned about the itching, especially since she could do nothing about it.

"Yes, itching is a very good sign indeed, because it means they are healing. You have probably noticed that effect before. When you have a cut and it begins to heal, it often itches a little." She nodded that she had. "However, in this case, we are doing magical healing, but at a very, very rapid pace, I might add. Thus, it itches much more, and you need to keep drinking as much milk as you can each day. Now I do need to change the bandages again. Shall we do as we did last night and get you a leg up on a good night's sleep?"

"Yes, but can you take this phone thing out of my ear and turn off my computer there? They've got it hooked up so I can do some of my homework during the daytime."

"Yes, that Pam is a whiz at computers isn't she," he commented. Soon, Lindsey was sound asleep, a deep refreshing, dreamless sleep, just what the doctor greatly desired. He was very pleased that she willingly allowed him this very private time to change her bandages and see how his magic was coming along. "Perfect, even better than I had hoped," he muttered, after he had removed all the bandages. A half hour later, all notes made, he turned out her light and left.

The next four days went well for her. During the mornings and afternoons, she reviewed all the notes her friends had taken for her and managed to get all her assignments in the three subjects completed. Evenings, she studied hard while they reviewed the three magic classes. She spent as much time as possible helping them with their science and math assignments. This was the very least she could do for their ceaseless assistance.

Friday night, after her friends had left, Doctor Caterwall came in whistling—a cheery mood indeed. "Well, how's my only patient tonight? How's that itching doing?"

"Oh the throbbing is gone now, but the itching is going berserk! It is even itching where my hands ought to be! Imagine that. It must be my phantasmal hands that are also itching."

"Well, I have brought some soothing cream with me tonight. That should relieve that discomfort. Okay then, I think that tonight we shall take the bandages off and leave them off. What say you?"

"I wish I could move my arms, you know, get up and walk around some. I'm so sore just lying here."

"I know; it could not be avoided, under these very special circumstances," he winked at her, but she had no idea what he meant. "Okay, close your eyes while I remove the bandages. When I tell you, you can open them. Okay?" She nodded and closed her eyes, preparing for some throbbing pain as he removed them. She felt none. "Yes, indeed. Perfect. You may open your eyes now, Lindsey."

She opened them, looked at her arms, and gasped. At the ends of each were hands, real hands, very pinkish and weak, but hands. She wiggled them to make sure they were real.

"Yes, real hands, Lindsey. Honestly, your parents ought to have had this done right after you were born, but as I understand it from the School Seeker, your parents were exceedingly poor and could not afford it. Well, just between you and me, I really shouldn't have done this for you. However, I have been extremely bored myself this term. You have been my only patient for weeks. With your arms so badly broken, I took the liberty of performing the magical operation myself. Even Governor Alister does not know yet that I've done this, not even the two nurses, though by now I expect that they have probably guessed that is what I've done. So yes, Lindsey, those are real hands, perfect hands, if I do say so myself."

"How can I ever thank you? This is a miracle for me. Thank you, thank you, Doctor Caterwall!"

"Yes, you are most welcome, Lindsey. No longer will you be at such a disadvantage here. Between you and me, I felt so awful for you. Now, then, when they get itchy, rub this cream on them. For the next two nights, I still want you to sleep with your arms up. After that, they should be finished growing. Unless something comes up, I will be releasing you to go back to your normal activities on Sunday night. How does that sound?"

"Fabulous, thank you, thank you." She gave him a big, long hug. He helped her up and to exercise for a while. Then, he got her back in bed and she took a sip of his sleeping potion. Doctor Caterwall wanted her to sleep soundly, with her arms raised for another two nights, just to play it safe.

Of course, by morning, the cat was out of the bag. Before noon, everyone knew what the good doctor had done. Lindsey sure hoped that he did not get into trouble because of it, however. Her roommates had all come at breakfast, once Pam had rushed down to tell them the big surprise. By lunchtime, the entire track team dropped by to see her new hands and to congratulate her. For Lindsey, this day marked a total turning point in her life; no longer was she unlike other people; no longer was she so helpless. Life took on a completely new dimension for her.

"Mom! I've got hands now!" she fairly screamed into her cell phone Sunday night when she returned to her room and called her mother. Life looked incredibly brighter to this twelve year old girl. The future could only be wonderful for her now.

Chapter 6—Samuel Rabnor

"Oh look, Lindsey's now got hands," sneered Deiter Cross, as Lindsey and Amanda walked into math class Monday morning. Of course, everyone in the room now stared at Lindsey and her new hands, whispering crescendoed. Professor Mac Elroy walked in and the noise died down.

"So glad that you are back with us, Miss Barron. I hate to do this to you, but it will put an end to it. Will you please raise both your hands high, Lindsey? Class look at them. Okay. Now then, that will be all. Detention for the next person I catch staring at her," he said both sternly and resolutely. Lindsey felt relieved. Most of these first years were in all her other classes, so perhaps the rest of the day would go better, somehow.

"All right, class. We have now completed our basic review of what you should have already known from your previous schools. From now on, it is new material for the majority of you. Today we embark on a study of fractions. For example, next year many of you will begin to study potion making. You will be asked to add one half cup of soy oil plus another quarter cup of soy oil. How much soy oil will you need? You see, you are being asked to add $1/2 + 1/4$ together. To do so, you need to find the common denominator of the fractions involved."

Kathy and Emilio groaned. This looked nearly impossible to them. While this particular problem seemed easy to solve, Lindsey knew that math was suddenly going to be much more difficult. The homework problems, she realized, were not going to be easily solved with her computer's calculator.

In science class, Professor Jasper Jones made an exciting announcement, however. "We have now completed our survey of our solar system and the constellations. For the next month, you are to plot the movement of Venus, Mars, and Jupiter on these star charts. This means for the next month, you will be allowed out of your dorm rooms until midnight.

Indeed, on the top of this very building is our observatory with a twenty-four inch telescope. At ten o'clock, you will all report to the observatory so that you can learn how to use it and observe the heavens above. Your Floor Monitors will bring you here and walk you back. I think that you will truly enjoy this bit of stargazing. I know that I always do."

Kathy groaned as they walked to their next class. "A whole month of plotting the stupid positions of the planets. Heck, I still don't know which is which!"

"Yes, but we will be allowed outside until midnight, that's something," Pam countered.

"But I need my sleep," Emilio countered. "I'm already falling asleep in math and science classes!"

"That's because you are always bored," Pam insisted. Emilio glared at her.

As they entered Professor Janice's spell casting class, Deiter Cross found a new way to tease Lindsey. "Lindsey has to use her wand now. She has hands. I wonder whose hands she stole?"

Professor Janice batted her long eyelashes at Deiter. "I'm sure that she has not stolen my hands, Deiter." She waggled them both daintily, displaying her long, cherry red nails to the whole class. The boys sitting in the front rows watched them closely.

"Well, Miss Barron, glad that you have finally returned to my class. I can see that now you no longer have any excuse for not using your wand properly. Therefore, in the future, Miss Barron, I will be docking you points for any wand failures. Now, class, open your spell books to page forty-two."

Leaving the class when the bell finally rang, Lindsey didn't try to mask her tears. She had just received a minus thirty for today's grade. Because she had missed a week's worth of spell training, she could not do today's spells at all. Professor Janice had been merciless in docking her points for every failure.

"Since we have to go to the observatory all month until midnight, I'll never have any time to catch up. By the end of the week, I'll be minus hundreds of points! I'll flunk for sure now," she wailed.

"That is sure not fair of Professor Janice! Honestly, all she does is sit there and flirt with the boys!" Pam said angrily.

"Why does she treat Lindsey so harshly?" Amanda wondered aloud. "Professors Herbert, Jasper, and Elaine are at least allowing her to catch up."

"Well, she is darn sexy," Emilio replied. Pam kicked him in his butt. "Ouch! That's the truth. You don't like her just because you are ugly," he retorted.

"Fine, then you do your own math and science papers!" Pam declared and walked quickly ahead of him, fighting to keep from showing her tears. For the rest of the day, Pam did not speak to Emilio.

Pam didn't join them for supper, however. Lindsey and Amanda went looking for her. They found her crying in the girl's bathroom, which was deserted just now, as everyone else was in the dining room eating supper.

"He didn't really mean it, Pam," Lindsey tried to console her friend.

"Yes, he did. I really am ugly. I'm not pretty like you, Amanda."

"You are the smartest engineer that I know, Pam," Amanda tried to find something to counter her declaration. That only brought more tears.

Lindsey felt heartsick for her friend. Indeed the parallels were too close for comfort. "Back in Plano, after that, I'd just run all the way home, Pam, an entire mile. I know how you are feeling; I've had that nearly every school day since first grade. Who cares whether you are pretty or not anyway?"

"Girls are *supposed* to be pretty!" she retorted. "*Everybody* knows that."

"Girls are *supposed* to have hands, too. Everybody knows that," Lindsey replied and waited to see how Pam reacted to this.

"Oh!" Pam looked at her, suddenly realizing that this was precisely what Lindsey had always been having to deal with every day here.

"Now I have hands. Has it made any difference to Deiter or Professor Janice?"

"Well, no, it may be worse with her," Pam conceded.

"How do you manage it, Lindsey? I mean, well, it hurts so."

"It sure does. I try to ignore it as best I can, but mostly I just go on being me and doing what I like. I sure as heck am not going to let them ruin my life!" Lindsey said angrily.

"Darn right! I won't let Emilio ruin my life. So I am not pretty. Tough. He can just shove it!" Pam glared.

"Right," Amanda jumped in. "Besides, perhaps we will learn spells that we can use to make ourselves better looking. I bet half of what we see with Professor Janice is just a magical alteration, somehow. Maybe she has an ugly wart underneath all that magic."

Pam thought that was a curious notion. Could it be that all that glamor of Janice's was merely magical alterations? Anyway, Pam felt somewhat better now and the three went down to get Pam some dinner.

Between six and nine that night, Lindsey began working hard to catch up on the spells she was supposed to have learned during the week she missed. Since Pam was not speaking with Emilio, she also took a little time to look over and correct his math and science homework.

Later, Sandy led them all over to the Science Hall and up to the observatory. Absolutely all the class thoroughly enjoyed looking through the telescope! In fact, Lindsey became fascinated with stargazing. Midnight came altogether far too soon for her. Sleepily, Sandy led them all back to their dorm. While her friends went to bed immediately, Lindsey stayed up until two in the morning studying her spell casting, finally giving it up when she nearly dozed off and fell on her wand, nearly poking out her right eye.

Unfortunately, she found herself almost dozing off in both math and science class as a result. Nevertheless, Professor Janice continued to dock her points in spell casting, though not as many. Today she was only minus five when the bell rang.

Wednesday night, right after supper, Bill came up to her. "Say, can I have a private word with you, Lindsey? It's not about track or soccer, I promise." She had her fill of his coaching tips already. Nearly every day he had dropped some new tip on her plate. Right now, she was more worried about spell casting than running.

They ducked downstairs into the giant tunnel complex, which was empty now. "Remember those strange lights that we saw around midnight?" She nodded; she'd already forgotten all about them.

"Well, I've been asking around about them. Strange indeed. I asked Professor Cho Lin about them and she said that I must have been dreaming. I asked Governor Alister about them and he said that Bradbury's is enchanted against any airplane coming over, against any helicopter landing, and against any flying wizard for that matter. He said I must have imagined it all and that no such thing occurred! Lindsey, we didn't imagine those lights nor were we dreaming."

"So I started asking around, being clever about it, you know. No need starting more rumors about Yellow Hall and imaginary flying machines. Guess what? Tom Spade of Black Hall, a fifth year student also saw the lights at the same time as we did. Only Black Hall faces south. He swears that the lights hovered or landed in the parking lot! He swears that he saw lights for a short time appear in the Administration Hall! We did see something, and I think that we were not *supposed* to see what we saw!"

"Curiouser and curiouser," Lindsey replied. "Someone is up to something and we aren't supposed to know about it. I've not been in the Administration Hall. What's in there?"

"I've only been inside there a couple times. Mostly just offices I think. Probably got our school records in there as well. Guess that's why students don't go there often. Anyway, I thought I ought to let you know that we weren't dreaming. Got to run. Don't forget the soccer match on Saturday afternoon. Bye."

That night, while they were studying before the nine o'clock hour came and they would have to go to the observatory once more, Lindsey noticed that Pam was missing. Instead, she made Emilio work with her on practicing the spells that she didn't know and then corrected his math and science papers. Unfortunately, Kathy's work also needed to be corrected as well, but Lindsey managed to get another batch of spells operational.

When Sandy was leading them all to the observatory, Pam hastily ran up and joined their group, acting as if she had been there all along. "Where have you been?" Lindsey whispered to her.

"Around," was all Pam would say, very mysteriously. As they walked to the Science Hall, Governor Alister and Professor Jasper Jones were finishing up a conversation. Lindsey overheard a snippet, however. Alister was saying, "Honestly, Jasper, it's all blown out of proportion. Only a small about of gold was actually missing from Fort Knox. You know how the papers exaggerate so."

"Well, if you say so. Here come my students. We'll talk more later. Good evening class," Professor Jasper said cheerily, quite unlike a moment before, when he was dead serious, as if something was terribly wrong. Lindsey realized that she had not been listening to the news for many days now. She wondered if this was on the news and decided to listen when she got back at midnight.

That night when everyone else was in bed, she plugged in her earphones that Pam had hooked up to her radio. She whispered, "Tune to KMAG." At once, she was hearing a rebroadcast of the news.

"Yes, today Dominus Malefic has struck once more. This time, he attacked the US Treasury at Fort Knox. This heavily guarded, top security facility holds the nation's wealth in gold, silver, and platinum. Three guards, including a wizard from the Department of Defense, were brutally slain during the robbery. Fort Knox holds billions of dollars. Just how much was stolen? KMAG has spent the day questioning anyone who works there, but all that we were told was 'No comment.' Does this mean that the country is broke? That the entire nation's wealth is gone? Speculations are running wild."

Lindsey yawned, turned off the news, and tried to practice a few more spells while sitting on her bed. She had the curtains pulled and performed them under her covers, trying hard not to wake her three roommates. At last, she fell asleep on her spell book.

The next day, Pam was still not talking to Emilio and he was ignoring her, though he still sat close to Lindsey and

Amanda. Lindsey, however, didn't much care; she was trying hard to stay awake all morning. In spell casting class, she did better, earning ten points today, instead of the one hundred that she desired. At least it wasn't negative as it had been the first two days back.

In her conjuration theory class, things got interesting for a few minutes. Someone in Brown Hall asked Professor Blake Smith about the recent robbery of Fort Knox. He replied, "No, our country is not broke. It's been blown all out of proportion." Lindsey realized he was merely repeating what Alister had been saying to Professor Jasper.

"Gold is very heavy, though wizards can deal with that. After all, how often do you buy a candy bar using a gold coin, eh? Even if he stole tons of gold, what's the point? You cannot go around spending it, like you can this dollar bill?" His wand activated and a dollar appeared in his hand.

"Say, can we learn how to make money?" asked Deiter. "Now that would be a *useful* spell!"

"Mr. Cross, you don't want to go conjuring dollar bills. If that were allowed, it would totally wreck the world's economic system. Hence, the Department of Defense has installed numerous magical safeguards against any wizard or witch trying to pass off conjured money. However, class, this makes an excellent topic for your research. By next Friday, you are all to write an essay on 'Why conjuring money would wreck the world's economic system.' This ties right into our conjuration theory." He launched into his lecture, but the whole class groaned over the lengthy assignment, with only ten days to do it.

"There goes my weekend," Kathy whispered to Lindsey.

On their way to supper that evening, Amanda asked Lindsey, "Say, Jim is taking me on a tour of the Trophy Room over in the Admin Hall. He wants to show me the various cups that Yellow Hall has won over the years. Want to tag along?"

Having a chance to look inside the Administration Hall wetted her curiosity, but the fifty points out of a hundred in spell casting had her more than worried. "No, I have to get the rest of the spells that you learned last week worked out. I'm sure to flunk anyway, but I have to try." She really wanted to go with them, but with the soccer match on Saturday and all these late nights at the observatory coupled with the numerous essays, not to mention she had not yet started on them, ruled the evening. Amanda dashed off with her brother, while Lindsey went to eat before cracking her books.

She had just finished her stroganoff when Amanda came running into the dining room looking for her. "Lindsey, Lindsey! That picture you have on your desk, that's your family, right? I mean it's a picture of your father?"

"Yes, it is the last one I have, taken when I was five, just before, well, I found him." Images of that horrible day returned when she had found their tractor lying on his crushed body out in the small field of their ranch.

"Well, you just have to come with me, now!" Amanda said excitedly, "Come on!"

She pulled Lindsey by the arm until she got up and began following her. "What is the matter, Amanda? Where are we going?"

"To the Trophy Room, that's where. You just *have* to see this." Amanda would not say anything further about it, however. It took them only a few minutes to race to the southwestern corner where the Admin Hall was located. Just inside the northeast door was the Trophy Room. Jim was still standing there, waiting for them.

The room was shaped like a pentagram, which Lindsey did not find unusual anymore. Each side of the room was one of the colors of their dorm, exactly in the same order. Black Hall trophies were right here where the main door was located. Lindsey could see Yellow Hall's wall of trophies to the northeast. "Come on, over here," Amanda pulled her to a specific section.

Shelves held various golden trophies shaped like cups, runners, and even a soccer player kicking a ball. Behind them were photographs of teams with their names clearly marked. Across the top were the corresponding dates. Amanda led her to a large cup won by the Yellow Hall track team, some twenty years ago. "What?" asked Lindsey, who could not imagine what Amanda was so excited about, just a stupid trophy from twenty years ago.

"Look at the boys in the photograph, the older ones. I know it was twenty years ago, but look anyway," Amanda insisted, pushing her close to the picture. "Doesn't that look. . ."

"My dad? That looks like my father!" Lindsey exclaimed. She looked at the names below the pictures. "No, it can't be, Amanda. Look, it says this boy is Samuel Rabnor. My father was Samuel Barron, not Rabnor. It just sort of looks like him, that's all."

"Look at the letters of his last name, r a b n o r. Now look at the letters in your last name, b a r r o n. Shuffle the letters around, Lindsey! They are the same! This must have been your father!" Amanda said triumphantly.

Jim broke in, "Hey, while you were gone, sis, I found four more pictures of Sam. Here, here, here, and here. This Sam fellow was quite good at track and soccer. He was captain of the Yellow Hall soccer team in his sixth year, and they won the Hall Trophy that year. He and Yellow Hall won the school track and field trophy three years in a row. This one is for winning the National Long Distance Relay Race in his sixth year. The fellow was quite an athlete."

Lindsey, her mouth open, went from picture to picture, staring at each in complete and utter disbelief. There was no doubt about it. The resemblance was uncanny. True, he was thirteen years older when he died, but the body build and the face were nearly identical with Lindsey's photograph. His eyes were green, just like hers. "It's probably an uncanny coincidence," Lindsey finally suggested.

She took out her cell phone and took a picture of each one of them, sending them to her computer in her room. The three left and headed back to the dorm. "If that was your father, why would he change his name?" asked Jim.

"He was obviously a wizard, sixth year at least, but he probably graduated. I don't think they let you play if you flunk out," Amanda added.

"Yes, but my father was a norm. He never did anything magical. I never saw him with a wand or spell book or anything," Lindsey countered and sighed, "but then, I was only five when he died. I don't remember much about him, just that he loved to hug and hold me, and play with me. If that was him, why would he change his name and hide being a wizard? It doesn't make any sense at all. It is probably just one of those crazy look alike situations, really that must be it."

When the two got back to their room in Yellow Hall, they found Kathy buried in her books, but Pam was working on her computer. Pam looked up with a sly, satisfied look on her face. "Lindsey, tomorrow I believe that Professor Janice will be treating you fairly. In fact, she will be fair to you from now on!"

"Huh? What are you talking about?" asked Lindsey and Amanda together. Pam sometimes made little sense. After all, her mind was that of a techno-geek.

"Oh, I just sent a little something to Professor Janice, a little something that will ensure that she treats you fairly from now on, Lindsey," Pam declared proudly. However, unable to contain her excitement, she just had to show them what she had emailed Professor Janice.

"You know how she is always pulling up her robes, showing off her legs to the boys in class, well, I guessed there might be more to it than that. I, er, I put a minicam, a Spy Cam, in her classroom, stuck it to the back wall on my way out yesterday. It's been feeding live video back to my dad's server. My laptop doesn't have enough hard disk space for that much video. Anyway, I fast-forwarded through hours and hours of her room images. Then, I found this tidbit a little while ago. Da ta!" She pressed play and the four crowded around her monitor.

"This was shortly after the supper bell rang. Her last class has just gone. Now watch this," Pam said gloatingly. A sixth year Black Hall student came walking into her classroom.

"Oh my god, what is she . . ." Lindsey didn't finish her sentence. Professor Janice was passionately making out with this student. However, they actually did little more than kiss and hug. "I wish they had gone a bit further, for that would have clinched it. I sent this to her in an email telling her that this would appear on the Internet if she did not begin to treat you fairly, Lindsey. I also told her that this video was not on my computer nor anyone else's here at Bradbury's. It is on my dad's secure server in the Department of Magical Misuse in Sterling. Access to it is password protected, so she can't find it or delete it." Pam sat back with a very satisfied look on her face.

Lindsey hugged her and thanked her. "Will you get into trouble over this?" she asked suddenly realizing the Pam was blackmailing a Bradbury's professor of magic.

Pam stated in her official voice, "The video was shot in a totally public location, where no one could possibly expect any kind of privacy. The law is completely on my side. If she tries any kind of retribution against me, the video will be sent to my father along with a request to have her arrested for pandering with underage students. That is a crime and she knows it. If she behaves herself, nothing at all will come of it. Matter closed. Never mess with a techno-geek!" Pam stated flatly.

"Well done, techno-geek!" Amanda declared. "Now, we have another interesting thing for this techno-geek witch to sink her fingers into!" Quickly, she related what she had found in the Trophy Room.

"Honestly, you think this Sam Rabnor and her father are the same person?" asked Pam, now very curious about another mystery. "Let's see the pics, Lindsey." Quickly, Lindsey brought up the five images she had sent herself via her cell phone. All four girls compared the images on her monitor with the photograph Lindsey had on her desk.

"Amazing similarities. What we need is an anthropomorphic comparison. Send me those images, Lindsey, while I scan in this one of your father," Pam ordered, very excited to be into a big mystery. Soon, she had all six images on her machine. Kathy, Amanda, and Lindsey had no idea what she had just said that they needed.

"Now that comparison software is way too expensive for one of us to buy and besides it takes up way too much disk space for these laptops. I will just hack into my dad's system and run the comparison on his machine and have it send the results back to me here." She typed rapidly, Lindsey watched as the Department of Magical Misuse, Sterling, Colorado, welcome page appeared, followed by the familiar enter user id and password. Pam flew threw that page and was into the server in short order. A few more clicks and the six images were sent. It took a bit of time for her to find the special program and nearly five minutes for her to work out the specifications for this comparison run. Finally, she hit the Go button and sat back, another satisfied look on her face.

"Since these pics are so small, it shouldn't take too long for the results to come back. The program is used to predict how some norms will age. You know, so dad can catch criminals who try to disguise themselves. It is also use by the anthropologists to get an idea of how early men and women may have looked, though why they would want to know that is beyond me."

"Won't you get into trouble using your dad's computer like this?" Lindsey asked, afraid that she was getting her friend into big trouble.

"Nah, dad will understand. I've been doing this for years now, using his server. Besides, he has never said that I can *not* use it."

Amanda asked, "Yes, but does he know that you are breaking in to the Department's computer system?"

Pam blushed, "Well, not exactly, but I'm sure he won't mind. After all, it is for a good cause. Hey, here come the results." Many numbers flashed onto her screen.

Kathy asked, "What's that all mean? Just a bunch of numbers. I hate math. Why can't the computer just tell us outright?"

"Oh it does. This one here. It says that these are the same person to a 95% certainty! Lindsey, this Rabnor fellow, he must have been your father!"

"But, but, why? Change his name? Do no magic? I don't understand at all," Lindsey complained, totally confused; her nicely ordered world was crumbling down.

"Well, there is only one way to find out," declared Pam, her fingers now rapidly typing. "We Google him." This was the mammoth search engine, which had now become the universal search engine for the entire World Wide Web. Not Found! appeared on her screen. "Now that *is* weird!"

"Why?" asked Kathy.

"Look." Pam typed in "Kathy Townsend" and pressed

Enter. Shortly a screen of results appeared, one of which she clicked to display:

> Kathy Townsend. Born Limon, Colorado. Attended Smith Elementary Grades K-6. Now attending Arthur Bradbury's School of Magic.

Pam explained, "All of our public school records are online. That's where this info came from; we're all in it."

"Hey, try me next," Amanda asked, very curious to see what it said about her. Pam cleared the info box and entered "Amanda Whitewater" and pressed Enter. All four read the results screen.

> Amanda Whitewater, (Apache), Arapahoe, Colorado. Attended Tribal School #28, K-6. Now attending Arthur Bradbury's School of Magic.

"Do Lindsey's next," Amanda asked. Shortly the screen showed the following:

> Lindsey Barron, Plano, Colorado. Attended School #19, 1-6. Now attending Arthur Bradbury's School of Magic on a full scholarship.

"Now yours," Amanda asked. This, she found very interesting. The web actually knew a little about each of them. The screen then showed the four this information:

> Pamela Betts, Sterling, Colorado. Attended Rollingbrook, K-6. Now attending Arthur Bradbury's School of Magic. Winner: MS Student of the Year in 4th, 5th, and 6th grades.

"Hey, what did you win there?" asked Kathy.

Pam blushed, "Microsoft gives out this award for the best student computer user in each state each year. I got it three times." She obviously didn't want to talk about this subject at all!

"But why isn't Rabnor in there?" asked Amanda.

"That's my point," Pam stated hotly. "He *should* have been in there. However, let's check MAG Google, but I need to get back into my dad's computer first." Her fingers flew over the keyboard and soon she was at another Google screen. Only this one had a heading just above Google: Magician's. "This version searches the wizard and witches databases. He surely will be in there! I'd use the one our school provides, but this one has no restrictions on it, while ours does. You know, no porn, but they have locked out other things besides porn. They didn't tell us that."

Two minutes later, the screen showed Not Found! "What?" screeched Pam. "That's *not* possible! Look ladies!" she typed in "Alister Broadwell" and hit Enter. A huge listing appeared in the search results, part of which read,

> Broadwell, Alister. Age: 50. Governor Bradbury's
> School of Magic, twenty-five years. Order of Merlin,
> Knights of Truth.

His biography was extensive. None of the four realized Alister was such an important wizard. Pam then typed in each of the four girls and found the same information they had just seen on the norm's Google, but an additional line read for each:

> First Year Bradbury's.

"Even we are listed. Rabnor is not listed in the norm Google nor is he in the Magical Google. This is not right!" Pam declared.

Kathy suggested, "You know, it's like someone has gone in there, wherever 'there' is mind you, and erased all traces of Samuel Rabnor! Is that even possible?"

"Darn it, you are right, Kathy!" Pam cried out excitedly. "That must be what's happened here! Now let me see. Surely, they have missed something."

"Well, maybe dad's name really was Barron. Try looking for Samuel Barron," Lindsey suggested. Pam typed that in and all four girls were shocked to see the results on the screen.

> Samuel Barron. Norm rancher. 2010-2070. Sterling, Colorado.

"He died over a hundred years ago! Now I *know* something very fishy is going on here! I'm going to check our own school's web. I should have done this sooner." Pam rapidly entered the Bradbury's School of Magic home page, went to the archives, looked up former students, and picked twenty years ago for starters. She entered "Samuel Rabnor" and pressed Enter.

None of the four was ready for what appeared on the

screen next!

Restricted Access.

Enter User Id and Password.

Pam stared at the screen in total disbelief!

"Hey, try our dad, Running Bear Whitewater," Amanda suggested, more out of curiosity than anything else. He had attended Bradbury's a long time ago. Now his children were following his example. Pam did as she asked and was surprised at the lengthy listing that came back. It included the fact that he was their tribal chieftain as well as being a competent wizard, who was also awarded the Order of Merlin and the Knights of Truth.

"Well, that clinches it," Pam said enthusiastically.

"Clinches what?" asked Lindsey, completely baffled. None of this was making any sense to her.

"Your father did exist as Samuel Rabnor! Why else would they make his school records completely hidden? If the screen showed nothing, the trophies would tell a different story. So they had to just make his records password secure, that's all. He did go to school here, only they don't want anyone to know about it! Further, someone has gone to extraordinary lengths to erase all traces of your father from the informational databases."

"Why?"

"Dunno yet, but I aim to find out! They have not reckoned with a three time, MS Honor Student!" Pam declared with a passion. "What I need is a web spider."

"A what?" asked Lindsey, who looked at Kathy and Amanda. All three had no idea of what Pam just said. They watched as her fingers flew over the keyboard. She entered the Voodoo Underground Website as "Madam Fingers," though they could not see her password, only *'s filled that box.

"You guys *haven't* seen this screen, all right?" Pam whispered. "There, it is running." She turned off her computer and looked at the three staring at her. "You didn't see that website I entered. Promise me you won't mention it. It's an underground hacker's site. I'm not supposed to be in there, but I'm known there *really* well, you see; Madam Fingers is my handle."

"Okay, but what's a spider?" asked Kathy.

"I've just launched a little spy program that is going to visit every web page in both the norm world and our world, searching for any mention of Samuel Rabnor. Whoever erased these main entries probably did not have the knowledge to erase absolutely everything everywhere. My spider may take days to visit everywhere, but it will give us back everything that has not been wiped out. Now I wonder how I can get the login and password to Bradbury's entry on your father, Lindsey? There must be a way. I cannot directly hack into it; they would catch me in a blink. I must be cleverer than that. Have to ponder that one. Say, hadn't we better get to our homework before the observatory time comes?"

By the time that the four headed down to go to the stargazing class, Lindsey had finally mastered all of last week's spells. Now she only had half of this week's to learn; she was slowly catching up to her classmates. If only she wasn't docked any more points, perhaps she could raise her grade at least to passing.

The next day, Thursday, Lindsey was on pins and needles, excited about, but dreading her next class in spell casting. How would Professor Janice react to Pam's blackmail, for that was really what it was. Would she really give her a fair deal?

In their History of Magic class, Professor Thalmus gave them a huge homework assignment. "I want you to do some original research. As you know or may not know, we wizards and witches have some unique jobs or employments that are not found in the norm society. For example, a professor of magic instruction, such as your teachers here at Bradbury's, is one of these. Write that one down. I want you to create as extensive a list as you can, noting the name of the position and a few words about what that job entails. Also, where possible, note what magical skills are prerequisites for that job. This is a very important exercise, class. When you graduate, you will want to find employment and I am sure that you will not want to become a norm ditch digger or waitress at Mc Donald's. It will be due on October 15; three weeks should be enough time."

Lindsey had never considered this aspect. He was right. When she graduated, what would she actually do? Until now, she figured she would return home to her ranch and help her mother with the chores. Now that seemed rather a silly use of her new skills. For once, she thought she would really enjoy doing this essay.

After lunch, they headed to their Beginning Spell Casting class. Lindsey bit her lip and hoped that all would go well. As the thirty students filed into the classroom, Professor Janice was not sitting in her usual position on top of her desk. Rather she sat formally behind it, a stern look on her otherwise gorgeous looking face. Several of the boys in the front row grumbled a bit, but she couldn't hear what they were saying.

"Good afternoon class. Some of you evidently believe that I'm not being fair in my grading practices. This is a free country so you are entitled to believe as you wish." Her eyes flittered over the class, but lingered for a moment on Pam, who squirmed slightly.

"I'm sorry to have to say this, but children, life is seldom fair. Yes, here at Bradbury's you're being insulated from the real world and all of its troubles, the least of which is this rampage of Dominus Malefic. Let me assure you that in less than six years you'll be out there facing it on your own! There will be no professor to back you up when you get into trouble." Again, her eyes flittered from student to student, but lingered this time on Lindsey, who also squirmed unpleasantly in her chair.

"Proper wand activation may mean the difference between life and death." Deiter snickered and glanced at Lindsey. "Likewise, proper spell use may spell the difference. With this in mind, today, we are going to review all of your basic grade 0 spells, which all of you should have completely under your grasp." Everyone groaned. "Yes, all sixty of them. Twin up with your partners. You have forty-five minutes for each of you to perform all sixty of these spells. That means between you and your partner, you have to get off nearly three spells each minute, twenty seconds apart. I will be monitoring them on this chart," she waved her wand and a large chart appeared in front of the class. It was so large that even Lindsey, sitting in the very back row, could clearly read it. Each student's name was listed down one column. Going across the top was the name of each basic spell.

"As you successfully complete a spell, a check will appear on the chart accordingly. Each spell completed is worth one point, sixty points will be perfect. No points will be awarded for any spell in which the student's wand fails to activate, whether or not the spell is successful." She looked straight at Lindsey when she said this.

"On your marks, get set, go!"

Lindsey made her downward motion with her wand and said clearly, "Chill." She and Amanda looked up at the chart. A checkmark appeared on her line under that spell. "Cool!" Soon the room was loud and raucous, spells flying off in all directions. Dirt appeared on the floor and then disappeared. Lindsey suggested that they use the Dirty spell first, then Clean, so that they did not have to waste time trying to get a box of dirt.

Worse, no one had any time to stop and look up a spell, not at a spell every twenty seconds. Instead, everyone looked at the huge chart to see what spell was next and tried to perform it. It was hectic and frantic in the classroom. Sweat began to pour down Lindsey's face, Amanda's too. Amanda looked over at Lindsey and said "Chill." Relieved a little, Lindsey returned the favor.

"Ten minutes remain," barked out Professor Janice. Pressure, that's what she is using on us, Lindsey thought as she colored her desk bright green. Amanda immediately turned it back to its normal yellow-brown. A pair of checkmarks appeared beside their names, though they both had stopped paying any attention to their appearance. "Five minutes remain," came the warning.

Lindsey looked at the chart. Rapidly, she scanned across to see what remained to be done. None, all boxes were checked. Amanda stared in disbelief. Then, the two smiled at each other and shook hands. "We did it!" she said.

The two now looked over the chart. Pam had only one more to do, Kathy, three. Emilio had six. They were fascinated with how this chart worked. "Time's up!" barked Professor Janice. Instantly, the chart stopped recording successful spells. Deiter groaned; it failed to count his last one.

"Well, you can see the results for yourselves. Clearly, some of you have learned how to cast spells, amazing." She stared at Lindsey. "Ten of you have a perfect score. Mr. Armstrong, you should seek a tutor very soon, if you want to pass this course." Lindsey glanced at his line; barely half of the boxes were checked.

"It's all Barron's fault; she tripped and I got a month's detention," Lyle argued.

"I believe that you didn't need her help in earning yourself detention, Mr. Armstrong. Class dismissed."

Lindsey saw that Deiter had only a few empty boxes remaining. Pam and Kathy also had perfect scores, while Emilio only had one empty box. He had forgotten how to Clean and Kathy teased him about it all the way to their next class.

As they left the classroom, heading for their theory class, Pam said, "Well, that went better than I had hoped. Actually, that was the best time I have ever had in her class!" Lindsey agreed wholeheartedly, but wondered if at the end of the year she would be doing something similar with all the Grade 1 spells, much more difficult spells indeed.

Emilio at last said something to Pam, "Yes, well, she didn't actually say anything, just called off the minutes, now did she?" Pam had to agree with him.

In the couple of minutes before class started, Pam checked on her spider, but it reported nothing as yet. Professor Blake Smith entered the room in his usual grand manner. Several of the girls swooned slightly. Lindsey didn't see what their fuss was all about. She wasn't interested much in boys, not yet anyway.

"Now class, before we begin, I have been asked by Governor Alister to make two announcements. This first one is very serious indeed. Quote. Any student caught hacking into the Bradbury's website will suffer an expulsion hearing. Unquote. I assured him that none of our students would ever try to hack into the school's secure side. As you may well guess, your academic records, your grades, are very well magically protected. Yet, it seems someone has been trying to do just that, hack into our system. Now then the second announcement. Governor Alister has canceled your nightly observatory classes. From now on, no student, regardless of age, is allowed to roam on the campus after ten p.m. Is that understood? I'm sure none of you will regret this one." He smiled and many in the class cheered. Two more weeks of midnight hours were eliminated.

"Why?" asked Deiter, rather belligerently. "I bet Lindsey had something to do with our good class being canceled."

"Well, I believe this time Miss Barron is not to blame. It is a matter of security—what with this madman Dominus on the loose. I suspect Governor Alister is being overly cautious for your safety, Deiter. Now then, let us get on with our lessons for today."

It was about eight o'clock when Lindsey hit the showers, physically exhausted. Bill had insisted on a full soccer practice right after supper. Even though she was swamped with homework, Lindsey had gone. She felt an obligation now, since she was on the team. Emilio had enjoyed the practice, asking for many more. This was a good excuse for not doing his homework.

Amanda and Lindsey walked up the stairs to their room, wearing their bathrobes, their long hair wrapped in towels. As they stepped into their long hall, Kathy was waiting for them. "Hey, I just discovered something, Lindsey. What with all those pictures of soccer players and all, I started looking at all these portraits of Yellow Hall former students. Follow me. Notice the dates on these here by our room, recent graduates. As we walk along, watch their dates."

"What are you talking about?" Amanda asked, slightly irritated; she wanted to dry her hair and do a bit more on her essay before bed.

"The dates, see the dates get progressively older as we go along." They were now halfway down the hall, where many of the third and fourth year students had their rooms. "See, the dates are about twenty years ago. See anything unusual?"

"No, but there must be or you wouldn't be dragging us down here," Lindsey replied.

"Well, there's a portrait missing," Amanda observed. "See, Lindsey, you can see the outline of where it used to be." She looked, and sure enough, one portrait was missing.

"I bet there used to be a portrait of your father hanging right there!" Kathy declared triumphantly.

"Ah, they could have just taken it down for cleaning," Amanda countered. "Or perhaps someone spilled a coke on it and they took it off for restoration."

"I know, I know, or it could have fallen down and gotten damaged, and they are repairing its frame," Kathy added. "Still, don't you find it just a little strange? This is the only one that is missing and it is in the right date range." Lindsey shrugged, why all this secrecy about her father, if indeed it was her father. She still was not convinced her father had been a wizard. The three returned to their room.

Pam looked gloomily up at them as they entered. "Nothing from the spider yet."

Lindsey sat down at her desk, looked at the old photo of her father, and then turned on her computer. She opened her essay, *Potential Jobs for Wizards and Witches*. She had one entry, professor at a school of magic. She sighed; this was a particularly tough assignment for her. She had been raised as a norm without any idea that there was an entire world of magic around her. She typed in a second entry. Doctor, healing both magic-caused injuries and norm injuries, such as growing my new hands, very rewarding career because you really do help people.

Pam looked over her shoulder and grimaced. "Here, try this." She opened up FoxFire500 and did a quick Mag Google on "employment, magical." A lengthy list appeared.

"Thanks!" Lindsey began examining the lengthy listings. "Oh, these are normal jobs, like maid, only you get to use spells to do the work!" Pam just grinned. Lindsey began copying many into her essay.

After a time, Lindsey said, "I was thinking that perhaps there were some special kinds of jobs that we might have. These are just enhanced norm type jobs, really. I mean I can round up our cattle using my horse. I really don't need magic for that."

"How many do you have on your list?" asked Amanda.

"One hundred sixty-two," Pam replied.

"Darn, I've only got sixty-three. Have you got Tracker on yours?" Amanda asked. Pam nodded.

"I don't," Lindsey replied. Kathy shook her head no as well. "What's a Tracker?"

Before Amanda could answer, Pam didactically explained, "Right now, those wizards are being used to hunt down and locate just where this escaped convict, Dominus Malefic is at. A Tracker is a highly skilled person who has uncanny skills that enable him or her to sniff out and follow the trail of a magic user or norm for that matter. The Departments of Law, Defense, and even Magical Misuse make heavy use of Trackers. They're very highly paid, but there aren't very many of them. Honestly, you all should have that one on your lists. Let me see what you do have." She rapidly scanned over the other three girl's essays.

While she was doing that, Amanda added, "My father is a Tracker. He says we Apaches make the very best Trackers in the country. Both Jim and Tom want to become Trackers when they graduate." Lindsey was impressed.

"Oh good grief! Are you all norms here? Except for Amanda and her Tracker, you have missed all the most highly paid jobs! Okay, look. When you graduate, you can start making magically enchanted items to sell to others; that's an Enchanter. You could become a Showman, but while they make money, I think it is cheap doing magical stunts for entertainment. You could become a Charmer for hire. I bet that's what Professor Janice would be good at." She couldn't resist taking a dig at her teacher.

"But the really cool, top jobs are seven. Amanda already has one of those, the Tracker. Closely allied to them are the Sleuths—that's what I want to do when I graduate, become a Sleuth. We track down people and things, not by following their physical trail, like the Apaches do, but by other means, such as using the computer. Trackers and Sleuths are in great demand at all three of the departments."

"Then there are three others: Lawman, Dispeller, and the Eliminator. The Lawman is really a glorified policeman, but is able to arrest the evil-doers, such as Dominus. However, the Lawman is never going to succeed unless he is accompanied by either a Dispeller or an Eliminator. The Dispeller is cool, because they can dispel nearly every kind of magic thrown at them. They have to be very quick or they are blasted. I mean if one was trying to arrest this Dominus guy, he's likely to start shooting any number of horrible spells at you, trying to kill you. The Dispeller has to react very fast to nullify those spells. I swear when they arrested this Dominus fellow the first time, they must have been using not only Trackers, but a bunch of Dispellers, or the Lawman would never have been able to arrest him."

"I don't much care for the Eliminator, because they do what their name suggests. They eliminate or kill things. Well, it's okay if they want to eliminate a rat infestation, but I bet that the Department of Law has now hired a bunch of Eliminators to go after Dominus."

"Finally, the other really high paying jobs are the Diviners and the Nous. The Diviners are able to predict things, as their name suggests. People will pay large sums to know or have a good guess at what the future holds. I know the three departments are now employing a number of Diviners to try to figure out Dominus Malefic's next move, so they can send Eliminators, Dispellers, and Lawmen to catch him in the act. My Aunt Petunia is a Diviner. Gosh, is she rich now."

"The Nous are highly intelligent, and using their mind philosophies, they can solve incredibly complex problems. Naturally, people pay highly for such solutions. Go to Magical Google and enter Employment, Magical, High Pay." Pam finished up and watched her three friends typing away and then looking at the listings on their screens.

"I think you are already a good Sleuth," Lindsey commented after reading the lengthy description of that job. Pam flushed.

"Hey, there is a little online test you can take that will tell you which of these jobs is best suited for you," Kathy called out. Quickly, all four went to that page and began taking the test. Ten minutes later, the job best suited for them appeared on their four monitors.

Pam's showed Sleuth, as she knew it would, having taken the test at least fifty times, changing her mind on several of the test answers. Yet, it continued to show Sleuth. "Well, I am not surprised," Pam said as she saw Tracker appearing on Amanda's screen. "Diviner? Really, Kathy, I would never have guessed that one!" Pam said surprised.

"Me either," Kathy replied. "I'm going to find out more about it. What's yours say, Lindsey?"

Lindsey stared at her monitor and the single word, Dispeller. "Well, that figures," Pam explained. "Look, Dispellers have to be lightning fast with the counter-spells. Already she can do nearly all the Grade 0 spells without using a wand or speaking the command words. That's nearly a prerequisite for becoming a Dispeller. There are so very few of them, you know, terribly hard to become one." She didn't mention that they often had short lives. Miss one spell and they have had it.

Just then, Pam's computer made a beeping noise. "Hey, the spider is done. Gather around; let's see what it found about this Samuel Rabnor. Well doesn't this beat all! Gang, there are over five hundred broken links to the Bradbury's web page that we don't have the password to!"

"What's a broken link?" asked Lindsey.

"In the past, someone made a link to another web page, where you could go to find additional information. His name is on well over five hundred pages, all linking to the one here that we can't get into without the password. I told you someone had been erasing all traces of him from the Net! But they were not as good as me! Look at this! We got something here!" She clinked on the link, while all three gathered around her monitor, looking over her shoulder.

"Anyone read Swedish? It's an obscure Swedish web page." No one did. Lindsey felt crestfallen; they were so close to finding out who this man was, only to be thwarted by a foreign language.

"Oh well, you tried," Lindsey sighed, ready to give up the search as a dead end.

"Oh don't be silly. Where's your computing skill?" Pam looked at the three glum faces of her roommates. "Are you all dopes? I'll have it all in a jiffy." She selected the entire web page, copied it to the clipboard, and then Googled for another web page called the UT.

"What's UT?" asked Lindsey.

"Universal Translator. Here, I paste in the web page. I select translate from Swedish to English. Press Do It! Viola, here we go." All four began reading the article dated some fourteen years ago. "Oh my god!" exclaimed Pam as she read the first few lines.

Samuel Rabnor, a graduate of Arthur Bradbury's School of Magic, USA, is the world's leading Dispeller and was recently hired by the USA's Department of Defense to assist in tracking down the worst criminal the magical world has ever known, Dominus Malefic and his band of Death Stalkers.

Officially the fourth member of the Rat Pack, Sam's work made it possible for these criminals to be taken into custody. This Rat Pack is reputedly the world's finest. Besides Sam, the Rat Pack's other members include the famous Tracker, Able Monument, the Diviner, Mabel Pruit, and the incredible Eliminator, Bill West.

On August 1, Mabel divined that these criminals would strike against the Wisconsin Hall of Justice. The Rat Pack moved in for the kill, with Able picking up their scent and leading them to this most malevolent group. Only because of the incredible skill of Samuel Rabnor was Bill able to subdue these thirteen men, finally taking them into custody.

On August 10, the Rat Pack members were officially given the highest honor that can be bestowed on civilians, the Knights of Truth medals. Because of

their valiant efforts, tonight the world is once more
at peace.

"Wow! If that was your dad, he was, well, famous
indeed," Pam said, somewhat awed by what she read. "I
wonder. . ." She quickly Googled the three new names.

Able Monument: Not Found!

Bill West: Not Found!

Mabel Pruit: ten links were shown.

Quickly, Pam chose the most likely one. They read and
gasped.

Pruit, Mabel, Diviner, Knights of Truth, graduate of
New York's School of Magic, member of the famous
Rat Pack that tracked down and arrested Dominus
Malefic and his Death Stalkers, murdered one month
after receiving her medal. Also slain were her mother
and brother.

"No need to hide information on a dead person," Pam
whispered. "Maybe the others are still alive."

"My dad is not," Lindsey whispered, though she didn't
know why she they were whispering.

"Curious that she and her family were killed days after
they captured Dominus," Pam whispered.

"Why are you whispering?" asked Amanda.

"This is scary stuff," Pam replied. "Well, whether or not
he was Lindsey's father, this Sam fellow was a *very* powerful
wizard indeed. Now we have tons of information that we can
use to extend our search. I bet some of this might actually be
in the library, you know hard copy, books, old newspapers,
magazines."

"Okay, I will volunteer to look," Lindsey said. "I can do
that, but I sure cannot do all this computer stuff that you have,
Pam. Thanks a whole lot!"

Pam yawned, "Well, I want to be a Sleuth, and this is
what they do, find out things that others cannot find for
themselves." The four retired for the night, pondering this
wealth of new information that hardly anyone knew. Why was
it all made secret?

All four were sleepy as they entered Professor Mac

Elroy's math class. However, they were instantly awake when he began. "Miss Betts, will you accompany me to the Administration Hall during your PE hour, please? It is very important, but you will have to miss your PE class today." All eyes suddenly turned to Pam. Embarrassed, she nodded, her face reddening, her stomach knotting.

Deiter called out, "Pammie's in big trouble now!"

"That is in error, Mr. Deiter. She is not in any trouble. We need her services. Now then, it is time for a pop quiz on common denominators." Everyone groaned, especially Emilio and Kathy.

Between classes, the five chatted about what Professor Herbert could possibly want from Pam. Had her attempt to look up Samuel Rabnor on the web site been detected? Surely not, she had only just taken that one link and done nothing, not even attempt to enter a user id or password. The five eventually gave up. They had no clue. Pam didn't mention it, but she wondered if it had anything to do with her blackmail of Professor Janice.

"Bye," Pam said worriedly as she headed south to the Admin Hall, while her four friends headed for the Stadium.

As she left her new friends behind her, Pam suddenly realized how much she depended upon them. All by herself, she was not brave. What did they want of her? Well, if it was over the blackmail, she thought, the Law would be on her side, assuming that they followed the Law. As she approached the Admin building, Professor Mac Elroy caught up with her, jogging to get there after his last class. "Long way from the Math Hall," he panted, very much out of shape. "I'm getting too old for all this hustle and bustle. Come on; we are probably the lasts ones here." He opened the east door for her. Four other students, all older than Pam, were inside the door waiting for them.

"Harry Wright, Black Hall," he introduced the students rapidly. "Tom Feld, Brown Hall. Monique Blackburn, Red Hall. Silas Bentz, Brown Hall. Pam Betts, Yellow Hall. Now then, if you five will follow me, I'll take you into our campus computer room. It's a secured area, so you will need to wear these visitor's badges." He handed out five badges quickly and got his own out of his pocket. He led them to the stairs and they went down a flight. At the locked door, he slid his badge through the reader slot and the door opened.

Inside were three rooms. One held a number of computers, the servers for the campus. Pam eyed them greedily; raw computer power always impressed her. Another held a bunch of monitors, and the third was a meeting room, into which he led them.

"Have a seat, please. Now then, as you may or may not know, I am in charge of the computer system here at Bradbury's. Two nights ago, we had a serious breach of our system. Someone attempted to break into our secure server side, making some five thousand attempts, before my program was able to lock down that entrance portal. I have been trying to make some sense of this break-in attempt, but frankly, it has me stumped. You five are the sharpest computer savvy students on this campus. I have asked you here to see if you can look over the break-in and shed some light on it, give me some clues about what they were after, who they might be, where they are located, anything that I can use to continue the investigation."

"Wow. So the rumors were true! Someone did try to break-in," said Harry.

"Yes, I've got these five laptops hooked up to the server logs. Help yourselves. Do your thing. See if you can find out anything useful, please."

At once, the five hopped onto a computer. Pam was exceedingly relieved. They were not after her after all. Harry called out, "Definitely an automated hack program was in use."

"They are using IP spoofing," Monique announced. Harry quickly agreed with her. Five sets of keyboard keys were flying.

"Coming in from all over the country," Silas added. For ten minutes, they exchanged bits of information, but something was not adding up in Pam's mind.

"Something's wrong with all this," Pam said. "We are missing something."

"Oh yea, first year?" Harry taunted her.

Pam shut up, determined not to say any more until she

could prove it. She scrolled down the huge list of hack attempts, along with the IP addresses from which the signal had come. "Wait a minute, these are totally fake addresses! This one is mine and I know my computer was powered off at the time this log says it was sending this request. See if you can find others that you recognize as fakes," she suggested.

"Darn it, Tom, she's bloody right! Here's one from my old system back home. It is not even operational, 'cause I blew its motherboard just before the bus came early to pick us up. I didn't have time to replace it yet. She's right. These are fakes."

"Must mean they are using the Amafrodyte Algorithm," Monique suggested. "There is no way to trace that one, is there?"

"No, I think that we are out of luck," Harry answered her.

Pam grinned and thought, *Oh no we aren't! The underground has already broken that algorithm.* Soon, the others were ready to throw in the towel, so Pam spoke up. "Professor, may I use my computer to make an outside connection? I need to look up something." He gave her the go ahead. The other four looked at her quizzically.

Quickly, she brought her laptop up and zoomed into her underground site as Madam Fingers. Carefully, she made sure that the others could not see her monitor. A few clicks later and she found what she needed. She scanned through the hack of the Amafrodyte Algorithm. Bingo. Hastily, she turned her computer off and began scanning down the server log. "No. No. No. No." she said to herself.

Now the other four crowded around her, watching as the log entries flew by. "Bingo. There is the real one! Got you, you hacker," Pam declared.

"Huh?" Monique muttered.

"You see, this algorithm has one fatal flaw. Periodically, it accidentally forgets to alter the real IP address. You can spot that one visually because there is no second message that follows the original one. See all these others above this one are in pairs. This one here is all by itself, but immediately followed by pairs again. If we search down from here, we will periodically find this real one popping back up. Yes, here it is again. Professor, here is the real IP address that the hacker was using. Now I wonder who it belongs to."

"I got that for you," Harry declared, quickly entering it into the WhoIs website. He wanted to salvage some face—a first year girl had already bested him!

"This cannot be," Harry exclaimed, as all five and Herbert stared at the results. The screen said this IP address belonged to the White House. It was the President of the United States' personal address! "Why would our president hack into Bradbury's?" Harry said.

"He wouldn't, he knows. . ." a very disturbed looking Professor Herbert answered. He sat very still, holding his chin in his hands for a minute, lost in deep thought. At last, he raised his head. "I must make a secure phone call immediately. I thank you all very, very much. I will see that each of you receives a personal commendation from the Governor. Now if you will please see yourselves out, I must make this call at once. Thank you. Oh, leave the badges just inside the basement door. Thanks." He looked terribly worried and distracted, thought Pam.

The five walked out of the room and over to the entrance door. "I hate to give this badge up," Harry teased. "Could prove most useful." However, all five dropped their badge onto the floor, each one making sure that the others also left their badges behind. They realized what they were doing as they climbed the stairs and all laughed.

As they walked back toward the dorms, Harry said, "Darn good bit of sleuthing there, Pam, especially for a first year." He meant it as a compliment.

"Well, I wouldn't have figured it out, if Monique had not recognized what algorithm was being used. Good going, Monique." She smiled and said thanks.

"I cannot believe that we all just got to see the schools secure server system! Darn cool!" Silas said, excitedly. "Server redundancy times six at least, wouldn't you say, Tom?"

"Yes, at least six. Five have to crash before the server is seriously threatened. Man, what a setup they have here. I never knew they had that kind of computer power. Impressive," Tom replied.

"Say how *did* you figure out what algorithm was being used, Monique? That was very clever," Silas asked her.

She raised her eyebrows under which she wore a dark blue shadow, which contrasted sharply with her cherry red lips, and said coyly, "My little secret." They all laughed.

At supper, Pam related what had happened. Of course, Lindsey was relieved that Pam had not gotten into trouble over her blackmail attempt. Still, none of the quintet could fathom why the president of the United States would be trying to hack into the school's computer system; it made no sense.

A while later, the quintet took up their usual study positions in the Yellow Hall Study room. However, when Pam sat down and checked her email, her face went white. "I have to go run an errand. Back in a short while," she made up an excuse and left her things there on the table.

As she walked to the Formal Gardens, she went over that email in her mind. It was from Axelrod, one of the members of the underground with whom she had occasionally exchanged online chats. Everyone who logged into the underground website took on an alias name. Hers was Madam Fingers. However, each logon was anonymous, so no one knew the real identity of any who belonged to this underground site. The email she just received was from Axelrod. It said, "I know who you really are, Madam Fingers. If you want your identity to remain a secret, meet me in the Formal Gardens at 6:30 p.m. tonight." Pam had no choice. She certainly didn't want her identity known.

At this hour, there was hardly anyone in the gardens, so she stood near the entrance and waited very nervously. This should not be happening, she kept telling herself. Just then, bright red lipped Monique Blackburn of Red Hall walked up, a twinkle in her eyes. She whispered, "Madam Fingers, follow me." Pam's heart skipped a beat! Axelrod was not a boy, but Monique? Her mind raced with this news.

Monique was a third year student, who knew just where they could walk without being overheard. "Yes, Axelrod here. I've always wanted to meet you, Madam Fingers, ever since you really set that goofy Mad Max fellow straight. What a put down, you did. Very well done."

"How, how did. . ." Pam started to ask.

"Find you? Simple. When you used your laptop to look up something and then came up with your clever discovery, mind you, that was really clever of you, I'm always looking for ways to put those boys in their place, anyway, I wondered if you had just gotten that clue from the underground. So I logged on before I went to supper and checked the activity log. Sure enough, Madam Fingers logged on just when you were logging on and was on for only a couple minutes, just as you were. Two plus two. Don't worry. Your secret is safe with me. We women have to stick together. Besides, you now know who Axelrod is. I bet you thought I was a boy, right?"

Pam flushed, "Well, yes, you always sounded like one, though you never said some of the really dumb stuff that the others often say in the chat room. I guess I ought to have guessed."

"Well, the boys sometimes say the stupidest things, you know. Even though I'm pretending to be one, I just couldn't bring myself to type such drivel. Friends?" Monique held out her hand, a big smile on her face.

"Friends." Pam replied and they shook hands.

"If you ever need anything, let me know," Monique offered. "I've got to get back. Tons of homework to do. It just gets worse and worse each year!"

A little later Pam rejoined her friends in the study room. Pam forgot that she wasn't speaking to Emilio and began correcting his astronomy charts for him. He grinned and thanked her, wondering why she suddenly was being friendly. He had not apologized yet. "Thanks, Senorita Pam. I'm sorry about upsetting you. I didn't mean to call you ugly."

"Well, that's okay. I'm really not very pretty, now am I? But you need to pay more attention in class, Emilio. You have Venus where Mars is located. Venus is close to the sun, it can't ever possibly be this far from the sun."

Chapter 7—Black Hall Versus Brown Hall

Saturday morning, Governor Alister met with Doctor Caterwall. "Well, you just had to do it, didn't you, Frank."

"Meaning her hands, well, of course. You've seen the tremendous difficulties the poor young woman was facing here. My god, man, she deserves better than that. Besides, with those broken bones, it was the perfect time to perform the operation. After all, Governor Alister," he used his formal title to suggest that he was not going to allow the Governor to reprimand him for taking the initiative, "I took an oath to heal. She, more than most, needed my talents."

Alister sighed, "Well, of course, you are quite right. If you hadn't done it, I was going to ask you to do it during her summer vacation, when there would be fewer problems. I'm not the old heel you may think of me. Perhaps this way is for the better, Frank. Now what was it that you wanted to see me about? You said it was urgent and most unusual."

"Can we be overheard, Governor?" Frank asked, looking around the office.

Alister flicked his hand. "I've engaged the scrambler. No one can hear us now. Why all this mystery?"

"DNA, Alister."

"What?"

"As you know, it is required of us doctors to take a DNA sample from every patient we treat. It goes into the MMDB, the Magical Medical Database. This way we can guard against fraud—one person claiming to be another by magically altering their appearance any number of ways. As required by law, I entered Lindsey Barron's DNA sample into the registry."

"So? Is she somehow defective?"

"No, no, nothing like that. When we submit a new sample, the protocols that are followed insist on verifying that DNA is not already in the system."

"Hers was already there?"

"No, no, will you let me finish? As part of that process, it does a comparison, linking up a genealogical hierarchy. The search discovered that Lindsey Barron is the daughter of another who is in the database, not this norm whom she claims to be her father. Lindsey's father is Samuel Rabnor."

"What? That cannot be!"

"DNA doesn't lie. Further, Alister, the very second the computer returned this result to me, it instantly flagged the entire data as top secret, refusing to allow me to enter any further data. Of course, I don't have that kind of security clearance. Someone has intentionally been watching for just such an event and has now locked it down tighter than a drum!"

"We both know who Sam Rabnor is or was—the Dispeller who originally captured Dominus Malefic and the Death Stalkers—part of the Rat Pack, as I recall the events. They were all over the news fourteen years ago. Now it seems that even KMAG cannot find their videos from that era. Our own school website does not list him as having been here. It's as if Sam has vanished from the earth. Well, I suppose that is none of my business. I just save lives and grow hands, but this is sure strange."

Alister drew himself up to his full height. "You didn't tell her about this, did you?"

"Oh no, it isn't my position to do so, sir."

"Wise of you, Doctor. Who else have you told about this or spoken about it to?"

"No one. Well you sir. I didn't think the nurses needed to know. Isn't this incredibly strange?"

"Very good of you, Frank. You could have caused a huge security breech, if you had started telling others about this. You ran into the Department of Defense's security, Frank. They have erased all traces of Sam Rabnor. Clever of them to think about putting in a DNA watch. As far as our website, Herbert handled it for me. My orders. While I could order you to keep quiet about this or even magically alter your memories, national defense you understand, I will not. Instead, I will tell you a little and trust to your good judgment. Let us sit down, Frank."

Sitting across from each other, Alister relaxed and explained, "After Dominus and his men were captured, Dominus swore that he and his minions would go after everyone in the Rat Pack and all their families. Of course, we hear similar threats from nearly every criminal that is sent to prison. However, less than a month later, Mabel Pruit, the Rat Pack's Diviner, was brutally murdered, along with her mother and brother. She had no other relatives. The sign of Dominus was on their bodies, though that fact was never released to the public. All hush, hush."

"The Department of Defense decided that the Rat Pack deserved to be protected from this murderous man and his followers. Thus, they changed their names and disappeared, vanished from sight. Meanwhile, the Department of Defense erased all traces of them from the world's informational databases, and they asked us to do it as well here at his old school."

"Now you can see the incredible mess that we are in with Lindsey. Dominus is on the loose, swearing on TV that he will get revenge on the Rat Pack who captured him and sent him away for fourteen years. Dominus does not know the whereabouts of any remaining members of that group, though I know he must be seeking them out for revenge. If he finds out that Lindsey is Sam's daughter, he will come after her, if nothing else but trying to use her to get at Sam. However, according to Lindsey, her father is dead, some kind of ranching accident. No matter, Dominus will snuff out her life in an instant, either way."

"So you see, right at this moment, Lindsey is far better off knowing nothing about her father. Here at Bradbury's we can keep her safe, while she grows up. If we are lucky, Dominus will never know about her. As long as he knows nothing about Sam having a daughter, Lindsey is safe. I wouldn't give a hoot for her life once he finds out about her. Now do you see why it is imperative that no one, and I mean no one, finds out about the connection between Sam and Lindsey?"

Doctor Caterwall wiped the nervous sweat from his brow. "I, I had no idea. God, I could have blown it completely!

In trying to do right by her, I could have caused her premature death. Good god man, what have I done?"

Alister relaxed and said soothingly, "You have given a young girl a whole new chance at life. You have worked a magical miracle, as you should. Personally, I'm very proud that you took the initiative and did so, Frank. I like that in a wizard, initiative. In this case, there has been no harm done, so I should be thanking you for your compassion, doctor."

"Still, I could have blown it wide open," Frank began to get his nerves under control.

"Now you best make sure the Infirmary is ready for soccer casualties. I understand that the first game of the season starts in a few hours."

"You are right. I should be prepared. They should pick a safer sport." Both men chuckled and the doctor left.

At once, Alister waved his wand and said "Cho Lin Sung." Magic flashed.

Cho Lin was still in bed with her husband when the magical flash occurred. A tiny piece of paper drifted before her eyes. She grabbed it and read:

My office. Immediately. Top Secret. Alister.

"What is it love," Huan asked, as he watched her climb out of bed, her long, thick black hair flopping from side to side as she rose.

"Alister needs to see me immediately. I'll be back shortly. Keep the bed warm, dear." She waved her hand and an elegant bedroom gown appeared over her silk, thin nightgown. She waved her wand and spoke, "Door, Alister's Office." A door appeared in front of her and she opened it and stepped into Alister's office, where Doctor Caterwall had just been.

Alister looked up, as the door appeared in the middle of his office. He watched Cho Lin step out. He smiled, "Sorry to interrupt your private time, but something extremely urgent has come up. Please have a seat." She did so.

"When the good doctor sent in the required DNA sample from Miss Lindsey Barron, we all received quite a shock. It seems that her father is not Samuel Barron at all, but Samuel Rabnor!"

It took a moment for the significance of his

pronouncement to register. Cho Lin had not heard that name in over fourteen years. She gasped, "Not the Rat Pack Sam Rabnor?"

"Yes, Rat Pack Sam. Lindsey is his daughter. If she is to be believed, her father was killed in some kind of ranch accident."

"Yes, she had the horror of discovering his dead body, lying beneath a norm tractor. Awful way to die, crushed his whole body, I expect. Good god, does she know this? Who else knows? Dominus is on the loose!"

"As far as we know, Lindsey has no idea who her father really was, Cho Lin. When Frank entered the DNA sample, the Department of Defense immediately flagged that whole transaction top secret and password protected it. Thus, that information is now secure, I hope. Frank has had the good sense to tell no one about this, just me a few minutes ago. I trust Frank to keep his mouth shut on this matter. Now you also know."

"The fewer the better, Alister. You know that. If Dominus finds out, he will most certainly go after her."

"Precisely. I hate keeping this from the girl, Cho Lin, but for now, it is in her own best interests not to know this critical information. You are in charge of Yellow Hall students; I want you to keep an eye on her. I'm sure she knows nothing at all about all this. Let's keep it that way for the time being. Just as soon as they catch Dominus, then it will be safe for me to tell her about her father."

"Agreed. Who else knows?"

"No one."

"Who else will you have to tell?"

"No one."

"Good. Do we need to jinx the good doctor to make sure he says nothing?" Cho Lin asked.

"I think not. I have explained the situation fully, and he understands full well the dire consequences for Lindsey, should this information become public knowledge."

"It is most unfortunate that she doesn't yet have a class with me. It would make keeping an eye on her much easier," Cho Lin lamented.

"Couldn't be helped. Janice is good at what she does, but I don't dare have her do something else."

"Well, in a way, I'm beginning to understand Lindsey better. This explains so much. You know that she has already demonstrated many of the qualities that Sam Rabnor had, don't you?"

"Yes, and we must provide a safe place for her to blossom. Now, I fear I've kept you from Huan for far too long on this early morning." Cho Lin bowed and stepped back through the magical door, her robe disappearing as she stepped into her room.

"Come on; we don't want to be late," Emilio tried to hurry the four girls up. "Have you got your stadium horns? I have mine."

"What's it for?" asked Pam.

"We can make a very loud noise to cheer them on, Brown Hall that is. No way am I giving one clap to Black Hall; they are a bunch of creeps!" Emilio declared. Already, they had merged into the vast crowd of students heading for the Stadium for the first soccer game of the year, Black Hall versus Brown Hall. Nearly every student at Bradbury's had turned out. After all, there was little else to take them away from their studies.

As they entered, Bill waved to them, motioning for them to come to him. He had reserved a pile of seats in the top row. From here, one had an eagle's eye view of the game below. He wanted the new recruits to have the best chance at seeing the overall game play—specifics they would work on later.

Soon, Professor Blake Smith began announcing the match, using a magically created PA system. "Welcome one and all to Bradbury's first soccer match of the year, Black Hall versus Brown Hall! Our referees today are Hank and Betsy Hall. Let's give them a round of applause." A small amount of noise greeted the two who appeared on the field wearing black and white checkered shirts and pants, waving at the crowd.

"And now Brown Hall takes the field. At goalkeeper, fifth year Jane Bateson!" The Brown Hall students cheered, along with many from Yellow Hall. Lindsey noticed that she was heavily protected with padding and looked nearly twice her normal size. She gave a wave to her friends in the stands and moved to her position in front of the Brown Hall goal, which was all brown today.

Blake continued, "At left fullback, one of the returning hot twins, Zena Horne, fifth year." Again, many cheers followed each person on the field. "At right fullback, Charlize Turnbow. At left middle field, fourth year Francesco Lopez." Emilio just had to blow his stadium horn as loudly as he could for his brother. "At right middle field, second year Lilly Wisenroot."

"Out to score big time this afternoon are the four forwards for Brown Hall. First year Riley Wrench, sixth year, Gene Truegood, the other half of the fifth year twins, Lisa Horne, and finally team captain, sixth year Elmer Dalton. Let's give them all a big hand!" Hoot! Hoot! Hoot! went Emilio on his loud horn. Of course, many of the Brown Hall students blew their horns as well.

When the noise died down, Blake continued. "Now for the reigning champions five years in a row, Black Hall, with fifth year Gallager Watson at goalkeeper, fifth year Art Merryweather at left fullback, first year Ben Dingle at right fullback. Look at the confidence Black Hall has, putting a first year back to defend their goal. At left middle field, fourth year Herman Freeze, right middle field, second year Henry Fielding. And now the top scorers, the Black Hall forwards. Phillip Royston, fourth year, the other half of the twins, Jennifer Watson, fifth year, Hektor Sanches, fifth year, and team captain, Larry Sacks, sixth year." Now it was Black Hall's turn to make a loud racket, which they did.

"Let the scoreboard and timer appear!" Instantly a giant scoreboard appeared along with a huge clock that counted down the first half, beginning at forty minutes. "And now Betsy is throwing out the soccer ball, as this game gets under way." She tossed the ball high into the air.

Lindsey watched as a Brown Hall player suddenly began levitating up into the air, sure to intercept and catch the ball first. Just at the last minute, Larry Sacks' arms grew enormously, and his arms caught the ball just in front of the outstretched hands of Elmer Dalton. Larry immediately tossed the ball far down the field, where Jennifer was waiting in the open. She bounced it down to the ground before her by using her head and began to kick it toward the goal area. Zena raced towards her and was all over her, lunging at the ball. Just as she was about to kick the ball from Zena, Zena kicked it backwards with the back of her foot, right into the onrushing feet of Larry Sacks, who quickly moved in to take a shot.

Suddenly, the Brown Hall goalkeeper saw five Larrys before her, each with a ball. "Which one does she block?" yelled Lindsey. All five kicked and it appeared that five balls were headed into the net! Jane dove for one and tried to block it, but she fell into thin air. The real ball flew into the net. Stadium horns blew loudly and the scoreboard showed Black Hall 1, Brown Hall 0. Again, the ball went into play. Lindsey, Emilio, and Amanda stopped listening to Blake announcing the game and concentrated on what was going on down on the field. It was a lightning fast game.

Elmer now had the ball for Brown Hall; he levitated high above the field and faked a throw to Riley, and passed to Gene, who was open. Now five Genes began moving the ball down the field, giving the middle fielders fits over which one was real. Herman cast a spell and only one Gene was now visible, he immediately side passed to Lisa, who brought the ball down into scoring position. The Black Hall left fullback suddenly raced up to her, kicking at the ball, viciously. Suddenly, three Lisa's appeared, moving the ball in three different directions!

Compounding the confusion, all three appeared to be passing the ball to three different forwards! All three attempted to kick a goal at the same time, Elmer's kick was real, and the poor goalkeeper chose the wrong ball to stop. Horns blared and the crowd yelled, as the scoreboard displayed 1 in the Brown Hall column.

"Good god, Lindsey, what have we gotten ourselves into? This is madness," Amanda yelled to her friend. Lindsey had never seen such displays of magic before.

Now Black Hall was bringing the ball back down

towards Brown Hall's goal. Francisco swept in and nearly stole the ball from Hektor, who retaliated by throwing the ball high into the air and then magically jumping twenty feet up after it, pounding it towards Larry with his fists.

Bill yelled to his team, "See, the right fullback was out of position, leaving Larry totally open. Indeed, five Larrys again appeared to be kicking a goal. Once more, Jane blocked the wrong one. 2 to 1 was the score.

As Lisa brought the ball down towards Black Hall's goal, Hektor came up behind her and deliberately kicked her hard in her shins, knocking her down. Immediately, the ref's whistles blew, hands raised, indicating a foul. Lisa could not get up. Doctor Carterwell rushed onto the field, his wand at the ready. He examined her; she was definitely in pain. The crowd was hushed as if trying to hear the doctor. His wand waved and her leg was bandaged securely, and he helped her to her feet. She limped around for a time before play resumed. She was given a free kick, but was in too much pain to be effective at her magic. Gallager easily blocked her shot, and the wild game resumed.

Gene passed across the field to Riley, who was in the open, but Henry suddenly extended his arms some twenty feet and intercepted the ball and threw it at once all the way down field to Hekor. But Zena was on to him and dove for the ball, knocking it from him, giving it a tap towards Lilly. Just as she was about to kick it to her forward, Herman's foot grew ten feet and pushed the ball out of the way of her foot, causing her to miss. In the mad scramble for the ball, Herman managed to tap it across to Henry, who shot it way down field to Hektor, who took it in for a goal, kicking it so hard that Jane's dive for the ball was a split second late. 3 to 1.

This time as Gene brought the ball down the court, Hektor slid in from behind and kicked him hard in the leg, just as he had done to Lisa, who was still limping around the field in pain. Down went Gene. Out came Doctor Caterwall once more.

Bill explained during this relatively quiet time, "That's their whole strategy. Take a foul by deliberately hurting all four forwards, maybe even break one of their legs. That removes all their offence. Larry's fancy multiple images lets him score most of their goals. I bet that Elmer is next." Sure enough a few minutes later, Elmer went down. Philip did the dirty deed this time. Naturally, hurting like mad, they were unable to conjure much magic and their free shots amounted to nothing, easily blocked by Gallager.

"They sure don't play a fair game, do they," Lindsey commented, very disgusted with Black Hall's team and mentality, win at all costs, even cheat.

With only the first year forward left who could run, Black Hall ignored him and began working on the two fullbacks. Once they were hammered very hard, they had the field pretty much to themselves. The goals continued to mount. Lindsey was never so glad to see the time for the game run out as she did this day. Final score, Black Hall 21, Brown Hall 3. Five Brown Hall players had to be carried magically to the Infirmary.

"That was the most disgusting performance I've ever seen," Lindsey spat on the ground as her team walked back to the dorms.

"Yeh, I know. If you want to quit now, it is okay by me," Bill said with a sigh. "I am asking you to come out there and get beat up by Black Hall. The other teams play fair, not these guys."

Amanda asked, "Is that their entire strategy? Injure the players and let Larry do most all the goal kicks?"

"Yes, it has won them the championship five years in a row now," Bill replied. "Kind of takes all the fun out of the game, doesn't it. It used to be fun, but not when you know they are out there intentionally trying to injure you."

"If we could somehow nullify those two things, Bill, Black Hall would be complete losers," Amanda replied.

"I'm all ears," Bill replied eagerly. Just now, she had no answers for him.

A little while later, the quintet headed for the Library to do research for their various essays, hoping to make some headway before dinner. Each split up to scrounge their own information from the thousands of books. The Library was indeed huge on the inside. Much of it was automated. One went to one of the many computer terminals, typed in what you desired, in one of many different ways, from ISBMN numbers (magical numbers), to author, to title, even searches. When you clicked the Fetch button, the book was brought to you. Of course, when you finished, the book was placed in the conveyor belt system, which soon put it back where it belonged. Once you had the book or books you desired, you had your choice of ten study rooms in which to spend time with your book.

After getting *Merlin's Choice for Job Applicants* being sent to her, Lindsey entered Samuel Rabnor. Of course, the system turned up nothing. She then entered Rat Pack. She was surprised to find three entries. Two were on how magically to eliminate packs of rats, but the third sounded more interesting, a historical essay by Eleanor Whiteridge. She sent for that one as well.

Eagerly she scanned the essay, one page out of the whole book of short essays. However, it didn't yield much information that she did not already know from Pam's search. Sighing, she went back to doing her homework essay. Time flew by and soon the bell rang, indicating it was dinnertime. The five got back together as they walked slowly next door to the dorm.

"I am on to something," Amanda said conservatively. "Perhaps I will have an idea how to stop Black Hall." However, they could get nothing more out of her. Being so conservative, she would not speak until she was certain.

After dinner, she and Lindsey returned to the Library. Both girls went their separate ways. After trying other ways to find information on Rabnor, Lindsey suddenly had an idea. What if they had only taken the information off of the computerized database? Surely, they would not have removed all the books that mentioned the Rat Pack. She went up to the Librarian, Lillian Angel Jones. "Hi, Lindsey Barron, isn't it? So glad to see you. Personally, I am so happy that the good doctor restored your hands for you. I cheered when I heard that good news. How can I help you?"

"Well, I was wondering, is the only way to get a book by using the computer system? I mean, well, back in Plano at norm school, we walked around the stacks of books, looking at their covers, leafing through them to see if they might be of interest. I'm having a hard time knowing what's in some of these and I seem to be wasting time getting books that are useless for my essays."

"Oh sure, dear. Only be alert for the mechanical arms that often pass by, retrieving books for others. If you are in the way, a red light flashes at you. Good hunting. I hope to see you here often." Lindsey thanked her and headed into the stacks. Soon she discovered this was far more workable. Right away, she found a book that caught her interest: *Dispellers: All About Staying Alive, a Handbook for Would Be Dispellers*, by Arthur Tonnelby. Fascinated, she took this over to a study desk and began reading.

> Of all the occupations for a witch or wizard, none is more demanding, more life-threatening than a Dispeller. He or she must be prepared at all times to expect the unexpected spell cast against them. The would be Dispeller is advised to know every defensive spell in the book! Object: stay alive, when the evil doer shoots his attack spells at them.

> However, the keynote of the Dispeller, the one thing that places him or her miles above the rest of us wizards and witches is his or her command of the Dispel Magic and related spells. While Dispel Magic is taught to all fourth year students, in the heat of combat, a Dispeller must be able to repeatedly let lose volleys of these spells in rapid-fire succession.

> We all know that dispelling another magic spell is always chancy, never certain. Indeed, a beginning wizard has only a slim chance of actually dispelling a powerful wizard's spell. Yet as his skill and practice increases, so do their chances of success. A Dispeller, on the other hand, takes this to new heights of success.

Yet by all reports, in order to be effective, a Dispeller must be able to cast this spell non-verbally and without a wand. Why? His opponent may have entangled him or sound dampened the area in which he or she is standing, even gagging the poor Dispeller. He or she must still be able to get off this spell!

So demanding is this profession, that few choose it, and rightly so. The wizarding world is lucky to have five Dispellers alive at one time in history! Unquestioningly, the best Dispeller ever was Samuel Rabnor, the man most responsible for the apprehension of Dominus Malefic, five years ago. As of this writing, his whereabouts are unknown, however.

The book then went into a lengthy discussion of the various spells that the author thought any good Dispeller ought to have at his or her command. He even suggested various training regimens to follow. It was not a thick book and Lindsey wondered if such books could be purchased and if so, where and how much this one might cost, though she had no idea where she could get the needed dollars to pay for it.

Carefully, she wrote down the name of the book, its author, and anything else she could think of that might help identify the book. She sighed and placed it on the conveyor; she had to get busy on her real homework. At ten, she and Amanda headed to their commons room to see how the others were doing. Quickly, Lindsey looked over Pam's essays, correcting several wrong tenses. Then, she looked over Kathy and Emilio's math problems, correcting half of his.

Later in their room, while preparing for bed, she asked Pam if it was possible to buy books. "Sure, the best place is Mag-Amazon.com. They have the best prices. What's its ISBMN?" Lindsey got out the paper on which she had jotted it down. Pam entered it and found that it cost ten dollars, plus one dollar mag shipping. Lindsey, of course, did not have the eleven dollars. Yet she was excited to find out that magical books were offered for sale, if only she could earn some money.

As she fell asleep, she suddenly got a bright idea. Maybe she could get some kind of job here at school, working in her spare time to earn some money with which to buy some books!

Chapter 8—A Visit with Cho Lin Sung

Sunday morning, right after breakfast, Lindsey decided to try to find out. She reasoned that the best person to talk to about this would be Professor Cho Lin, since this was not a House Mother sort of question. She walked over to the Hall of Illusions and went to her office. The door was locked, but a sign said to go to room 301.

She climbed the stairs and found the room. It was actually their living quarters. She knocked on the door. "Be right with you, Lindsey," the voice of Cho Lin came through the door. Lindsey wondered how she could possibly know that it was her, since she had only knocked!

A little later, Cho Lin opened the door, patting dry her long, black hair. "Come in. I was just washing my hair. Now, it's drying. Have a seat. How can I help you?"

"Can students take on some kind of jobs here at school to earn some money?" she asked.

Cho Lin chuckled. "You don't think we assign enough homework, do you?"

Lindsey realized that she was teasing her. "No, it's not that. You see, I don't have any money and I would like to get some."

"Whatever for, if you don't mind my asking."

"Books. I found aninteresting book in the library last night. I would really like to own it and study it all the time. Pam showed me that I could buy it on Mag-Amazon.com last night for eleven dollars, but I've never had more than fifty cents in my pocket my whole life. So I thought maybe I could wash dishes or something to earn eleven dollars so I could buy this book."

"Gracious me, your House Mother, Ann, is such a scatterbrain at times! She must have forgotten to explain to all you first year students about your weekly allowances! Each week that you are here, Lindsey, your full scholarship provides five dollars for you to spend on anything you desire. I'm so glad that you aren't wasting it on lipstick and perfume as the girls in Red Hall so frequently do. Let's see, this is the start of your sixth week here, so you have thirty dollars accumulated that you can spend! However, Lindsey, I am very curious. What magical book has so gotten your attention that you wish to own it?"

"This one," Lindsey showed her the paper on which she had jotted down all the key data.

"Dispellers?" Cho Lin said, very surprised at her choice.

"Yes, Professor. I'm doing an essay in history class on all the possible jobs we might pursue once we graduate. Pam showed me all the interesting ones and my list is now about one hundred seventy long. Of all these jobs, being a Dispeller really interests me the most. I know that in this book he says it is one of the most dangerous jobs in the world and that there are very few of them. I think he said five for the whole world."

"Yes, it is the most dangerous of all occupations! Why on earth does this so interest you, if you don't mind my prying?"

"Oh I don't mind. Well, ah, I, ah, don't know how to say this."

"Say what, dear child? It is safe to tell me anything. It will just be between me and you."

"Well, this is so hard to say, but I think that my dad might not have been my dad."

"Huh?"

"This is so confusing, so hard to explain, but we found pictures of Samuel Rabnor, the famous Dispeller and part of the Rat Pack who captured Dominus Malefic fourteen years ago. He looks just like my father! Besides Amanda pointed out the spellings: b a r r o n and r a b n o r. Just shuffle the letters. Also, less than a month after Sam Rabnor and the Rat Pack captured Dominus, their Diviner, Mabel Pruit, was murdered along with the rest of her family, her mother and brother. Right after that, Sam Rabnor disappeared. My dad came to Plano with a carpetbag in his hand not very long after that in time. Mom's told me all about that many, many times. However, I don't know for sure, you see, my dad never used any magic, no spells and no wand. He never ever spoke of magic, so it might just be some weird coincidence, you see. All this has gotten me very interested in finding out all I can about Sam Rabnor and Dispellers. Besides, of all those jobs I have listed on my essay for History Class, the only one that really interests me is the Dispeller."

"My goodness! How on earth did you find out about all this?"

"It started by us seeing the pictures in the Trophy Room of all the Yellow Hall track trophies. Jim was showing them to us, because we're on the team. There are five pictures of Sam Rabnor there, and they look so alike to my picture on my desk of my dad, mom, and me. What is so weird is that all the information on Sam Rabnor seems to have disappeared utterly. Even I'm in the database, saying I'm a first year student here. Actually, all traces of the others in the Rat Pack have also gone missing, except for Mabel, whose entry says that she was killed. However, we found out all of this detailed information on a Swedish web page. Its title contained six typos, but the text was just fine. We translated it and that's how I know about this man. Like I said, my father didn't ever have anything to do with magic that I know about anyway, so this is all probably some weird coincidence."

Lindsey had not noticed Cho Lin's face growing very white, while she was explaining all this to her professor. *What should she say? Lie to her, telling her that her real father was not her father?* No, she couldn't lie to this girl. Yet, she was under orders not to divulge this information, because it would put her life in dire jeopardy! What made matters far, far worse for Cho Lin was the simple fact that she had known Sam Rabnor! He was a sixth year student here at Bradbury's when she was a third year student. If Lindsey discovered this additional fact, she was sure to ask her if she had ever seen him! How could she possibly lie about that? He was one of the school's track stars! Never in her life had she been in such a predicament!

Cho Lin picked up on the single possible line of reply. "Well done indeed, Lindsey. Yes, it does seem like a remarkable coincidence indeed. I know that Sam Rabnor did disappear back then. What we lack, Lindsey, is any information that might somehow link him to the father that you know, such as a bus ticket from where he lived to Plano or someone in whom he confided that he was heading to Plano. I'll make you a deal, Lindsey. If you leave all this alone and concentrate on your studies, I will make a number of inquiries and see if I can somehow prove or disprove whether he was your father or not. I believe that I might be able to do this."

"You will? Wow! Thank you, Professor Cho Lin! That would be the greatest thing! I'll work really hard on learning everything here. I've already caught up on my spells, but I'm still a bit behind on all the essays. I know so darn little about the magic world. I must be the dumbest student here. I'll work hard though."

"Good girl. I know you will. In the meantime, about this book you wanted. If you are really interested in learning about the Dispellers, I know of a much better book. I'll loan you my copy. You can keep it until next May. Then, if you really want your own copy, you can get it before you leave for summer vacation. Now, if you want to buy other books using your allowance money, just go to the bookstore and take them the information as you have written here. Tell them the money comes from your allowance fund. They will order it through Mag-Amazon.com for you. It will come in one day by mag messenger. How's that?"

"Great! Just great! I never knew that there were so many magic books until I began wandering in the stacks last night. There is so much to learn!"

"Yes, dear child there certainly is. A little tip from me, Lindsey. You just keep on learning new things even after you graduate. I'm still learning new things nearly every day that I'm here! Now here's the book I would recommend to anyone who wanted to learn about being a Dispeller." She made a motion with her hand and a large, leather bound book appeared in her hand. Cho Lin handed it to Lindsey, whose eyes opened as she read its title. It was written by an actual Dispeller!

"Now run along and do try to do some homework today and not devour this whole book." Lindsey giggled and promised she wouldn't. Lindsey ran all the way back to her dorm, happy as a lark. She told her friends all about her chat with Professor Cho Lin and how she had promised to help prove or disprove Sam Rabnor was her father. Everyone cheered. This was the best news they had had yet.

Lindsey did not see the sign on Cho Lin's office door suddenly change to "Out of the office, back shortly." A bit of paper floated past Alister's nose, while he was reading the morning paper. At once, a door appeared near his table, and Cho Lin, still wearing her bathrobe, appeared, her hair wrapped in a towel. "You old sentimental old fool! You blew it! She and her friends know the secret and all about it, as well!"

"Calm down, Cho Lin. Who knows what? Tea? Brandy?" he teased her. He knew she never touched alcohol and that she loved green tea.

"Tea please. Lindsey, she and her friends know all about Sam Rabnor! They've compared pictures and are this close to proving that he was her father! And it is all your fault! You left those darned pictures of him in the Trophy Room, where the track team stumbled on them."

"But how?" Alister grimaced, handing her a cup of tea he'd just conjured for her.

"I don't know. She said something about finding a Swedish web page that told them all about Sam, the Rat Pack, its members, and what they did with Dominus. They know that Mabel was murdered and that Sam disappeared shortly after that. Lindsey knows that her father appeared at their ranch right after that. They've discovered that someone has deliberately removed the key information on these men from the databases. Next, she will be telling me just who removed them! Honestly, Alister, how could you leave those photographs out there?" Cho Lin finally calmed down.

"I see that you have had a little excitement this fine Sunday morning, Cho Lin. And how did you handle her?" Alister said calmly.

"She wants to become a Dispeller, just like her dad! She found a book on the profession in the Library and came to me wanting to find a job here so she could make some money so she could buy it. House Mother Ann forgot to explain to the first years about their allowances and how to use it. I loaned her my copy of Broadwell's. If she is serious, she ought to read about it from another Dispeller."

"Excellent, but how did you handle her?" he repeated softly. She'd not answered his question.

"Oh," Cho Lin flushed, realizing also that she had not answered his question. "I played off of what she told me. She had no way of proving a direct connection between the disappearance of Sam and his re-appearance there in Plano. I told her if she would forget about this and leave it to me, concentrate only on her studies here, that I would investigate and see if I could provide a link to prove or disprove it. She accepted that very readily, I might add."

"Well done, Cho Lin. You have saved me from my foolish mistake. Now I'm in your debt. I owe you one."

"Yes, but not only does she know, but also her four roommates and very likely the entire track squad! We might as well broadcast it to the whole school, Alister. Eventually, one of them is going to mention it to someone else, and gossip like that will sweep through the whole school in a day! Especially because it involves Lindsey!"

"You do have a point, Cho Lin. What would you recommend we do about the situation now?" he asked quietly.

"Tell her the truth, but then you are the Governor, not me," she retorted. "Eventually, she's going to discover that I was a student here when Sam was here and come asking me about him. I won't lie to her if she does this, Alister."

"I know you don't like secrets, Cho Lin. Neither do I, for that matter. Yet, in this case, I truly don't know the best avenue to follow. For one thing, we need to find out if Sam is really dead. Who knows; it could have been staged. Perhaps he found out someone was getting too close to him and needed to disappear once more, faking an accident."

"In front of his own child, who had no hands? Sam would never do that! Not the Sam I knew here. I was shocked beyond words that he did not somehow get her hands regrown, allowing his own daughter to grow up a helpless cripple."

"Well, perhaps he had his reasons, Cho Lin. First, we

must uncover what actually did happen. If he is truly dead, alas, we have lost a most valuable wizard. If he is truly dead, then there is the matter of Lindsey's inheritance. He left behind much when he fled for his life. How much, we don't know, and we'll have to be extra careful finding that out, what with Dominus on the loose once more."

"Ah, professor, I have a plan," he added with a smile.

"You always do, Alister. I guess that's why I like you so well," she admitted.

"For a time, we need to keep her occupied so she can't go off searching for more data about her father. Are we agreed on this?" Cho Lin nodded; this was obvious.

"You said that she was keenly interested in becoming a Dispeller. We both know what that means, don't we, Cho Lin? She must be able to cast nearly every spell without the use of her wand, without words, and in rapid fire. Further, she must be able to sense what spell she should use next with only tiny moments of time in which to make that judgment call."

"Yes, but that training comes in their sixth year, Alister."

"Already Lindsey can cast all the Grade 0 spells without a wand and probably without speaking, if Janice is to be believed. I would suggest that you invite her to spend a couple of hours right after supper with you. Work with her on getting each of her Grade 1 spells mastered in the same way, no wand, non-verbal. From what I have seen of her and from all the reports I've gotten, you'll find her up to that task. What with her track and soccer activities, this should keep her more than busy for the time that I need to discover more information. Will you do this for me Cho Lin?"

"Well, yes, it does sound like a reasonable approach to take. God knows if Dominus comes after her, she will need every bit of training we can cram into her head to stay alive! I'll do it."

"Thank you and thank you again for saving my butt over the trophies. Now where did I put my out of office sign? I must get busy quickly and it was such a nice morning to read the paper." Cho Lin smiled and stepped through her magical door back into her room.

"Trouble, dear?" Huan asked her.

"Alister has asked me to give Lindsey Barron some extra training right after suppers as often as she can spare the time. Sorry dear."

Chapter 9—Sports

"Well, it's about time that some teacher started lending you a hand, Lindsey," Amanda replied. Lindsey had just told everyone that Professor Cho Lin was going to help her with her spells every evening for an hour after supper. "We'll just have to have Bill schedule soccer practices a little later in the evenings. I can't devote five nights a week to his training schedule. How about you?"

"Me either, the assignments are getting harder," Lindsey replied.

"Well, Emilio ought to spend more time on his math and science, not running around. Where's all that running going to get him once he graduates?" Pam added. She still had a tendency to pick on Emilio. She hadn't forgotten he thought she was ugly. Even though she knew she wasn't pretty, that wasn't something you say to a twelve year old girl!

"Still, that is a pretty cool book that she loaned you. None of us knew about the allowance money we have accumulating in the bookstore. It will help me replace my Spy Cam that I lost. I'm sure that Professor Janice smashed it. I found the pieces on the floor," Pam continued.

Indeed, Bill grumbled about the difficulty of scheduling practices for track and soccer. Trying to fit in times that were free for nine students was becoming a chore for him. Graciously, Sally lent him a hand, working out a spreadsheet and blocking out all the known times that everyone was not available. They would have one practice on Wednesday night before the track match on Saturday, and only two practices, Sunday and next Wednesday nights, to get ready for their first soccer match against Red Hall. Bill only moaned, sure this season would be no different from the last bunch. He longed for at least one victory before he graduated, and he'd long given up all hopes of winning a championship cup.

Saturday afternoon came quickly. Buoyed by her successes with Professor Cho Lin during the week, Lindsey felt more than confident about the race. Today, they were racing against Brown Hall, while Blue Hall, coming off a victory over Brown Hall last time, which she missed because of her injuries on the track, tackled Red Hall. Unlike the lengthier soccer matches, the track meets were much shorter events. This allowed two competitions per meet. The October afternoon was quite chilly, as her companions were warming up for the event. The large crowd wore cloaks with hall-colored scarves. She saw Sally waving to Bill.

As before, Professor Blake handled the announcements, but she barely listened. Her nerves began to tingle her stomach. The last time she ran, she was tripped and forced to spend a week in the Infirmary mending her broken arms. Well, she how had hands as a result, but still, she felt nervous about the race. What if she managed to trip herself? She could never live that down! "Focus, Lindsey," Bill said as he jogged in place. "Okay, Sally, you are up. Go beat them! You can do it!" Sally smiled and moved to the starting line for the 100-meter dash.

"And how about that folks. Miss Sally Ridgeway has done it! First place in the 100-meter dash goes to Sally and Yellow Hall. Can this young team actually do it this year? Yes, that is the question that we are all asking. Ah, the runners are getting in place for the one-mile relay race! Remember, Yellow Hall took this one from Black Hall just a few weeks ago. Can they do it again? Brown Hall fans say NO!" He introduced the runners for both sides and gave them the countdown.

Lindsey, Amanda, Jim, and Tom stopped their warm up exercises to watch. Soon they too were yelling their team on. It was a close race all the way. However, Brown Hall edged out a victory by two feet, and Bill looked dejected as he came off the field. Lindsey moved into the starting block, while her three mates moved back to their pick up starting locations.

Next, Red Hall and Blue Hall ran their same two competitions, with Blue Hall taking both of them from Red Hall. Lindsey ignored those races, concentrating on keeping her nerves in check and warming up for her long race. Soon, Professor Blake did his usual introductions of the long distance runners. As he announced them, Lindsey looked at her opponent, Emilio's brother, Francisco. "Good race,

Lindsey," he said with a smile.

"You too," she said back to him. She took a deep breath to calm her nerves. Go! Echoed across the field and she and Francisco took off. As before, Lindsey worked very hard to find that pace that Amanda and Jim insisted she take. When she finished the first of the ten laps around the whole field, Jim was giving her signs to slow down a bit. She had been pushing it a bit too fast. Indeed, she realized she had been trying to keep pace with Francisco. By the third lap, she had her pace perfect and Amanda gave her all thumbs up as she swept past her.

Now it was just a chilly wind on her face and the crisp, clear Colorado air. Ah, Lindsey loved just running like this. No cares, no worries, no problems, just herself flying along. Suddenly the whistle sounded, bringing her out of her reverie. It was the last lap; she began to increase her speed, gaining on Francisco steadily. As she rounded the last curve and headed into the straightway, she gave it everything she had, overtaking him. Jim began to run, soon matching her speed along her right side. She held out the baton and felt him snatch it. Simultaneously, she began slowing down, as he pulled on out ahead of her. She saw the other Brown Hall runner doing the same, though he was significantly behind Jim. At last, she moved off the track and began her cool down jog. "Good run," panted Francisco, jogging nearby.

"Nearly got suckered into your speed at the start," she replied.

"Yes, I have longer legs, but you're darn fast. How long have you been running?"

"Seven years."

"That explains it. Never been beaten by a first year, but then you really aren't first year, in terms of running," he complimented her. She thanked him. Both moved over to their teammates to watch the rest of the race. The crowd was noisy and yelling, and soon she was yelling as much as anyone else was. Jim had lapped his opponent!

The handoff to Tom went perfect, as if they had been doing this for years, Lindsey thought. Perhaps they had, she realized, since they were brothers. When Tom handed off to

Amanda, Tom was two laps ahead of his opponent. Now it was in Amanda's hands. She watched her Apache friend get her pace down. She looked like a fleet footed master, racing along the track, smooth motion, sleek, and trim. When the whistle blew signaling the last lap, Lindsey watched her carefully, hoping to pick up some tips. Smooth, steady increase in speed, no instant forcing as Lindsey had done, just a gradual pickup in speed. Amanda was flying down the finish line. As she crossed it, she held the baton high in victory. The crowd yelled and hollered for some time, giving Amanda time to start cooling down. Her brothers and Lindsey jogged alongside her congratulating her and each other.

Professor Blake called out loudly, drowning out the crowd. "Yes, it's a new school record time for the twenty-mile run! 110:31! Incredible, Yellow Hall has broken the ten year old speed record! Just incredible and you saw it happen! Let's bring those four magic runners out here for a bow!" Holding each other's hands up in triumph, the four stepped on to the grassy field to a wild celebration.

By the time that Red Hall and Blue Hall long distance racers finished, few were paying their slow times any attention. Blue Hall won in 130:22, a long way from Yellow Hall's new record. Literally, everyone was commenting on Yellow Hall's stunning times, though most somehow chalked it up to the invasion of the Indians. Just why the Apaches should be such good runners, categorically, Lindsey had no idea. As the celebrating group of runners headed back to the dorms surrounded by will-wishers and a few autograph seekers, Bill realized something, "Hey, Professor Alister said if we broke the school record, we would get to go to the Nationals in Des Moines, Iowa. We did it; we're going to the Nationals!" Lindsey wondered what that meant and when it would be.

Deiter whizzed past them can called out, "Gee, now Lindsey has no excuse for not signing autographs." She ignored him, but Amanda glared at him.

"Give it a rest, Deiter," she spat at him.

"Well, that's all the racing until spring," Bill explained to his team. "One more set of races happens in two weeks, but we sit that one out—Black versus Red and Blue versus Brown.

Promise me that you will keep on working out during the winter, gang. We've got Nationals in May, yes!" he pounded his fist in the air. Lindsey wondered how that would be possible in the winter snows, but didn't ask, just glad that she would not have to worry about more track meets for months.

Back in the quiet of her room, Lindsey realized that her first soccer game was one week away. She knew she could barely bring the ball down the field. Amanda was somewhat better at it, though Emilio had taken to soccer like a pro. "Next, week, I make a fool of myself before the whole school again," she complained to Pam, whose essay she was correcting.

"Are you any good at it?" Pam asked, making some of the corrections Lindsey was suggesting.

"I'm terrible at it. I hardly even know the rules. There is so much magical faking going on, but it won't take magic to steal the ball from me! Oops, you misspelled wonderfully, Pam."

While she changed it, Pam replied, "You know, I have been asking around some of the older girls, and they say that most of the spells that we saw in the game last week were done by the fifth and sixth year the players. It seems that that's when they start working on doing the spells non-verbally. According to Lucy Potts of Brown Hall, almost all the spells her team uses, non-verbally, are Grade 1 spells. She says that the players have a hard time doing all that running around carrying their wands. Is delicious spelled right? I mean isn't there a 'c' in it?"

"Yes, you spelled it right."

"I looked in our book and Jump and Create Phantasm Illusion are both there. Even the Enlarge spell is there. You remember when that guy got his arms stretched ten feet long to get the ball? They are using spells that we are going to be learning; maybe that will help you, Lindsey." Pam wanted to sound a hopeful note; she certainly didn't want her friend to make a complete fool of herself next week.

"There, your job listing for Professor Thalmus is done. Good going, Pam. You have two hundred and fifty-three lines! That's a hundred more than I found. I'm sure you will get an A on this one," Lindsey complimented her.

"That was quite a race you ran, Saturday, Lindsey. Well done," Professor Cho Lin complimented Lindsey Monday evening, when she reported for her extra lessons.

"Thanks, this Saturday, you can watch me make a fool of myself, though. I can barely bring the ball down the field. I've never played soccer before and honestly, I don't play very well at all. However, if I don't play, Bill won't have enough players on the team and would have to forfeit the game, so I will do my best."

"I know you will. This week, Lindsey, I thought it might be wise for us to work on some spells you might find useful in your soccer game," Cho Lin said with a wry smile. She was not above helping her team members. She had grown tired of the taunts from Professor Delius Dogs, the Black Hall guardian.

"Really?"

"Yes, now I think the first one we should learn is Jump. I believe Janice will be covering that one later this week, but we will get the jump on her." Lindsey giggled at her pun. When Lindsey returned to her study hall that evening, she was cheerfully able to Jump, using her wand. By Wednesday evening, she could Jump without saying any words or using her wand to activate the magic. She knew this would be of immense help to her in the soccer match.

"I have given considerable thought to the next spell, Lindsey. We still have time to begin another yet tonight. We both know that soccer can get quite rough. I certainly don't want a repeat of last time, when you fell and broke your arms. Since it is likely that you are going to get knocked down one or more times during the game, let's see if we can get you a safety spell."

"Normally, we use this spell when we are on top of a building or cliff and need to get safely down. The spell is called Gentle Fall, and you fall and land as if you were light as a feather. Now I have brought this box for you to stand on, and I want you to jump off of it and land on your feet once, without magic, just to get the feel of it."

When she left for the evening, Lindsey was able to cast

Gentle Fall using her wand, a very good step forward. By Friday night, Lindsey was very proud of the fact that this spell too she could cast non-verbally and without a wand. Cho Lin cautioned her to work on speed; if she were tripped, she'd have only a split instant to get the spell off.

"What are you doing, Lindsey?" asked Pam Saturday morning. Lindsey was practicing falling off her bed and Gentle Falling to the floor. "I can see that it's a cool spell, but why?"

"I'm going to try not to get hurt this time. I expect to be tripped and I don't want to spend another week in the Infirmary," Lindsey stated flatly, as she again jumped off her bed, only to land gently.

Amanda walked in on them, "Well that's going to be useful today. Have you looked outside? It's pouring down rain! Maybe they will take pity on us and call it off!"

Later at lunchtime, Amanda asked Bill about it. "No, we play rain or shine, mud or snow. It's actually humorous to play soccer when the field is covered in snow. That happened once. No one could stand up for long, hilarious. Glad I wasn't on the field, though. You all ready?"

"Lindsey is so nervous that she can't eat," Amanda replied. "I expect I'll get my face full of mud today. Honestly, with three first years, two of which barely know the rules, we don't stand a chance, Bill."

"Yes, but against Red Hall, so it will at least be fun," he tried to sound cheerful. "Just make sure you use a lot of Dry spells today; it's going to be wet out there!"

A little later, the nine made their way to the Stadium to get ready for the match. Only die-hard soccer fans showed up to watch, conjuring all manner of umbrella-like contraptions to keep themselves dry. At least the wind wasn't blowing hard, just a good downpour, which had made the grassy field extremely wet and slippery.

Lindsey relaxed for two reasons. First, it was obvious that every player was going to be slipping and sliding everywhere. Second, very few would see her make a fool of herself. Besides, it would likely be masked by the inclement weather. "Remember, Lindsey, you move around in the red zone trying to get open. We will all keep an eye on you and pass it to you when you are free. Just take your best kick at the goal. If you get into trouble, remember try to pass it to one of us somehow. I have you at this position because I know that you really are not yet up to speed with the game and all that." Now she finally understood why she was playing forward: he took pity on her poor skills and had given her the easiest position to play. She was thankful for that, since Emilio seemed to have hundreds of rules that he had to follow and didn't know how he could keep half of them straight.

Barely fifty students braved the rain and were in the stands, as Professor Blake, who had conjured a complete tent over himself, began introducing the two teams. At last, Betsy tossed out the ball and the game began. Bill grabbed the ball, but the wet ball slipped out of his hands and went rolling away from him.

Rocky Jones, fifth year, began kicking it to move the ball down to the yellow end. However, he soon began slipping wildly and decided to pass instead. As he delivered a good kick over to Phyllis Bellington, also fifth year, he slipped and fell into the mud. Phyllis waved her wand and five images of herself appeared, just as the six Phyllis's kicked the ball toward the net. One of the images, however, fell flat on her butt, the real one, Lindsey guessed.

Sally dove and caught the ball, but came up soaking wet. At once, Sally heaved the ball far down the field towards Bill. Lindsey marveled at Bill's skill. He positioned himself and when the ball came to him, he batted it across the field to the left forward, Tom. Whitewater then tried to move it closer to red's net, using his feet. He too saw this was not going to work at all well. Ella Himes, fifth year fullback, closed in on him. At the very last instant, Tom kicked the ball over to the right side, where Jim was. Rocky Jones, their fifth year fullback, narrowly missed stealing the ball, however.

Lindsey tromped around the middle of the field. No one paid much attention to her. The next thing she knew, Jim had kicked the ball over to her. As she tried to quickly stop it with her feet, she discovered what everyone else was discovering: quick moves caused one to slip. She stopped the ball, but began falling backwards. She cast her Gentle Fall and landed safely. However, Ella was splashing her way towards her ready to steal the ball from her. Lindsey grabbed the slippery ball and cast Jump. High in the air, she threw the ball over to Jim. Ella certainly was not expecting this move from a first year! Jim had a clear shot and he took it. Wham! He kicked it as hard as he could.

Red's goalkeeper, the husky Maribell Jones, fifth year, dove for the ball, but missed it. Professor Blake yelled, "Score one for Yellow Hall on a brilliant kick by Jim Whitewater! Now Rocky Jones has the ball for Red. Can he tie this game up? Let's see what brilliant move he makes." Unfortunately, Rocky slipped and fell and everyone piled up on him and the ball. Lindsey watched as the ref threw the ball back into play. She was now soaked completely and shivering. "Warm," she said determinedly. "Warm."

"No, Amanda has just stolen the ball. Will you look at the grace of this first year player," Professor Blake commented. Just as he said that, Amanda slipped and fell flat on her face in the growing mud. At least she managed to move the ball over to her brother Jim. He grew a few feet taller and passed across the field to his brother Tim. The ball slipped out of his hands, and Ella, the Red Team Captain, stole the ball, lobbing it far down the field to Phyllis, who promptly lost control of the slippery ball. Becky latched onto the ball and lobbed it far down the field the other way.

Ella jumped for the ball to intercept it, but Bill waved his wand, leaped high in the air, and grabbed it just as it was heading for Ella's open arms. "Great pass and catch," yelled Professor Blake. Unfortunately, Bill could not hold onto the slippery ball. It slipped out of his hands. Ella grabbed it, but she too slipped and fell into the growing mud pool. The ball rolled away from both of them. Lindsey saw the ball come towards her and she just gave it a wild kick closer to the goal. Tim saw the direction of the ball, waved his wand, and made a half-field jump, landing softly as the ball arrived where he was. He pivoted and kicked for the goal net.

Maribell, suspecting some trickery, had enlarged herself and now she easily blocked his kick. She got up and heaved the ball back down the field. Steadily, the field became brown instead of green. Mud puddles grew like small lakes as the players continued to slosh around the field. Even in this downpour, Lindsey saw that this was one fast moving game!

A little later, Lindsey was open and was passed the ball. She took her time and kicked hard for the goal net. Her feet went out from under her and she began falling backwards. Gentle Fall, she thought, and landed lightly in the mud puddle. Maribell had effectively blocked it, and by the time that she got back on her feet, the ball and play was far down at their own goal net!

Late in the last half, again Lindsey had the ball in her hands. She was close to the net. Ella was charging her. She knew that she had no time to lower the ball and kick it. Besides the last time she did that, she had fallen backwards into the mud. Jump! She commanded and rose high in the air. Partway up, she threw the ball as hard as she could at the net. Maribell did not expect this move; she was guarding against another horizontal kick. The ball came down at an angle. Though she hit it, she only deflected it and the ball flew into the net. Score to Yellow Hall.

By the time that the buzzer announced the end of the game, all eighteen players were laughing their heads off! Eighteen players were totally covered in brown mud with only their eyes visible. Professor Blake cheered out, "And Yellow Hall claims its first victory in many years! Congratulations to Yellow Hall. Let's give all these players a great round of applause. They have all been great sports to play in this downpour. Wait a minute, I cannot tell who is who anymore. Are all these the Brown Hall students?" The small crowd laughed as the players on the field looked from one another.

As they walked off the mud field, Amanda said, "Thank god for magic! Otherwise, I'd never get my hair clean! Quickly, dozens of Clean spells began flying right and left. Dry spells were pointless in the downpour. However, Lindsey noticed Professor Blake standing by the mud field with his wand. She paused and watched as the muddy mess turned back into the green grassy field, as if they had never played on it.

"Well, we won a soccer game!" declared Bill, enthusiastically, as they all entered the stairs of Yellow Hall.

Everyone chuckled. It had hardly been a soccer game, not the way Lindsey expected a soccer game to go.

An hour later, warmed up pinkishly from the hot tub, Lindsey and Amanda joined Pam and Kathy in their room. "Way to go, Lindsey, I saw you score a goal!" Pam complimented her.

"Only because I didn't fall down that time. Honestly, we shouldn't have even been playing in this rain! Boys and their games," she said. All four giggled. Lindsey felt relieved because their next soccer game was not until the spring. Now she could concentrate on her studies, which just seemed to be getting more difficult with each passing week.

Chapter 10—Halloween

Sunday evening, Sandy dropped by to see her first years. "Two weeks and it's Halloween! There will be a very special dinner at five. Then, while we're all conjuring up our costumes, the professors will be re-arranging the dining hall. At six, the Halloween Ball begins. It is a costume dance." Naturally, the four asked many questions about it.

When she left, Lindsey said, "Gosh, I don't know how to dance. Is it hard?"

"Me either," Pam admitted. Now that Lindsey had come forth first, she felt braver in admitting it.

"The only dancing I know how to do is tribal dancing. I don't suppose that's what Sandy means," Amanda added.

"Oh good grief! Don't any of you know how to dance to rock and roll?" asked Kathy in disbelief. "Well, I certainly do. I guess I will have to give you all dancing lessons, in that case." They giggled.

In their spell casting class, the first years had now begun their study of Grade 1 spells. They had mastered Sound Control, Alter Self (which allowed them to grow or shrink a foot or so and to manipulate their appearance), Understand Languages (now they could read Swedish directly), Moving Lights (simulating lanterns complete with visible light and useful at night), Detect Magic, Erase (to make corrections to their writings), and Light (direct creation of a globe of light).

This week, the class moved outside underneath the tall marble columns, where they had lots of space in which to perform their spells. Per the warning from Professor Janice last Friday, all wore their heavy cloaks over their robes. Though the day was sunny, it was late October and quite chilly.

The students were chatting excitedly. They were outside, which could only mean they were going to work far more interesting spells this week. "Now then class, you will notice that over there are ten small fires burning. Any good wizard or witch must be able to increase those flames or reduce them down. After all, if your house catches on fire, you want to be able to put it out before it burns down. The spell is Alter Fires. Over on your right are small fireplaces. On chilly nights, you might want to start a fire. The spell is Finger Flames. It will shoot flames out from your hands. Please, students, point your hands at the logs. If you catch someone on fire, you will get detention!" She stared at Lyle, who stared at the ground. "This half will work with the ten burning fires and this half will begin lighting the fires. Grade 1 Spell Book, page 52. Get started."

"Looks like we get to start fires," Amanda whispered to Lindsey, as they got their spell books out. "Isn't she going to show us how it is done?"

"Lyle!" shrieked Professor Janice. "Do not burn down the Hall of Charming and Summoning!" Everyone turned to see what was going on with his fire. Flames reached the marble ceiling! He had turned the small fire into a roaring inferno. While his eyes were transfixed upon the flames, Professor Janice quickly lowered the flames to normal. "Deiter, work with Lyle. The spell did not say create an inferno!"

Amanda read from the book. "Your wand should make a sharp upward thrust as you say the command Fire Emit." Lindsey tried it; flames shot out from her other hand, which was pointing at the ground.

"Oops. It says you should be pointing in the direction you want the flames to shoot towards first. Sorry," Amanda cautioned her. Lindsey tried again and got the flames onto the logs. After a few more attempts, Amanda began trying. Like Lindsey, she forgot to point her hands first and very nearly caught her own robes on fire.

A while later, Professor Janice came over to watch the two. "Professor, may I ask a question?" asked Lindsey. She nodded, but not a hair of her blonde locks moved out of place with the motion.

"Well, if you should point this at a person, wouldn't this harm them, I mean they'd get a bad burn or worse. Their clothes might catch on fire."

She forced a smile from her cherry red lips. "Well, it most certainly would do that, Miss Barron. You can attack another with this spell. I remember once I went to Montana to visit a cousin of mine, who lived in the wilderness. Why on earth she should choose to live out there in the middle of nowhere I will never know. Well, I was on the porch just putting another coat of nail polish on my nails, when out of the woods came this large, grey wolf, great fangs and all. I shot this spell at the wolf and set his fur on fire. He ran off and I was safe. Very useful spell. Now let's see your wand activate as you do it, Miss Barron." She did not mention that she had also set fire to the forest and burned down her cousin's log cabin.

As the bell rang ending the class, Professor Janice proclaimed loudly, "Do not try these spells in your dorm room. If you set fire to your dorm, you will face a *very* lengthy detention!" Half of the class giggled. Who in their right mind would cast these in their bedrooms?

During the week, they also learned Fan of Blindness (which often caused temporary blindness in the victim), Enlarge or Shrink (most useful in soccer), Jump, and Gentle Fall. These kept them rather busy, as these spells were more difficult to master. Lindsey thought that Professor Janice took great pleasure seeing her students becoming temporarily blinded, when their partner's spell finally worked. Many girls screamed in panic when they suddenly could no longer see. However, all quickly realized that always there was some chance that the victim would recognize the spell for what it was and thus avoid the spell's effect. By the end of the week, Lindsey was rarely affected by Amanda's spell.

Friday night before the Halloween party, the four girls sat back catching their breaths. Kathy had been teaching the three how to dance to the heavy rhythms. A few Chill spells later, Pam said quietly, "I know what Dominus was after."

"What? No way," Amanda declared. "How could you?"

Grinning mischievously, she replied, "Goed oud Zweden." Huh? Three exclaimed, then waved their wands and had her repeat it. "Good old Sweden," Pam repeated in Swedish, the four giggled. Their new spell was quite useful.

"I've been using my spider, only this time—well, you know, I wanted to find out more about this nasty criminal who's on the loose, Dominus Malefic. That Swedish webmaster is an awful speller. That's probably why whoever tried to wipe the information from all the databases missed his. Keep your spell active and read what's on my monitor," she said, puffing up proud of her find.

> When the Rat Pack closed in on Dominus Malefic and his Death Stalkers, Dominus was engaged in stealing an ancient relic uncovered during the recent archaeological digs along the Tigris River. The relic was identified by Professor Smythe Diggs, Order of Merlin, as the Rod of the Apocalypse. The relic was in the secure vaults of the Wisconsin Hall of Justice, where it was being studied by Professor Diggs, in hopes of understanding its precise magical properties, repudiated to be apocalyptic in nature.

Pam clicked on another tab in her browser. "At least no one had tried to eliminate information on this relic. There are dozens of references to it. This one is good. Besides it is in English."

> Rod of the Apocalypse: The wielder of this ancient artifact dating from 200 BC calls forth one at a time and in succession the seven Horsemen. The first Horseman brings forth a great pestilence upon the land. The second Horseman brings forth a great drought, where all things perish. The third Horseman brings a great plague upon all peoples. The fourth Horseman brings with him a great flood over the land. The fifth Horseman brings fires beneath its feet as it rides over the land, burning everything in its path. The sixth Horseman brings a great darkness upon the earth, an eternal darkness. The seventh Horseman brings death and a mighty conquest, bringing the wielder of the rod his final conquest of all peoples of earth.

"Well, that does sound like something a madman would like to get his hands on," Amanda declared flatly.

"It's awful! He'd wipe everyone out!" Kathy said more than a little fearful.

"Yes, but there is one more thing I came across. I wonder why it wasn't in the news last week?" She clicked on the third tab displaying the Wisconsin Daily Magical News. It was dated last weekend.

> The secure vaults of the Wisconsin Hall of Justice were broken into last night. Five guards were slain. The vault, which at one time contained the ancient relic known as the Rod of the Apocalypse, was rifled. Minister Able Wisenham issued a statement that the rod had already been relocated to a more secure location just after Dominus Malefic broke out of prison.

"I'll bet anything that Dominus broke in there and killed those poor guards," Pam declared authoritatively, though she had nothing with which to back up her declaration.

The four chatted about these revelations and praised Pam for her clever detective work. Lindsey had the strange notion that maybe those peculiar midnight lights that she had seen were the great wizards bringing that rod relic here for safekeeping. Why she had this thought eluded her, but perhaps it was all the talk of Bradbury's being so secure and safe.

Finally, they picked up their things and headed down to the study hall. Emilio was very patiently waiting them there. They found him with his head down on his spell book, dozing very nicely. Pam teased, "Emilio, trying to pick up the spells by absorption I see. Is it working well?"

Red faced, he woke up, muttering, "Where you been, senoritas? I've been waiting. Kind of fell asleep. I'm ready to practice spells, if only someone will look over my math problems. I don't think any of them are correct. Do you have Professor Thalmus's essay done?"

"Here, I'll look over Kathy's and your math problems, if Lindsey will check my essays. You three can work on your spells," Pam took charge.

"Thanks, Pam," Emilio replied and became the guinea pig for both Amanda and Kathy's spells.

Just before they ended for the evening, Emilio asked them, "Have you figured out what your costumes will be for tomorrow night? I'm using my Phantasm spell to make me look like a skeleton, you know, just bones walking around. Creepy, right?"

"I ought to go looking exactly like a miniature Professor Janice," Pam teased. The girls giggled. To be honest, none of the four had yet decided upon a costume for the party.

Saturday morning, girls of Yellow Hall headed for the bathtubs and showers at nearly the same time. Objective: get ready for the evening's party. By the middle of the afternoon, the four had their hair dried and were still trying to figure out their costumes.

Finally, Amanda gave up in disgust. She waved her wand and she was dressed like an Apache princess. "How do I look?" she asked. Now all she had to do was brush out her hair and work out how she wanted it to look.

Pam, must have waved her wand two dozen times, trying out this look and that look, never really satisfied with any. "What would you really like to look like?" Amanda finally asked her, becoming annoyed with the dozens of different looks that Pam kept asking her about, with her ceaseless "How's this look?"

"Well, I'd really like to look pretty, you know, just once, look really nice," she admitted. Amanda waved her wand and dressed up Pam.

She looked in the mirror. "You have me looking like some movie star. It's rather cool. I don't look half bad this way."

"Come here. I'll fix your hair so it looks good with this outfit," Amanda replied, glad that Pam was at last satisfied.

"How do I look?" asked Kathy, who now looked like a queen, complete with a glittering tiara. Now only Lindsey had yet to work out her costume. Finally, she decided to look like her idea of a fairy, complete with dainty little wings.

They went down to dinner only to find that their dining room had been decorated for Halloween. Spiders, webs, and pumpkins dominated the scene. Even the food was cut or baked or pressed into Halloween shapes. Everyone had fun eating the meat pumpkins and French fries in the shapes of bones. At last, they dashed back to their rooms to make their last minute preparations to their outfits, eagerly awaiting the six o'clock gong, which would announce the start of the Halloween dance party.

The lighting was dimmed. Candles within pumpkins overhead provided the illumination. Whoever did the decorations had really gotten into the spirit of play. The back wall contained tables with hundreds of different kinds of snacks, many in special shapes as befitting the season. The music was provided by a magical console, which even took requests. Six hundred students filed onto the floor, along with the House Parents and all the professors and staff.

Lindsey noticed that many of the fourth, fifth, and particularly the sixth year students were paired and dancing close together in the center of the floor. She spied Sandy and Tom dancing so close that mere inches separated their lips. She looked away. Lindsey was not interested in boys very much just yet.

Monique from Red Hall came over to Pam and whisked her off to the dance floor. Monique was dressed as a woman impersonating a man, a bit strange, Lindsey thought. She did notice that they were whispering to each other and from the looks on their faces, were having a good time.

Amanda dragged Kathy, Lindsey, and Emilio, who was intent on stuffing his face with all the sweets, onto the dance floor. Soon, all four were dancing and enjoying the party. For Lindsey, this party was very special. It was the finest party that she had ever attended. True, in Plano, there had been some school parties, but she rarely attended them, not wanting to endure more teasing and taunting. She had never gone trick or treating. Plano was a mile away. Besides, with no hands, she would only be more embarrassed going from door to door. Thus, tonight was a night for her to remember.

The costumes were as varied as the students were. However, uniformly, those in Black Hall wore "darker" costumes; headless horsemen, undead zombies, and skeletal nightmares predominated. Everyone could tell a Red Hall girl, regardless of her costume, just look for the cherry red lips.

Around ten p.m. everyone heard the sound of breaking glass, followed by screams of terror! Lindsey jumped up to see over the heads of the hundreds of students. A pack of huge wolves burst through the windows and growled at the nearest students, saliva dripping from their huge canines. Everywhere kids screamed and rushed for the exits.

Above the din, Alister's voice called out calmly, "Floor Monitors, lead your students to their rooms now." Mass panic and a small stampede followed. Lindsey and Amanda were forcibly pushed along the nearest path to the stairs. Twisting and turning, trying to keep their feet on the floor, they struggled in vain, only hoping not to fall down and get trampled!

When the mass hit the stairs, Lindsey and Amanda fell down the steps toward the basement, as the crowd of panicking kids pushed and shoved to get up the steps. Lindsey grabbed a hold of Amanda and said, "Gentle Fall." Both girls landed awkwardly, but unharmed on the lower landing. On their backs, they looked up at the terrified faces pushing, shoving, and yelling to get up the stairs.

"Let's go down and find a safer way up," Amanda suggested. "Thanks for catching me. You are hot, Lindsey." She flashed a smile.

"Gosh, those were sure big wolves. I saw them when I jumped," Lindsey said as the two hastened on down the steps into the giant tunnel area directly below the dining room, where twelve side tunnels fanned out to all the other buildings. "Where did they come from?"

"Dunno, maybe the mountain? We were nearly crushed in the stampede! Wonder what stairs would be the best ones to try?" asked Amanda, who could hear the howling of the wolves even here in the basement.

"Oh no!" Lindsey gasped, as they entered the giant tunnel room. All the hundreds of lights were turned off! It was pitch black. The two girls stood holding each other's hands, staring into the blackness.

Lindsey was about to create her Light, when they heard voices, strange voices that they did not recognize. Fear seeped into their minds, as they stood motionless, holding their breaths.

"It's working, master, just as you said."

A cold voice said, "Quiet. Let's see, which is the right passage?" A dim light outlined two heavily cloaked men. The light came from the tip of the taller man's wand. Slowly the light moved from sign to sign, resting finally on "To Admin Hall." "This way, Rubius," the cold voice whispered. Slowly the footsteps of the two men trailed away down the now dark tunnel.

"Who—who was that? Rubius? Could that have been Dominus?" Amanda said, her voice breaking and trembling. Lindsey felt her legs going weak on her.

"We—we should tell someone," whispered Lindsey.

"But we cannot get through the crowd of kids rushing up the stairs. Besides there are wolves running all over up there," Amanda whispered back. "What are we going to do?"

"Maybe, maybe we should follow them and see what they are up to. Then, we can find another exit and go warn Alister or Cho Lin," Lindsey suggested.

"If that's Dominus and he finds us, we are as good as dead!" Amanda whispered back.

"Well, if that rod is here and he gets a hold of it, everyone is going to be dead," Lindsey rationalized. "Come on; let's use our Blue Lights. They're not likely to be seen. Besides we have slippers on and won't make any noise." Still holding hands, wands at the ready, the two cast their Blue Light spells, holding the origin point on the tips of their wands. It provided just enough light that they could barely see where they were walking.

"This way," whispered Lindsey, as she saw the sign "To Admin Hall." They moved very slowly and concentrated on being as silent as they could. For Amanda, who was also wearing moccasins, this was natural. She whispered a quick spell and Lindsey now wore similar moccasins. She grinned at Amanda, realizing what her friend had done for her.

It was a long walk down to the Admin Hall from the center of campus, where the dorms were located, long, but perfectly straight with no other exits. This worried the two somewhat, because if the men returned, they would have no choice but to run. There was nowhere to hide! Step by silent step, the girls made their way to the hall.

After what seemed hours, they arrived at the end of the tunnel. Steps leading upwards lay in front of them. Two other tunnels angled off to their right and left, heading for the Infirmary and the Hall of Invocation and Evocation. However, they heard noises coming from just up the steps. They moved closer to hear.

"Of all the. . .!" the cold voiced man cursed. He was trying spells that was for sure. The girls heard all manner of commands that they had never heard, including one that jarred the entire walls, vibrating the solid stone walls and floor that they were standing upon.

Nearly falling down, Amanda let out an involuntary squeak. "What's that?" the voice of Rubius called out. "Thought I heard something."

"Well go down and check on it. I'll keep trying to get past this ward." Heavy footsteps thumped down the stairs. Hearts beating furiously, the girls had no choice but to turn around and begin running back down the tunnel. They heard yelling behind them.

"Come back here!" yelled Rubius.

"Go get them! Leave no witnesses," called out the cold voice. The heavy footsteps of Rubius echoed in the tunnel. His Light spell was enormous and suddenly both girls found themselves illuminated!

"Run!" shouted Amanda, and they both broke into the fastest strides they could take! Unfortunately for them, the tunnel was very long and very straight, with no exits, except back at the junction below the dorms. The only advantage they had now was distance—they were considerably ahead of the racing Rubius. Suddenly he barked out a spell. Lindsey looked back over her shoulder and saw an explosion of fire billowing their way.

She screamed, "Faster!" Both stretched themselves to their limits. Closer and closer, the exploding flames came to them. Just as Lindsey thought they were about to become fried utterly, the explosion ceased. It had reached the limits of the spell's distance.

Amanda looked over her shoulder and saw that Rubius had now cast another spell. He was running twice as fast as the two girls were! She screamed this to Lindsey. Both girls panicked but continued to run. What else could they do?

The next instant two things happened nearly simultaneously. Lindsey called out, still holding her wand, "We need a place to Hide!"

Rubius waved his wand in a zig-zag motion and barked, "Lightning Come Forth!" An enormous bolt of lightning shot down the tunnel at the two fleeing girls. Just as the electrical bolt struck the two girls, they both disappeared completely from the tunnel. Rubius walked up to where he had last seen them, looked around, and saw nothing. He chanted several spells. Fear slowly crept into his mind. He sent a spell message back to his master, who instantly rejoined him.

The man with the cold voice said, "We've got to get out of these tunnels immediately. They are coming. Hold my hand. Door." A door appeared and he opened it. The two men stepped through the door and arrived in the Formal Gardens. Quickly, they raced for the outer walls and the tunnel that they had made underneath the barrier walls, protecting the school's perimeter.

The two girls lay on cold stone, numb; they couldn't move. The electric current, which had hit their bodies and should have slain them, had only temporarily numbed their nerves. Though they didn't know why they were still alive just now, they had been spared the full force of the current because they were simultaneously in transit into this room.

It was black, utter and complete darkness. It was cold. Neither could move a muscle of their own volition, yet each heard the other's labored breathing as their bodies recovered from their sprint for life. Lindsey was very happy to hear Amanda still breathing, though terror tried to swamp her own mind. She couldn't move. What if she could never move again? Where was she? No one even knew where they had gone during that panic rush up the stairs. Time, in time, someone would find out they were missing and come looking for them. Slowly that thought gave her some comfort and the building terror began to subside.

After a long time, her foot wiggled. She tried to wiggle it more and it moved a little. Lindsey tried to speak but couldn't yet. Eternal minutes passed while slowly she regained control of her body. Finally, she could move her arms, and she felt for Amanda, who was also feeling for her. Their hands touched and latched onto each other. Both were making groaning, gasping sorts of sounds.

Minutes later, both were able to sit up and their voices returned. Immediately, Lindsey cast her Light spell, thanking the day that Cho Lin had worked with her on learning how to do this one without her wand. They looked around. They were in some kind of storage room. Dust lay thick on everything, including the floor. Both their wands were near them and they instinctively latched on to them and stood up.

"Where are we?" asked Amanda. "What happened to us?"

"Why aren't we dead?" Lindsey asked. "Where is this? What is all this stuff?"

Desks, beds, chairs, and tables were piled in an enormous stack that defied all logic on how they were so positioned here. They looked around for a door and found none. "There has to be a way out of here, there just has to!" Amanda cried. "We got in here somehow. I have to go badly."

Slowly, they walked around the walls that they could reach and found no slightest trace of a door or anything remotely resembling a way out! Next, they began tapping on the walls, hoping to find a hollow spot, but everywhere they tapped, they met what seemed solid cold stone. Already they had to renew their Light spells ten times, because the spell only lasted about ten minutes.

Unable to find any way out, they each removed a chair from the pile and sat down. "We should think," Amanda said half determinedly and half hoping against all hope this was the right thing to do. "We were running and then Rubius cast that electrical spell at us and it hit us, but we are in here, wherever here is. How did we get in here? Did you cast any spell?"

"No, I just said, 'We need a place to Hide!' Then, it hit me," Lindsey replied, thinking about what had happened.

"Well, you got your wish. We sure are 'Hide!'" Amanda replied. "It's probably what saved our lives, Lindsey."

"Unhide!" Lindsey commanded, but nothing happened.

"Open Door!" "Let us out!" "How about a little help here? What else could be the spell command words to get us out of here?"

They tried a number of possibilities, but nothing happened. Amanda lamented, "Not only do we need the command words, but also the right wand motions to make, Lindsey. It's hopeless."

"Light! Well, sooner or later we will be missed and someone will come looking for us," Lindsey sounded hopeful, having recast her light spell again. "I wonder if that really was this Dominus fellow. The Death Stalker was called Rubius."

"What were they doing here? I bet they were behind all those wolves! That certainly distracted everyone so they could rob the Admin Hall, but what were they after? Our student records?"

"No, what would they want them for? Remember, I told you that I saw those weird lights around midnight. Well, someone in Black Hall saw them too and whatever it was, it landed in the parking lot and a light was on in the Admin Hall. Someone came here. I'll bet someone brought something here. You don't suppose that they brought that relic thing that Pam showed us here, do you? That rod thing?"

"Who knows, but at least that would make all this make some sense to me," Amanda admitted. "Say, that was a good run you did there. You kept up with me. Very few can do that. During summer vacation, how would you like to come and visit us?"

"Cool! I've never had any real friends before nor traveled anywhere. I have no idea how I would get to your home. I suppose I could ride Betsy, my horse, if I knew the way."

"We can work something out. Dad has an old car. Maybe he or Tom can drive us. How are we going to get out of here anyway? Light!"

"I guess we just have to wait until someone finds us. Light!" Lindsey replied.

Bored, Amanda began looking at the piles of unused junk. Old school desks from perhaps a century ago caught her attention first, but they were mounded behind worn, but fairly new desks. She moved around between the newer ones, trying to get a closer look at the antique ones. "Lindsey, these back there might be antiques and worth some money on EBay2000. I wonder why they are keeping them when they could get some money for these?"

"Light. What's an antique anyway and what is EBay2000?" asked Lindsey, who had never heard of these before. However, she moved over to where Amanda was exploring.

"Antiques are really old things. People like to buy really, really old things. I can't imagine why though. EBay2000 is the biggest Internet buying and selling site. My dad once sold his old rusted out Ford Galaxy 200 truck on it for five hundred dollars. Honestly, it was junk and hadn't run in fifty years at least. Why someone would buy that I don't know."

"Maybe Bradbury's doesn't need any more money," Lindsey ventured, "and that's why they are keeping all this stuff."

"Maybe they are pack rats, just like my father. He keeps everything, even old newspapers. I can hardly get him to pitch the trash out. He says one day it might be just the thing he needs. Say, what's this?" In climbing over the more recent desks to get a closer look at the quaint antique desks, she slipped and caught herself on one desk. However, her hand felt some paper on the underneath side of the desk top.

"Light! Hey, something's stuck underneath here. Yeu! Chewing gum. Dried out. Yeu! Hey, a paper." Amanda became excited over her find. It was a highly folded paper. She climbed back off the desk pile and the two of them began opening it up on the floor.

"Light! It looks like someone had drawn a map of Bradbury's," Lindsey said, noticing the similarities at once.

"These are the tunnels. It is a map showing all the buildings and the tunnels. Wait a minute. There are all these other things drawn on here in pencil," Amanda became very curious. "Look, under the dining room, it shows a big bunch of rooms labeled kitchen and pantry. We've never seen them down here!"

"What's that tiny writing there beside that room?"

asked Lindsey.

"Kitchen Please," Amanda read it to her. "Maybe, maybe that is the password or magic word that opens the door to the kitchen," Amanda speculated. "Light! It would make sense to keep the kitchen and pantry hidden from us. After all, we would constantly be running in there asking for a snack or things. Mom sometimes says I just get in the way when she is cooking."

"Hey. Look and see if where we are at is on the map," Lindsey suggested. "Light!"

"Hum, we were running along here, but I don't see anything. Wait a minute. Look, here's something. Could this be it?" Amanda asked, pointing to a side room on the west side of the tunnel to the Admin Hall.

"Maybe, what's the writing say?" Lindsey asked.

"Hide Please and Exit Please," Amanda answered. "Maybe those are the command words. Shall we try them?"

"Let's, but we better fold up this map first. No telling how long the door will stay open, if it does open." The two folded up the large map. Lindsey insisted that Amanda try it, since she found the map.

Not knowing exactly where the door might be, she stood in the center of the area and waved her wand, saying "Exit Please." Just to their right, a door appeared and the bright lights of the tunnel suddenly entered the room. They cheered and stepped out into the long tunnel.

The door shut behind them. "Lights are back on. That is a good sign. Oh, you are very dirty, Lindsey. Clean." Amanda removed the accumulated dust from Lindsey's fairy costume. Lindsey returned the favor since Amanda's was also very dusty. The two barely began walking back to the dorms when Professor Cho Lin came running down the tunnel, her wand held at the ready. Her robes were ripped and torn. She did not look in a good mood at all.

"Thank heavens you two are all right! Whatever possessed you to run off like this? Never mind. I had better let Alister and the others know I've found you. The entire staff is out looking for you two!" She waved her wand and said, "Message. All Staff." Found girls. Returning to dorms. CL. A flash of magic indicated her message was sent. Looking them over, she noticed several large bruises on their arms and legs. Cho Lin was about to ask them if they were all right, when a flash of magic appeared near her head and a small piece of paper floated past her eyes. My office. Immediately. Alister. As soon as she read the words, the paper vanished.

Cho Lin waved her wand and said, "Door: Alister's Office." To the utter surprise of the two girls, a door appeared right here in the middle of the tunnel! "Take hold of my hands and we will go through this door. This is a Grade 4 spell, which you will be learning in your second year, assuming that you manage to stay alive that long." Cho Lin was annoyed, slightly angry, and worried, a jumble of emotions right now. The girls obeyed and were surprised to find themselves stepping into Governor Alister's office, somewhere in the Admin Hall!

Both exclaimed, "Wow! Cool!"

At nearly the same time, another magical door opened and a very worried looking Alister stepped into his office. His robes, too, were torn, his hair disheveled, something neither girl had ever seen. "Found them half way down the Admin-Dorm tunnel, heading to the dorms," Cho Lin said curtly. "I just noticed these bruises on them as I came here."

"Very well, Professor. I suggest that we all have a seat," he said kindly and softly. At once, three chairs materialized across the desk from his chair in which he swiftly sat. The three followed suit. "Now then are you hurt? You gave us all a terrible fright, running off like that, disobeying my direct orders to return to the dorms. Did you not hear me?" he asked.

The two had not noticed their bruises and quickly glanced at them and rubbed their legs and arms a little. Lindsey decided to speak for them both. "We're okay, I think. Yes, we heard you and tried to get to the stairs, but the stampeding kids knocked us down the stairs. I used my Gentle Fall to keep Amanda and me from getting hurt when we landed near the bottom, sir. We didn't mean to run off. It's just that we couldn't get up those stairs and so we went to the tunnels to go up a different stairs to our rooms. We weren't trying to run off."

"But you have been gone for hours, girls. Surely, it

didn't take that long to find the other stairs," he replied.

"No, well, all the lights were off in all the tunnels and we couldn't see."

"She's right; all the lights were off, and just as we were about to make our lights, we heard two men coming and saw their lights. One was Rubius and he was the one who tried to kill us!" Amanda interrupted, getting to the main point at once. "We think it was the Death Stalker and the other one was Dominus! We followed them, and they were trying to break into the Admin Hall to steal the relic, that rod, whatever it was called!"

"Apocalypse. Yes, the Rod of the Apocalypse," Lindsey added.

From the shocked look on Alister's face and the gasp from Cho Lin, they knew something was wrong, just not what. "How do you. . ." Cho Lin started to say, but Alister cut her off.

"Dear me, dear me. Perhaps, you should start at the beginning and tell us everything that happened, just as it happened. No jumping around, please." Since he was smiling, the girls relaxed and felt more comfortable relating their tale.

Amanda began again, starting when Lindsey used Jump to see the wolves crashing in through the windows. She did a good job of describing the details of what happened. "Then, Rubius came down the steps after us and we ran back down the tunnel as fast as we could. Suddenly, this explosion of red fire came swooshing down the tunnel at us. We ran as fast as we could! Just when we expected to get burned up, it stopped and disappeared!"

Alister said softly, "That was a Ball of Fire spell, a Grade 3 spell. You will learn that perhaps late next year. Not many first years could possibly survive that blast. You were exceedingly lucky, both of you. Continue."

"Well, we kept on running and then he shot something at us, kind of like a lightning bolt in a thunder storm, only there wasn't any storm and we were in the tunnel."

Cho Lin gasped. Alister said calmly, "That was a Lightning Bolt Grade 3 spell as well. You should both be very dead."

"Well, it was all Lindsey's doing. At the same time—well

we did have our wands out—anyway she said, 'We need a place to Hide!' Just as we got electrified, we just disappeared, falling hard onto a cold stone floor! For the longest time, we couldn't even move! It was pitch black. We couldn't see anything. After a long time, we could finally move, and we both made our lights to see where we were. Did you know that you have a whole lot of valuable antique desks in some storage room down there? You could sell them on EBay2000 for a lot of money, I suspect."

"Professor, that explains why we couldn't find the girls for so long. Yes, I had forgotten about that old storage room. EBay2000 you say?"

"Yes, my dad once sold a beat up, rusted out, old junk car on there for five hundred dollars!" Amanda explained.

"I see, and then you finally said Exit Please and began walking back when Professor Cho Lin found you?" Both girls nodded.

Alister rubbed his chin and said, "You both were incredibly lucky this evening. You could have been killed twice, but only have a few bruises instead. Lindsey, Professor Cho Lin has told me that you are interested in becoming a Dispeller when you graduate." She nodded enthusiastically. He added, "Well, just so that you know, Lindsey, what you did tonight, managing two very narrow escapes, is just the kind of thing a Dispeller must be able to do. I am very proud of your level thinking in a time of crisis. Both of you did very well. Commendable, in fact." Both girls beamed.

"Now about the identity of those two men. Were you able to see their faces? Did they look like either of these two men?" He held up a prison photograph of two men. Both positively identified the one on the right as the man who had nearly killed them, the one called Rubius. Neither had seen the face of the other one, unfortunately. Cho Lin merely held her hand over her mouth as the girls made the identification.

"You only heard the other, cold voice you say? Would you mind if I heard what you heard, Lindsey, Amanda?" Alister asked calmly and politely.

"Yes, but how?" asked Amanda.

"Repeatio: Cold Voice." Alister said. Suddenly, both

girl's minds went back to their memories of the few times they had heard him speak. The room echoed with his words.

"Quiet. Let's see, which is the right passage?"

"This way, Rubius."

"Curse them!"

"Well go down and check on it. I'll keep trying to get past this ward."

"Go get them! Leave no witnesses."

Then, the spell ended. Cho Lin now had both of her hands covering her mouth. Alister nodded grimly. "Yes, I recognize that voice. It belongs to Dominus Malefic." A squeal emitted from Professor Cho Lin's covered mouth anyway.

"Tell me, how is it that you know about the Rod of the Apocalypse? I was under the impression that Professor Cho Lin had asked that you cease searching the past, Lindsey?" he asked sternly.

"I'm sorry. I didn't go searching. Pam, she came across the whole story about how the Rat Pack finally captured Dominus, when he went to steal the Rod of the Apocalypse at the Wisconsin Hall of Justice. She found it on some Swedish website, where the webmaster does a lousy job of spelling his page captions."

Alister smiled and winked at Cho Lin, as if to say, "See, she lived up to her part of the bargain." He then asked, "Very well, but why should you think that this rod was being kept here at Bradbury's?"

She related what she had seen: the strange lights coming down by the mountain at midnight, shortly after Dominus had escaped. She told of the Black Hall boy who had seen it too, and her thoughts that something had landed in the parking lot, and that one light was on somewhere in the Admin Hall.

Alister said, "See Professor? Once you have all the pieces, it is clear how sharp minds fit them together. It would seem that you have would-be Trackers, Dispellers, and Sleuths in your hall. In light of these revelations, I believe that you should be giving more extra lessons."

Professor Cho Lin opened her mouth as if to say something and then shut it just as fast. Alister sat back in his chair and sighed. "Revelations. Yes, I suppose that this is the time. Lindsey, we have known that Samuel Rabnor was indeed your father." Lindsey gasped.

"When Doctor Caterwall regrew your hands, by law, he had to submit a sample of your DNA into the medical database. When a new sample is entered, the entire database is searched for any matches. You see, this way, we can find criminals, who are trying to alter their physical appearance or trying to assume some new identity. It came back with the data that Rabnor was your father. However, at that very instant, all of that information was instantly classified top secret and wrapped with a secret password to prevent anyone from finding out."

"I chose not to tell you for your own safety. As you already know, Dominus is an evil wizard. He swore revenge on those that had captured him, those in the Rat Pack. You have found out that he did indeed kill their Diviner, Mabel and her family. We believe that is when your father decided to go underground, to go into hiding for a time. I purposely withheld this from you, Lindsey, because as soon as Dominus learns that you are the daughter of Sam, he will very likely come looking for you to kill you as he promised to do fourteen years ago. Now that the cat is out of the bag, so to speak, I will have the Department of Defense send someone to protect and look after your mother. Dominus may well want to harm her, although that seems highly unlikely. However, we ought to take every precaution."

"Mom! Not mom! Oh no! She knows nothing about magic!" Lindsey cried.

"We know. I will see that they send a very good protector to look after her. Would a new ranch hand work as a disguise?" Lindsey nodded, since that was how her father had come there long ago.

"As I promised Professor Cho Lin, I am still researching your father, trying to determine what exactly happened after he went into hiding. As soon as I know for sure, Lindsey, I will come and tell you all about it. Is that acceptable to you?"

"Yes, but does this mean he knows about me and will come into my room at night and kill me?" Lindsey asked, becoming rather scared.

"Oh no. I have many protections on Bradbury. This is perhaps the safest place in the world for you right now, Lindsey. You see, Dominus could not get past my magical defenses in the Admin Hall. I admit that was a clever move on his part to get through my outer wall defenses. You see, he dug a tunnel underneath the walls. That's how he got all the wolves into the campus. I believe he then shattered the windows so that the wolves could interrupt our festivities. That was a clever ruse to hide his real actions. He turned off all the tunnel lights so they could see anyone coming. Yet, he did not expect the Guards and Wards I have within the Admin Hall. So in the end, he failed once more."

"We were distracted by the wolves. Yes, you can see that they attacked us, but we got rid of all them. However, I am sad to say that three students were bitten and are now in the Infirmary. They will all recover and be as good as new by tomorrow. Once we had that handled, your House Mother reported that you two were missing, and I have had all the staff out hunting for you for hours now. It has been quite an eventful evening, but with no real harm done, I'm very glad to report."

"Finally, I do owe you this, Lindsey. Tonight, you handled yourself just as your father would have. Yes, I knew him. I was Governor when he was here at Bradbury's. I believe that Professor Cho Lin was a younger student while he was here as well. She may be able to tell you a little more about him, though remember, she was three years behind him. How many fourth year students do you know well?" Lindsey smiled; she only knew a very few, but the prospect of hearing anything about her dad from Professor Cho Lin filled her with excitement. Indeed, "just as my dad would have done" filled her mind!

"Now I believe they have had enough excitement for one night. Professor, would you please escort them safely to their rooms? And do make appointments for Amanda here and Pam, if you will be so kind. Oh, I'm sorry. I guess it is already tomorrow, 1 a.m. already! My, my."

Cho Lin nodded, waved her wand, and said, "Door:

Yellow Hall, Room 2." A door appeared and the three stepped thought the portal into the girls' room.

"Wow! Way cool! You are alive! Oh!" came the rapid fire words of the startled Kathy and Pam, as the door appeared and the three stepped into the middle of the room.

Professor Cho Lin said, "Here, they are safe. They can tell you all about their narrow escape with death. However, starting tomorrow night, after I finish with Lindsey's special lessons at seven, I expect that you, Amanda, will be there waiting yours, and at eight, Pam, I expect that you will be at my office waiting your turn. It seems all three of you will be having extra lessons with me for some time. Now I am very tired. See you tomorrow evening." She created a door to her room and left them.

"He *is* my dad! Alister told me so!" Lindsey fairly screamed her delight. All four girls began to talk at once. Finally, Pam insisted that only one of them talk at one time. It was three in the morning before the four finally went to bed.

Of course, at Sunday Breakfast, the dining hall showed no signs of last night's disastrous attack. Gone were the decorations, however. Hundreds of students discussed the attack of the wolves, but Yellow Hall's track team insisted on hearing what happened to their two players. Half of Yellow Hall's students listened in as well. They of course spread the word to their friends in the other halls.

Sunday evening, Amanda nervously waited outside Professor Cho Lin's office for Lindsey to complete her private lesson. She kept vacillating between the exciting possibilities of maybe learning new spells versus being in very hot water because of their foolish escapade last night. Lindsey came out and smiled, "Your turn. See you in our room when you get done." Rats, that gave her no clue which way this meeting would go. Timidly, she went into her office.

"Ah, right on time, have a seat Amanda," Professor Cho Lin said. She had a smile, so perhaps this is good, Amanda thought. She sat down and fidgeted with her robes. "Now then, first I want to compliment you on your quick thinking, putting moccasins onto Lindsey last night. That certainly helped you two move silently down the stone tunnel. Alister believes that you have Tracker abilities. It is my responsibility to find out if this is true or not. Are you ready?"

"For what?"

Cho Lin waved her wand and Amanda swore that they were out on the high plains. "A man has been through this area, I want you to see if you can follow his trail and lead us to him."

Amanda relaxed at last. Finally, here was something that she had been doing all her life on the reservation. "He is going this way. He is about two hundred pounds and is being careful to hide his tracks. He has a slight limp in his left leg." She bent low and suggested, "About an hour ahead of us. This way." To her keen eyes, the trail was unmistakable. However, soon he walked over a rocky patch where he left no impression on the ground. "Wait here, please," she said and quickly continued in the same direction the man had been going. When she got to softer ground, she realized that would have been too easy. He had deliberately changed directions. She moved around in a large circle and soon picked up his trail once more. "He's veered to the right."

Cho Lin stopped her at this point, saying, "Excellent on this test." She waved her wand and Amanda found that it was night and quite dark. The moon, behind a cloud, allowed her at least to see the shape of the ground, but without using her Light spell, she could not see the trail. "This test is to see if you can track using only your sense of smell. I know you are not a dog, but a good Tracker must use what is at hand to follow his prey. Close your eyes and tell me what things you can smell."

Amanda rattled off several things before saying, "There is a hint of lavender in the air which is out of place."

"Precisely, I want you to see if you can follow her trail." Once more Amanda set off; only this time, she found it exceedingly challenging. The only real clue she had was that, if she were moving in the right direction, the smell became a little stronger. At last Cho Lin halted the test, "Very good, Amanda. Now for the final test." She waved her wand and she found herself in another location at night.

"A wizard has been having a spell combat with another wizard. I want you to see if you can tell from which direction the two wands fired. I know that you have not studied anything about this in your classes. It is a fifth year subject that few can master. Just use your magical senses and take your time."

Amanda could not see how she could possibly do this one. "I have no idea what to look for, Professor Cho Lin. I guess I flunk this test before it even starts."

"Watch. I will cast some magical missiles using my wand. I will shoot them over there towards that rock. Watch the magical lines of energy flow as I do it. Later this spring, you will be learning how to cast this spell." Amanda did as asked, four bluish, projectiles sprang from her wand, arced through the air, and struck the rock, harmlessly. "Did you see the faint energy lines? I'll do it again." This time Amanda saw the very faint lines. "Now look around here and see if you can find where the two wizards battled."

After a good deal of looking, Amanda replied, "I think I see a blue one coming from over there and a red one going back towards the blue one."

Cho Lin waved her wand and they were both back in her office. "Very well done indeed. Very few fifth years would have been able to spot those. Indeed, it would seem that Alister was right. You do have the innate skills of a Tracker. Those three places were just illusions that I created to test your skills. Perhaps one day if you are keen on casting illusion based spells, you may learn that one. Now then, I have a book for you to study and each evening we will work on these skills and drills, Amanda."

"Cool! Thank you, Professor."

"For your information, the Tracker of the Rat Pack was also an Apache. Now then, let's get to work."

Pam walked up to the office door, awaiting her turn. She was sure that Governor Alister had made a grave error. Either that or she was being somehow punished. "Perhaps I deserve it. After all, I was using dad's server for some of it," she thought. Pam decided that this must really be some form of punishment and resigned herself to accepting whatever Professor Cho Lin dished out to her. Amanda came out looking very thoughtful, but smiled as the two girls passed each other.

Pam wanted to ask her about it, but there was no time.

"Hello Pam, come on in and have a seat," Professor Cho Lin said, as Pam set foot inside her office. "Alister seems to believe that you have sleuthing skills, so why don't we find out." Pam nodded, wondering what form the punishment would take.

She waved her wand and Pam found herself in a grizzly looking room. A dead man lay on the floor on the other side of a table, littered with all kinds of papers and items. Cho Lin was beside her. "Two wizards had a battle in this room. One killed the other. Wizard A was tall and thin; Wizard B was short and thin. When the Department of Law arrived, Wizard B claimed that Wizard A attacked him and he had to fight back, killing Wizard A. I want you to examine this room and tell me if that is what happened, please."

"Oh, I see, like a detective, find the clues. I like puzzles. Let's see, weird, the dead man's pants are too short on him. That doesn't make sense." She knelt down and examined the dead man more closely. He had a nasty wound in the small of his back. Pam said, "I think Wizard B is really Wizard A. He switched pants and he shot this man in the back. If they had a fight, he would be more likely to have been hit in the front, not the small of his back."

"Very good observations. Now look over this room and tell me what the two men were fighting over. All the clues you need are in here."

She rummaged through the papers and various objects. What she found curious was that there was a woman's hand mirror lying smashed on the floor. She looked but saw no other signs that a woman had been in the room, however. She even sniffed the air and Cho Lin asked her why. "Trying to sense if a woman was in here. No perfume, so maybe not." One of the papers had strange writing on it, which of course really caught Pam's attention. Across the top of the page was: enim dlog. There were lines sketched on the paper and more of these nonsensical groups of letters.

"Repair Mirror," Pam said firmly and the glass shards of the mirror mended themselves. She held the paper up to the mirror and read, Gold mine. The other strange letters gave directions on how to find the gold mine.

Cho Lin grinned and replied, "Well done, Pam, that was very quickly done indeed. Finally, I want you to tell me what spell the wizard used to kill this man. I know that this may be way beyond your skill and learning. It is a sixth year subject that only a few can really master."

Pam looked at the wound and sighed. She had no way of knowing this answer. Suddenly, she thought of an idea. "May I use my computer, professor?"

"I don't see why not, though I don't know how that will help you solve this riddle."

Pam didn't pay her any further attention. While her laptop was booting, she kept whispering to herself, "Now where did I see that? I've seen it somewhere. Guess I'll have to Google it." She typed in: "visible effects of spells." The third entry was what she was looking for, but unfortunately, it was on her father's secure server. A minute later, she was in and looking at the hundreds of pictures. She found one that matched fairly well, but the spell was called Lightning Bolt. She categorically ruled that one out; the room was far too small to fire off such a spell. She examined the shirt the dead man was wearing more closely. Around the entry wound, the fabric had been burned, but not by fire. "Ah," she exclaimed and scrolled rapidly down. She stopped at another spell and compared the image on the screen and the shirt. "I believe this one is it, but I want to make very sure, so I have to look at all the others too," she declared. One thing defined Pam; she was always thorough in her work.

At last, she said, "I believe that he was hit in the back with an Acid Arrow. It is a kind of . . ." Pam began her lengthy explanation.

"Yes, I am familiar with the spell. That is indeed what was used here. Well done, even if you used rather unorthodox methods, you achieved the result." She waved her wand, and the two were back in her office. Again, Cho Lin explained about illusions. "Now then, it does seem that you have a knack for sleuthing as Alister suggested. Hence, during our sessions, it will be my responsibility to improve your skills, Pam. Here is a book that I recommend," she handed Pam a thick volume.

"Hey, I just bought this one right before the bus came to pick us up. I brought it along in case I had some spare time to read it, but I haven't yet."

"Well, good girl, this one is the best text on the subject. Now you will have time to start in on it. Begin with chapter one. Of course, it is written as though you were a sixth year student, so expect that there will be quite a lot that you will not readily understand. We will work on it together during our study periods. Let's read the first sentence Professor Bottlehoop has written on page one, shall we."

Pam dutifully read: The cardinal rule that every Sleuth must always follow is always observe and not formulate conclusions based on a cursory examination. In the next several paragraphs, Professor Bottlehoop went on to back up his statement from cases that he had worked on during his youth.

"Now why do you suppose Professor Bottlehoop made that statement?" Professor Cho Lin asked. Pam was off and speculating. The hour passed altogether far too rapidly for her!

When she finally got to their room, she discovered the others were there. Lindsey, Amanda, and Kathy had already helped out Emilio with his many math and science blunders, had corrected Kathy's nearly equally dismal math errors, and Lindsey was nearly done helping smooth out Amanda and Kathy's science descriptions of planetary effects observable to the naked eye and how those could be used to tell in what part of the world the observer actually was.

Quickly, Pam told them all about her lesson and Amanda told Pam about hers. Finally, all four began to look at the map. "Curious that no mention of this map came up," Pam said. "I wonder if they know about it?"

"I wonder if we are supposed to know about all these hidden rooms?" Lindsey asked. "Who is Looney and Green anyway? Former students?" Their signatures were on the bottom of the map; perhaps they had made the notations.

"Well, maybe none of these hidden rooms actually exist," Kathy suggested. "After all, it's only a map. We've never actually seen these, well except for the storage room that you two found."

"There are so many. It would take ages for us to check on each one of them," Amanda said.

"I know, why don't we divide up and each one of us take a section and see if it's there and the doors work as the map says?" Pam suggested.

"We can't go opening the door to the kitchen with all the other students around," Kathy replied.

"You're right. We will have to do it in secret, when no one's watching," Pam said with a mischievous hint of glee in her voice.

"But kids are always around during the daytime," Kathy protested.

"Then, we will have to do it other times, like at night. Not too many kids use the tunnels at night. That's probably the best time to try, unless you want to break the rules and go down there in the middle of the night!" Pam suggested. None wanted that.

"Now we each need a copy of the map. Copy Map," Pam stated, waving her wand. Thrice more she cast the spell. "Now we each have a copy and we can keep the original safe in here. Perhaps we should hide it." Lindsey didn't know why all this secrecy was needed, but went along with Pam's ideas, hiding the original under her bed.

Chapter 11—Work, Work, Work

By Monday, word had spread throughout the entire school. Dominus and Rubius had been here and had caused the wolves to attack. The three girls, who had been bitten by the wolves, were released, but were upset because no one would listen to their stories. Everyone was now talking about how Lindsey and Amanda had encountered Dominus and Rubius in the tunnels, along with their narrow escape. Worse, everyone seemed to know that Lindsey's father had been Sam Rabnor, the famous Dispeller who had been instrumental in capturing Dominus fourteen years ago.

As the four entered Professor Janice's spell casting class, Deiter teased her. "Lindsey thinks she's a Dispeller, just like her father, thinks she's going to catch Dominus herself." Many classmates either laughed or giggled at his taunt. "What spell were you going to use on him, Gentle Fall?" More laughs followed, as Professor Janice, finished touching up her red lips and stood up to start her class.

"Well, yes, Miss Barron or should we now call you Miss Rabnor? What spell *did* you use on Dominus? We would all like to know?"

Lindsey's face grew hot, probably red she thought. "I, I didn't use a spell. We ran for our lives." Deiter's side of the room laughed heartily.

Amanda whispered, "Ignore them." She found that hard to do, however. Lindsey had gone through six grades of school in Plano and never had a friend, only taunters or sympathy givers. Now, she realized that she had a number of friends. Amanda was actually sticking up for her. She gave her friend a smile.

"Well, then, perhaps you should study your spells more diligently. Class, open your spell books to page fifty-nine," she said, bringing a satisfied look to her red lips.

The spells were now much harder. The essays on magical theory seemed impossibly long and tedious. Math had moved onto the basics of trigonometry, a new area for all.

Science moved from astronomy into elementary earth science, which many found at least a bit more interesting. The only redeeming action was PE. Lindsey discovered that there was an entire underground gymnasium below the Stadium field! Now that the weather had turned cold, PE classes were held there. Thankfully, Lindsey was given a choice and chose to continue running laps, along with Amanda. Pam and Kathy chose volleyball instead, probably the most favorite sport among the girls at Bradbury.

Combine this with the extra hour of private lessons with Professor Cho Lin, and the first years found little time for anything except constant study. For the first time in her life, Pam found herself actually behind in answering her emails!

Fortunately, they discovered they had a four-day weekend around Thanksgiving time. The older students were allowed a day trip into Telluride. For nearly a whole day, only the first and second year students were on the campus. The five friends spent the day in the Library doing research on their many essays, which were due when school resumed in four days.

Emilio grumbled, "What a way to spend our vacation, nose to the books."

"Well, it would help, Emilio, if you read them instead of putting your nose on them," Pam teased him. He grinned as the Librarian glared at them to be quiet.

When the Library closed at ten that night, the five walked back to their rooms using the tunnels. Already the snow blanketed the campus six inches deep. Wearing parkas and heavy boots to class was just too cumbersome, so everyone went back and forth via the tunnels. However, from her window, Lindsey saw that several kids had been outside playing in the snow. Three snow angels stared up at her window.

Because of their schedule, none of them had time to check on any of the hidden rooms. Of necessity, it had become sidetracked even before they had a chance to begin.

The next morning, Lindsey learned an entirely different aspect of the magic world, the Mag Postal System, or MPS as everyone called it. Once again, House Mother Ann had neglected to tell Lindsey about it, assuming that she had no magical friends, or any friends for that matter. While they were gathering up their books to cart down to the study hall, a paper magically appeared in front of Amanda's nose. It fluttered around her nose until she read it.

MPS delivery for Miss Amanda Whitewater.

As soon as she read it, it disappeared.

"What was that?" asked Lindsey. "A message from Professor Cho Lin?"

"No I've got some mail, magical delivery," her long, black haired friend replied. Seeing the confusion on Lindsey's face, she had her follow her to the Bookstore, while she explained. "You see Bradbury's is not on the maps of the norms. Hence, when you want to send mail to us here, you can't use the norm mail system. Instead, there's the MPS, Mag Postal System. When someone wants to send you a letter or package here, they use the MPS. The item is delivered to the Bookstore, and they send you a message that it's arrived, and you go pick it up. You can send anyone something from here too. In fact, we hardly ever use the USPS anymore. You can send anything via MPS to any wizard or witch anywhere, as long as you know the destination."

She stopped in front of a small counter on the first floor, one that Lindsey had seen before when she was getting her schoolbooks. "MPS for Amanda Whitewater, please," she said to the woman behind the counter. A minute later, the clerk handed Amanda a bulky package. Lindsey noticed how it was addressed.

Miss Amanda Whitewater

Bradbury's School of Magic

"Oh, it's from mom. I bet I know what it is, another blanket to wear. She's always making us throw-over blankets for the winters. They are colorful, but totally out of style. No one wears these off the reservation." Back in their room, she opened it up. A short note from her mother asked her to stay warm in the snowy mountains. Indeed, Lindsey thought it looked more like a poncho; it had a head hole and a tie sash around the waist.

"Cool!" Lindsey commented.

"I'd look like—well, weird, if I actually wore this around here. 'There goes Miss Indian,' the kids would tease me," Amanda commented, tossing it onto her bed. She had an idea. "Say, Lindsey, we should exchange addresses with everyone; that way we can stay in touch with each other over the summer. Soon Lindsey had three names in her new address database on her computer.

When they joined Emilio in the study hall, he had a tip for them. "My brother just gave me a warning. When we get back from this short vacation, Professor Janice is going to be throwing another one of those surprise tests. We have to know all the Grade 1 spells that she's covered! Maybe we should work on them too. I didn't have time to get them all done last time or maybe we can wait until Sunday night to practice them." He had thought about all the work involved and thought better of spending three days on them. One night sounded better to him.

"Oh good grief!" declared Pam. "Thanks for the warning, Emilio. We should get started on them right away! They are so much harder than the little useful spells!" Emilio groaned in mock protest.

At once, Pam began constructing a list of the spells she had to know perfectly. Her list consisted of the following: Alter Fires, Finger Flames, Gentle Fall, Control Sounds, Create Fog, Reproduce Simple Object, Understand Other Languages, Enlarge, Reduce, Erase, Create Grease Patch, Jump, Light, Mend Object, and of course the two spells that had been cast hundreds of times during Halloween, Spook and Taunt Another.

"Golly, I hadn't realized we've learned so many of these," she declared proud of her accomplishments thus far.

"We should put them into order for the most efficient casting," Amanda decided. "Remember, last time she only gave us forty-five minutes to do all them. We should do Jump followed by Gentle Fall. Finger Flames and then Alter Fires, don't you think?"

The five found working on their spells far more interesting than their math, science, and literature homework. Indeed, they had to read one very thick book and write a three page essay on it by Monday. Plus, Professor Thalmus had assigned them another lengthy research topic, which would require their spending hours in the Library as well. Lindsey sighed. This was going to be a long weekend and certainly not a holiday!

Saturday afternoon, Emilio did not go with them to the library, "I've got something better to do on such a fine day, senoritas. I'll show you just before supper."

Pam thought that he was just being lazy, "We just have too much homework to do, Señor Emilio. Don't go asking me to do your science homework tonight!" He grinned sheepishly, as if that was precisely what he intended to ask her later that night.

When the four girls left the Library just before supper, Emilio hit Pam in her chest with a snowball. "Snowball fight!" he yelled. Indeed, half of the school was out on the grounds just north of the dorms. Snowballs were flying in all directions! "This way to safety," he called out.

"Hey, over here, Lindsey, Amanda," Jim Whitewater called out to the group. Five snow forts lay arranged in a pentagram form, mirroring the dorms. Some, including Amanda's brothers, Jim and Tom, were raiding other forts, throwing snowballs as fast as they could make them. Ducking and dodging, the four girls trudged over the slippery ground to the Yellow fort and ducked inside for cover. Sally and Sandy were making snowballs, while Bill lobbed them over the walls at other forts. The four joined in the great battle. The war ended when the dinner bell sounded, which was followed by hundreds of Warm and Dry spells.

Monday afternoon brought the anticipated pop test from Professor Janice. Forewarned and prepared, the five easily accomplished all the spells. However, Emilio just barely got his last one done before the time was up. Lindsey and Amanda had ten minutes to spare, which raised the eyebrows of Professor Janice, who had to recheck her grading spell to make sure that the two had not circumvented her rules.

"Tomorrow, class, you are to report over to the Hall of Divination. Professor Mary Ann Thornby will be teaching you about Divination Magic, and she'll be working with you until the Christmas break. I warn you, be on your best behavior. She will be attempting to teach you three divination magical spells, one of which you'll find quite challenging indeed. While you are gone, I'll be teaching some advanced Charm spells to second year students."

The five speculated over this exciting news for the rest of the day. "I will not regret not being here for a few weeks!" Lindsey declared. That was the consensus of the five. None of them particularly liked Professor Janice. Anything would be a pleasant change, they thought.

On Tuesday, the five wandered into the Hall of Divination, excited about this welcome change. "Welcome first years, I'm Professor Mary Ann Thornby." Her eyes darted from student, as if she thought one of them might be about to attack her. Her brown hair flew off in all directions, as though she were somehow electrically charged. Her socks didn't match, Lindsey noticed. Neither did her skirt and blouse. She wore an odd-looking number of rings and with two broaches on her chest. Amanda guessed that she was probably in her forties. She had a pale complexion, totally unlike that of Professor Janice. She wore no makeup either, for that matter.

Apparently satisfied that no one was about to attack her, she began. "For the next few weeks, I am to teach you about elementary divination magic. When, when I say divination, I do *not* mean the norm's reading of tea leaves, their habits of reading palms, or even astrology, or the tarot cards. We will *not* be using crystal balls either, though some of you may wish we were before we finish here. Does that cover it?" she asked herself.

Apparently, because she continued, "Divination means to foretell or foresee by magic and signs. First, we will learn to both read and to write magical inscriptions. Books, rings, cloaks, boots, all manner of objects can be endowed with magical properties, so you must be able to read any potential magical inscriptions they may have on them. Yes. Indeed you must." She again looked around the room making sure it was still safe.

Lindsey found herself glancing around the room wondering what Professor Mary Ann might be sensing. She saw Deiter making flighty gestures, imitating her to his small group in jest. She didn't think it was funny. Professor Mary Ann continued. "Once you can read and write magical inscriptions, then we must learn how actually to detect if some object is magically endowed." She lowered her voice and glanced around the room once more, "Then, we must learn to Identify what those magical properties of that item actually are!"

"Now then, can anyone give me an example of a magical item?" This was news to Lindsey—that there could be such things as magically endowed items. Since no one was volunteering, she raised her hand. "Miss Barron?" she said, her voice with a slight shake in it.

"The Rod of the Apocalypse that Dominus Malefic wants to steal." As soon as she said it, Lindsey wished she had not volunteered. Poor Professor Mary Ann began shaking and trembling, as though the very mention of that rod scared her half to death.

"Yes—yes, er yes. However, let us not speak of such awful magical items. Anyone else with *n-normal* items?" she hastily bypassed Lindsey's answer.

Deiter raised his hand and bragged, "My father had a ring which can turn him invisible!" His companions nodded, as if this was an important answer.

Kathy, surprising Lindsey, added, "My dad has these boots that allows him to make super huge jumps."

These seemed to calm Professor Mary Ann down. "Yes, yes. During the next weeks, I will be handing out items that have been magically enchanted. It will be your task to identify properly what each of them does. It, it, it won't do to copy off your neighbors. Each one is different. Yes, they are. First, you will each get a magical ring to identify. Each ring is different. Don't bother asking your fellow students. It won't help you to i-identify y-yours. N-now open your books to page sixty-one, Read Magical Inscription." Dutifully, the class of thirty pulled out their spell books and began reading about this new spell. Meanwhile, using her wand, she wrote something across her blackboard, a magical bit of writing.

For the five friends, this turned out to be one of the

easiest spells they had learned thus far! By the end of the class period, they were reading each of the lines Professor Mary Ann had written on her board. On Wednesday, they tackled writing magical scripts, which went nearly as well. On Thursday, they learned a most valuable spell, Detecting Magic.

For Pam, this was more than useful—it was pure fun! Each student had a box of knickknacks, three of which had been magically endowed by Professor Mary Ann. Using their spell, they had to pick out which of the items were magic. Of course, this brought out the Sleuth in Pam, who at first tried to see if she could pick them out without using the spell. Each time, she was alarmed to discover she was wrong on all items!

After class, this was all that Pam could talk about: how looks were so deceiving when it came to magical properties. However, one detail caused her to stay after class to ask Professor Mary Ann, "Excuse me, Professor, but I noticed that whichever item has been enchanted, it is always of the highest quality. Why is this? I mean I would never have guessed that the mother of pearl button was enchanted, though it was really well made."

After glancing around the room, perhaps looking for invisible spies, she said in a whisper, "We will go into that more tomorrow, but if an item is to retain its magical endowment, it must be of high quality manufacture. You can always enchant a common matchstick, but it will not hold its enchantment for but a few minutes. Now you had better run along to your next class. Hurry, hurry." She shoed her out of the room. Pam quickly caught up to her friends and chatted about what she'd just learned.

On Friday, Professor Mary Ann hastily shut all the windows and waved her wand to increase the illumination in her classroom. Lindsey thought that she was more nervous than normal, though just why this might be, she had no clue. "P-page sixty-four. T-today we will start in on learning the one spell that o-ought to be in every wizard and witches employ, the Identify spell. W-with it, you can eventually learn the magical properties that h-have been endowed into an i-item." She looked around the room; satisfied all was in order, she handed out a ring to each of the thirty students.

'T-this is the s-spell that you will be w-working to i-improve upon during your entire career. Y-you can never g-get too good with this one." She lowered her voice, "With this spell, you can determine just what magic has been endowed into an item and how it is to be activated and used."

"What's the old bitty afraid of anyway?" Deiter whispered to his buddies, rather too loudly.

"A-afraid? M-Mr. Cross, if you should e-ever get as g-good as I am at this divination Identification, y-you will perhaps understand. Everyone wants you to assist them, either willingly or u-unwillingly. I-I hope and p-pray that it n-never happens to you. E-evil men do e-evil things and," she again lowered her voice to a bare whisper, "t-there are e-evil magical items out there in the world, t-that can do very bad things to y-you."

Lindsey began to wonder if something dreadful had happened to Professor Mary Ann, and she made a reminder to herself on her computer to ask Professor Cho Lin this evening at her special session.

Evidently, she regained her composure and explained, "I want you to read the spell and cast it upon the ring I gave you. Each ring has a different enchantment placed upon it. After casting the spell, you then study the object, diligently and observe it well. If you are very lucky, you will pick up one of its properties after an hour's study. S-some of you might not get it worked out until the end of next week. Identification is a spell that you just have to work at diligently. Observation and diligence pays great dividends with this spell. Haste makes waste with the Identification."

Lindsey and Amanda read the spell's casting rules. "Seems simple enough to do," Amanda commented. Both girls cast their version of the spell and began to stare at their rings. Certainly, they were magical; Lindsey did a quick check first, just to be sure, recalling the Professor's admonition from yesterday, detect if there is any magical enchantment first, before you attempt to Identify it.

"What's supposed to happen," Pam whispered after staring at her ring for a half hour; her eyes had become crossed.

"Dunno," Lindsey whispered back. "Mine is turning greenish. Wonder what that means? There isn't anything in the text about that."

Suddenly, Deiter called out, "Fire!" At once, the ring he was holding let forth a giant ball of fire, just like the one that had nearly incinerated Lindsey and Amanda in the tunnel. Lindsey had never seen anyone act as quickly as Professor Mary Ann did. As the ball of flames exploded to a foot in diameter, a wooden staff, which had been sitting in the corner of the room, flew into her hands and seemed to suck the entire spell into the staff.

"M-Mr. C-Cross! I did *not* say that you were to activate the item! If I had not intervened, that ball of fire would have killed every student in this room, including you!" Deiter's scorched face reddened even more. He muttered that he was sorry.

Pam's hand shot up! "Professor, professor? Is that one of those Staves of Power that I've heard about? Did it suck up the spell from the ring?"

"Yes, Miss Betts. This is my Staff of Power." Because many of the class had no idea what it was or how it worked, she explained didactically, "A Staff of Power stores magical energies, allowing its owner to cast spells using that stored energy. However, it must be periodically recharged by absorbing the energy from other spells that are cast. I keep it over here in the corner for just such emergencies. Now class, please do not attempt to activate the power contained in your rings once you have identified them. Yes, Mr. Cross correctly identified his. It can cast Balls of Fire spells. Next, Mr. Cross, you are to determine how many such spells it can hold and how many remain and if it can be recharged and if so, by what means." Deiter looked upset; he'd been the first to identify his, only now he faced what he thought was an impossible task.

When the bell rang ending the fifty-minute class, no one else had gotten theirs identified yet. Pam saw that this was indeed going to be their hardest spell yet! All five talked about it the rest of the day. Lindsey and Pam decided to visit the Library over the weekend to find out more about this spell and how best to perform it.

When they were getting ready for bed that night, Lindsey said, "Gosh, I never knew that there were such things as magical items. Are they expensive? Where do you buy them?"

Pam explained, "Oh yes, there are any number of items. Some are, well the usual, like rings that can store spells. My father has one of those. However, wizards and witches are always inventing new enchantments to put on items. My father once had to confiscate a bar of bath soap that was enchanted to give the bather warts! Magical Misuse, you see. Usually, they are very expensive to buy. Mag-Amazon.com is the first place to look for normal, routine items."

Lindsey typed in the URL and clicked on the Magical Items list. Her mouth dropped wide open. "Wow! Oh, wow! This is utterly unbelievable! Look at all these things! Who would want to by a Love Dress? Oh," she blushed, reading aloud, "It is guaranteed to make your man fall in love with you or your money back." All four girls looked at her screen, while she scrolled down the extensive list. The prices ranged from five hundred dollars and up, way up from there.

During Lindsey's session with Professor Cho Lin, her computer reminded her to ask about Professor Mary Ann. Cho Lin said, "I will say only what is common knowledge. Fifteen years ago, she worked for the archaeologist, who was trying to unravel the mysteries around the Rod of the Apocalypse. She was kidnaped by Dominus and forced to reveal some of what she knew about its magical properties. She is very lucky to be alive." After hearing this, Lindsey and her friends felt much more kindly to the fearful professor. Both Lindsey and Amanda understood what such an encounter might do to a person.

On Monday afternoon, when they were back identifying their rings, Pam and Lindsey began reciting repeatedly what they had discovered from several books in the Library. "Relax, focus your mind solely and only on the object. Be the object."

After relaxing and focusing on her ring for another ten minutes, Lindsey began to see the room fill up with a fog, a dense fog. She blinked and saw that there was no fog in the classroom. Professor Mary Ann was near her, so she ventured a guess, "I believe that my ring emits a dense fog."

Her professor smiled, "Yes, that is correct. Now find the activation word, how many of those spells the ring can hold, how many it has left, and whether it can be recharged, and if so, how that may be done. You see, any magical item may have many properties; it takes diligence, time, and patience to discover them all."

"Class, this is an important point. It is utter folly to obtain one or two of an item's properties and then proceed to use it. For example, Lindsey here has determined that her ring will cause a dense fog. Suppose that she goes no further, but decides to use the ring. Some norm muggers are coming after her, and she decides to use the ring. After all in a dense fog, she can easily elude the muggers. Only not having obtained all the properties of the ring, she discovers that although she knows the word of command to activate it, nothing happens, because the ring has exhausted it charges and needs to be recharged. Always, always, *always* determine all the magical properties of an item before you attempt to use it! Write that one down. I guarantee you will see that one on your test." She waved her wand and the rule appeared nicely written on her blackboard.

Always determine all the magical properties of an item *before* you attempt to use it!

Pam's ring would make her invisible, she discovered. Amanda's ring would provide light. Kathy's ring would help her to fly like a bat. Emilio's ring would allow him to be very lucky, and he decided that he needed just such a ring! However, Pam showed him the cost of one of these Rings of Luck on Mag-Amazon.com, and he forgot about that wish: ten thousand dollars.

Slowly, everyone improved their identification process. However, Professor Mary Ann continually gave them new items to identify, urging them to become faster at it. They had until Christmas vacation, now a few weeks away, to be able to pass the speed test. In three class periods, they would have to identify completely one magical item with all its properties. All thirty students were used to having to spend a day or two at the most to learn a new spell. This Identification spell was an entirely different matter!

Further, as a reward incentive, on December 1, Professor Mary Ann announced, "Class, as soon as you passed your speed test, you don't have to come to class until after the Christmas break!" Such an incentive! All thirty worked very hard to pass just as soon as they could. Emilio, Lindsey, and Amanda passed within a week. All the class was finished by the second week. However, Pam insisted on coming to class every day, being the only student for the entire middle of December. Why? She had long ago passed her speed test. Rather, she found this detection and identification absolutely the most fascinating, useful thing that she had learned, and insisted on practicing every chance she got. She had to identify everyone's rings!

With the hour free time they now had as Christmas was coming up, all thoughts centered on holiday plans. All would be heading home to their families for three weeks, coming back on January 4. Pam explained that the five should stay in touch via email on their laptops. However, Lindsey said, "Sorry, mom and I don't have any Internet connection at our ranch."

"Silly, our computers use the MagWirelessNet, MWN. No matter where in the world you are at, you can instantly connect to the Mag side and from there to the norm's side," Pam explained.

Presents were another aspect that was quite new to Lindsey. Until now, she and her mother were exceedingly poor. Yet, even though she at that time had no hands, Lindsey had still worked very hard to make her mother simple things during art classes at her Plano school. These had been the only presents she could give to her mother. Now she had not only hands, but also she had her allowance, which now mounted to nearly eighty dollars, more money than she had ever seen in her life!

Further, Lindsey had something equally as precious to her as her hands, four very dear, close friends! In her twelve years at Plano, she had no one but her mother. Lindsey now desired to give all her friends and her mother a special Christmas present. She took to spending time on both Amazon and MagAmazon looking for just the right presents for everyone.

Her mother's present turned out to be the easiest one to find. She knew her mother's horse bridle was nearly worn out; its leather nearly rotten. She spent thirty dollars on a new one, having it gift wrapped as well. For Pam, based on some advice from Professor Cho Lin, she got Mumfrey's *Guide to Sleuthing*. Kathy liked jewelry; Lindsey found a heart shaped gold locket and, with Pam's assistance on the sly, got their desktop picture of all four girls miniaturized and into the locket. For Emilio, she got a book, Maxwell's *Top Tips to Make a Wizard's Homework Simpler*, figuring it might help him get more done. For Amanda, she bought a very well made knife with leather sheath, the kind you can strap onto your leg. She had each of her presents delivered to their home addresses by Mag Post, marked "Do Not Open Til Christmas." Her mother's present, she would take with her.

Indeed that last week before the Christmas holidays, little schoolwork was done. Everyone was excited about going home for the holidays. Surprisingly, the Smith professors, Blake and Janice, conjured a huge Christmas tree in the dining hall, and Professor Janice decorated it beautifully. All that week, the dining room was festively decorated. Even their evening meals contained treats for the season. Lindsey particularly loved the chocolate drop cookies shaped like tree ornaments. Amanda preferred the ginger snaps, which looked like Santa Claus. Emilio was not particular, helping himself to all kinds of cookies as frequently as he could. "Growing boy," he explained to the girls, who giggled.

The only "unholiday" actions were the final exams in math, science, and grammar classes. Lindsey was very glad that they didn't have homework to do over the holidays!

Chapter 12—Christmas Holiday

Lindsey found that saying goodbye to her dear friends and Bradbury's very emotionally charged. Even though they were only going to be separated for three weeks, she felt a deep loss when Pam got on her bus that went to the northeast corner of Colorado. However, the rest boarded their bus together. On the return trip, Deiter and his friends were too excited about the holidays to bother insulting Lindsey. Thus, the trip was very pleasant indeed. Lindsey felt pangs of loss when Kathy and Emilio departed first. One by one, she was losing her friends, if only for a short while. When the bus stopped at her ranch in Plano, only the Whitewater bunch remained onboard. She hugged Amanda and then stepped off the bus, carrying her duffle bag and wearing her school parka. Six inches of snow blanketed her ranch.

Her mother was on the porch waiting her daughter, but she allowed Lindsey to wave as the bus left before rushing up to her and hugging her tightly, tears of joy flowing. "Just look at you, Lindsey! You've grown inches and your hands. Oh, I have thanked the Lord a hundred times for you over that incredible gift! Come on inside and warm up. We even have a tree this year!"

Lena had warm cocoa and Christmas cookies waiting for Lindsey. She looked at, felt, and rubbed her daughter's hands, but just could not keep from crying. Time flew by as Lindsey told her mother all about her new friends and the school. Lena was very proud of her daughter when she found out about how she had helped set a new school record for the twenty-mile relay race.

"Mom, I can now do so many really useful things, like starting a fire easily, cleaning, dusting, polishing, and mending my clothes with my new magic skills!" She just had to show her mother some of her new skills. Then, she finally spied the large Christmas tree. "A tree? Mom, it is so pretty! How did you. . ."

"The man from the Department of Defense, Lloyd

Compton—he's a wizard; he told me. He's been such a help for me around the ranch! Oh, you've heard of that prison break, that nasty criminal, Dominus something or other—for some reason the Department thinks he might try to harm me or you. I never thought that the Department of Defense would ever send someone here, not in a million years. It must have something to do with you going off to magic school, I reckon. He insists on being around me all the time, dear. Now that you are back, he will probably want to be around you as well."

"Mom! I found out a whole lot about dad!" Lindsey just couldn't restrain herself from telling her mother all about what she had learned about Samuel Rabnor. Lena listened incredulously as Lindsey outlined who her father had been and what he'd done and more importantly, why. "You see, mom, he came here to hide from the henchmen of Dominus, who were going around killing the families of those who had captured their leader. That's why dad came here to hide from them. That's why he never did any magic around here, because it would give him away. That's probably why he didn't take me to the Healers when I was a little girl, because as I said, they have to run a DNA comparison whenever they re-grow hands, and he would have been discovered. Probably, those nasty men would have come here and tried to kill us all, once they found out. Mom, I've got five pictures of dad when he was in school!" Quickly, she booted up her laptop and showed the photos of Sam with the teams at Bradbury's. Her mother just stared at them and cried. They brought back both the happiest memories of her life and the saddest ones as well.

Just then, Lloyd came in the front door. He wore a heavy parka, and Lindsey could barely see his face, but his eyes twinkled, however. His soft, kind voice said, "Lena, the new well is now operational. Want to take a peak? I'll show you both how it works. Hello, you must be Lindsey." Hastily, he pulled off his heavy work gloves and they shook hands. He pulled down his hood so she could see him better. Lloyd was about the same age as her mother, with rather long brown hair and blue eyes. He had thick eyebrows, and one of those kindly faces, which aided first appearances. Hastily, the two donned their parkas and followed him outside. It had already begun to snow once more; large flakes flittered down, settling lightly on their brown canvas coats.

"I've put in a new deep well, bypassing all the contamination areas. While the water is a bit hard, it is pure, not even traces of agricultural chemicals or pesticides. Now this pump sends water out to the barn and this smaller one routes it to the house. The fuses are there in the barn, safely out of the weather. If there is ever any trouble, just pull this emergency shutoff lever; it will kill the juice to the pumps. Of course, the pumps will have to be serviced probably once every five years, Lena, but come spring, you should at last be able to irrigate your crops. More water, more grain, more income. Triple would be my first estimates, Lena."

"I don't know how to thank you, Lloyd! Lindsey, he's been doing so many things around here to help. Thank you, Lloyd. Now we should all get inside; the weather is turning nasty. Blizzard is on the way, according to the weather station on the radio."

Once inside, Lena refilled Lindsey's cocoa cup and brewed a pot of coffee for Lloyd and herself. She began explaining to her daughter all the wonderful things that Lloyd had done for her around the ranch. "Of course, I told him I could only afford to pay him minimum wages, but that seemed fine with him, though I surely don't know why."

"My main job is to protect you and your daughter, when she is here on vacations, Lena. Yet, it is to your credit that you insist on paying me for my work. Say, Lindsey, how do you like Bradbury's? I went to school there many years ago."

Lindsey talked for hours about her friends and school. She showed Lloyd the pictures they had found of her father. Lloyd was keenly interesting in seeing them, however. "Your husband, your father, was a very great man and wizard. He with the help of his friends captured Dominus Malefic and his evil companions some fourteen years ago. Lawmen had been trying to capture him for years, but it was Sam who finally managed to bring him to justice. Now, unfortunately, this serial killer is on the loose once more."

"But why didn't they execute him?" asked Lena.

"In hindsight, perhaps he should have been. Lord

knows he certainly deserved it, but capital punishment has been abolished for over a century now. I, for one, think that they ought to make an exception in his case, that is, if he can ever be captured again."

"I agree, such murders ought to be put to death. Just look how many more innocent people the news has said he has killed since his escape!" Lena declared. "I sure do not want anything to happen to Lindsey!"

"That's why I'm assigned here, to protect you both, though I doubt very seriously that he or his men would be after either of you at the moment," Lloyd took a stab at relieving her worry.

Later, when her mother went out to the barn for the evening chores and insisted that Lindsey stay put at least today, Lloyd volunteered, "You know that you have quite a mother. I can see what Sam saw in her. She's a hard worker, fiercely independent, knows ranching well, compassionate and caring, and enjoys the peace of the open ranch. Quite a woman, your mother." Lindsey grinned; she already knew that.

On Christmas day, both Lena and Lindsey were surprised to find that a few presents appeared under the tree. "Mom, you have to open mine first!" Lindsey insisted. "This is the first time in my life I could actually get you a present mom! I saved all my allowance money at school so I could get some presents for you and my new friends."

"Honey, you shouldn't have. Lord knows you're going to need all that money, dear." Nevertheless, Lena excitedly opened her daughter's gift, wondering what she could have gotten her. Memories of the little paper and cardboard art gifts that Lindsey had awkwardly made in grade school for her came back to her. She cherished the thought and love behind those presents. Indeed, she still had all twelve sitting on her dresser in her bedroom. "Oh my, Lindsey. How did you know I needed this? It's beautiful, thank you!" She hugged her daughter tightly while holding onto the new bridle for her horse.

"Now you open yours. I had a tip from Lloyd and I do hope you like it." Lindsey tore through the wrapping paper, realizing that this was the first time in her life she didn't have to have her mother open them for her. A tear formed as she and her mother both realized this at the same moment. Lindsey pulled out a sky blue, silk, formal prom dress and gasped.

"Lloyd told me that there is a formal end of school dance at Bradbury's each year. I sent off to Denver for the pattern; they assured me this one is the latest fashion. I know that I splurged a little; it is silk, dear. I made it with growth in mind. It should be a little loose fitting just now, but you are growing so fast that by May it should be perfect. However, all the seams have extra material so that with your new skills you can enlarge it for next year too." She hugged her mother and then just had to try it on. She reappeared a little later wearing the beautiful prom style full-length gown. From the radiance in her face and eyes, Lena knew that Lindsey loved it. Indeed, this was the first "real" dress that she had made for her daughter.

There were still three presents under the tree. Lindsey looked and exclaimed, "Lloyd, here is one for you. It's from mom."

"I hope you enjoy it. As you know, we haven't much money, so I got you a little something I figured you could use," Lena explained.

"Hey, perfect! Thanks Lena, you are absolutely right." He held up two tins of his favorite pipe tobacco. "I promise to smoke outside as usual," he teased. "Now Lindsey, open the one from me first."

"But I didn't get you anything, Lloyd. I didn't. . ."

"I just wanted to give you a little something, Lindsey. Of course, you didn't know about me. Don't worry about it. Open it." She did so and gasped.

"Oh my! Terrific, just what I need." It was a copy of Thompson's *1001 Tips on Identification of Magically Enchanted Items*. She gave him a big hug in thanks, and he flushed.

"I figured you could use it. I certainly could have. Did you have the three week session with Professor Thornby trying to identify all those knickknacks she enchanted?" She nodded she had. "I took the whole darn three weeks to get them right! Hope this helps you. Now, give that small one to your mother for me, please."

"Honestly, Lloyd, after all that you have done for us, you shouldn't have," Lena protested.

"Look, what else has an old bachelor like me got to spend his money on anyway, but two pretty women," he teased. "It is going to be a useful present."

She opened her package and read the paper inside. Tears started flowing, "You shouldn't have—this is too much!"

"Not for such a deserving woman. Come on; get your parkas on. We need to go to the barn to see her present, Lindsey." Lindsey looked at the note and read, "Lena, your present is very much needed here. Spotty is out in the barn."

A few minutes later, the three saw a beautiful quarter horse stallion named Spotty because of his brownish spots on his hindquarters. "Now we can breed, Lena. He has an excellent lineage and in a couple years, you'll be able to begin selling foals for extra income." Lena gave Lloyd a big hug, tears of gratitude streaming from her eyes. All three rubbed Spotty down, introduced him to the three mares of Lena's, and Betsy as well.

"I think he likes it here, mom," Lindsey said. Indeed, he nuzzled all four mares as if they were his private harem.

When they went back inside, Lindsey discovered that while they were out, the MagPost had arrived with four presents for her! "Look, mom! This one's from Amanda. There's one from Pam and Kathy and Emilio too!"

Pam got her a book, Herman's *A History of Dispellers*. A note told her to look at page forty-five. She did and gasped! One whole chapter was devoted to the exploits of Samuel Rabnor! Both she and her mother read this chapter together!

Amanda gave her a homemade Apache saddle for her horse—her brothers had made it for her. Kathy sent her a golden necklace, her first ever piece of jewelry. Kathy knew that Lindsey could never have afforded to get anything like this. Emilio, having gotten some tips from Kathy, gave her a bracelet of gold and turquoise, commonly found in Pueblo and made by the Navaho.

For the next few hours, Lindsey sat at her computer, emails flying back and forth between all five. Her mother watched from the kitchen as she prepared the Christmas dinner. She had never ever seen Lindsey so excited, so happy. She was still wearing her new blue dress and her new jewelry, while typing messages madly to her friends. Lloyd came inside from having a smoke and whispered to Lena, "What an incredible daughter you have there." Lena cried even more. This was the best Christmas she had ever had. If only Sam had lived to see his daughter now, she thought.

A few days later, Lloyd gave Lindsey a few tips. "Near the end of the year, Professor Janice Smith loves to give the speed test. You have the class period to see how many of your Grade 0 and 1 spells you can properly cast. 70% is what you need to pass. Only a few students have ever gotten all the spells cast in that short a period. Your dad was one of those hotshots who did it. I think just to spite her, because I don't think he liked her at all. If the rumors are correct, he constantly caused her trouble. I remember one story in which he put a thick layer of lipstick, red of course, on her seat. Later after she had sat in it and was then roaming the classroom, everyone was giggling behind her back. It looked as though she had kissed her, well you know, her butt."

"Another thing that they don't tell you is about the Colorado High School Tests that you must pass to get your degree. Most students expect that at the end of their sixth year, they will have to take some huge test to pass. However, each term the math, science and English teachers give you that relevant portion of the State exams as part of their last tests. Thus, at the end of your sixth year there, you only need to pass the last three tests for that spring term to get your degree. They don't tell you that because I think they want you to study harder or something like that. Say, I heard also that you are going to the Nationals in Des Moines in May. Is that true?"

"Yes, we set a track record in the twenty-mile relay race, and Governor Alister said that if we did that, we would be going to the Nationals," Lindsey replied modestly, not at all sure what this really meant.

"Terrific, Lindsey. You know the Rat Pack, that's what

your dad used to call his circle of friends, they went to the Nationals once as well. You are rather following in your father's footsteps, Lindsey, whether you know it. Keep up the good work!"

Lindsey had much to ponder. Her father had also disliked Professor Janice. Now Lindsey felt much better about her own dislike of that teacher! However, she couldn't bring herself to begin to make trouble for her or to play tricks on her. Again, she looked over the five photos of her father, taken with the winning track teams. She would have given anything to talk with her dad just now.

Finally, she had to pack her things to return to school. The snow outside their ranch was now over a foot deep, and she wondered if their bus could even make it down their road to pick her up. She wore her parka and had her duffle bag packed and ready to go. She and her mother stood on their porch waiting for its appearance. Right on time, the bus suddenly appeared. She hugged her mother and tromped through the snow to the bus.

Their familiar bus driver, Jimmy Jones hopped out to put her bag in the lower storage compartment. "Merry Chris'mas, Miss Lin'sey. Have a good 'ime here?" He sure was hard to understand without his front teeth. Again, she wondered why he didn't get them fixed somehow.

"Yes sir. Fabulous!" She climbed on board and headed to the rear seats. Amanda waved to her. Both Jim and Tom moved over to make room for her. They began to chat, and one by one, her other friends joined them, as the bus made its way across the east central part of Colorado. Before Lindsey realized it, they were back at Bradbury's.

Chapter 13—Attacking Spells and Spring Sports

"Dominus killed Beach Limmer, the Keeper of Possessions at the Hall of Justice in Denver. It seems this was the one person who knew just where the magical item possessions that Dominus had when he was captured were stored. According to MagNews, he also stole his id card," Pam was explaining the latest news to her friends. During their holiday vacation, the others had forgotten to watch the news. "He must have used a spell, probably a Self-morph, at least that is what most authorities now believe. Impersonating Beach and using his id card, Dominus entered the vaults and retrieved his things. MagNews has discovered that he had a Staff of Power, a number of magical rings, a broach, and amulet impounded. Now Dominus has gotten his powerful magical items back, which makes him even more dangerous than before."

"I find that hard to believe," Emilio replied rather bored with the news. "I thought he was dangerous enough as he was, Senorita Pam. Hasn't he killed a fair number already, I mean before he got his stuff back?"

"Yes, but now he is even more unstoppable. After all," she said rather didactically, "it took the likes of Lindsey's father to capture him. According to my father, there is not another Dispeller living today who is as powerful as Sam Rabnor was."

"Surely, they will be able to catch him somehow, won't they?" a concerned Kathy asked, her voice slightly wavering, with a note of pleading in it.

Pam just shrugged. She had never seen her father so worried in her life, but Pam didn't want to alarm her friends further.

First days back at school can be rough. This one was no exception. Evidently, all the professors must have thought their students' brains had turned to mush over the vacation. Every one of them assigned lengthy homework that first day!

In math, geometry was now the topic, and the class groaned when they were told to return tomorrow with a proof that the shortest distance between two points is a straight line. "Everybody knows that, yet how do you prove it?" Professor Mac Elroy asked. Everyone groaned, but it made no difference.

Science was now covering all about rocks, geology, to be precise. While Amanda found this a fascinating subject, Lindsey was quite bored with it. Kathy could not see any reason for studying rocks; they were just pretty, that's all. In literature, a very thick novel was assigned to be read by Friday!

Professor Janice woke up the class by announcing, "This term we will be taking up the Grade 1 attacking spells. Some of you whose wands fail to activate will most definitely find that most painful indeed. Each year, several first years manage to wind up in the Infirmary. I expect this class will be no different. Some of you might move your personal belongings into the Infirmary today, so that they will be there when you arrive for an extended stay. Unfortunately, there are only two defensive spells to help you survive the attacks, and neither are much good, really. I don't know why we bother teaching them, but then, I don't write the spell books, now do I? Today, we will learn two spells. Create Body Armor will help you, if only slightly, and Provide Protection from Evil is useless, unless your enemy is actually evil in nature. Nevertheless, I expect you to learn these spells today so that we may commence learning spells that you can use to attack beginning tomorrow. Now take out your spell books and your wands. I will tolerate no wand malfunctions today," she looked at Lindsey, who wondered why. Since she had gotten her hands, her wand seldom failed to activate.

Wands began waving and voices called out "Create Body Armor." Professor Janice's shrill, piercing voice cut through the dim, "Lyle, don't you think that is several *centuries* out of date?" Everyone stopped to stare at Lyle, who now wore body armor. Girls giggled. He looked like a tin man, something from the Middle Ages, a knight in armor.

From inside his helmet, Lyle muttered, "But I happen to like it. Can't harm me this way." More giggles followed.

"Miss Peggy West," Professor Janice's voice continued

to cut to the quick, "this is not a beauty pageant. You are creating armor for protection from harm!" Everyone turned to look at this Red Hall girl. Emilio whistled. She looked stunning in her outfit, rather like the ancient norm TV show Zena. Bits of carefully made leather covered her torso, leaving her arms and legs in full view, along with her cherry red lips as well. Now, a bit of red also highlighted her cheeks, and she quickly returned to her normal robes over her school dress, ready to try again.

"What's it supposed to look like?" whispered Pam to Lindsey and Amanda.

"It says here that it is a magical force field," Lindsey read to her.

"Miss Barron, let's see yours now," Professor Janice interrupted her explanation to Pam. Lindsey waved her wand and it activated. Neither Pam nor Amanda saw Lindsey's appearance change. She still wore her robes over her school dress.

"Well, I *never* thought that I would be using you as an example for the class, Miss Barron. However, for once, it does seem that you have managed to get everything correct. Class, this time I want you to look over here at Miss Barron; she has her armor properly done."

"But I don't see anything different," Deiter protested.

"Cast your detect magic on her and observe how she has her magical armor about her," Professor Janice replied covertly. "I would, however, suggest that she put a bit more protection around her head, which is a common target of magical spells and attacks."

As the class headed out the door when the bell rang, Deiter catcalled, "Miss Barron, don't forget to protect your head!" Several laughed.

Two days later, things got far more interesting in spell casting class! The class was held outside beneath the tall marble pillars. At least, there was no snow on the stone floor, but it was cold, and the students frequently cast Warm! Thirty targets, shaped like some wild animal stood at one side of the building opposite each student. "Today, we will be learning to cast one of the more powerful magical attack spells, one which each of you must master and one which all your lives you'll be seeking to improve, Magical Missiles."

When this spell was properly cast, a magically conjured missile, which looks like an arrow, shoots forth from the caster's fingers toward a target that the caster is seeing. For once, the entire class began to enjoy the class period, immersing themselves thoroughly in the task.

"This is really, really cool!" exclaimed Amanda, who had been waiting all year for a chance to learn this spell. Even Lindsey appreciated this spell; she could at last do something useful to defend herself from wild animals, such as the wolves that had interrupted their Halloween party.

Professor Janice walked among her students and commented, "Don't get too overly dependent upon this spell. While each year you will improve and be able to cast more than one missile at a time, remember that the damage each missile does varies from strike to strike. Sometimes, its effect is much like a good solid fist blow to one's head. At best, it is equivalent to a moderate sword hit or cut."

A bit later, everyone in the class was very happy; their missiles hit the target. However, Professor Janice cut in once more. "Don't get so cocky, class. Only when you become far more experienced is this spell really effective and deadly. Watch children," she emphasized that last word. She waved her wand and six missiles shot at her target, machine gun style, bringing a lot of "oh's" and "ah's" from the students.

Amanda whispered to Lindsey, "That could kill a wolf!" Lindsey, for once, was impressed with her teacher's skill.

During the next weeks, the class was put through its paces, learning how to potentially blind someone with the Blinding Spray. Lindsey got quite good at avoiding its effects when cast upon her, however. Electrifying Touch had a good chance of shocking the recipient, dealing wounds nearly as bad as a large sword, if one were very lucky. If not, it was more like a large fist blow to the one's jaw. With both of these spells, a good, attentive, alert wizard or witch had some chance of avoiding the damage or blindness, unlike the magical missiles, which always struck the intended target that the caster was seeing.

At first, Lindsey just thought Professor Janice was sadistic, enjoying seeing her students harming each other. Everyone, including Deiter, was shocked when she ordered the class to break into teams and cast these at one another! "Defense, you know it is coming. Attempt to avoid it," she explained. "We begin with the Blinding Spray, because it is relatively harmless. If you are blinded, its effect will only last a few minutes. You must learn how to avoid being hit by harmful spells." She didn't add, however, "the hard way."

"I can't see!" Betsy screamed in panic after her twin's spell made contact with her. Indeed, Professor Janice was kept busy undoing many of the effects, especially when the end of the class period was near. She couldn't have blinded children fumbling their way to their next class.

However, Doctor Caterwall joined her when the class began casting the Electrifying Touch spells on each other. It took both adults to keep the harmful damage to the students to a minimum, though screeches of pain were constantly heard during these periods.

Remarkably, by the end of January, Amanda and Lindsey were routinely able to avoid these two spells' effects on them, as long as they knew it was coming. When Professor Janice saw this, she ordered the class to begin mixing up the spells, and once more, Lindsey found herself temporarily blinded or hurting like mad. So did most of the class as well.

By the end of February, everyone in the class finally reached the passing level, able to avoid these two spell's effects at least half of the time. Only Amanda and Lindsey now avoided them all the time. Secretly, Lindsey practiced these both as non-verbal spells and without using her wand, but only when she was sure that Professor Janice was not looking her way.

During this time, Valentine's Day came, complete with fancy decorations in the dining room. Third years and above got the day off to take their second trip into snow-packed Telluride. Emilio sent all four girls a surprise magical card from MagGreetingCardsOnLine, which the four giggled over, as they watched the funny antics of the cartoon figures on their screens.

Much to her surprise, Pam received a heart shaped box of chocolates from her admirer, whom she refused to name. Her face reddened every time someone mentioned it. She vanished the card that came with it as soon as she had read it. It was from Monique.

When March came, Bill called a meeting of his team. "Gang, here is the spring schedule. Take note of when we play." Everyone crowded around the poster.

March 25 Soccer: Blue Hall versus Brown Hall

April 7 Track: Yellow Hall versus Red Hall

April 14 Soccer: Black Hall versus Yellow Hall

April 21 Track: Red Hall versus Black Hall

April 28 Soccer: Red Hall versus Blue Hall

May 5 Track: Playoff if needed

May 12 Nationals: Yellow Hall

"Bill, don't make us run in the slosh! We have until April before our first match," Amanda complained. Considering there was still substantial melting snow on the field, he relented. However, he did insist on once a week runs on the underground, indoor track, located beneath the Stadium.

The first soccer match of the spring was as bad as the last one had been. The field began as a mixture of snow and mud but slowly turned into one giant mud puddle. Players were lying in the mud more than they were running. Only standing still ensured one of remaining out of the mud. Having suffered through a similar mess last fall, Lindsey felt sorry for all the players. In the end, Blue Hall won by one point.

The following week, their track meet faired a little better. The track was still soggy and though Yellow Hall won all three events over Red Hall, their times were less than spectacular. "Well, you can't expect us to run fast in the muck," Jim countered Bill's chiding them for having such a slow time in all three races.

All during the next week, the Black Hall students teased Lindsey, Amanda, and Emilio relentlessly. "Be prepared to be creamed come Saturday. Hope you have your Clean spells ready. Your face will be in the mud all the time. Pretty Amanda fall down and get an ouchie. Lindsey will need her hands to help her get up after all the times she gets smashed into the mud." On it went, taunt after taunt.

At their last practice session on Wednesday, a grim faced Bill explained, "Come Saturday, I'm not worried about winning. After all, Black Hall has a huge winning streak. They play nasty. With Nationals coming up, I want you all to play it safe. Do what you have to do to avoid getting hurt! I've spoken to Hank and Betsy, and they assured me that they will be very alert to fouls this game. After all, it is in their best interests that none of us gets hurt playing these Black Hall beasts!" The team found this a little encouraging.

Both Amanda and Lindsey were unusually silent. Professor Cho Lin had coached both on defensive spells, and Lindsey had been working very hard during her extra lessons with the professor, perfecting her Phantasm Illusions.

On their way to the Stadium on Saturday, Deiter Cross caught up with them and said, "Are you all ready to get your beatings?" He and Lyle laughed loudly and raced on ahead of the small group, most of who were dreading this afternoon, wondering just how badly they would be pulverized and embarrassed.

Once the team was in their locker room, Amanda put on her special ring on loan from Professor Cho Lin. She went from player to player, saying "Skin of Stone" and touching them. "What's this tingle, Amanda? What are you doing to us?" Bill asked, more than a little annoyed. After all, he was the team captain here, not her.

"According to the rules, there is nothing amiss in our casting defensive spells on us before the match. Now, I have given each of you a Skin of Stone. This means that when they intentionally miss the ball and try to kick your legs, they will connect with stone or rock not your fleshy legs! Of course, you still need not to get tripped up by the force of the blow, but this way, we'll not be injured by their illegal kicking and hitting."

"Wow! This is great! How long does it last?" asked Emilio.

"Darn it, sis, this is brilliant! Why didn't we think of this, Jim?" her brother Tom asked.

"A lot of kicks, I reckon. When it stops tingling, then the

spell is gone, so then you have to be careful," Amanda explained.

"Incredible, I could hug you, sis!" Jim exclaimed. He did so to her embarrassment.

"Hey, when the spell ends, let us know. Some of us know that spell," Bill said in an attempt to regain control of his team.

"Good, then you can recharge my ring. It only has nine charges, one for each of us," Amanda suggested. Bill, Tom, and Jim waved their wands and cast that spell back into her ring.

"There, you have an emergency supply of three more, Amanda," Bill explained, feeling like he was back in charge of his team once more.

Now Lindsey spoke up, "I'm supposed to be scoring goals, right Bill?"

"Yes, sure. Why?"

"Well, I've been working on ways to fake out the goalkeeper. I think that I might be able to give them a dose of their own medicine," she replied.

"Okay, just get yourself in the open, Lindsey," Bill kindly ordered. "At least, they've dried the field for this match. No more of that slipping and sliding mucky mess. Come on; there's the stadium horn." The nine marched out on to the field. The sunny afternoon brought nearly all the students out to view the match. Most expected to see Black Hall cream Yellow Hall, what with their lengthy record of victories spanning a number of years now. Secretly, Amanda touched her other ring and hoped that it would work.

Professor Blake Smith, the announcer, called out the Black Hall team members, who jogged onto the field when their name was called to a near deafening noise of stadium horns, cheering, and yelling. "At goalkeeper, Gallager Watson. At left fullback, Art Merryweather. At right fullback, Ben Dingle. At left middle field, Herman Freeze. At right middle field, Henry Fielding. At left forward and captain playing his last game, Larry Sacks. (He was a sixth year student and about to graduate from Bradbury's.) At right forward, Hektor Sanchez. At center forward, Philip Royston. At center forward, Jennifer Watson. There you have the championship Black Hall team!" The noise was now even louder.

"And now for the challengers, coming off their first victory in years, Yellow Hall." Only the Yellow Hall students cheered, a much lower noise level indeed. "At goalkeeper, Sally Ridgeway. At left fullback, Becky Salinos. At right fullback, Jake Rattlebeam. At left middle field and captain also playing his last game, Bill Ferny. At right middle field, Emilio Lopez. At left forward, Tom Whitewater. At right forward, Jim Whitewater. At center forward, Amanda Whitewater. Soon the Whitewaters will be able to field their own team." His joke received only a few chuckles, so he continued. "At center forward, Lindsey Barron. Let's give Yellow Hall a big hand." They received a bit of noise from Yellow Hall, but that was only a fraction given to Black Hall.

"Betsy throws out the ball. Looks like it's going into the hands of Black Hall's Herman Freeze. No, look at that sensational interception by Bill Ferny! Arm stretch, wow. Nice move Bill, who passes across field to Emilio. Oh, it looks like Henry Fielding is about to clobber Emilio; lookout lad!" Indeed, Henry, upset at Bill's interception, charged into Emilio, kicking deliberately for his leg, though missing the ball. Instead of hitting a leg, his toe hit stone! He fell flat on his butt, crying out from the sharp pain in his right toes. The force of the blow nearly knocked Emilio off his feet, but he managed to lob the ball to Tom, who had fallen back to support him.

"Tom's got the ball, bringing it down field. Lookout; here comes Art Merryweather to steal the ball. Look at Tom leap out of the way, but he is holding the ball, so his options are limited. Sensational pass into the center to Amanda. Look out Amanda, here comes Ben and he looks mad." Amanda watched Ben close in on her. Art was still recovering from his attempt to steal from Tom, leaving Lindsey completely open there on the right center area. Amanda gave a quick kicking pass to Lindsey, just as Ben tried to kick her in the leg. Ben went down howling in pain, his toes aching from the unexpected blow. Amanda lost her footing and fell back onto her butt as well, but hopped up rapidly.

Lindsey moved the ball just a little to line up her shot. Now she concentrated and Gallager moved to block her kick.

Lindsey's spell activated. Gallager and the crowd saw Lindsey begin to make a Jump, hoping to get a better angle to throw the ball for a goal. The instant Gallager reacted, jumping up to block the toss, Lindsey kicked the ball as hard as she could. At the very last instant, Gallager saw the two Lindseys. One was in midair; the other one on the ground had just kicked the ball. The horn sounded as the ball hit the net.

"Will you look at that! Lindsey Barron scores for Yellow Hall! 1 to 0 is the score. Incredible fake out of Gallager! Now Art throws the ball deep down field for Black Hall. Do they feel the pressure? When haven't they had the lead? Now the ball goes across the field in a brilliant pass to left forward, Larry Sacks. Can he get Black Hall on the boards?"

"Lookout Larry, Bill's coming on fast! Look at that pass to Hektor; he's in the open. Will he take a shot?" Amanda, way down the field, saw Hektor's magical energy flash, five Hektors appeared, and one would take the shot just as soon as Sally was sufficiently confused as to which one was real. Amanda whispered, "Be Gone." Her ring energized just as Hektor was about to kick for the goal. Suddenly the five Hektors became one, and Sally dove to block his kick, catching the ball. She got to her feet and heaved the ball as far as she could down field. Hektor, totally upset, came charging into the goalkeeper's zone and smashed into Sally. Two whistles blew simultaneously.

Hank and Sally made the signs for foul, and Blake reported, "Foul on Hektor for entering the goalkeeper's zone. Free kick for Sally." While the players took time out and tried to catch their breaths, Sally made the long walk to the other end of the field, where she would get a free kick. Of course, Gallager was sure to block it, but Sally had never kicked the ball when she had this Skin of Stone on her body. Unless one had a lot of fake-out type of spells at the ready, about all one could do was to kick it hard and hope it somehow got by the goalkeeper. Sally never carried her wand on the field, because it interfered with her goalkeeping skills. Thus, she made no effort to use any fake magic; besides she was upset that Hektor would deliberately charge into her protected zone. She kicked it with all her might, but the Skin of Stone added to her kick. Wham! The ball flew so fast that the diving Gallager missed it completely. The horn sounded again.

"Amazing free shot! Sally scores. 2 to 0! Amazing, looks like this Yellow team is all fired up. Black Hall is now down two goals. They are going to have to get moving!" Once more Betsy threw out the ball. Herman got it away from Emilio and passed cross-field to Herman. Out of position, Emilio raced to get back across the field to his position, giving Herman plenty of time to bring the ball down the field and pass to Larry.

"It's the usual four against two situation. Larry has the ball, but Yellow Hall's two fullbacks are not moving out of their positions to chase him. Wise move. Now Larry's bringing the ball closer in; he passes to Hektor. Becky moves to block him. He tosses it over to Philip, forcing Jake to move to block."

Now Larry saw his opening and dashed toward the scoring line. Philip faked a jump and bounced the ball between Jake's legs straight to Larry, who was now open. Larry faked right and kicked left. The horn sounded. Black Hall was on the boards.

Jake brought the ball up toward middle field, but Hektor rushed him and kicked him in the shins, a complete mis-aim for the ball. He howled in pain as he hit the ground hard. Jake grabbed the ball, kept his footing, and took his time passing to the open Tom. At once, Art rushed in to block him, smashing hard into his body. Art now bleeding profusely from his nose, which struck stone not flesh, stopped to deal with his face. Tom passed cross-field to the open Jim who raced the ball into scoring position, bringing a rushing Ben towards him as anticipated. At the last instant, Jim punted the ball lightly to Lindsey who now had a clear shot.

Once more, she made a phantasm illusion of herself. One, she sent rushing with the ball to her right, while she moved left. Both seemed to kick at the same time. Gallager could not block both and chose the one on the right. The horn sounded as Lindsey's kick entered the net from the left. Blake enthusiastically announced, "Goal. Lindsey's second of the afternoon! How about that one? 3 to 1 it stands. Now there appears to be a time out on the field. Yes, Larry has called for a time out. Oh, on the backfield, it's Hektor. He's on the ground. No, they are carrying him off the field. Injury time. Yes,

Wizard Soccer can be dangerous. Let's hope it's nothing serious folks."

Doctor Caterwall, Hank, and Betsy joined the nine Black Hall players on the sidelines. Inside the huddle of people, the doctor removed Hektor's right shoe. "It's broken son."

"Gimme somethun; god it hurts," Hektor replied. "We can't play with just eight players."

The doctor gave him a potion to drink. "Son, it will begin healing, but you are still going to be in some pain for a while yet. I urge you to sit out the rest of the game."

Hektor grimaced as he put his shoe back on, and Larry helped him to his feet. He could barely walk but was determined to continue to play. Blake announced what had happened and shortly play resumed.

Art threw the ball down the field to Herman, who quickly shot it over to Larry, who pulled Becky out towards him. When she was slightly out of position, he raced around her and drove the ball towards the goal. At the last instant, he waved his wand and five images of Larry appeared: two were in the air about to throw the ball, while three were about to kick it at three spots along the net. Poor Sally didn't know which was which. Once more, Amanda had maneuvered so that she could see the far action and said, "Be Gone." Sally saw the real Larry as he kicked the ball; she made a brilliant dive and trapped it against her chest, knocking the wind out of her momentarily. Slowly, she got to her feet to toss the ball back.

Her two fullbacks were now being double-teamed by Black Hall's forwards. Hence, Sally did the only thing she could; she gave the ball a running kick, sending the ball high over the heads of the players near her, sending it into the middle field. Henry and Bill collided over the recovery of the loose ball. Henry fell to the ground; it felt like he had run into a stone wall. The wind was knocked out of him, and he was slightly stunned. Bill was knocked flat, but recovered to grab the ball and passed it on down field to Lindsey. Art rushed at her, viciously kicking at her right leg, but the ball was on her left side. Art howled in pain, hopping around on one foot. Lindsey was knocked over. Whistles blew.

Blake announced, "Intentional foul on Art Merryweather. Kicking. Free shot goes to Lindsey Barron." Once more, the field cleared, and Lindsey got to her feet and tested her legs to be sure they were still unharmed. Gallager stared and glared intently at her, wondering what fast move she would try on her this time.

Lindsey saw that Gallager was now fully expecting some magical fake out. Just as she kicked the ball as hard as she could, she yelled "Boo!" Gallager stared at her, wondering what that was all about. That split second cost her dearly. She dove for the flying ball, but it ricocheted off her arms into the net. The horn sounded.

"Incredible! Lindsey Barron scores again, three goals so far. Wonder woman this player is! 4 to 1. Now it's half time."

Black Hall needed this ten-minute break. Since Art had not gotten up on his own, he was also carried off the field. He'd broken two of his toes. Doctor Carter gave him a potion and asked him not to play, but Art just glared at him as if he was an idiot. By the time that the second half began, Hektor was able to get around better, but Art was still limping badly. Larry issued the orders, "Get Lindsey. She's scoring like mad. Be sure not to foul her and give her any more chances. Block her; she's never to be in the open, got that Art, Ben?" Both agreed.

During the second half, wherever Lindsey ran, both Art and Ben followed her. During the entire second half, Lindsey rarely got the ball. Instead, Amanda took up the slack, as well as Jim and Tom who found themselves frequently wide open. When the game finally ended, the score was 10 to 2, a sound thrashing by Yellow Hall. Art, Hektor, Larry, Philip, and Herman all had one or more broken toes from attempting illegally to kick their opponents, arguably aiming for the ball. Jennifer had scored the second goal for Black Hall. Amanda, Jim, and Tom each had two goals for Yellow Hall.

Amid wild cheering from Yellow Hall fans, the triumphant team waved and raised their hands in victory. Bill pointed out that unless Blue Hall triumphed over Red hall and a playoff game was needed, Yellow Hall would actually win the Soccer Cup this year, for the first time in many years! No matter what, Black Hall would lose the cup for the first time in equally as many years.

Pam's commented to her friends as they walked back to the dorms, "You beat them at their own game. Clever. How did you get that third goal past Gallager, Lindsey?"

"I said 'Boo' to her. She was expecting me to use some magic so I just said Boo. Faked her out for a split second," Lindsey modestly replied and Pam giggled.

On Monday, Lindsey, Amanda, and Emilio received stares of hatred from their Black Hall classmates, particularly Deiter and Lyle.

As expected, Black Hall took the next track meet from Red Hall, but that did them little good. Yellow Hall had already won the Track Cup this year. A week later, Red Hall took the soccer game from Blue Hall, clinching the school soccer cup for Yellow Hall. No playoff was needed. On that Saturday afternoon, after the soccer game, the two trophies were presented to the Yellow Hall team. Photographs were taken, and the cups and pictures joined those from the previous years in the Trophy Room in the Admin Hall.

Lindsey felt very proud. No matter what happened in future years here at Bradbury's, at least one time, her victorious picture would be on the wall along side of those of her father. To her, this mattered the most, though she would have given anything for her father to have seen her games.

May Day came, bringing with it warm weather and flowers. Spring fever struck all over the campus. Once more, the third years and above got the day off to go into Telluride for some fun.

The five companions sat in the Yellow Hall study hall looking over their mountain of homework. Pam pointed out, "Gang, I have been going over our spell textbook, and the only spells we have left to cover are Charm a Person and Put to Sleep! What can we be doing for the whole month of May?"

"I could kiss you, Pam!" Emilio replied. "That's the best news I've had! Two spells for a whole month! I need a break; this geometry is absolutely impossible." Indeed, the geometry had been getting steadily more challenging, even for Pam and Lindsey.

However, the next day in Science class, Emilio got a

second, most pleasant surprise. Professor Jasper announced, "During this last month of science, we are going to study rocketry. Each of you will get to build several rockets, and we'll give them a test flight. The first two of your rockets will be from one of these pre-made, norm's kits. However, the last one will be of your own design." The boys in the class let out a war hoop of joy. Finally, science had turned to fun.

He added, "However, you will be graded on just how well your designed rocket actually performs." For the next month, the science class smelled of balsa wood, glue, and paint. Lindsey was very glad that she now had hands, for without them, she would have failed this portion of the class utterly; such fine work was needed to build the rockets.

When they arrived for Professor Janice's class, she announced, "Class, two spells remain: Charm a Person and Put to Sleep. Of course, I expect you will do simply grand on the first. Some of you may be wondering why a whole month on just two spells? Well, I was ordered by Governor Alister to make sure the class was quite ahead of schedule this year. It seems that some of you students would prefer to go run at the Nationals instead of learning your spells. After all what earthly good will running have to do with your careers as witches and wizards, eh?"

"After you have mastered these remaining two spells, during the rest of the classes, we will be reviewing all spells. As some of you have probably heard from your older siblings, near the end of the term, you will once again have a comprehensive spell test, just as you had with all of your useful spells. You will have only forty-five minutes to complete all and I do mean all your Grade 0 and 1 spells! And I can tell you all right now that all of you need all the practice you can possibly get, if you wish to pass this final test and move on to the second year spells. Now let's get to work."

"Today, let's liven this up a bit, shall we? Deiter, you are to twin with Lindsey. Amanda, you twin with Lyle." She had evidently been taking careful note of who disliked who all year long, for now she matched up everyone with someone they disliked. Soon, everyone was groaning about this unexpected twist.

"Now I want you to charm your twin and get them to say and do silly things. Begin," she said with an evil grin. Lindsey knew that Janice loved every minute of this class. Of course, casting a Charm a Person spell against someone you disliked was vastly more difficult than using it on a friend.

"Ha! Didn't work again," Deiter sneered at Lindsey, who had failed to make the spell work for the third time. "Le'me try it now, since you can't figure it out." She had no choice but to re-read the casting details. She knew she must be missing something. Deiter went to work waving his wand and casting away, mostly with no results as well. Suddenly, Lindsey heard Deiter say, "Lindsey, my boots are dirty. Please lick them clean with your tongue."

She found herself sighing and saying, "Oh yes, dear Deiter, my love, anything you say." In spite of her deep feelings against him, she found herself on all fours, licking away at his boots. Half of the class began laughing loudly, halting their own attempts just to see Deiter's brilliant move.

Satisfied, Professor Janice forcibly cancelled his spell. "Excellent charm, Mr. Cross. Now let's see if Miss Barron can possibly manage this spell. I doubt it, but you never know, do we, Mr. Cross?" He shook his head to say no, because he was still roaring with laughter. Lindsey's face went beet red, when she realized what she had done under the influence of his spell.

Two tries later, she commanded, "Deiter, kiss my hand, please."

"Oh yes, I thought that you would never ask me, my love!" he said eagerly. Once more, the class stopped theirs to watch this pair. He kissed her hand repeatedly. Lindsey couldn't think of anything else for him to do, so she said, "Now brush out my pretty hair, please." With the class roaring with laughter, Deiter fumbled with the task, until Professor Janice canceled Lindsey's spell. Deiter now went crimson and sat back seething with anger.

Halfway through the class, Professor Janice had them all switch partners once more. She knew from experience that if she allowed these same two to cast more Charm a Person spells, that they would get wilder and wilder. She wouldn't allow pornographic actions or even kissing of lips, since these were, after all, only first year students.

Lyle glared at Lindsey. They were now partners. Fortunately for Lindsey, Lyle was not too creative and had her kiss his boots, mimicking what Deiter had done. Lindsey charmed Lyle into dancing before the whole class. Other pairs also had their enemies doing similarly embarrassing things. Peggy, who had Deiter as a partner next, commanded him to put on her cherry red lipstick. The entire class roared with such laughter, that Professor Janice finally had to bring order, but only after she too stopped laughing. When Deiter found out, he was so livid with anger that he could not manage to cast his spell properly on her before the bell rang.

"Well, that surely was interesting," Pam chatted as the five walked to their next class. "It is *so* much more difficult to cast that one against someone you dislike." The four readily agreed with her observation. "I bet Janice really got her jollies out of us today!"

Later that evening in the study hall, Pam looked up from her books and said, "You know, we have been so busy that we have yet to check out one of these secret underground rooms!" Pam suddenly realized that they'd done nothing about that yet!

"We've not had time," Kathy pointed out. "Say, what's the latest news about Dominus? I've been so darn busy that I haven't been paying much attention to the news. Probably nothing much happening anyway or the school would have been talking about it," expressing mild interest in it.

"I only watch the sports channels," Emilio replied. "Nothing on there about him."

"That's just it! Don't you see?" Pam suddenly got very excited. No one "saw." "Look, he stole back all his magical items. Then what? Nothing! No murders, no robberies, nothing for months now. That I find fishy indeed. If I was him, I certainly would make another attempt to get the Rod of the Apocalypse! I've been doing a little research on the side, with the help of one of my dear friends in Red Hall. I've found out that Governor Alister sure has magical protection enchantments on this school! You can't even teleport in or out of the school pentagram walls! So even with his staff, Dominus couldn't just appear there in the Admin Hall stairs. He's already circumvented the spells by digging underneath the walls, making that tunnel and bringing in the wolves. After that failure, I'd bet anything that Governor Alister re-did his protections to disallow the digging of tunnels as well, though he ought to have thought of that in the first place."

"Next, I wondered what would keep someone from just flying over the walls or perhaps even climbing them. My friend, Monique, showed me some web pages where former students tried that. There is a whole site devoted to tips from former students, you see, Bradbury's-Tips.org. Of course, once she showed me, it made sense. After all, if you could just climb over the walls, what's to keep fourth years from hopping over them and taking a stroll into Telluride on their own?"

"So what does happen if you try to hop over the walls?" Emilio asked, now very interested in what she was explaining.

Pam said rather rhetorically, "Mind you, I haven't tried it, nor would I want to hop over the walls, but according to the website, you are just bounced back. It is dangerous to try to fly over them, because you just run into some kind of invisible wall that won't let you through."

"Darn, that would have been useful, you know, hopping over the walls and heading into Telluride," Emilio sighed, greatly let down. Another of his plans for the future was dispelled.

"So now we and the rod are perfectly safe?" Kathy asked.

Again, Pam said flatly, "Governor Alister certainly wants us to believe so anyway."

Lindsey saw that certain gleam in Pam's eyes and she asked, "But you don't think so?"

"Well, no." Pam said emphatically. "Think about it for a minute. This guy wants that rod with which he can cause no end of problems for the entire world, not just the US. He and everyone else knows that it is now being kept here somewhere secret. Would you say: oh well, now there is no way for me to steal that rod? Well, if I were Dominus, I certainly wouldn't, though after the last fiasco, I would *certainly* come better prepared. Besides, there may well be other security men hanging around here, though I have not actually seen any myself."

"But Pam," Emilio protested, "you just said that he can't climb the wall, go over or under the walls! How can he possibly get in here?"

"That's what everyone believes is the case. Yet, I would expect a powerful, clever wizard to find a way. I know I would certainly find a way in here. It's just that I haven't yet completely worked that one out. Only we students, faculty, and staff are allowed to enter. That must be the key somehow. Give me time. I will work it out."

"Say, have you all seen the calendar of events?" Kathy changed the subject to something that interested her. "The bus leaves for home on June 1. On May 31, we have a big end of school celebration dinner. May 30 is the End of Term Ball. I have a new dress to wear to the ball. Have any of you been asked yet? Of course, we can all go, even if we don't have a date."

"But none of us knows how to do those fancy dances," Emilio groaned.

"Speak for yourself," Kathy replied. "I do. How about the rest of you?"

"I've no idea how either," Lindsey admitted.

"Me either," Amanda added. Pam shook her head no as well. Amanda continued, "But Jim had told me that Professor Janice will be giving us all lessons in middle May instead of spell casting."

"Oh no! If sitting through her spell casting classes weren't bad enough, now I'm going to have to take dancing lessons from her too?" Emilio groaned in protest.

"Well, we *do* need to learn, Emilio. After all, you don't want to look like an idiot on the dance floor, now do you?" Pam retorted.

Emilio just groaned. He was had, no matter how he replied, so he said nothing, just groaning. "Will someone please look over my geometry problems?" he begged. The five got back into their study mode once more.

Chapter 14—The Nationals

May 11 came and the whole school assembled in the Stadium. The sun shone brightly in the morning sky, drying the dew upon the green grass. Governor Alister himself presided over the big send off for the Yellow Hall track team. "It is with the greatest pride that Bradbury's School of Magic sends these fine young athletes to compete in the Nationals. It's been years since we actually sent a team there. This time, we have a good chance to beat out many other schools, maybe even bring home a trophy."

"As I call your name, please step forward and I will place your official ribbon around your neck. Captain Bill Ferny." The students, having forgotten their Hall rivalry, yelled and cheered the competitors, who would be representing their school. Well, most did; some of the Black Hall students only went through the clapping motions.

Governor Alister went in age order, introducing Lindsey last. "Last but certainly not least, first year Lindsey Barron." She heard Pam and Kathy screaming loudly and smiled. He placed a yellow ribbon over her shoulders and she took her place at the end of the line of the nine track team members. "Today, they travel to Des Moines, Iowa. Tomorrow, they compete. Sunday, they return. Let us all root and hope that they can bring a trophy back with them!" They received the largest applause yet and they walked off the field.

Near the field, they picked up their small backpacks with a change of clothes, their track outfits, and their wands. Little else were they allowed to bring for security reasons. At the Nationals, there would be so many others there, that it was not safe to bring along anything of real value. Hank and Betsy were the last to board the bus in the parking lot.

Professor Cho Lin accompanied Hank and Betsy, since she was the Yellow Hall Councilor. Her presence did much to alleviate the worries and fears for Lindsey and Amanda. Though the bus was nearly empty, Amanda and Lindsey went to their usual seats in the very back. However, Jim urged them to climb to the top level and take the rear seats there. "You don't want to miss the view. You can see much better from up there." They did so and did not regret it.

As the countryside sped past them rapidly, they gazed in awe at the spectacular Colorado Rockies, which soon gave way to their homelands, the high plains. However, once they entered Kansas, the scenery, while new to both girls, rapidly became incredibly boring. They dozed off for a time. Around lunchtime, the bus came to a halt outside a giant stadium that dwarfed their own. "Wake up sleepy heads. We're here," Jim called out to the two. "Come on; it's noon."

"Two hours? But that means we must have been going hundreds of miles an hour!" Amanda exclaimed.

"Sh. Or Professor Mac Elroy will be making you do the math calculation on just how fast we made the trip," Jim jested. Here in the bus parking lot, Lindsey saw dozens of other school buses. She wondered just how many other schools were competing.

Hank led them into the large dining hall. A man asked for their school name and pointed out a banner. Hank said, "Hey, we are over there; see that big Bradbury's School of Magic banner? That's us. Come on."

A waitress came to take their lunch orders and, while they waited for her to return with their orders, Hank opened their schedule card and read it to the group. "Okay, we are up at ten in the morning. We go against New York City School of Magic. Sixteen schools are competing. It is an elimination style. If we win, we move on to join the next eight. This track supports four simultaneous team races. Half of the sixteen schools race at eight in the morning, the other half at ten. If we win, then at one p.m. we race one of the other winners and move into the quarterfinals. If we get into the quarterfinals, we are assured of a trophy. The top four teams get one. If we are incredibly lucky and win that race, then we race in the final race for first place, after the two losers race for third place, at two p.m. The final race is at three p.m. There is a banquet at five and then, first thing the next the morning, we head home."

"What happens if we lose our first race?" Jim asked. "Do we have to go home right then or can we stay and watch the other races?"

Hank smiled, "We stay. Ah, here comes our food."

Later, they were shown to their rooms and they changed into their track outfits. Hank and Betsy led them down to the track for a practice session. Many other students from the other schools were also on the field doing trial runs, getting the feel of this new, fabulous track. Lindsey thought that the running surface was the best yet. Their hopes high, the team had dinner and went to bed early, though many were very nervous.

Finally, around 9:30, they went to their warm up positions at the side of the track. Near them, the New York group was also warming up. Lindsey looked at her competition. Nearly everyone was black and at least a fourth year or higher student. She saw none that was her age. Indeed, she thought that the competition would be very stiff. Butterflies began appearing in her stomach. Hank, Betsy, and Bill gave them a final pep talk, but Lindsey heard very little of it.

Just as the New York school was being introduced, a strange man with a notebook and pen approached Lindsey. "Excuse me, Miss Lindsey Barron?" She nodded and looked at the young man, apparently a reporter from the hat he wore that said Mag News. "May I have your autograph?" Lindsey looked at him with a blank look on her face. She had no idea what he really wanted, but she did not like the coldness in his voice. Somewhere, somehow, she knew that voice.

Bill yelled, "Come on; just sign his paper; we're about to be introduced!" Lindsey mechanically obeyed, but as she picked up the pen, a tiny needle on its side pricked her finger, drawing a tiny drop of blood.

"Oh that darn pen is always giving us trouble. I'm sorry. Thank you. You'd better hurry up." He turned and walked away quickly. Lindsey rushed to the end of her team's line, behind Amanda.

"What'd he want?" she asked.

"Wanted me to sign my name on a blank paper. His darn pen bit me," she said, sucking her finger.

"And here comes the Arthur Bradbury's School of

Magic, Colorado," the announcer said enthusiastically over the loud speaker. Lindsey saw that there were thousands of people in the stands and her stomach really gave a lurch. After they were properly announced, the race began. One minute later, a dejected Sally walked back; she'd lost her 100-meter dash by a foot.

Bill encouraged the next bunch, "Hey we can still win if we take the next two events. Let's do it gang!" Bill, Becky, Jake, and Emilio went to their starting positions for the mile relay race. Meanwhile Amanda, Lindsey, Jim, and Tom took theirs for the twenty-mile relay race. As before, Lindsey would lead off, passing to Jim after five miles.

Amanda sent her a Message, a paper floated before her eyes until she read it.

Keep our pace. Ignore the other runner. Watch us as you go by.

The paper vanished and Lindsey smiled back at Amanda. She took her position beside the tall New Yorker, a fifth year boy. He gave her a sneer as if to say you are running???

The announcer gave the countdown and the two sprinted from the starting line. He tried to egg her to speed up, but Lindsey watched her pace, concentrating on bringing to mind her racing home along the gravel road from Plano. As she passed Amanda, she got a thumbs up sign and knew she was on the right pace. Here, the track was double the size of the one at school. Hence, the runners only needed to make five passes around the track. Hank located himself half way around so that he could signal his runners, when they were beginning the last half mile, at which point, they would pour on the speed.

Lindsey had been running all her life at the higher elevations of Colorado. While she didn't know that this was a benefit here at a much lower elevation, she knew she didn't feel as winded as she maintained her pace. At last, Hank's whistle brought her out of her mechanical run, the last half mile. As they had practiced, Lindsey slowly increased her pace. She was actually passing her competitor! Now she spied Jim begin his warm up run, matching her speed ready for the handoff. As she passed the finish line, Jim smoothly snatched the baton from her hand, and she began to slow down. Just then, her competitor banged into her left side hard. Fortunately, both players recovered from their stumble and continued to jog to a slow down. Once Lindsey was cooled down and back with her teammates, Bill looked at her arm. She had a nice bruise from the collision, nothing more.

At last, Lindsey could just relax, catch her breath, and cheer for Jim, Tom, and Amanda. "Oh, we won," Bill announced off handedly.

"Wow! Great! We have a chance!" Lindsey hugged him and yelled all the louder. Finally, Amanda flew across the finish line, and the victory went to Yellow Hall and Bradbury's! Time was a spectacular 105:33! They'd combined to shave an additional five minutes off their record setting time at Bradbury's. Jumping and cheering, the team celebrated their victory. Even Cho Lin yelled along with them. Then, it was off to lunch.

"The problem is, gang, we have to go back out there and race yet again, without a day's rest," Bill explained. "Then if we win again, we race on just a couple hours' rest. This is going to be grueling indeed!"

"But at least we are in the best eight schools in the country," Amanda pointed out.

At one p.m., they had to race Chicago's School of Magic. Again, all the team members were much older and none was less than fifth year students. Lindsey had serious doubts about winning a second time, for their competition looked terribly fierce indeed. As they were about to start, Bill whispered to Amanda and Lindsey, remember, these guys have also already raced once. They are getting tired too. Stick to the game plan."

Lindsey walked to the starting line and looked at her competitor. He was tall and thin, nearly twice as tall as she was. "Hi, I'm Fred, fifth year."

"Lindsey, first year," she replied hesitatingly.

"Good luck, Lindsey." She smiled and wished him the best as well.

Then the race began. Lindsey sprinted out of the block and hunted for her pace. It took her a little longer to find it this time. However, she noticed that Fred decided to pace her and wondered if he had some trick up his sleeve. After getting the thumbs up sign from Amanda, she knew she'd found her pace once more. Like a machine, she continued to speed down the long track, admiring how great the track felt beneath her feet. She'd never run ten miles in one day however and wondered if she could do it, if she'd have anything left for the stretch run. Minutes later, Hank sounded his whistle and she slowly increased her speed to the best she could manage. To her surprise, her competitor was keeping pace with her, though he was straining his utmost. Lindsey pushed all the harder, and then concentrated on making a perfect handoff to Jim. Finally, she slowed down to cool off and catch her breath. Fred was right beside her. They had been in a virtual tie the whole five miles.

"Looks are deceiving," Fred gasped. "You, good runner indeed. Tied me! Good job."

She grinned back. "You're good too! Going to be a close race." A while later, she joined the others. Bill reported Sally won her heat, but Bill's group lost. Once more, everything depended on this last race. Lindsey gave Sally a big hug. On cloud nine, Sally had finally won one sprint.

"Man, this Chicago team is good. Jim's in a tie as well!" Bill exclaimed. Sometime later, Bill moaned, "Still a tie. I can't believe Tom's only tied. Come on Amanda! It's all up to you." She, of course, couldn't hear him. She was facing a sixth year, veteran runner, who pulled ahead of her. Unwilling to break her pace, she allowed him the advantage, saving herself for that final sprint. As they got the final whistle for the last half mile, he was already several hundred feet ahead of her. Undaunted, Amanda increased her speed once more, drawing on her inner strength. Faster and faster, she flew down the long straightaway. She caught up to him and crossed the finish line one stride ahead of him!

The whole team began yelling and cheering. "That's our sister!" both Jim and Tom yelled. Soon the scoreboard displayed their time: 108:33. Just as Lindsey suspected, they were tiring and losing time. Yet, they knew they still faced two more races, but that no matter what happened, they would return with a National's trophy at least.

However, they only had an hour to rest up before the next race against the Los Angeles School of Magic. As they looked at their competition, Lindsey saw that they were up against an entire team of sixth year runners! Even Bill lacked any words of wisdom this time. Sally lost in short order. A little while later, the four one milers lost theirs. Much later, the twenty milers lost their heat as well, coming up a hundred feet behind. Amanda just could not catch these fleet footed men. Their time also showed what was happening to them: 114:29.

Hank cheered them up. "One more race gang. Will it be the third place trophy or the fourth place trophy?"

"Better be third!" declared Emilio, drinking an energy booster drink.

Their opponent for this last race was St. Bernard's of St. Paul, Minnesota. Lindsey noticed that they had a wide mix of students, from third year on up. The Los Angeles team was all sixth year; hence, Lindsey felt that they had a chance this time. As they moved toward their starting positions, Fred from the Chicago team yelled to her, "Go get them, Lindsey from Bradbury's!" She smiled; she had at least one other person rooting for her, something she had never had before— opponents rooting for her! She smiled back at him and positioned her feet into the starting block.

She'd already run fifteen miles this day! Could she even possibly run yet another five miles? She found it very difficult to find her pace, wasting nearly an entire mile before her aching legs found their groove once more. However, a glance at her opponent told her that he was having as much trouble as she was. This run was anything but enjoyable; her legs and lungs ached. After an eternity, she finally handed the baton off to Jim. She was nearly dead to the world. Fortunately, Bill and the others were right there with her, helping and insisting she jog to cool down.

"Hey, Sally won again," Bill reported. His voice then changed to a sour tone, "but we lost ours. It's up to you all again."

Jim had handed off to Tom before Lindsey was aware of much of anything. Emilio told her that Jim had a difficult time finding his pace as well. Now she didn't feel so badly. After all, if an Apache could not find the pace, well. . .

What saved their race was Tom, who fell into his pace at once. Slowly, he began to distance himself from the exhausted runner from St. Bernards. He handed Amanda a two hundred foot lead, hoping that she still had it in her to hold on to it. Like Lindsey, she too had difficulty finding her pace; she was as tired and sore as Lindsey was, unused to running twenty fast miles in one day. Still, she held on to the lead Tom had given her.

When the final whistle blew, Amanda tried to increase her pace, but found she had nothing left to give. It took extreme effort just to continue her normal pace. The older girl from St. Bernards valiantly pushed to catch her. Slowly she narrowed the distance. Try as she might, Amanda couldn't go any faster; if anything, she might be slowing! Ahead, she saw the ribbon across the finish line. She wished with all her might that she was across that line; it would all be over, one way or the other. Then, it was; she didn't even remember breaking the ribbon; she was completely exhausted and won by only one foot!

Bill and Emilio raced to her to keep her jogging and to help her cool down, knowing it was a disaster if she just stopped totally. The announcer said, "Arthur Bradbury's School of Magic has just taken third place! Time: 120:13! What a remarkable performance from two first year students! Competitors take note: Bradbury's will likely be coming to the Nationals for the next several years with a performance like we've seen today."

He continued, "And now for the final match of this National event. Los Angeles School of Magic takes on the Sam Houston School of Magic. Winner takes first place and this huge trophy."

Lindsey began walking with Amanda, as she finally got her wind back. A bit later, they joined the others, sitting down in their reserved seats to watch the final runs of the day. Houston's team likewise had mostly fifth and sixth year students. Bill said encouragingly, "Well, if you guys make it here next year, you won't be facing these guys, they will have all graduated. It's a shame that I will be too. I bet we could take first place next year!" Lindsey smiled, but she knew that, if she were going to continue to be a runner for the team, she was going to have to practice running at least twenty miles a day! She had never felt so exhausted in her entire life. Amanda, likewise.

Sometime later, Los Angeles took the race. Next, came the team presentations. Lindsey and Amanda's legs felt like butter, and they could barely walk onto the field. Thankfully, Sally and Emilio put an arm around each of them, supporting them. Bill grandly accepted the tall trophy amid the noisy cheering.

Then, they headed back to their rooms to bathe and change into their normal clothes. The dinner banquet was next. Lindsey went to the bathroom. Sometime later, she rejoined her group. "Hey, Lindsey, have a look at our super trophy!" Emilio said to her when she rejoined her companions at their long table in the fancy dining hall, all decorated in the colors of the top four winning teams. "Pretty cool, eh?"

Lindsey growled, "If you all would have run better, we should have had first place." She sat down and looked over the menu. Shocked by her reply, Emilio glanced at Amanda, who was sitting beside Lindsey. She shrugged her shoulders as if to say I don't know what's gotten into Lindsey.

"Say, Lindsey, did the doctor give you something for your arm? I see the large bruise is completely healed."

"What bruise? No, I just heal fast, that's all," Lindsey said rather annoyed at the question. Amanda looked surprised and shot a glance at Emilio. He shrugged his shoulders too. Just then, the waitress came asking for their orders. The banquet offered four main courses. Lean roast beef and gravy, New York strip steak, roasted chicken breast, and an artichoke deluxe.

Emilio asked for the steak, as did many of the others. Amanda and Sally took the chicken, along with Betsy and Cho Lin. Lindsey said, "The artichoke supreme, please."

Amanda looked at her in surprise. "I thought you didn't like artichoke, Lindsey."

Lindsey shot Amanda a glare, "Mom had it for us over

Christmas break a couple times." She said nothing more and Amanda dropped it.

After the meal, the officials gave several speeches, and each of the four winning team members rose and were presented a pin. Once the little ceremonies finished, they all headed to their rooms. Amanda was so stiff and sore, she barely could climb the stairs. "I've never been so pooped! My legs are like butter."

"You should get out and run more," Lindsey said somewhat picky. Amanda noticed that Lindsey had no difficulty with the stairs and was ahead of the team, just behind Hank and Betsy, while the eight others slowly climbed behind them. She thought this was curious indeed.

When the girls entered their room, each headed for their bed, while Lindsey held the door open for the others. Lindsey looked out the window for a time, glancing covertly at the other girls to make sure they were in their beds. With only one bed unoccupied, Lindsey then went over to it and laid down. Sally and Amanda began discussing some of the interesting runners they had met or seen today, but Lindsey pretended to be tired and shut her eyes.

After a time, Amanda said, "Well, Lindsey, what about that runner from Chicago; he was all over you. I think he really likes you. He even came up to you after the race. What did he have to say?"

Without turning her head to face Amanda, Lindsey mumbled, "Nothing really. I'm going to sleep."

Amanda looked curiously at Sally, who shrugged her shoulders. They chatted a bit more, and then they too went to bed. When they awoke the next day, Amanda was very stiff, her legs and thighs ached. Only with difficulty did she get her body dressed, her few things packed, and ready to get breakfast. Lindsey, she noticed, had evidently slept in her dress, and was moving about as if she were perfectly fine, no sore muscles. Amanda, remembering how she had growled at her yesterday, decided against asking her about it.

At breakfast, Lindsey ate well, perhaps twice as much as Amanda normally saw Lindsey eat in the mornings. Then, it was time for the bus trip home. Lindsey took their usual seat in the very back. "I'm going to take a nap," she said. "Wake me when we're home."

"Okay, but don't you want to watch the Rockies when we go through them?" Amanda asked.

"No, they're just mountains. I need to sleep. Thanks." Lindsey laid down on the seat to sleep, quite unlike her, Amanda thought. With effort from her sore legs, she climbed to the second story of the bus and sat at the back with her brothers.

Two hours later, the bus arrived in the Bradbury's parking lot. Lindsey still seemed to be asleep, when Amanda, Tom, and Jim climbed down. Amanda shook her gently, "Wake up sleepyhead. We're there."

Lindsey opened her eyes and sat up. She grabbed her small backpack and followed behind the other three. As they assembled off the bus, Professor Cho Lin told them, "We will walk to the Stadium directly. Hank and Bill will carry your trophy. The school has been assembled and will properly welcome the victors home. Enjoy your well-earned spotlight," she grinned at Lindsey, who did not smile back.

Indeed, the track team walked on to the grassy field amid the loudest round of stadium horns, applause, yelling and cheering Amanda had ever heard. Even Black Hall students clapped, though they didn't yell. She thought that they at least had some sense of school pride in them. Governor Alister said some welcoming words and gave them all a solid handshake. After displaying the trophy and the noise subsided, the short assembly broke up. Many came up to congratulate the victors. Sandy Rains, Tom's girlfriend, gave him a big hug and kiss right out here in the open for all to see. Amanda thought that was not the thing to do, however.

Pam gave Lindsey a big hug, "I knew you could do it! Well done, Lindsey."

Lindsey growled and said, "We should have had first place, if the others had really run. Let's go to our room. We have lots of homework to do. I've missed three days and am so far behind."

Pam shot Amanda a curious look; this was not like Lindsey at all. Kathy came up and congratulated her two roommates as well. Then the two gave Emilio a hug too. All five headed for the dorms and their rooms. Lindsey was the last to enter their room, having followed along behind the three. Inside, she went to the window and gazed out toward the gardens, while the others gathered up their stuff. "Coming to study hall, Lindsey?" Amanda asked.

"Be there in a while," she replied as if her mind were on other things besides homework.

As they went down the stairs, Pam asked, "What's with Lindsey? She's like so cold."

"Dunno, she's been acting weird since the race was over," Amanda replied.

"How so?" Pam asked. Amanda began to chat about it.

"Well, Emilio was trying to enthusiastically show Lindsey their trophy. He's always bored, but this really had his interest. Yet, she growled at him, claiming we'd gotten first place if we had all run better. Honestly, we gave it all we had. None of us had expected to run four races in one day and two were only an hour apart! Grueling indeed."

"Then there was the bruise that suddenly disappeared. She got badly bumped after the first race, a big bruise and swelling on her left arm. The New York runner banged into her. Yet, at dinner, her arm looked perfectly normal. I thought at first the good doctor had given her something for it, but she said he hadn't, that she healed fast. I didn't believe her; honestly, I've never seen a bruise like that go away in a few minutes."

"Yes, that is strange," Pam said, as they entered the study hall. They were alone; the others were outside enjoying the sunny May afternoon. "I've heard that a healing potion could do that, but if the doctor didn't give it to her, who could have?"

"Then there was supper, the banquet. You know how Lindsey hates artichokes—well that's exactly what she ordered for dinner. I mean, honestly, after putting our bodies through all that running, it needed some real nourishment. So Lindsey had the artichoke deluxe! I asked her about it and she said her mother made them several times over Christmas."

"Wait, those are expensive. I know Lindsey and her

mom are really poor. How could she possibly afford to buy artichokes in the middle of the winter? That makes no sense," Pam declared.

"There's more. After the dinner, we runners were sore and aching. I mean my legs felt like they were butter! Yet, Lindsey walked up the stairs after Hank and Betsy as though hers were just fine! And when I asked her about it, she said that I should get out and run more. I couldn't believe she said that to me!"

"That is curious," Pam replied. "Say, when you got to your room, did Lindsey go straight to her bed?"

"Well, now that you mention it, no she didn't. She looked out the window for a time. Actually, we all got into ours. Only then did she go over to her bed. Is that important?"

"Could be. It is so strange. What else happened?" asked Pam, now very keenly interested.

"Oh yes, in the second race, her opponent from Chicago—he seemed to like her, and he even came over to her and talked with her a bit after the race. Yet, when I asked her about it, she said it was nothing. I've seen that look in boys' eyes before. He really liked her."

"Another thing, when we got up in the morning, we were incredibly stiff and sore, yet Lindsey didn't seem to be. Plus, I swear that she had slept in her school dress, weird, don't you think?"

"Surely, I'd never sleep in my dress!" Kathy pointed out.

"Did she do anything else on the strange or unusual side?" asked Pam.

"Well, at breakfast, Lindsey ate like there was no tomorrow. We all know that she doesn't eat a whole lot in the mornings. Oh, yes, on the bus ride home, she laid down on the back seat and slept all the way here. She didn't want to see the Rockies! She said they were just mountains."

"Curious, besides when we all entered our room a bit ago, did you all see how she looked out the window until we were all set to come down here? I would have expected her to be grabbing her things. After all she was just before that complaining about all the homework she'd missed during the last three days," Pam added.

"So what's it all mean? Did something about the race really get to her some way?" asked Amanda. "I mean after the racing was done, it seemed as if all the life and warmth was sucked right out of her. How can that happen?"

"Maybe she just totally overdid it and is completely exhausted," suggested Kathy.

"Well, I can get grouchy when I get totally shot," Amanda agreed.

Pam stated flatly, "We'd best keep an eye on her for a while, that's what I think."

"Keep an eye on who?" asked Emilio, who had just entered, his arms piled high with books and papers.

"Lindsey, we think she has been acting strange after the race yesterday," Amanda explained.

"You can say that again, turned into a big grouch bag, if you ask me, a heartless grouch bag. I need a lot of homework help," he said, his eyes going from girl to girl, a pleading look on his face.

"You want me just to work your geometry for you?" Pam asked haughtily.

"Would that help?" Emilio asked, thinking that would be terrific. He'd have to do nothing at all if she did it for him.

"No, you are supposed to be learning this math, Emilio," she replied.

"Well who really cares how you can prove that two planes intersect anyway?" he complained.

"Well, it must be the norm air traffic controller's fault, if two planes intersect," Kathy suggested seriously, trying to be of assistance. Pam groaned; she was surrounded by math idiots.

The four worked on their homework until supper time. Lindsey had not joined them. However, she was not in their room when they got back and dropped off their books, before heading down to dinner. They found Lindsey sitting at the Yellow Hall table, already eating. However, she was not sitting in their usual spot at the head of the first table; rather she was sitting in the last table near the rear.

"Hi all, I fell asleep and woke up starving. I hope you don't mind my coming here sooner," Lindsey explained, when the four brought their trays to join her. "I guess I'm more tired than I realized," she added, a coldness or an ingenuousness in her voice, Pam wasn't sure which it was.

After a bit of light chatter, Pam asked, "Say, Lindsey, I've been meaning to ask you how you liked that necklace I gave you for Christmas? I really liked the book that you got me."

Lindsey stared at her plate, before answering, "Glad you liked it. Do you think that they will let us wear jewelry to the spring ball? I mean we are only first years, after all. I suspect that they would if we were sixth years, don't you think?"

Pam smiled; she knew that Lindsey not only evaded the question, but had no idea that it was Kathy who got her the necklace. "I don't know; we're awfully young, but by the time of the ball, we'll be nearly second years. I wonder if that helps? I'll ask Professor Janice about it tomorrow. If anyone would know, she would."

"Thanks, Pam. That's a good plan," Lindsey replied, returning to her meal. Kathy was about to protest, but Pam shot her a "don't you dare" kind of stare! "Well, I'm still incredibly tired, gang. I think I'll have a bit of a lie down for a while. See you in the room." Lindsey left, leaving her tray still on the table, instead of taking it over to the conveyor. Kathy was about to say something about it to her, when Pam gave her another dirty look. Instead, Kathy stared at her plate.

Once Lindsey had left the room, Kathy spoke up, "What's that all about? *I* gave her the necklace."

Pam said decidedly, "I don't think Lindsey is Lindsey, that's what I think. Clever the way she avoided my direct question about the necklace. I said that on purpose! If she was Lindsey, she would have known that I gave her a book and you gave her the necklace. So this Lindsey isn't Lindsey," Pam said flatly and decisively.

"But this makes no sense; she's Lindsey. I mean she looks exactly like Lindsey," Kathy objected, her nicely ordered, conservative world was being shaken slightly.

Emilio looked very worried, "If this Lindsey isn't Lindsey, then where is the real Lindsey?"

"Good question. An even better question is who is this

Lindsey," Pam added.

"You guys are befuddling my mind," Kathy declared. "How can Lindsey not be Lindsey?"

Amanda commented mostly to herself, "Well, that explains all these little things that I've noticed. It makes sense now if Lindsey isn't Lindsey, but then Emilio has a point. Who is this Lindsey and where is our Lindsey?"

"Maybe something scrambled her mind?" Emilio offered an explanation.

"Yes, that is a valid possibility, Emilio, except for one thing," Pam pointed out.

"What?" he asked perplexed and somewhat let down. He'd thought he had just solved it.

"Her bruise. She had a bruise during the afternoon, on her left arm, right Amanda?" Pam said triumphantly.

"Yes, from the New York runner collision. It was not there at dinnertime. You saw it too, Emilio," Amanda replied. Emilio groaned; he had indeed seen it, but had not realized it was now not present on her arm.

"It has to be something more than just a mind scramble of some kind," Pam said thinking. "Until we figure this all out, I think that we should keep an eye on her."

"Guess that leaves me out. I can't get into the girl's dorm," Emilio groaned yet again. He wanted to help.

"I have a plan, but it will take all of us to make it work," Pam said with a big, mischievous grin. "First, let's all go get our books and meet in the study hall. I bet that Lindsey will make some excuse not to come with us. I'm counting on that. See you all there in a few minutes." The group carried their trays and Lindsey's tray to the conveyor and headed to their rooms.

The three found Lindsey once more looking out at the gardens. "We are heading down to the study hall, Lindsey," Pam announced nonchalantly. "Wanna come with us?"

Lindsey made a huge yawn. "No, I think that I am still feeling exhausted from running twenty miles yesterday. I'm going to turn in early. Please don't wake me up when you all get back." The three headed down to the study hall. Emilio was already there and had their favorite spot near the back reserved for them.

Pam whispered, "I told you so." All three looked glumly at Pam, wondering what was going on and what her plan was. Pam didn't answer them, but quickly booted up her laptop. "Gather round," she whispered excitedly, "Spy Cam 2 is in operation."

"What? You didn't put one of those in our room did you?" Kathy asked, her voice a mixture of concern and displeasure. "How long have you been spying on us?"

"I just put it up there while we were getting our books, Kathy. Since you didn't notice, there is a good chance Lindsey didn't notice it either. Look, she certainly isn't sleeping! What's she doing?" Pam asked, the four hovered around her monitor, watching Lindsey, who appeared to be pacing the room.

"What's she doing with that pencil in her hair?" asked Emilio. "She's had that pencil there since, well at least yesterday at dinner." No one had any idea. "Well, now she is lying down at least."

"Yes, but not sleeping. Look, her eyes are open and she is staring at the ceiling," Kathy said, becoming more interested than before.

"Why don't you all get to work on your homework," Pam suggested. "I want to do a bit of research here. I'll keep an eye on her and let you know if Lindsey does something, well, weird."

"But I need help on my geometry," Emilio protested, knowing that Lindsey or Pam would normally lend him assistance.

"Okay, Emilio, I'll help you on that, but you have to help me on this infernal rocket design. I haven't a clue on how to design one," Amanda volunteered. Kathy needed help with both and soon the three were working hard.

Pam began searching MagGoogle. She had the small Web Cam window flagged as "Always on Top" so that she could keep one eye on it from time to time. At first, she tried "impersonating another person," but that led mostly to norm entries on the Web. For quite a few minutes, she tried this and that with no luck. She knew that she had heard the word for this, but couldn't remember it offhand. She sat back and tried to recall. The word she was looking for had something to do with her computer programming skills in C++, but what?

Suddenly, she remembered. It was the word that meant many forms, which had to do in C++ with functions that had the same names but were passed different parameters, polymorphism. Quickly, she typed in the word and finally began to make some headway. She narrowed down the search by adding magical spells to it.

A few minutes later, she had found what she wanted: some overall details on the spell called Morph Oneself into Another. She read, "By use of this spell, the wizard or witch can alter their entire appearance to look identical to another person. None can tell the difference. Caution, the use of this spell can easily be misused and is monitored by the Department of Magical Misuse."

"Rats, just not enough information," Pam said. "I've got to go to the Library. One of you, keep an eye on the Web Cam for me. Message me if something comes up." She left in a bit of a hurry for the next-door Library.

It took her an hour to track down the details of the spell. It was a Grade 4 spell, one that they might be learning next year. Just now, she was not looking to learn how to cast it, only what was involved, that sort of thing. "Bingo!" she said aloud, only to be admonished for making noise. Hastily, she copied down the key details and headed back to Yellow Hall's study hall.

It was getting late and only her friends were still in the study hall, when Pam entered, eager to tell them what she had found out. "Lindsey's not Lindsey, but Lindsey is still alive somewhere," she blurted out. She glanced at the Web Cam. The not-Lindsey was still resting on her bed, which was a good sign.

"It's a Morph Oneself into Another spell; that's what's very likely going on here. I researched the spell's details. We will learn it next year. It's a Grade 4 spell. According to the spell casting book, by use of this spell, you can turn yourself into a perfect likeness of another person. However, to cast this spell, you must have a sample of the other person's DNA, which the spell uses to make the replica identical to the original. Somehow, whoever the not-Lindsey actually is, he or she must somehow have gotten real-Lindsey's DNA. Further, the spell requires that the real-Lindsey or person you are replicating remain alive for the duration of the spell. If by accident the real person dies, the spell is instantly cancelled. That means our-Lindsey is still alive somewhere, probably being held prisoner somewhere."

"How long does the spell last?" asked Amanda, who had become increasingly worried the more that Pam spoke.

"As long as the caster desires, assuming the spell is not ended by the death of the real person or the spell is not dispelled by other magic, but I suppose that there are other factors that we will learn about next year," Pam said knowledgeably.

"Then who is the not-Lindsey? Why would someone want to pretend to be Lindsey anyway?" asked Kathy, who was rather confused by this whole spell.

No one had an answer for either question, however. At last, the ten o'clock hour approached, and they had to vacate the study hall. Ever since the attack by Dominus and the wolves, Governor Alister had insisted that everything was shut down by ten each night. Gone were the midnight hours.

"Emilio, when you get to your room, don't fall asleep for a while. If we need anything, I will Message you, okay?" Pam asked, knowing that girls were not allowed into the boy's rooms ever. He agreed and the four left the study hall, going up the two different stairs to their respective rooms.

When the three entered, the not-Lindsey pretended to be asleep, so the three were as quiet as they could be getting ready for bed. After a few minutes spent down in the bathroom brushing teeth, they returned to go to bed. At last, Pam canceled the last of the Blue Light spells. All three were snug in their beds. Unfortunately, Kathy fell asleep. Amanda lay pondering all that she had seen and heard. She was very worried about her dear friend. Where was Lindsey? Was she injured, hurt? Who was this not-Lindsey anyway? Why would anyone want to impersonate Lindsey, of all the students here at school? After all, she was picked on by so darn many other students. She began to doze off.

Similar thoughts raced through Pam's mind, searching for a reason for all this deception. She found none. She could make strong cases for impersonating a professor or even Governor Alister, but a lowly first year student? It made no sense at all. She too dozed off.

Around midnight, Lindsey, hearing the sounds of sleep from the three, quietly rose, cast a silence spell, and made her preparations. She tiptoed out of the room, being quite silent. Outside the room, she paused in the dimly illuminated hallway, listening for sounds. Hearing none, she cast another spell and her body disappeared from view. Her footprints in the deep carpet showed clearly that she was heading for the door and the stairs.

Pam's computer made a ding noise and Pam woke up from her doze. At once, she cast her Blue Light and saw not-Lindsey's bed was empty. She smiled at her own cleverness. Yes, all first years now knew how to set up a warning spell that would trigger. That is, she could have set a spell on their door that would have announced to all that the not-Lindsey had just left the room. However, since this not-Lindsey must be a wizard or witch, that would have been a dead giveaway. Instead, Pam had resorted to norm methods, installing an electronic monitoring switch, activated whenever the door opened. She'd programmed the alarm to wake her one minute after the door closed.

When clever Pam had gone down to brush her teeth, she'd moved the SpyCam 2 from her bed, sticking it just over their door. Quickly, she rewound the video feed back about two minutes and watched the door open and the not-Lindsey appearing. She closed the door quietly and stood silently for a moment. Pam noticed that some spell was cast and the not-Lindsey suddenly disappeared. However, she could see the not-Lindsey leaving footprints in the carpet as she headed for the door. The door opened and then shut. Pam stopped the recording and woke up Amanda.

"Come, look at this," she whispered, unwilling to wake up Kathy just yet. After all, perhaps the not-Lindsey was just going to the bathroom and might appear soon.

"Why would anyone want to become invisible just to go to the bathroom," protested Amanda, after Pam offered her lame suggestion. "She must be up to something."

"I'm sorry, Amanda. I could only afford to get another two of these Spy Cams. Professor Janice destroyed the only one I had, so I bought two more over Christmas. If I had lots of them, I could monitor many key locations."

"I know. I am going to see if I can follow her!" Amanda said resolutely. After all, she was certain that Lindsey, the real Lindsey, would do the same for her. She slipped on her moccasins so no matter where she went, she could move silently. Amanda took her wand and put on her dark cloak, figuring the dark cloak would make her more difficult to see. She pulled up the hood and looked in the mirror. Finally, she strapped on the knife that Lindsey had given her for Christmas and looked at Pam.

"I don't know where to tell you to start looking, Amanda. Just be very careful, please. If I can find out anything, I will send you a Message. If you find her and can safely do so, send me a Message, all right?" Amanda agreed and snuck out of their dorm room. She listened for any sounds. Hearing none, she moved to the door and listened again, her ear to the door. At last, she opened the door and peered into the stairs. Up to the House Mother made no sense, so she went down the steps. She cautiously peered into the commons and then the study hall. Both were completely deserted and only a very dim light illuminated the two rooms.

She went on down to the tunnel complex. Amanda reasoned the not-Lindsey had not worn anything but her school dress, so it was unlikely that she intended to go outside. Though it was early May, nights here were still very chilly. It had to be the tunnels. Soon she stood in the giant hub where the dozen tunnels connected here to the dorms. Twelve directions faced her; most likely, the not-Lindsey had gone down one of these, but which one?

She listened for sounds, but heard none. At last, she remembered her private lessons with Professor Cho Lin on Trackers. Determinedly, she began to put into practice what she had learned; she opened her senses fully and observed.

After a few minutes, she saw something remarkable, a faint trace of magical energy had moved off from about where she was standing toward that direction. Careful not to lose sight of this very faint trace, she followed it. All the lighting was dimmed for the night. With difficulty, she read "To Admin." What was Lindsey doing sneaking off in the middle of the night to go to the Admin Hall, she wondered. Nevertheless, the magical trace continued down the tunnel, so she began moving silently down that tunnel as well. Then, she stopped and cast her Message spell, before continuing down the very dimly illuminated tunnel.

Back in their room, a paper fluttered before Pam's eyes. She read Amanda's message.

Following magical trace down the To Admin tunnel. A.

The paper vanished from sight as soon as she read it. At once, Pam switched over to Spy Cam 1, which she had installed in the main stairwell leading to the various floors of the Admin Hall. When she had returned from Christmas with her new toys, she had gone to view the Trophy Room and installed the device at that time. Why? After Dominus Malefic's break in attempt last year, she was curious to see if he would try again. Pam stared at her monitor.

Only a very dim light outlined the steps; one set went up, and one set went down. At the moment, she saw nothing else picked up by her tiny camera. Still, even if the not-Lindsey had gone this way, there had not been enough time for her to get here, unless she had run all the way, which Pam doubted. The risk of noise was too great. She watched and waited.

Chapter 15—The Restroom

Lindsey, tired and exhausted beyond anything she had every experienced before, had to go to the bathroom. She had drunk too many energizing sodas today. Waving to Amanda, she veered into the women's restroom just before the large dining hall. They were heading to the victory banquet and celebrations. In spite of her aching legs, Lindsey was truly happy, for they had won third place in the Nationals. Now her picture would reside in Bradbury's Trophy Room, alongside those of her father. She was extremely proud of that.

She entered the restroom and came face to face with herself! Staring straight at her was herself, only this herself had a large wizard's staff in her right hand. Lindsey began to let out a scream of shock and total surprise, but the other Lindsey's spell activated. Wham! Lindsey felt like someone had just delivered a knockout punch to her face. She was stunned, unable to move, unable to speak, unable to flee, only to continue to stare at this other herself. Her mind raced to comprehend what was going on, but it felt as though her mind did a complete short circuit. After all, think about it. How would you react, if the next time you entered a bathroom to go pee, you suddenly found yourself staring back at you?

Though unable to move, not even her eyes, Lindsey heard the other Lindsey speak; it was her voice! "She's stunned now, so you can come out, Rubius." Peripheral vision soon revealed the man who had earlier attempted to kill her and Amanda down in the tunnels at Bradbury's. She had only been able to escape certain disaster by accidentally activating a hidden storage room's entrance spell. As the man moved in front of her, she had no doubt that this was the Death Stalker known as Rubius, a ruthless killer, but where was Dominus?

Her other self spoke again, "Rubius, you realize that she must remain alive at all costs. If she dies, I'm a goner."

"I understand, Supreme Visor. I'll guard her with my life. I'll allow no harm to come to her," Rubius replied, grinning evilly at her. Lindsey wanted to scream, to run, to do anything, but she was completely, utterly helpless; she couldn't move a muscle no matter how hard she tried!

"Now then, I will take certain safety precautions for you, Rubius. She is, after all, nearly a second year witch. She can cast simple spells, which might give you trouble. Besides, as soon as the stun wears off, she will likely start screaming her head off in a useless attempt to get help. We certainly can't allow that, not until you have her safely transported to the house, right?"

Rubius grinned. "Very true. I could punch her out with my fist."

"I've thought of that, but we just can't risk doing her harm. If she dies from your fist blow, we lose everything! No, you can't ever hit her. After all, she is a weakling girl. One punch of yours might actually kill her. No, I have better ways to ensure a safe trip and to guarantee that she doesn't try to pull any magic on you. Heaven help us if she should somehow escape."

"I promise you I'll not let her escape!" Rubius pleaded with his master.

"Well, you do have to sleep. With her ability to cast even her primitive spells, she might somehow elude you. We must keep her in the house and keep her alive, until I return with our prize. I have just the spells for this, Rubius. Hold both of her arms out in front of her, yes, like that."

Rubius lifted Lindsey's arms up, while standing at her side. The Lindsey with the staff chanted and spoke "Remove Hands!" A flash of magical energy flew forth from the staff. Searing, excruciating pain shot through Lindsey's arms! Still, she could not move a muscle or even cry out! In slow motion, she watched her new hands separate from her arms, as if instantly surgically removed, and fall to the ground. Blood seeped onto the bathroom floor from the ends of her hands. Pain, pain, unbearable pain shot through her body, but her body could not react physically in any way. She couldn't even pass out!

Once more, the other Lindsey spoke, "Sew Lips Shut!" Again, the staff energized, and suddenly Lindsey saw a large needle with a thick string in it moving to her mouth. She felt the needle plunge into her upper lip, felt the string pulling through the hole it had made, felt it pierce through her lower lip, and the string sliding through that opening. Slowly, her lips were sewn together! At last, she saw the needle separate from the thick string and the two ends of the string magically tied themselves into a knot. She couldn't open her mouth now, even if she were able to move, not without ripping her lips apart. Her body was wracked in pain from her arms; her lips ached, but she could do nothing.

The other one of her said, "Okay, get a hold of her. I will release the Stun. She will probably pass out from the pain, which will give you time to make yourselves invisible and get her out of here. Remember, you can't use your teleport until you are miles from here. It could be traced, if anyone gets wise to what we are doing. Use the norm Chevy that we 'borrowed.' When you get to about five miles outside of Des Moines, then you can safely teleport her to the house. I'm almost certain she'll pass out and not regain consciousness for hours. Just remember to keep her safe and alive until I return to the cabin, no matter how long that may be, Rubius."

"I understand fully," he replied. "I must say, this is an ingenious use of magic on her. I would have never thought of it! Positively brilliant. She'll not be able to cast any spells nor will she be able to scream for help later, though it is unlikely anyone will be anywhere near the house to hear her screams. You've made my task extremely easy, master. I will not fail you."

"I know you won't, Rubius. I have always known that you are the very best of the Death Stalkers. Are you ready to make yourselves invisible? I'll hold the door open for you to leave as I go join the festivities." Rubius nodded and the other Lindsey cancelled her spell.

Suddenly, Lindsey, entrapped in so much horrible, overwhelming pain, felt life returning to her body. She couldn't scream, though she tried; her lips were sewn shut tightly. The hideous pain slowly overwhelmed her as her arms lowered to her sides, throbbing in massive pain. She felt her legs weaken and she blacked out, sliding into the safety of a deep unconsciousness. The last thing she could recall was strong arms catching her body as she fell, along with her other self saying, "Clean." All traces of her bloody hands disappeared from the restroom.

She had some vague recollections of being jostled around, but nothing more, just the blackness of unconsciousness. Lindsey did not hear the car start or the sounds of traffic as it pulled out onto Interstate 80. She didn't feel the car turning off at the exit for Booneville, Iowa. She didn't sense the car pulling over to the side of the deserted blacktop, nor feel the strong arms lifting her from the trunk of the car. She didn't hear him cast his powerful Teleport spell either.

Lindsey finally awoke, consciousness returning, as if from some hideous nightmare. She tried to move and to scream, but the tight string kept her lips shut completely, only an inaudible sound came out into the world. It was daytime, though she had no idea how many days had passed. The ends of her arms ached terribly, and she raised her arms and tried to scream and gasp, but only a muffled noise came out of her sealed lips. Her hands, her new precious hands were completely gone, as if they had never been there! Pink, very tender skin covered the ends of her arms.

Lindsey was sitting on a hard, wooden chair. A rope went around her waist and the back of the chair, holding her securely to the chair. She looked down and saw that only a simple square knot tied the two ends of the rope. If she had hands, she would be free in a moment. Instead, she raised her aching arms to her face, feeling the heavy twine that held her lips tightly shut; she felt the string and began to cry. This was the worst nightmare she had ever had, and she wished that she could just wake up soon! However, it was not a dream. It was excruciatingly real!

Hearing the muffled sobbing, Rubius awoke. After rubbing his face with his hands, he went to the refrigerator and brought out a potion bottle. He inserted a straw into it and carried it over to Lindsey, sitting the bottle on the table before her. "Here, drink this. It will help you heal and make you feel a whole lot better. Ah, pretty thing, can't open your mouth now can you?" He inserted the straw between her lips. It just barely could squeeze through them. "Go ahead. Your body needs this after those spells, miss."

Lindsey had little choice but to comply with him. If there was any chance that he was telling her the truth, that her body needed this potion, then she had to take that gamble. She sipped in the liquid, which tasted more like medicine she had as a child. After drinking it all, Rubius removed the straw and pitched the empty bottle into the corner.

However, Lindsey now had to pee badly. She tried to say, "I have to go pee." Her lips sealed shut only let out a muffled bit of noise. She wiggled and eventually used her arms to point. At last, Rubius understood.

"You have to go pee? Well then, go ahead. Just pee right where you are. No way am I letting you loose!" Embarrassed, Lindsey had no choice but to pee her pants, she felt humiliated on top of everything else. When she finished, Rubius waved his wand and said "Clean." Lindsey was grateful for that tiny kindness.

Soon she felt the effects of the potion. Indeed, her body needed it. She felt the familiar itching of healing at the ends of her arms where her new hands had been. Even the pricks in her lips were itching slightly. She remembered Doctor Caterwall's admonition not to itch and resisted the urge to rub the ends of her hands. Lindsey was miserable.

Now her stomach growled. She had not eaten in . . . well, she didn't know how long. She had been starving when she had gone into the restroom, now she was ravenous. She tried to make signs to Rubius that she was hungry, using her arms, pointing to her stomach and then her mouth. "Hungry?" he asked. She nodded.

"Well, it's liquids only for you. No way am I going to undo that twine sealing your lips. I don't want you screaming for help, cursing me, pleading with me, none of that silliness. It's best that you can't say a darn thing. Hold on while I get you a protein drink." Soon, she was sucking up another bottle. After drinking two, she was finally full.

Rubius went back to his bed and lay down, reading some newspaper. Lindsey began to look at her surroundings. She was inside a one room, wooden cabin, crudely built, perhaps a log cabin. In one corner was a stone fireplace, made from rough creek stones mortared into place. The floor was crudely hewn logs, rotting in places. One rickety door beckoned on the right wall. One small window behind her allowed some sunlight inside. The table in front of her looked like it would collapse any minute, though it did not. Three chairs were in the room surrounding the table; she was tied to one of these. Unlike the table, these two chairs looked solid and sturdy, not easily broken, so unfortunately that idea vanished at once. To her left was the only bed, a crude affair, whose blankets were not fit for human use, though Rubius apparently didn't mind them.

Lindsey concluded this crude cabin could not be within any city or village limits, because it would surely be condemned and torn down at once. Thus, she reasoned they must be out in the country somewhere, but where? How could she, sitting tied to a chair inside here, figure out where she might be? Sounds. She should listen for outside noises!

For a long time, Lindsey listened for any sound. She heard winds rustling through pines! In fact, she now realized she was smelling the scent of a bunch of pine trees. Pines were not often found in quantity within cities, certainly not in the farmlands of Iowa. Could she be back in Colorado? She took a deep breath and it felt normal, not like the denseness she had been breathing in Des Moines. The air was thinner! No fire was going and the temperature was a tad chilly, just like the mornings had been at Bradbury's before she had left for Nationals. She concluded that this shack must be at a high elevation, probably in a pine forest in the Rockies. Yet, that could mean anywhere along the entire range from Canada to Arizona and New Mexico for that matter.

Yet, if the other Lindsey was indeed Dominus Malefic, it made sense that she was now in Colorado, in all likelihood not too far from her school. She suddenly realized that Dominus was once more after the Rod of the Apocalypse! But why kidnap her? *No, I am not kidnaped, he **was** me!* She thought. Now she realized what must be happening at Bradbury's, and she tried once more to scream, but only a muffled noise came out. Rubius took no notice of her.

Lindsey's hope sank into the pits of utter despair. Alone, crippled, she could do absolutely nothing. All her friends would be in the gravest of danger as well. She did the only thing that remained for her; she cried and cried. Rubius commented after a while, "Dominus, this has got to be your greatest use of magic yet! She can't even make a noise to bother me. Easiest assignment you've ever given me!" Lindsey cried even harder.

Twice more, he interrupted her crying to feed her more liquids. Once it was a juice and then more protein drink. She pooped her pants after the second feeding, and Rubius didn't even get up; he waved his wand and said, "Clean." Lindsey felt more miserable than she had ever felt in her whole life. Besides, now her butt began aching, forced to sit on this hard chair all day.

Finally, the sun began to set and Rubius cast a Permanent Light spell on an old, worn out lantern. He set about fixing himself a proper meal. Lindsey's mouth watered, as she smelled his steak cooking on his magical fire. He fed her another protein drink, while he sat across from her eating his thick, juicy steak, teasing her a little.

Finally, he said, "Time to sleep. First, I make sure you can't escape." He waved his wand and began casting spells. "Lock. Lock. Alarm." Lindsey saw a magical energy surround the door and the window, locking them securely. The Alarm spell would wake him if either were opened. Even if she could move, she couldn't leave the cabin.

He threw some filthy blankets on to the floor next to his bed. "You sleep there. I will untie you and tie you to the bed. No funny business, you hear, or I will bash you a good one!" He untied her and she stood up, grateful for the release, her butt ached badly and she rubbed it as best she could with her arms. He forced her to the bedside and then forced her to lie down. He tied one of her legs to the lower bed leg and one of her arms to the upper leg. She could sleep on her side or on her back. Perhaps she could maneuver into other positions, but she certainly couldn't get up, let alone somehow attack him as he slept above her.

Lying there in the dark and miserable, Lindsey

continued to cry until at long last sleep overcame her. She awoke and peed her pants again long before Rubius finally awoke. "God, you stink," he said as he sat up. "Clean." He climbed out of the filthy bed and rubbed his bearded face. At last, he untied Lindsey and walked her over to the table, once more tying her to her seat. He stuffed another protein drink with straw in between her tight lips and went off to make his own breakfast. From behind her, Lindsey smelled fresh bacon and eggs frying, as she sucked on the straw.

This was a new day. The utter hopelessness of yesterday was gone. *Look, I am no worse off than I was before I came to Bradbury's, no hands, but I can cast nearly every one of my spells even as I am now! Dad faced Rubius and Dominus and so can I. I do have one thing going for me. I can cast all my spells just as I am and they don't know that! Somehow, I have to use that to escape. What if he gets the rod? He'll probably bring it here. Here must be near the school. The rod! I can't let him have that rod; it will mean the end of the world! I should bide my time and wait for Dominus to appear, then make my move. Both of them will now think I'm utterly helpless. I bet anything they will mostly ignore me, until they are ready to kill me. That's when I strike. Yes, Lindsey, but strike with what? A single magical missile? Get real! These are powerful wizards who can kill you in a blink! Well, I'll think of something. I just have to. Besides, dad would have thought of something. I know he would. I just know it.*

Rubius inserted a second protein bottle beneath her straw. "Drink up little lady. Don't this bacon and eggs look scrumptious?" he teased her. As she drank, she began mentally arranging the spells that she would cast, beginning with the simple Untie.

"Well, it's 5 a.m. Dominus ought to be back shortly, miss. Not long now." He gave her an evil grin.

Shortly after that, the door burst open and not-Lindsey stepped into the cabin! She looked absolutely terrible. Her hair was mostly burned off; great blisters covered her arms. Her legs were bleeding from several large gashes. Only with great difficulty did she stagger into the cabin. Lindsey noticed, however, that she carried a long, silver rod in her other hand, while in her other, she used the tall staff to hold herself upright.

Chapter 16—A Thief in the Night

"I just know I'm right! It just has to be, there is no other reasonable explanation. It just has to be this one!" Pam whispered to herself as she stared at the Spy Cam 1 images flicking by on her Web Cam screen, ten seconds apart. She had set it to send a new image every ten seconds, a good compromise, she thought. Not too much data not too fast, surely, it would capture the appearance of anyone entering that stairwell. It just had to. Still she needed it to show her Lindsey—it just had to!

She glanced at the time display on the bottom right of her monitor. Five minutes. It had been five long minutes since Amanda's hasty Message had reached her. "Long enough," she whispered to herself. "Any second now. Come on. Show me. It has to be Lindsey. Come on, where are you?"

She saw some movement at the bottom of the Web Cam image. Pam stared. There! The next frame show her the familiar form of her dear friend, Lindsey, rather the not-Lindsey, she reminded herself. The next frame showed her standing still for a brief time. Lindsey held a wizard's staff in her right hand! The next image showed only her back as she went down the stairs. This had to be Dominus again attempting to steal the Rod of the Apocalypse!

Since he or she was now heading down the stairs, Pam sent Amanda a fast message. He or she could not see her getting it. She waved her wand and said, "Message. Amanda Whitewater." Dominus. Down the stairs. P.

While Pam wondered what was the best course of action to take, she continued watching her Spy Cam 1. Yes, there went Amanda down the stairs as well. Pam noted the time difference. She was about three minutes behind him. Pam knew that she needed to sound the alarm. Governor Alister had to be informed immediately. Professor Cho Lin, as well. Suddenly, Pam realized the fatal flaw in her lengthy plans: she'd not uncovered how to notify these people! She had no idea at all where the Governor's residence might be located.

Did Cho Lin actually live somewhere in her hall?

She tried to rouse Kathy, but she was a heavy sleeper. Instead, she sent a message to Emilio, hoping that he had not fallen asleep too. *I have to do something fast. I have to get to Alister somehow; he'll know what to do.* At last, she grabbed her wand and headed down to the commons room. The deserted, dimly lighted room offered no ideas at all. Pam paced back and forth, cursing her stupidity. Lindsey was kidnaped or worse! Amanda was alone hot on the trail of Dominus and might be killed any second now. Pam had no idea how to raise the alarm!

The boy's door burst open and a half-dressed Emilio, wand in hand, appeared, a terrified look on his face. "D-D-Dominus? Y-You sure?"

"Yes, I saw the not-Lindsey going down the Admin Hall stairs to the basement and she was carrying a wizard's staff in her right hand. Lindsey doesn't have one, now does she? It has to be him. We have to sound the alarm. We have to let Alister and Cho Lin know immediately!" Pam burst into tears. "It's all my fault! I forgot to figure out how to alert them!"

"Come on. We better get to Amanda and tell her to retreat," Emilio said, trying to be practical. No sense in putting Amanda into greater danger now. "Maybe we could just Message them," Emilio suggested.

Half-heartedly, Pam did so, sending a rather lengthy message to both Governor Alister and Professor Cho Lin. At least when they awoke in the morning, they would know what horrible things had happened here in the middle of the night. The two rushed down the stairs to the tunnels.

"Blue Light," Emilio commanded. "Follow me, Pam." He began running down the long tunnel towards the Admin Hall. "We have to reach Amanda before she is discovered and killed!"

Amanda quietly stepped down another step towards the basement. She'd already passed the floor, which held the campus computer networks. She remembered Pam telling her about this room. In her moccasins, she moved silently down another step. Amanda kept all her senses alert. She could still sense the magical energy trail being left by the not-Lindsey.

She wondered why she could still sense this however. Was he somehow continually using magic? If so, what could it possibly be?

At last, she reached the bottom floor. Here the stairwell ended. A door, which had a complex locking system, was open; the remains of the lock lay in pieces on the floor. Even more interesting, she saw soot from a fire covering a portion of the floor and wall near the door. Had there been a fire here? As quietly as she could, Amanda opened the door wide enough for her to slip through it.

She found herself in a long hallway. It was pitch black, but now she detected strong signs of a magical energy residue. Her nose definitely smelled smoke. Something had burned in here recently. She listened for any sounds, but heard none. "Blue Light," she whispered, but forgot to wave her wand. Amanda was more than a little surprised to see that her spell actually worked without her wand activating! This was the province and skill of Lindsey, not her. Now she could see black soot markings all down the long hallway. Firetraps. These had to be firetrap spells, designed to defend something. She didn't need to guess what. In this case, it had to be this rod.

Amanda had a choice to make. If she went forward into this hall, would she also trigger these firetraps or were they a one shot kind of thing? While she wanted to go forward, the danger of triggering these traps a second time scared her. Finally, she decided to observe the traps very closely. She spotted the tiny origin points from which the flames had suddenly erupted. Amanda couldn't help hoping that Dominus got badly burned by them.

Then, her geometry lessons kicked in. If the flames shot out from such a tiny hole, they would likely come out cone shaped. Yes, that fit the pattern of soot she saw on the floor. Here, close to the wall, the flames would occupy only a tiny area. There were two possibilities: the traps were done and it was safe for her to pass or the traps would fire once again if she passed them. Only one way to find out, she thought. Carefully, Amanda moved the tiniest portion of her left little finger in front of the hole. Her reasoning was if it fired again, she would only be burned in this tiny spot; perhaps she could tolerate that without getting badly harmed or killed.

Amanda held her breath. Nothing happened. She moved more of her hand past the opening. Still nothing. At last, she rapidly moved into the room past this first blast spot. Nothing happened. Whew. They were not going to fire a second time, she concluded, and began moving on down the hall, now trying to hear what was ahead of her. She heard another loud noise and high-pitched scream, followed by a curse.

Minutes before, Dominus reached this long dark hall. Commanding Light from her staff, she/he saw nothing but a long hallway. Determinedly, she began marching down its length. Suddenly, great cones of flames shot out at her/him from the walls, first from her right, then from her left. Her/his hair caught fire; her dress began smoldering. Pain, burning pain, swamped her senses. Dominus froze in place. "Extinguish!" she commanded and her hair stopped burning. "Show Me Traps!" she commanded and his staff energized once more.

Dominus wanted to get rid of this accursed little girl's body and become himself, but knew that he needed the little girl's body still. She would be the only way that he could leave Bradbury's once he or she, he reminded himself, got the rod. This whole sex thing was becoming a confusing mess for Dominus, and he longed to be done with the masquerade.

"Where's Thaddeous when you need him?" Dominus muttered. Thaddeous was his thief friend, who was an expert at disarming and setting traps, such as these. Thaddeous was still locked up in some prison. Dominus had not figured out yet where he was being held. "Trigger Traps!" she commanded of his staff. Great jets of flames erupted all along the hallway in front of him. Still hurting from the serious burns she'd just received, she moved quickly and safely along the hallway.

The hall turned and she/he stood facing another door, enchanted by magic. A large circular disk was swirling around where the doorknob might be. She saw a pile of glowing numbers moving or hovering around outside the disk. She tried to disarm traps once more, but nothing happened. She grimaced and set to work figuring out how to open this door. Frustrated, she energized her staff once more, "Open Door." Usually, this spell opened all doors, even hidden or locked doors. Nothing happened. "Darn you, Alister!"

Next, she activated her staff once more, "Disintegrate Door!" This most powerful spell ought to disintegrate anything, she/he thought. Dominus had used this spell to kill many people in the past, to open bank vaults, even end a car chase by eliminating the car following his. This time, the spell had an effect, only it was not what he/she expected.

A jet of sulfuric acid sprayed out of the revolving disk, covering her head and face. The burning pain nearly overwhelmed her. "Clean!" Dominus screamed. The acid vanished, but great burn spots covered her face and arms. She staggered from the pain. Slowly because of the intense pain in her hands, she withdrew a potion bottle from under her skirt. Shaking from the pain, she managed to remove the cork stopper. She drank it as fast as she could. Instantly, she felt relief from the pain, as the healing drought began to work its magic on her greatly injured body.

Now she examined the numbers. Obviously, she would have to work out this puzzle to get past this door. "I'm smarter than you, you old fool," her high-pitched soprano voice whispered. "God, I hate this voice," she/he added. Suddenly, she had it. She picked up the number 5 and placed it into the golden, swirling disk. It appended itself to the disk and the entire magic vanished, leaving a simple doorknob in its place. "You stupid old fool!" her high-pitched voice said. She opened the door and entered another room.

"Ah hide and seek time," her high-pitched voice said as she looked around the room. The twenty by twenty foot room contained a dozen boxes and chests. There were no other doors visible. "Enie meanie minie moe, catch a fairy by her toe. Games, Alister, games. One day, I will teach you another game: How to Die in One Easy Lesson. God, I hate this horrid voice! This accursed dress is letting my legs get unnecessarily damaged."

He began looking at the boxes and chests. Perhaps the prize was hidden in one of these. Again, he wished that he had

Thaddeous here to deal with these. Certainly, eleven of them would hold nothing but a dangerous trap, maybe even the one with the rod was booby trapped as well. Try as he might, he saw no way to ascertain in which box or chest the rod might lie. He failed to realize that the boxes and chests formed a pentagram. In fact, they represented the buildings that formed the outer pentagram of Bradbury's! The chest in front of him represented the Infirmary.

Staff at the ready, she commanded, "Open Box." Suddenly, a huge wall of water came gushing out of the box. In seconds, the entire room would be filled from floor to ceiling, drowning all occupants! "Dispel Magic!" her high-pitched voice called out, too late as the water was now up to her chin, generating intense pain as it came in contact with her raw fire and acid wounds. However, the water did vanish. She looked in the chest. It was empty.

Dominus was methodical to a fault. Indeed, this was the trait that Sam Rabnor had used to capture him so long ago, although Dominus had never realized this. He moved straight counterclockwise to the next one, which represented the Hall of Necromancy. Again, her high-pitched voice called out, "Open Box." Rotting fungus sprang out and turned into fifty rotting zombies—dead bodies now animated fighting machines, without any minds of their own. The room was too small to launch a ball of fire to kill all them in one shot. He could use his powerful Disintegrate spell, but he could not cast fifty of them. Instead, he began shooting volleys of Magical Missiles. These were cheap spells, and he could cast them by the cartload. However, the zombies began hitting him back, scratching and clawing into her flesh. Particularly vulnerable were her exposed legs. She again cursed the dress she was forced to wear. Three minutes later, the zombies littered the floor. Bleeding profusely from so many wounds, she had to reach under her dress for yet another potion bottle, guzzling its contents as rapidly as possible.

Methodically, Dominus continued her counterclockwise movement, bringing her to the next one, representing the Hall of Divination. She knocked this one open, prepared for another nasty trap. Nothing happened as the lid opened.

Dominus looked into the box; it was completely empty! She cast a spell, looking for any magic within the box. Nothing. She tapped around inside the box with her staff, looking for secret compartments, hidden dividers, anything, but the box was completely empty. At last satisfied, Dominus moved on to the next one, representing the Hall of Abjuration.

Ah, but the box that she judged empty was not empty! The instant she opened it, the spell triggered, though Dominus did not notice it. Time within the room slowed down to a snail's pace. Since nothing else in the room was moving except Dominus, she was not soon aware of this time effect. Seeing her body move on to the next box seemed normal. To someone on the outside world, an hour passed as her body moved from the empty box to the next one!

"What are we going to do?" whispered Pam to Emilio. The two had finally reached the stairs leading into the basement of the Admin Hall. Somewhere down there was Amanda and Dominus, but where?

"Let's go down and warn Amanda. She comes first," Emilio said, his heart pounding. At last, he was not bored. He couldn't tell if he was merely scared or if he was truly excited about this dangerous action. "Come on." He took Pam's shaking hand and pulled her on down the steps, slowly. Pam's heart raced. What was she thinking, going straight into mortal danger? She was a Sleuth. She used her skills to find out things, not put her very life in the gravest of danger. Pam was no hero, not a fighter. Indeed, she felt anything but brave just now, trying hard to keep her steadily rising panic under control. Only the solid grip of Emilio on her hand kept her from fleeing back up the steps.

They passed through the fire-blackened door, which gave Pam something concrete to analyze as they stared into the long, dark hallway. Emilio cast his Blue Light and saw all the fire cones that had blackened the hallway ahead of them. Now Pam, too, saw them.

"Come on. Amanda must be up ahead of us," Emilio whispered.

"Okay, her body is not dead lying on the floor, so these

must have been triggered by the not-Lindsey," Pam concluded, thankful to have something on which her mind could focus, another puzzle, which was very short lived. Two steps into the room, and her panic began to grow once more. Slowly, the pair crept down the fire-blackened hall.

As they reached the bend, both nearly screamed! Someone was backing around the corner two feet in front of them! If Pam's legs would have cooperated, she would have run for her life, but they froze! Emilio whispered, "Amanda?" The backside of the person began turning around.

Relief filled three faces as Amanda saw that the noise she heard was Emilio and Pam. "I thought you might be Rubius or something. Gosh! You scared me! She's inside the room just down there," Amanda whispered.

The three looked down the twenty-foot long side hall and stared at a blank wall. "What room?" asked Pam, her nerves finally calming. Here was another mystery, no door, no room.

"It was there. She went through a funny, magical door, but she got badly hurt. I heard her screams. After she went in there, the door—it just vanished!" Amanda exclaimed wide-eyed. She added, "But every now and then, I hear her scream again. I think that more bad things are happening inside, but I can't and don't want to go in there. What are you two doing here?"

Pam flushed, "We came to warn you! That's Dominus in there! Somehow, he is our not-Lindsey. Does he still look like Lindsey?"

"I figured that much out myself. Yes, the last time I saw her, she was still she. I mean he was still she, er, does this make any sense?" Amanda tried to explain her confusion.

"We have to warn Alister!" Pam said one more time. "I sent him and Professor Cho Lin a Message, but they probably will not see it until they wake up in the morning."

"He'll be gone with the rod before then," Amanda pleaded.

"Okay, I will get them," Emilio said determinedly.

"How?" chorused both girls. He grinned, pointed to the red fire alarm on the side wall. He pulled the switch down.

Suddenly, sirens began wailing throughout the building. Red lights began flashing as well. Above them, they heard strange sliding noises coming from the room with all the school's computers.

Grinning at his extremely simple, but elegant solution to alerting Governor Alister, Pam suggested, "That will be the Fire Prevention System kicking into action to protect our Bradbury Computer Network. It seals off the room and all the oxygen is being removed. I'm glad the rod was not hidden in there!"

"I wonder if she can hear all this noise inside the room," Amanda said, and continued staring intently at the blank wall, which had earlier been a wall.

Suddenly, a magical door opened and Governor Alister, wearing his pajamas stepped out into the room, his wand at the ready. "What in the blazes are you three up to in the middle of the night? What. . . Dominus is here! Kids, get behind me now!" He stepped out in front of them, moving closer to the door, which wasn't there. Another magical door appeared and Cho Lin appeared, wrapped in a silken nightgown. She had a staff in her hand.

"Pam is right. It's Dominus," Alister said grimly.

Cho Lin's face twitched nervously. Alister added, "We have some time. The dumb fool has triggered the Hall of Divination trap; that will slow him down. Now then, would one of you like to explain what you three are doing down here?"

"It's the not-Lindsey who is in there," Amanda gushed out, "I followed her magical spell trail down the tunnels to here. She's taken a whole lot of, well I don't know exactly, but she must be very badly injured; she screamed so terribly so many times now. We have to find the real Lindsey." Amanda suddenly realized that both Alister and Cho Lin were looking at her and not understanding her at all. "Pam!" she pleaded.

Pam straightened up and began to explain, "Yes, it began when we noticed that the not-Lindsey who came back from the Nationals was not really Lindsey. Amanda, Emilio, and I noticed that she was acting strangely, saying things that our Lindsey would never say. Then, I tricked her, asking about what I gave her for Christmas. She got it wrong. So right then, I knew this Lindsey was not our Lindsey, and that's when we started calling her not-Lindsey. Are you with me so far? It gets more confusing," Pam admitted.

"So not-Lindsey is not Lindsey?" Cho Lin asked, trying to get it straight.

"Yes, so then we started spying on her. She said she was going to go to bed early instead of doing our homework. Only she pretended to be asleep. I went to the Library. Sir, I believe that the not-Lindsey has used a Morph Self into Another to become a duplicate of Lindsey."

"Ah, I begin to see," Governor Alister interrupted. "As a duplicate Lindsey in every way, she would be allowed to enter the school. Clever, I had not thought of that deception. Please continue, Pam," he said kindly.

"Well, yes. This means that the real Lindsey, our Lindsey, is being held prisoner somewhere, kidnaped. She has to be alive or the not-Lindsey's spell would be broken. So we all are following the not-Lindsey hoping she will lead us to the real Lindsey. When we went to bed, the not-Lindsey snuck out of our room. My Alarm spell woke me, and I watched not-Lindsey become invisible, something our Lindsey can't do, you see. Amanda decided to follow the not-Lindsey to see what she was going to do and maybe lead us to the real Lindsey, before it's too late. Then, I saw the not-Lindsey going down the Admin Hall stairs to the basement. That's when I knew that the not-Lindsey must really be Dominus, trying to steal the rod once more. I warned Amanda that was who she was trailing, and Emilio and I sent you two a message. The only flaw in my plan was that I forgot that I didn't know how to find either of you—I mean in the middle of the night. Emilio pulled the fire alarm and that has worked. There, did I leave anything out?" Pam finally finished.

Just then, three other professors raced into the fire-blackened hall, faces full of fear and concern. The soothing voice of Alister calmly said, "False alarm on the fire. Dominus is in the secret room, attempting to steal the rod. Get the students safely locked down. Cho Lin, alert the Department of Defense at once. We still have time."

"But what about the real Lindsey?" Pam pleaded. "We've got to find her."

"I think it best if you three now return to your rooms," Governor Alister replied. They had no choice but to leave. "We must keep Dominus from obtaining the artifact at all costs, Cho Lin. How soon will help arrive?"

"Not for some time—most are in bed and have to prepare," she replied, more than a little concerned.

Climbing the stairs, Amanda pouted, "I don't think that they have any intention of rescuing our Lindsey. All they care about is that rod thing. I can't just abandon Lindsey to these vile men. We have to do something."

"I've an idea," Pam said, although her idea was only just then coming to her. She snatched up her Spy Cam 1 from its position overlooking the stairwell going downwards. "One of two things is going to happen, well maybe three things. One, not-Lindsey is going to somehow escape them and flee. Two, they are going to capture the not-Lindsey; if so, maybe they can find out where our Lindsey is located and rescue her. Three, the not-Lindsey is going to be killed."

"If she's killed, what will happen to our Lindsey?" Amanda asked, becoming very worried indeed. She had illusionary imaginings of her dear friend being brutally murdered.

"Dunno," Pam relied honestly. She had not yet given this third possibility any thought. Hastily she continued. "If the not-Lindsey escapes. . ."

"Then I am going to follow him," Amanda interrupted her. "I have been able to follow her magic energy trail so far."

"Right, she's got to leave via the main gate into the parking lot. I'm going to setup my Spy Cam 1 so that we can monitor the gate," Pam replied, outlining the part of her plan that she had just figured out. "You find a safe place to hide, and I'll Message you if we see her leaving via the gate."

"Super!" Amanda replied, giving no thought at all to breaking school rules about either being out of the dorms after ten at night or even leaving the campus illegally. Her friend's life was at stake. "I'll follow her if she leaves through the gate."

Emilio added, "If that happens, I'm going to rouse Jim

and Tom. They can set out after you, following your trail. I know that they will want to help their little sister." She smiled at his thoughtfulness.

"If they capture him, I guess we can't do anything but wait it out," Pam added. "On the other hand, if they kill him, we've got to figure out another plan and super-fast! Our Lindsey might not have much time left before they, well you know what I mean." She was loathed to say murdered. "So while you are hiding, we two will return to the dorms like he asked; only Emilio and I will begin to formulate a plan if the worst happens and the not-Lindsey is killed."

By now, they were at the ground level. They exited the Admin Hall and while Amanda and Emilio kept watch, Pam repositioned her Spy Cam 1. "Okay, battle stations everyone. I'll make a pillow dummy up for you Amanda, in case they come into the room and do a head count. Message me if you see anything."

Like a dark shadow in the dead of night, silent Amanda moved across the grounds, looking for the perfect place to hide and still be able to see the main gates, which were securely fastened. She found a tree and crouched in its shadow. Now she could only wait.

Pam and Emilio raced back to the dorms, then up separate stairs to their rooms. At once, Pam booted her laptop and began observing the cam screen. She had a good view of the main gate. She sat back and began to tackle the third eventuality, not-Lindsey being killed. How could they possibly find the real Lindsey, let alone in time to keep her from being murdered?

Not-Lindsey began to suspect something was terribly wrong. She had moved on methodically to the next chest, corresponding to the Hall of Abjuration. However, it seemed to her that she had just thought an enormous number of thoughts in the short space of time that it had taken her to walk over to this chest. In a flash, Dominus knew something was indeed wrong. She decided to touch the chest and see how many thoughts she could think during that split second. "Time flow has been altered! Magic Dispel!" A flash of magical energies came from the staff and once again, Dominus conducted her experiment. Only a single thought occurred before her badly burned hand touched the chest. Relieved, she began to open this next chest.

As the chest opened, magical energies once again ignited. Braced for the worst, she saw nothing at all happening, no balls of fire, no clouds of noxious gas, nothing. Having become alerted to "nothing happening" with the time slow down magic, Dominus knew something had happened and quickly tried to work out just what. Soon, she found the problem. As she tried to approach the next chest in the line, her body was thrown back from it. She tried to approach the other boxes and chests, all with the same effect; her pain-wracked body was thrown back away from the boxes. "Magic Dispel," she commanded and moved to the next box, that of the Hall of Charm and Evocation.

When she opened this box, a great ball of fire exploded, filling the entire room. The noise was even heard outside by Alister, who knew precisely which box had been opened. These were his traps, after all. Not-Lindsey smiled; she was prepared this time. Her counter-spell worked to perfection, and the inferno did not harm her in any way. She ignored the flames, which quickly died, and went to the next chest, that of the Hall of Conjuration and Summoning.

As she opened it, out flew an enormous creature, some kind of giant cat with great fangs. The cat leaped upon Lindsey and sank its fangs deep into her chest. For a minute, the staff shot a great number of spells onto the cat, which proved more difficult to slay than she had guessed. As its body finally lay dead before her feet, she watched more magic flash, and it disappeared. Her deep wounds, however, did not. Hastily and in great pain, blood seeping out of the deep tears, she gulped down the last of her healing potions. Presently, the gashes began to heal, and she was no longer in danger of bleeding to death. However, she still coughed up a considerable volume of blood.

Dominus moved on to the next one, the Hall of Math. When she opened it, a head appeared. "Answer my question please. What is the formula to find the volume of a sphere?"

"I don't know!" the high-pitched voice of Lindsey painfully answered. Her chest throbbed relentlessly; she could barely think properly.

"Wrong," the head replied, and a bolt of lightning shot from its eyes. Again, the protection spell she had on her body completely repelled its effects. Longing eyes peered into the empty box. Leaning on her staff, Lindsey hobbled over to the next box, that of the Hall of Alteration. This time when she tried to open the box, the magical spell attempted to turn her into a frog! Because of her protective spells, this also failed, and she continued to hobble to the next chest, that of the Hall of Illusions.

Opening that chest caused a giant demon to appear, ten feet tall with huge fists. Before she could react, the demon swung its fist, smashing her in the side of her face. The force of the blow sent her flying across the small room, hitting hard against the far wall. Dazed, one eye out of its socket, and her jaw cracked, she stood and commanded, "Magic Dispel." The demon disappeared, and her eye was in fact not out of its socket, her jaw was not in fact broken. However, the pain of the blow was there; the left side of her face began swelling rapidly.

She moved over to the next box. Only three remained. She knew she was about to claim her long sought victory! However, she cast several more defensive spells before opening this one, the Hall the Humanities. A head appeared and asked, "Who wrote Moby Dick?"

Lindsey's high-pitched voice now sounded garbled because of the rapid swelling of her left cheek. "Who cares?"

"Wrong." Immediately, a giant whale appeared overhead and began falling down. "Disintegrate!" Lindsey screamed. The whale disappeared one half inch from her head. She wiped her badly burned forehead with an equally burned left arm; both hurt badly when they touched each other. That had not been a good idea; she let the sweat trickle down her head after that. Lindsey moved to the next one, Hall of Invocation and Evocation.

After forcing it open, a giant cloud of a greenish poisonous gas quickly filled the room. Choking and coughing,

Lindsey commanded, "Vanish!" The gas disappeared, but her lungs now ached and throbbed. Breathing was terribly painful for her. She could barely stand, let alone walk. Indeed, not-Lindsey was very close to death and needed healing very soon now.

Yet, glee filled her eyes and mind. One box remained; this had to contain the ancient relic that Dominus had so long sought. With it, she would rule the world! "Open," her voice barely able to speak now, commanded. The lid flew open, and there lay the silver rod, about a foot in length; the prize of prizes was now hers!

Dominus lowered her left arm and grasped the cool silver rod, metal, she thought. "Now to get out of here," she was barely able to whisper. The door, which had vanished the instant she had entered this room, now reappeared. Limping badly, her right arm using the staff to support her pain-ravaged body, her left clinging tightly to the rod, Lindsey opened the door and walked out.

"You look pretty bad off, Dominus," the soft voice of Alister spoke. He was waiting at the corner of the two halls, some twenty feet in front of not-Lindsey. "I'll take that rod, if you don't mind. You may also surrender your Staff of Power."

Leering in utter contempt and disgust at Alister, the barely alive body of Lindsey spoke, "I wish you were stunned!" Wham! Evidently, Alister had misjudged Dominus. One of Dominus' most powerful spells was granted. Alister's body lay smashed in a heap on the floor in front of her. "Old fool!" the soprano voice added. "Door to Gates" came next, followed by the appearance of a magical door.

At that instant, the face of Professor Cho Lin appeared around the corner. She waved her wand and commanded, "Magic Dispel!" However, she was a fraction of a second too late. Dominus had already stepped through the door and was gone. Cho Lin rushed to Alister's crumpled form.

Sitting in her room staring at her monitor, Pam nearly fell asleep! It was dawn now; the sun had already risen, ruddy red on the horizon. Suddenly, a door appeared out of nowhere, and the badly wounded not-Lindsey stepped out, standing before the entrance gate! So startled was Pam that she just gaped at the image on her screen.

"Fist: Break Gates," Lindsey commanded. A giant fist three feet across appeared and began pounding hard against the wooden gates that led to the parking lot, just outside the walls of Bradbury's. Soon, the gates splintered into fragments. Leaning heavily on her staff and still clutching her prize, Lindsey stepped out into the parking lot and freedom. A shadow darted across the lawn, stopping at the gate, watching her. She didn't see the form, however.

"Oor ou abin," her voice began to fail her completely. Her staff failed to activate. She was getting weaker. Worse, she saw the telltale signs of a number of people beginning to appear, using teleport spells. "Door to Cabin," she mustered all her strength to utter this one last command. The door appeared, and she stepped through it and vanished from the parking lot.

Amanda raced to where she had last seen not-Lindsey, as she had stepped through the door. Amanda concentrated on the tiny, nearly invisible magical energy trace left by the spell. Fortunately, this particular spell did leave a trail for her to follow. It led off up the side of the mountain that lay behind the school, up and to her left. Amanda began to run after her, following that almost invisible trace of magic, a trace that nearly none could see.

Seeing Amanda appear and then take off in a run startled Pam back to her senses. She sent a message to Emilio, Jim, and Tom, though she didn't know if they could find a way to go after Amanda. "What's happening? I fell asleep," the sleepy voice of Kathy startled Pam. From the look on Pam's face, Kathy knew that she had missed something. Pam began talking ninety miles an hour.

Ten Department of Defense wizards and witches suddenly appeared at various points around the parking lot. "Look at their gate! I think we are too late yet again, Fred," one tall, thin man, wearing a dark tweed suit said.

"Dunno, look there. Some girl is running up the mountainside, Fred. Guess we should check with Alister and get the full story. Come on, everyone; the Admin Hall is this way," Gary replied. He was a well-built, muscled young man, perfectly suited to the job of providing defense, both norm and magical.

In the basement hallway, Cho Lin worriedly examined Governor Alister for serious harm. He was not bleeding, just stunned, she concluded. "Magic Dispel," she commanded once, then twice, then thrice. At last, Alister groaned and moved. "Alister, are you all right? You had me worried for a second! Let me help you to your feet. He got away. Dominus took the rod. I was a hair too slow in stopping him."

"Not a problem, Cho Lin. So far, it is all going as planned." She looked at him, and her mouth fell open; a strange noise emitted from deep within her throat.

She swallowed and tried again, "Plan? What plan?"

"Yes, my traps very nearly did him in, Cho Lin. Actually, they would have killed him, had I not intervened and greatly lessened the effects of that last trap on his behalf."

"You did what? You let him escape with the Rod of the Apocalypse? Alister, you didn't?" She was terrified of what he had done.

"I had to for the safety of our student, Lindsey. You see, Professor, he still had that one spell remaining, uncast as yet, the one spell which could have made all the difference in the world to him and to us. I had to get him to use it on me. I was counting on his thoroughness and methodical nature, that and his ego. He could not kill me outright, for that would spoil his seeming victory over me. You see, he wanted the whole world to see me in utter disgrace. The rod was in my safekeeping, and he stole it right out from under me. Yes, I knew that he could not kill me today."

"But now he has the rod, Alister! He'll unleash a reign of terror this world has never seen!"

"Oh he may well unleash a reign of terror, Professor. I have no doubt about that, only the story of the rod is not yet finished. Another has a role to play before it is finished. Come; help me get up the steps and into some fresh air. It smells of sulfur down here." She allowed him to lean on her. His legs were still a bit weak from the stun spell.

They had no more than gotten to the stairs, when the ten Department of Defense, six men and four women, came rushing down the stairs, two at a time. "Alister, we got your message. Looks like we are too late yet again. Are you injured? Did he?"

"Yes, he did take the rod with him. Yes, he did escape, but he is very near death as we speak, very weak, in great pain, likely incapable of casting much of anything. Prime time to capture him, wouldn't you say?"

"Yes, but where is he?" asked Gary. "We saw a young woman racing up the mountain side as we arrived. Is she connected to all this?"

"Interesting, interesting indeed. Well, then, that makes my job even easier. I'll be an old buzzard!" Suddenly, an old buzzard sat at the side of Cho Lin. He quickly resumed his normal form, "That was a joke, by the way." No one was laughing, however.

"Okay, you would do well to go and follow that young lady. Amanda Whitewater is her name. She is hell bent on rescuing her friend Lindsey. You see, Dominus kidnaped one of our students when she was at the Nationals in Des Moines. He morphed into her and assumed her identity to gain access to our campus. As you know, the young woman he kidnaped must remain alive for his spell to continue to operate. Hence, Miss Lindsey Barron is still alive. I believe that Amanda will be able to lead you to where they are. I suggest you be quick about it. Dominus will not linger around here for long."

"Great tip! Great work, Alister. Men, women, after that student!" They raced up the steps two at a time. To follow her, some chose to use a Fly spell, while others used magical doors, taking giant steps at one time. None ran on foot, however.

"Cho Lin, I need to be in my study and alone. Will you be so kind as to stand guard outside my door? Let no one interrupt me. This is very critical. Lindsey's life may well hinge on my work now." While she had no idea of his plan, she did as he asked, casting a door to his study spell and stepping him through it into his study.

"Tea Please," he commanded and a tray with a steaming pot of tea and two cups appeared on his desk. He poured Cho Lin a cup, "Here, this will help warm you up. Remember, no one, not until I come out." She nodded and left by the main door. There she stood vigilantly on guard, wondering what the old man was up to anyway. She had much to ponder. He'd told her far more than he ever had in the past!

Doggedly, Amanda kept on the trail of that faint energy line. After three miles of heavy running, all uphill, she was becoming winded. Yet, ahead cradled against the side of the mountain, nearly hidden from view in a patch of pine trees, was a beat up, rundown log cabin, probably one room, she estimated from its small size—a line shack or emergency shelter perhaps. She headed straight for it.

When she was within a hundred feet of the cabin, she heard an awful racket. Smoke billowed from the broken window; fog drifted out of the front door; men were screaming. Just as she was about to rush in there, the Department of Defense wizards and witches caught up to her.

"Amanda Whitewater?" Gary asked. Out of breath from her long sprint up the mountain, she just nodded. "Okay, you stay back here. We'll take it from here." She nodded again and watched as Gary ordered his forces to surround the rickety cabin. Then, they began to move in on the building.

Chapter 17—Lessons in Confusion

"Well, it's 5 a.m. Dominus ought to be back shortly, miss. Not long now." Rubius gave her an evil grin.

Shortly after that, the door burst open, and Lindsey stepped into the cabin! She/he looked absolutely terrible. Her hair was mostly burned off; great blisters covered her arms. Her legs were bleeding from several large gashes. Her chest showed huge bite marks, but what could have made such a bite, she had no idea at all, except that it must have been absolutely huge! Only with great difficulty did the wounded girl stagger into the cabin. Lindsey noticed, however, that she carried a long, silver rod in her left hand, while she used a tall wooden staff to hold herself upright and keep from collapsing.

"It's done. There it is!" Lindsey heard her own voice weakly proclaim victory. This was incredibly unnerving for Lindsey to be sitting there staring at herself on the other side of the table! She reminded herself that this must be Dominus.

"Cancel!" her/his voice said, and Lindsey watched as the short girl body suddenly began transforming back into the tall, thin man in the photographs, Dominus Malefic. His true appearance was also terrible. None of the wounds and burns disappeared. They were real! He was in great pain, barely able to stand. Very little of his hair remained; great blisters disfigured his face and arms. Blood covered what little remained of his filthy robes.

"Fabulous, Master. Congratulations are in order!" Rubius ecstatically exclaimed, eyeing the Rod of the Apocalypse. Now they would control the entire world, bring it unto their mercy!

Dominus looked at Lindsey tied by the waist securely to the chair, her handless arms lying uselessly in her lap, her mouth still sewn shut tightly. He grinned, "I see you didn't have any trouble with her." He laid the rod onto the table and leaned on it for support as his legs began to give way. "Healing potion, fast, Rubius!"

Rubius dashed off to find their last bottle of their stolen

healing potions. Lindsey saw her chance. She would only have this one chance, of that she was certain. Soon they would be leaving and probably just kill her or perhaps leave her to die here alone. No one knew where she was, not even her for that matter. Rescue was certainly not coming. However, seeing the rod on the table, she altered her carefully planned sequence of spells. She thought "Identify Rod." Lindsey blocked out all other thoughts and looked intently at the rod.

She picked up the phrase, "First Horseman" emanating from the rod. Satisfied of its authenticity, she silently began her rehearsed sequence of spells, beginning with Untie Me. Next, came Fog followed by Servant: Bring Rod to Me. She saw an invisible magical shape move to the rod. It brought it to her. Now she began her litany of spells. One after the other, she cast all her helpful spells, though using many in the reverse, such as Dirty instead of Clean. Rubius was Chilled. Dominus' forehead was Polished. Salt and spices flittered down upon both men's heads, coming out of the rolling fog. A magical needle was busily sewing away at the tattered remains of Dominus' clothes, while at the same time parts of it were Unraveling. Rubius' teacup Spilled over his face and then Shattered on the floor, only to Mend itself.

The rope, which had tied her up, Changed into a model of a rattlesnake, lying near the feet of Dominus, who couldn't see it because of the fog. He cancelled the fog spell, so Lindsey cast it once more. A loud Belch came from the right of Rubius, who turned to see who was there, taking him by surprise. Near the door, a Giggle sounded, followed by a Sneeze. Rubius' left arm suddenly twitched, and he very nearly dropped the potion bottle. Now Bees and Bugs began swarming at the feet of both men, crawling up their legs. The fireplace Burst into flames. Footsteps sounded as though someone was coming in the door. A Whistle followed, perhaps a signal to others outside. A large pile of Grease appeared on the floor, as Rubius brought the much needed healing potion to his master. He slipped, but held onto the bottle, cursing all the while.

A Magical Missile hit him in his forehead as he handed the potion to Dominus. Both men cursed loudly. The fog was canceled by Rubius, and both men stared at Lindsey, who simply was looking innocently back at them. Obviously, she could not be causing this confusion, for she was utterly helpless. Fog, she commanded and then Horse. Yes, a horse appeared in the doorway, adding to the confusion. Now all the sounds became greatly magnified, echoing loudly in the cabin. Lights began to Dance around the fog, the fireplace grew twice its normal size; its crackling sound of burning greatly enhanced, sounding like a roaring inferno.

Holding the rod tightly in her arms, she Jumped backwards across the room. Light suddenly shown from the bed where Rubius had been sleeping. An illusion of three rattlesnakes coiled to strike, complete with tails rattling, appeared beneath the two men's feet. All the spiders in the room fell asleep, but their slumber went totally unnoticed. She cast three more Fogs, before a voice in her head said do it now.

Holding the rod, she commanded by thought, "First Horseman." Magical energies, which had been shooting right and left from the ends of her arms, now hit the rod in her arms. Lindsey was not prepared for the activation, however. Suddenly out of nowhere, a black robed man upon a black horse appeared in the tiny cabin, crushing the table as it appeared.

Lindsey couldn't see the actual face of this man, hidden within the dark folds of its hooded cloak. Eyes like lanterns shown out, piercing into hers. She stood there transfixed, while in the background the two wizards were calling out a litany of "Magic Dispel!"

A voice in her head said, "Give the rod to the horseman now!" Without arms, she found this difficult, but leaned forward with the rod, trying vainly to hand it to him. At last, the black gloved hand reached out to her and touched the rod. A disembodied voice came from somewhere within the folds of the cloak hiding its head.

"You wish to give me the rod?" it said clearly and distinctly.

"No!" screamed Dominus, who finally had all of Lindsey's spells eliminated and saw the First Horseman standing there, its hands upon his prize, his rod. "No! No! No!" he screamed. Rubius stared in utter shock and disbelief.

Lindsey, lips sewn shut could not speak, but nodded yes instead. "Very well. It is done!" the hollow, deep bass voice replied.

"No! No! No!" screamed Dominus, as he lunged to grab the rod from the First Horseman.

A giant flash of magical energies replaced the First Horseman, who vanished as suddenly as it came. The Rod of the Apocalypse vanished from sight as well. The concussion of the explosion sent Lindsey flying backwards, crashing into the back wall. Gentle Fall kept her from serious injury, however.

Dominus was at the center of the magical explosion. He too was sent flying, up to the ceiling in his case, and quickly came crashing down, unable to manage even a simple first year's spell at this point. "Potion, quick!" he called out to a still shocked Rubius, who finally had a command that he could obey. He jumped to his Master's side and poured the precious liquid into the throat of Dominus, who was very nearly dead. At the last instant, his body finally responded to the healing draught, and he could stand on his own now.

He turned to see where Lindsey had gone, finding her in a heap in the distant corner. Just at that instant, both men heard many feet running up towards the cabin, coming from all sides. "Of all the things to go wrong!" Dominus exclaimed. "Get us out of here fast, Rubius! Now man! Now!"

Rubius held on to the still badly wounded, but alive Dominus, and waved his wand. "Teleport. . ." he commanded. Lindsey couldn't hear where the destination was to be, however, and wondered if that was part of this powerful spell—not hearing where they were going.

The door, nearly off its hinges from Lindsey's many spells, crashed open and fell onto the floor, which now had many holes in it, also from her spells. Men wearing business suits rushed inside and began looking round. Then, Lindsey saw the most wonderful sight she could imagine! Amanda quietly stuck her head in as well, looking for her.

Unable to speak, Lindsey made muffled voices, which got their attention. Strong hands lifted her up and helped her to sit down. Amanda hugged her and cried, as she saw Lindsey was once more handless and her mouth was sewn shut. "Do something for her, please, I beg you!"

"In due time, she is otherwise uninjured. We must see if there is any chance of capturing Dominus first," Gary replied, while the others were casting various spells neither girl had ever heard before. Amanda just continued to hold on to Lindsey as if she were her baby.

Shortly, in a fit of anger, Gary smashed his fist into one of the remaining chairs, breaking its seat in half. The two halves of the chair fell in opposite directions. "We missed getting them by three seconds! Three lousy seconds! Just three miserable seconds and we would have had him!"

One of the witches, named Wanda, said, "Gary, the girl." She nodded towards Lindsey. He calmed down. His anger vented. Gary walked over to her and said, "Lindsey Barron? Just nod if you are her." Lindsey nodded.

"I know that you want us to free your lips, but we had best leave that to more competent wizards. If we just cut that thread as Amanda is considering (Amanda turned beet red and replaced her knife back into her leg sheath), worse damage might occur. Inside the thread may well be poison, which would then kill you. Perhaps cutting the thread will cause an explosion blowing your face off. We can't take that chance out here in the middle of nowhere. I'm going to take you back to Governor Alister and your Infirmary. We'll let the good doctor work his magic. Is that acceptable to you, Lindsey? Just nod if it is." She nodded.

"Good brave girl," Wanda added. "Say, was that you causing all that confusion?" Lindsey nodded. Wanda raised her eyebrows. Gary, who had been doing something else, stopped and stared at her. Wanda asked kindly, "Did Dominus leave with the Rod of the Apocalypse?" Lindsey shook her head violently no!

Hastily, all began looking around the room for the precious rod. Lindsey wanted to tell them it had simply vanished, but could only mumble through her lips. Amanda suddenly was inspired, "Message me, Lindsey." Shortly a paper appeared in front of her eyes. Amanda read the message aloud.

I summoned the First Horseman and gave him the rod. He

and the rod just vanished. Dominus does not have it. L.

Everyone in the defense group looked utterly stunned! Finally, Wanda found her voice, "Leave it to a helpless first year to do what piles of us adults never could do! Lindsey, by giving the rod back to the horseman, you managed to rid our world of this hideous relic from the ancient past. Well done, my dear. Many, many adults knew that had to be done, but not one of them could bring themselves actually to do it." Wanda leaned over and kissed Lindsey's forehead.

Wanda then said, "Gary. Get with it. She needs to get to the Infirmary pronto!"

"Yes, Wanda. Okay, Wanda. Anything you say, Wanda," he teased her, and she poked him in his rear.

Since Amanda was not about to let go of Lindsey, Gary put his arm on both girls' shoulders and said, "Teleport: Bradbury's School of Magic, parking lot." Magical energy flashed, and the three were standing in the parking lot.

"This way ladies," Gary said, walking the girls through the smashed remains of the main gates. Lindsey stared at the sight, however, wondering what on earth had happened to them. As they walked along the sidewalk towards the Infirmary, a door appeared and out stepped Governor Alister and Professor Cho Lin. One look at Lindsey and Cho Lin was all over her, putting her arms around her, even offering to carry her to the doctor.

"Catch him?" Alister asked.

"Three lousy seconds, Alister. Just three lousy seconds and we would have had him. That close! Clean get away; no trace of where they went, though he looked to be very near death as he left," Gary replied sadly. "I'll leave the girls in your care. We'd like to question her when she has recovered, with your permission of course."

"Of course. Now I think that Lindsey needs to spend some time with the good doctor. If you will excuse us?"

Gary teleported away. Lindsey suspected that he rejoined the others, searching the cabin for any possible clues that the duo may have left behind.

As they closed the distance to the Infirmary, Lindsey wanted to say something, but could only mumble inaudibly.

Frustrated, she messaged Alister. He smiled and replied, "We can see that Dominus cut off your new hands, and, while you say you can live with that, there is no need. The good doctor will just have to work his magic once more, only this time with my permission. As far as the threads tying up your lips are concerned, we will have to take a very close look before we remove them. I ask you to have a little more patience with us, Miss Barron." His tone did wonders to alleviate her growing fears. She had so much she wanted to say and to ask, but walked along with them into the Infirmary.

"Oh dear god, what have they done to my patient?" Doctor Caterwall exclaimed as they led Lindsey into his examination room. "Well don't just stand there gawking! Nurses, prepare the exam table immediately." The three nurses who were staring at Lindsey hastened into the next room. "Well, we will have you fixed up in short order, Miss Barron. Alister, I will need your able assistance."

"I presumed so. Professor, will you escort Miss Whitewater back to her dorm? I think that classes ought to be suspended just for today. Have the staff begin repairing our gates, please." Amanda, though she wanted to stay at Lindsey's side, reluctantly followed Cho Lin.

"Will she be all right? I mean they can somehow cut the string thing? How awful she must have been all this time," Amanda asked.

Cho Lin replied, "Yes, she has been through quite a lot, I'm afraid, and so very lucky to be alive and not in worse shape than she is in now. She's very lucky to have a friend such as you, Amanda. If it hadn't been for you, they would have killed her before they left with the rod. I'll leave you here at the door. I trust you can find the way to your room?" That was a tease, and Amanda smiled, rushing inside to find Pam, Emilio, and Kathy.

Instead, the entire Yellow Hall came down to the commons to greet Amanda and to hear firsthand what was going on and what had happened. Not too many actually believed all that Pam had been saying. "Sis, over here. Are you all right? Lindsey?" Jim waved and got her attention, as students mobbed her, pelting her questions the instant she set foot in the room.

Amanda made her way through the well-wishers to her brother. Tom, Kathy, Pam, and Emilio were with him. "I found her, Jim. I really did. The Defense people and I got to her just in time. They said if we had been three seconds faster, we would have been able to capture Dominus and Rubius! Lindsey's in terrible shape though. He cut off her hands and sewed her mouth shut. Gary—that's one of the Defense men—said the twine holding her lips shut might be poisoned, so we can't cut it. She's with the doctor now."

"Then it's true, what Pam has been saying?" asked a fifth year boy. Now everyone was clamoring for her to tell them everything.

Bill groaned, "Not her hands again. God!"

Amanda had no choice but to try to explain all that had happened. Pam had already told them much of the events, but it was so wild that few had honestly believed her. Now they totally changed their minds about Pam's story. An hour passed rapidly, especially with the announcement that all classes were canceled for today only. Someone called out, "Let's have a look at the broken gates! Most of the students raced out of the dorm, heading for the Admin Hall area for a firsthand look.

"Sis, I'm proud of you; you saved Lindsey, no question," Tom said, now that the small group was finally alone. "At first I thought it was ridiculous to think that you might have dad's Tracker skills. I'm sorry I ever doubted you, Amanda. I think one fifth year over in Red Hall can also see magical energy trails. Trackers are so rare. You have a unique gift, sis!" She beamed; having her brothers finally believing in her meant the world to Amanda.

Just then, a breathless Monique from Red Hall came rushing into the commons. "Pam, Pam, is it true? The rumors? Dominus kidnaped Lindsey, stole the rod?" she exclaimed totally out of breath and rather scatted about what to ask first.

Once more, Pam began to outline what had happened. She no more than finished when a dozen others from neighboring halls came in, and she had to start over once more. However, Pam, who had never had this much attention before, thoroughly enjoyed each retelling. Amanda quietly exited, escorted by her brothers and Emilio. Sandy joined them, having been to see the smashed gates. She suggested they go for a walk in the gardens. No one would likely come there looking for Amanda.

Doctor Caterwall slid his chair out from under the illuminated magnifier, focused on the ends of Lindsey's arms. "Very clean cut, Miss Barron, no infections, though that must have really hurt." Lindsey nodded vigorously. Her lips were still held tightly together by the threads of the spell Dominus had used on her. "Well, growing new hands will be no problem. Now let's have a closer look at these threads."

He moved his apparatus up to her head, positioning it over her mouth. "You can see what I'm seeing on that screen, Alister. Or if you prefer, you can have a direct look yourself. This one is devilishly tricky. The spell he used is not in normal usage. In fact, I've never actually seen an example, though we did have some photos in our medical texts."

"We may be in better shape than normal, doctor. The spell Dominus used required Miss Barron remain alive and safe. She was in the custody and care of Rubius, who is not known for his brilliant intellect or wisdom. Dominus is not stupid. I hope that he didn't booby trap these threads. After all, Rubius might have tried to cut them loose himself."

For several minutes, Doctor Caterwall studied the threads carefully. "Simple slip knot ties off each end here at the edges of her mouth. Might be simple to undo."

"Allow me to have a closer inspection, please." Governor Alister took the doctor's place, staring long into the magnifier at the thread. "You see, often the thread is hollow. Inside can be a poison or an explosive powder, for example. You cut it and then the poison gets into their system or their face explodes. However, there is no end of counter spells that could have been piggybacked onto the thread, designed to take effect, if the thread is cut or untied. However, in this case, I believe we can rule out poison—too great a risk for Dominus. If she had died, his spell would have been instantly canceled. The thread does not appear to be hollow either. I think that it is safe to rule out having her face blown off." Relieved, Lindsey sighed and mumbled a thanks.

"Now allow me to check for piggy backed counter spells. He waved his wand and said, "Reveal." He studied every visible portion of the thread carefully, holding his wand just above each section as he viewed it. At last, he said, "I do believe, Frank, that we have gotten a break with this one. I can see no indication of counter spells. Dominus probably didn't trust Rubius that well. I would suggest untying it as a first step to be on the safe side."

"Untie Thread," Doctor Caterwall commanded as his wand made a circular motion, as if the wand were untying the thread ends. Nothing unexpected happened. Next, using a sterilized pincher, he began the slow process of pulling each thread section back through the holes in her upper and lower lips. He went extremely slowly, not wishing to injure further the tender puncture wounds or to cause her any undue pain. A half hour passed before the thread came out of the last hole in her upper lip.

"There! A successful operation! Let's have a look inside your mouth now. Say 'ah' please," he asked. Lindsey gladly opened her mouth wide! It felt so great to be able to open her mouth again that she didn't want to close it right away. "Just fine, nothing amiss inside her mouth. I will go prepare the potions now."

"Good, I would like a word alone with Miss Barron anyway," Alister replied. As soon as the two were alone, he said, "You have done exceedingly well! You did as I asked there in the cabin, summoning the First Horseman and then handing him the rod, as I desired. I so hoped that you would follow my hints."

"That, that was your voice I heard in my head telling me what to do?" she asked, remembering what had happened.

"Yes, I tried for years to convince them to destroy this relic, but no, the knuckleheads kept saying not to worry, Dominus is in prison. Well, together, you and I have managed to rid the world of this evil artifact. You see, when you gave this highly charged magical item to itself—the horseman was part of its own enchantment—we sort of turned magical energies back on themselves, resulting in its nullification or destruction. We will talk more of all this later. Yet there is one more thing that I wish you to know. Your rescue in time was due in a very great measure by Miss Whitewater, whose Tracking skills shone this morning. She was able to follow the magical traces left by Dominus's Dimensional Door spell that he used to get from our parking lot to the cabin. She led the Defense people straight to you."

"Wow! That means she is on her way to being a Tracker! Doesn't it?"

"Oh very much so, I would say, indeed so. Just as you are well on your way to becoming a Dispeller. That was quite a performance you gave Rubius and Dominus. I do believe you cast every spell in your Grade 0 and 1 spell book, did you not?"

"Well, yes, I did. I had plenty of time to work out what sequence I wanted to use, starting with Untie Me, but when the rod appeared, I had to change the order a bit, to Identify the rod as being the rod, you know. Hey, how do you know all of this?"

"Because I was there with you, Lindsey. There's no way I'm going to allow one of Bradbury's students to be permanently harmed, if I can avoid it. I was prepared to rescue you myself, if Amanda had not been able to follow the trail that Dominus left. Now here comes the good doctor. I'll leave you in his hands for now. We will speak again later. Oh yes, I'll see that you do not have to cast all of those spells again for Professor Janice in her lengthy final exam." He had a twinkle in his eye. She grinned, knowing she wouldn't have to do them all again so slowly by using a wand to make them happen.

The doctor entered carrying a tray of bottles. After Alister left, he said, "Miss Barron, there is one final tiny detail I should ask you. It's about the holes you have in your lips. Do you wish to keep one or more of them? I mean to get metal rings or spikes in them? What is the term the norms use, oh yes, the gothic look."

"Huh? What are you talking about?" Lindsey had no idea what he meant.

"Here, I brought you a photograph showing one young woman's fine set of body ornaments." He showed her a picture. The girl had numerous rings going through her lips, a silver spike sticking out of her bottom lip and even a ring through her nose.

"Yuck, no way! I get enough teasing just looking the way I am. I don't need more!"

"Good girl. I didn't think so, but I owe it to my patients at least to ask them. Now then, I have three potions for you to drink, and then I have your straws coming."

"Yes, I know, drink all that funny kind of milk that I can, right?" she replied with a smile.

"Good girl, but please promise me that you won't make a habit of losing your hands!" Both of them laughed.

"Will I have to have my arms taped upright for a week like last time?"

"Oh no, no, no. That was because the bones were broken in three places in each arm. This time, there are no broken bones. I'll wrap the ends just so that the newly forming hands are not easily bruised or damaged by a bump against something hard. I do want you to say here in the Infirmary for several days, but you are not going to be confined to total bed rest like last time. It should be much more pleasant for you this time. I will send a message to Pam to bring your study things here once we are through, okay?"

She thanked him and drank the awful potions down. Almost at once, she began to feel a tingling sensation at the ends of her arms. Within a few minutes, she saw the faint outlines of her new hands growing at the ends of her arms. Now that they were beginning to become substantial, Doctor Caterwall bandaged them up to protect them. Then he finished up with "Clean. Sterilize."

"There now, all done. You can get up and move around; just be careful not to bang them into anything. Come with me. I'll take you to your room for the next few days." This time, she had a room with a bed, table, and several chairs, along with a window that looked northward onto the green lawn and swimming pool. She saw quite a few going for a dip on this unexpected day off.

Ten minutes later, the entire gang came hesitantly into her room. Pam, Amanda, Kathy, Emilio, Tom, Sandy, Jim, Bill, Sally, Becky, and Jake all tiptoed into her room. Amanda carried a clean set of clothes for her, while Pam lugged her computer and schoolbooks. "Okay to come in?" Pam asked timidly, unsure what she would find.

All were shocked to see Lindsey up walking and coming over to hug them. "I just have to be extra careful not to bump these into anything," Lindsey explained, as she hugged each in turn. "I thought that I would never, ever see you all again. I was sure they were going to kill me. What I still don't understand is why did they kidnap me and how come Dominus looked like me?" she asked.

Pam had all the answers. Again, she went through all their observations and deductions, occasionally amended by Amanda or Emilio. When she finished, Lindsey said, "Pam, you are one terrific Sleuth! And Amanda, gosh, that makes you a beginning Tracker for sure!"

Both girls smiled with pride. Emilio added, "And that makes you a beginning Dispeller, Lindsey. Alister told us that you cast every spell in our books, there at the end."

"Yes, I couldn't speak, and with no hands, it was the only thing I could think of doing. I knew that our spells were not going to harm them at all, but I figured that if I could create enough confusion in the cabin, I could somehow slip out the door and run for my life. That is, until I saw the rod. Then, it all changed. I couldn't let them keep that rod."

"Three cheers for Pam, Amanda, and Lindsey, the best first years ever!" Tom declared, and the little group cheered and clapped, while the three smiled, but felt rather embarrassed.

"Now then," Pam cleared her throat, "we all should use this extra free day to catch up on our homework. There's less than three weeks left now!"

"Yes, Tom, we should get to work on ours; only twenty days left, and two of those don't count," Sandy added. Grumbling, the others left the five to work together on their homework.

"Gee, Lindsey, since you don't have to do all the spells," Emilio suggested, "then you have more time to help me with my geometry problems. I'm still trying to figure out how to prove that two planes intersect. Kathy said it was the air traffic controller's fault, but I don't think that is what Professor

Herbert is asking."

Pam snickered and giggled. Kathy gave a "Well it *is* their fault" kind of look, and Lindsey burst out laughing.

"You two really do need our help with this one!" Lindsey teased. "See that wall there and the ceiling there." Both Emilio and Kathy looked where she was pointing with her heavily bandaged hands. "Well where the two planes meet, they form that line."

"Oh!" Kathy exclaimed, her face as red as Pam's friend Monique's lips.

"Oh, that's simple enough to see, but how do you prove it?" Emilio asked. Pam and Lindsey began remedial geometry lessons. A half hour later, both finally had their proofs written out.

"Now, Emilio, it's payback time," Lindsey declared. "There's no way I am going to be able to get my rocket designed and all glued together, not with my hands like this. I need some help."

"Me, too!" added Amanda and Kathy. Emilio gladly looked over their paper designs and glued the fins onto Lindsey's rocket.

The nurse came in to tell them it was lunchtime and to admonish Lindsey for her failure to drink the quart of milk she had sitting on her table. Hastily, Lindsey drank the whole thing. Amanda stayed behind to help feed Lindsey and then took off to get herself something. Finally alone, Lindsey marveled that it was only noon on Monday, so much had happened this morning! She'd gone from being convinced of her eminent death, to rescuing the rod, to destroying the rod, to being rescued, to being healed, to being nearly back to normal with her dear friends. She knew now just how much the friendship of these four meant to her; it was the most precious thing she possessed, excepting for her mother.

On Friday, she was released from the Infirmary and allowed to resume her normal activities. When she entered her first class, math with Professor Herbert, the whole class stared at her. Slowly, one by one, her classmates began clapping for her. She was shocked to see that even Deiter was clapping for her! Her face became quite red indeed, before Professor

Herbert began the class.

In science class, the entire class carried their personally designed rockets outside to launch them. Emilio and most of the boys were terribly excited with this entire study, very anxious to launch theirs. Indeed, the boys shot off their rockets first. Amazingly, Deiter's rocket flew the highest, although his recovery system needed improvement. The nose cone shattered from its impact with the ground. Emilio's rocket with fancy fins flew the second highest, while landing perfectly.

The best that can be said for Lindsey's rocket is that it at least worked. Excessively heavy, it did not gain much altitude, but landed safely. Pam's rocket flew off in a screwy path, but landed okay. Kathy's rocket lost its fins part way up and there was not too much of it left but a tube when it finally landed. "More glue" was the notation the professor wrote on her design paper. At least, they all passed, but Emilio's project received the top marks in the class. He felt fantastic over his achievement.

After lunch, Lindsey entered Professor Janice's class, a little unsure of what her reception would be. "Next week, on Monday, you'll have one period to cast all the spells that you should have learned this entire year. Regretfully, Miss Barron will not have to participate with the rest of you. Apparently, Governor Alister is vouching for her skill level and has asked me to waive this test."

With everyone looking at her, Deiter called out, "Is it true that you cast every one of our spells with your mouth tied shut and no hands?" Lindsey saw that he was actually quite serious this time, not teasing or taunting her. Hence, she decided to answer him, especially since the rest of her classmates from the other halls were eagerly awaiting her reply as well.

"Well, Miss Barron? Are you going to answer Mr. Cross or not?" Professor Janice asked her rather nastily.

"Yes, I did them all that way, trying to confuse Dominus and Rubius so I could escape from the cabin and not get killed."

Many oh's and ah's greeted her ears. She suspected that

many now understood fully that she did indeed possess skills of a Dispeller. Even Professor Janice's eyebrows rose slightly. Lindsey fully expected her to make a comment about her wand failing to activate, but she did not.

Instead, Professor Janice said, "Today, we will begin our dancing lessons. After all, the formal ball is coming up in just a few days, and you all must learn to waltz properly. I assume that you, Miss Barron, are also an accomplished dancer and can show us all how it is done properly?"

Lindsey's face felt hot again. "I don't know how to dance," she said quietly. However, her discomfort was short lived. All the boys groaned loudly, while the girls mostly giggled at them. She was off the hook, so to speak.

"Now then, formal dancing does not consist of shaking your butts around, wiggling your waists, or even shaking your topsides, as so many of you did at Halloween. It is stateliness and elegance that counts." She put on a waltz. "Boys, step forward with your left foot and girls, back with your right foot. Then, bring the other up to it and close them together. One-two-three. Boys, line up here. Girls, line up facing the boys. Now get closer. They won't bite!" Indeed, the line of girls was about ten feet from the boys. Closer, closer, closer." Lindsey was now only two feet from Emilio. "Remember boys forward on your left, girls back on your right. Here we go, one-two-three." The music began, and the klutzes became overly apparent almost immediately.

Within minutes, the girls had the basic steps down pat, while the boys continued to have immense trouble with it. The incessant giggling of the girls didn't help the boys any, only making it worse. Above the blaring music, Professor Janice called out, "Boys, practice, practice. One-two-three."

The boys were very glad when the ending bell rang! "Remember to practice. Think how embarrassed you'll be at the dance, if you step on your partner's foot!"

Deiter muttered as he left class, "Maybe I won't go then." Several nearby Black Hall girls heard him and giggled. His face grew perceptibly pinkish, and he rushed on to his next class.

On the other hand, Emilio was going, "One-two-three,"

repeatedly, as he walked along with the four others. "Say, maybe I'm getting the hang of this dancing thing."

"Yes, you were doing lots better than Deiter," Kathy said encouragingly. "Say who have you asked to go with you to the ball?"

Emilio's face grew a shade of red, he muttered, "No one yet. I haven't gotten the courage to ask anyone."

"Well, don't wait too long or we will all have been asked," she replied.

At suppertime, Jim came by their group, "Lindsey, may I have a private word with you?" Lindsey got up, and the two walked out of overhearing range of their friends, who were indeed trying hard to listen in on the two. Lindsey flushed as he spoke and nodded. Jim returned to his group of third years, and Lindsey sat back down to finish eating.

"Well, what was that all about?" asked Amanda, very curious about what her brother wanted of Lindsey.

"He's asked me to the ball," Lindsey whispered.

"Well?" Pam asked. After a pause, she added, "Did you accept?" Lindsey nodded.

"Great! He's rather cute you know," Pam stated.

"Has someone asked you, Pam?" Lindsey asked.

Now it was Pam's turn to be somewhat embarrassed. "Well, yes, I've been asked and said I would." She refused all attempts from her friends to divulge who had asked her to the ball.

Amanda quickly explained, "Henry's asked me to go with him. He's the quiet one in our class. I hope he can learn to dance. He didn't do at all well today." A short silence fell around their group, as they recalled the fiasco in Professor Janice's class. The boys had made a complete mess of the lessons.

Kathy broke the silence, "Well, I'm still available, for the dance, that is."

Emilio, who had just seen all his prospects for a dance date rapidly evaporating, quickly said, "Kathy, wannagotothedancewithme?"

"Huh?" she asked, not understanding a word he had said, other than her name.

Emilio took a deep breath, as if this would be his last one, "Want to go to the dance with me?" His face was also rather pinkish as well.

"Sure, Emilio, I thought that you would never get around to asking me," Kathy replied cheerily, secretly very happy that she had finally been asked to the ball. She'd been extremely worried that no one would ask her.

Now the table conversation turned to what the girls would be wearing, and Emilio became his usual bored self once more. He'd wear clothes, what else? Why all this fuss over clothes anyway? He was sure that he didn't understand girls in the slightest.

Chapter 18—End of Term

"Lindsey, you've made MagNews!" exclaimed Pam over breakfast on Saturday morning. "I recorded it on my laptop. Come on." She led Lindsey up to their room and double clicked on the mp4 file, labeled "Lindsey."

Hugo Whitefield's handsome face appeared on the screen. "Good morning you witches and wizards. I have breaking news for you today. A KMAG exclusive! As widely reported last week, Dominus Malefic broke into the Arthur Bradbury School of Magic and stole the relic Rod of the Apocalypse. However, KMAG has just learned from a reliable inside source that Dominus used a Morph Self into Another spell to break into the school. Who did he use? We've just learned that he kidnaped a Miss Lindsey Barron, a runner who was at the Nationals in Des Moines, Iowa, over the weekend. Yes, Dominus, disguised as this school girl, was able to break into the secure vault and steal the rod."

"Yet, this first year student apparently completely turned the tables on Dominus, by activating the rod and giving it to one of its Horsemen! Magic into Magic—it was destroyed. Many of you know that for years now a great many wizards and witches have been pleading for its destruction. Seems they got their wish."

"Now does it seem possible that a first year student could pull this off with Dominus Malefic and his Death Stalker Rubius right there with her? This reporter did not believe a word of this, not until our source inside the school of magic revealed this tidbit."

Hugo leaned into the camera giving the effect that he was leaning closer to you. "Her father was none other than Samuel Rabnor! Yes, you heard me correctly, Sam Rabnor, the famous Dispeller, who originally captured Dominus some fourteen years ago. Although he has been confirmed as dead, it seems his daughter is following in his footsteps!"

He leaned back. "Of course we heard some other preposterous stories about Miss Barron's feat. Some are saying that Dominus cut off her hands and some even say that he sewed her mouth shut, but that seems completely at odds with her having been able to defeat Dominus and destroy the rod. After all, how many of you out there can cast a spell with your mouth shut, eh?"

"KMAG has attempted to obtain a live interview with Miss Barron. However, Governor Alister Broadwell has declined to permit it, saying it is not in the best interests of his student. Well, KMAG can be persistent. We will continue our efforts to disclose the truth of this entire matter." The video ended at this point.

"God, I don't want to be interviewed! Now the whole world knows I'm Sam's daughter! Mom and I will never be safe ever again!" Lindsey broke down and began crying. Pam had no idea how to comfort her. She had spoken the truth. Now everyone knew.

Amanda joined them, having just seen the replay along with many others in the commons. "How's she taking it?" she whispered to Pam, rather obviously not well, since Lindsey was lying on her bed crying into her pillow. Pam shook her head and pointed to her.

Sitting on the edge of Lindsey's bed, Amanda put her arm reassuringly on her best friend's shoulder. "Maybe you should speak with Governor Alister about this, Lindsey. He might have some ideas or maybe he can get some extra Defense protections for your mom. At least, you have to try."

Have to try. That thought registered in her mind. Yes, she would have to try anything to help protect her mother and their ranch. She wiped her tears on her sleeve and sat up. "You are right. I can't lie here and do nothing, not while mom is in danger. I'd better go see him right now. Walk there with me?" With Amanda and Pam on either side of her and Kathy rushing to catch up with them, they headed towards the Admin Hall to hunt for Governor Alister.

Along the way, Lindsey thought that many other students walking on the campus lawns were staring at her. Probably by now, all six hundred students would have seen the news. As they approached the building, Governor Alister was just walking into the building himself, coming from the direction of the Infirmary. "Ah, Miss Barron, I was just about to send for you. I would like a few words with you, though I suspect that you and your friends have come to see me." Again, he had that "knows all" twinkle in his eyes, which made you wonder just how much more this old wizard actually did know. At least the gesture and manner put the girls more at ease.

He opened the door to his office for Lindsey, motioning for her to take a seat. This was a private conversation; her three companions waited just outside the door for her, whispering to themselves about how awful the situation had become and how rude Hugo was to her in his newscast.

"Well, Lindsey, how are the hands and lips doing?" he began.

"Fine, you can't tell where they were tied shut anymore, and I'm still getting used to the new hands. Doctor Caterwall says it will just take a little time, sir."

"Good, good. Your report agrees with the good doctor's, I'm glad to say. I believe that we can forget all about that awful mess now. On the other hand, I'm afraid the MagNews has gone a bit too far. I presume that you have already seen that so called newscast about you today?" Lindsey nodded. "Well, let me give you a bit of wisdom about the news industry. It's all about the ratings, attracting and keeping viewers, and very little about reporting truthfully what has happened. Death, destruction, controversy, conspiracies, these things people have a morbid fascination with, I've always seen. Hugo just had to twist the whole story around so that his viewers would continue watching him. I refused to allow them to interview you."

"Thank you, sir. After seeing that today, I never want to be interviewed. From what he said, someone here at school leaked many of the details to him. Do you know who it may have been?"

"That's good of you, Lindsey. I hate to be interviewed as well, avoid it as much as possible, myself. As far as who may have leaked the story, there are many possibilities. As yet I do not know who it may have been. We probably never will, but I will continue to try to find out. We do have freedom of press in this land, though I do wish they would stick to the truth of matters and not pervert it to their need to sensationalize."

"Water over the dam, as the saying goes. We've tried to keep the connection between you and your father a secret, mostly for your own safety and that of your mother. Alas, I'm afraid that the time has come for us all to face the facts. The world now knows. Hence, Dominus and his gang surely know. The question becomes what will they do about it? At the present, I suspect nothing. I believe Dominus has far more urgent needs than to go looking for the young daughter of the deceased Dispeller, who captured him a long time ago, let alone some norm wife that he married years after that. Though I admit that he may be a little incensed that you and I destroyed his precious relic, that rod. At some time, he may well wish to settle that score with you and me, but not in the near future is my educated guess."

"Just between you and me, I believe that you and your mother are in greater danger from the MagNews people hounding you both for interviews, which, if I know anything about your mother, she will refuse to be interviewed." Lindsey grinned. She could see her mother brandishing her shotgun, ordering Hugo with the white, grinning teeth off her ranch.

"Lindsey, this is all part of growing up. As we begin to leave our carefree childhood behind, we have a choice to make. Do we accept the responsibilities of being an adult and all that comes with it or not? Red Hall students prefer to operate only upon the strong emotions and passions that they feel. Right now, I'm sure that you have some very strong emotions swirling through your body and mind. Yet, Yellow Hall students believe that thought should rule their lives, not their passions. Yes, you may wish to smash that smiling face of Hugo right now, even beat up the person or persons who betrayed our confidence to the press, but you and I both know that we would not give in to such passions, such emotions. Rather, we use thoughts and ideas to form our world. Right now, we need some good ideas." Lindsey grinned; yes, some good ideas were just what she needed, ideas, ways to protect her mother.

"Life is all about change, Lindsey," he went on, leaving her wondering where the good ideas went. She had hoped he would offer her some. "Some have a very hard time with change. Mr. Cross, for example, is having a most difficult time of it. Here at school, we are constantly challenging so many rigidly fixed ideas he has held since his early childhood. You, I'm afraid, have taken the brunt of his rebellion against many of these fixed opinions. You see, he was raised to believe that women are nothing more than a mother, a raiser of children, and a cooker of meals, nothing more. His father is the essence of self-power, a self-made man, proud of his strength and might, and his ability to control others. That you can do all the spells he can and yet do them non-verbally and without a wand is crashing and smashing his viewpoint of the world. Naturally, he is lashing out at you. However, here at Bradbury's, we will try our very best to temper that, to educate him, to allow him the opportunity to alter his fixed ideas, and to overcome his insistence of self-importance, that might, strength, and effort alone are enough to conquer what life throws our way."

While Deiter's actions towards her now began to make some sense to her, this was not what was bothering her. Rather, it was the dire peril that she and her mother were in on their isolated ranch. "Ah, I see that you are not so concerned with philosophy than with your present circumstances," he replied, almost as if he were reading her thoughts.

"There is a point that I'm about to make with this. Life presents us with many changes. You are facing one of those this very minute. What I am trying to suggest to you, Lindsey, is not to fight against those changes. Embrace them and find ways to make the changes work to your betterment. While it may seem like the end of the world to you at this very moment, in fact, it may well work to you and your mother's advantage somehow. That is the challenge that you face, Lindsey. How do you make this work to aid and assist your survival?"

She replied, "Oh, I see. Yes, that is what I need to do, but I don't see how it can ever help. It seems to me that we need a hundred guards around our ranch at all times to keep us safe from Dominus and his henchmen."

"That is because you are not embracing the whole, only

one tiny portion. Have you discussed all this with your mother? I thought not. Perhaps you should, when you return home for the summer in just a few more days. However, there is another aspect in all this. Remember last fall when we discovered that Sam Rabnor was your father? I said then that I needed to do some research to fill in the gaps, so to speak. Well, I have finished that task. Yes, your father was killed that day that you found him. However, that story is not yet finished. You and the world believe that he was crushed beneath that tractor, correct?" She nodded. She'd been the one who found him that fateful day.

"I've had his body examined by some friends of mine. I would like you to read their report. For their protection, you will not be able to see certain portions of their report where it gives their names." He handed her a short, handwritten document.

> Alister,
>
> In regards to the matter of the death of Samuel Rabnor, alias, Samuel Barron. At your request, we have exhumed his body and done a complete Mag-autopsy. You were right in your hunch. While his body was indeed crushed by some very heavy object, he was quite dead before being so crushed. Our analysis is that he was killed by the spell Power: Kill, which as you know is one of the most difficult spells ever to learn. The ministry has a ledger of all those who are known to be able to use that spell. I've attached a copy with this report.
>
> Sincerely,

As Lindsey read this, her mind began to race over the implications! Her father had been murdered! It was not a ranch accident after all! However, from the beautiful, flowing script, she guessed that a woman had written it.

"Now you have a new mystery in which to sink your teeth, Lindsey. I strongly suspected that this might have been the case. Knowing that your father was a powerful Dispeller, this is about the only way, short of a Wish, that he could have been murdered. I suspect that whoever did the slaying took him by complete surprise. Otherwise, the perpetrator would have been killed, not your father."

"But I'm not always the bringer of bad news, Lindsey. It seems that your father had set up a secret bank vault in Denver before he went underground into hiding. I've been in contact with Lloyd's Secure Vaults. As the next of kin, I have been assured that the entire contents of his vault now belong to you. With your permission, I will delay your return home to your ranch by one day so that you and I may take a quick trip to Denver and see what may be inside his vault. Who knows, it may be completely empty. Don't get your hopes up, it may be nothing at all, but then again, he may have left you something. We'll see on June 1. I've already notified your mother that you will be returning a day later than expected."

"Wow! Thank you! This is incredible news. Maybe, well I don't know what to hope for, really."

"Yes, that's the proper way to approach this news. His vault may be empty; then again, it may not. The one thing of which you can be certain is that only he could entered it. No one else could possibly access it without destroying the entire bank. Now I've taken up a lot of your nice Saturday morning. I should let you get back to your friends. However, I will tell you this. I have asked that the Department of Defense supply your ranch with additional security measures. Don't expect dozens of norm armed guards, Lindsey. We wizards work in much different ways." He smiled reassuringly. She thanked him several times and left.

Her three friends outside the door had grown to four. Emilio joined them, while she was inside with Alister. "What news? Is he going to insist on better security?" Pam asked the second she walked out and the door was shut.

As the small group walked back, Lindsey began to retell what she'd heard. When she got to the part about her father having been murdered, Pam became all ears, asking her to go over all that she had read and what he had said. Pam now had a new mystery to solve!

"Incredible, Lindsey! Your father left you a Lloyd's Secure Vault!" Emilio said excitedly. "Wow, that's super. Those are very expensive vaults, you know. Surely, he must have left you something quite valuable."

"Yes, but I was only five when he died. Besides, he got the vault before he went into hiding, so he wouldn't even know he was going to marry mom, let alone have a daughter," Lindsey countered, trying to remain objective about it.

"Still, he may have left behind some pretty cool stuff," Emilio insisted, full of life instead of his usual boredom. The five speculated what might be in the vault all the way back to their rooms. While the others got their books and headed for the study hall, Lindsey decided that she needed to call her mother.

"Hi mom. Yes, it's me, calling a bit earlier than normal. Yes, everything is all right. How's everything at the ranch? Good."

Lena said, "Dear, are you sure that you are all right? I know that you were on the news. Lloyd Compton showed me a replay on his funny handheld computer thing. It's apparently all the rage, now, these tiny little handheld things. Anyway, I didn't like the attitude of that Hugo fellow, too self-centered, must think he is god's gift to women. Already some reporter fellow came snooping about, but I ran him off. He didn't take kindly to a shotgun blast warning. Anyway, Governor Alister Broadwell called to say that he is taking you into Denver before you come home. What's this about Sam having a safe deposit box there? He never mentioned any such thing to me, ever."

"I know mom; he never told me either, but I was only five, so I don't suppose he would have anyway. Governor Alister says for us not to get our hopes up, 'cause it could well be completely empty."

"Wise man, this Alister. Yes, dear, it is probably just something your father forgot to get rid of when he came to Plano. By the way, I have some surprises for you when you get home. You know me and these phones. I want to tell you in person. Good surprises. I have to move the horses to the greener pasture now. Call me again tonight if it is not too expensive for you. I love you."

"Love you too, mom. Bye." Lindsey felt more relaxed now. Her mother had seen the broadcast and also didn't think much of Hugo, and she also didn't believe much of what he'd said. That was a good sign, she thought. Plus, she'd run off a reporter. Lindsey wished she could have seen that one. Smiling, she grabbed her books and headed for the study hall. Curse the news anyway—it wasn't going to ruin her life.

Today, the study hall was rather empty. It was the last day trip to Telluride for the older students. Tom and Sandy were off on a date in the town. Lindsey told the others about her mother running off a reporter, and Amanda laughed at that. Then, they all traded papers, correcting each other's mistakes. Kathy corrected several oversights in Lindsey's report for their History of Magic course. Pam and Lindsey found numerous math errors in Emilio's project and corrected Kathy's misconceptions in her math project. Emilio looked over all four girl's History of Rocket Design papers, correcting their errors. Soon it was lunchtime. For once, they had all their homework done.

Over lunch and ignoring Deiter's taunt of "Even Hugo doubts you, Lindsey, and he ought to know," the group decided to spend part of the afternoon going over all their spells. "Really, you should work out the proper sequence of casting them, because that way you waste as little time as possible," Lindsey pointed out.

Pam added, "Save any that you have a hard time casting for last; don't waste precious seconds on them at the beginning. You have to cast as many as possible in the forty-five minutes that she gives us, you see."

Back in the study hall, Lindsey watched and made suggestions as the four wrote out their lengthy lists of spells, in the order that they wanted to cast them. "Emilio, I'd suggest you create the fires before you try to enlarge them and shrink them, less wasted time," Lindsey suggested. Around two, the five headed outdoors to practice many of them.

Most of the other first years were also outside, enjoying the sunny afternoon while practicing theirs. Peggy West and Janis Smelter, from Red Hall were near the five, working on their spells as well, their cherry red lips animatedly commanding spells. Peaches Colt from Black Hall and Lilly Rains from Brown Hall were also twinning together on the other side of Lindsey's group. Peggy, taking a bit of a break and greatly desiring to satisfy her curiosity, asked, "Lindsey, it's true isn't it? I mean what everyone is saying, that you can cast all of our spells without your wand and non-verbally?"

"Yes, Peggy," Lindsey said modestly.

"That must have been just awful having your lips sewn together! Just awful," Lilly said sympathetically. "I know I would have been just mortified, if it had been me."

"Yes, but maybe she was just lucky," Janis said rather icily.

"Well, I agree with Hugo," Peaches added snidely. "You can't cast spells without a wand and with your mouth sewn up! That stretches everyone's imaginations to the limit."

"But Governor Alister would not have given her a total, complete pass on the test if she hadn't done that," Lilly pleaded with the two. "She must've."

Pam interrupted their discussion. "Look here. Wouldn't you all be somewhat scared of Lindsey if she could cast any one of our spells on you without uttering a word and without even having her wand with her? What if at any time, Peaches, she could set fire to your knickers? You'd have no warning at all, no wand, no words. Wouldn't you be just a little bit scared around Lindsey?"

She hit the tender spot. Peaches' face crimsoned. "Well, er, well, sure I would be, who wouldn't be?" she defended herself. Lindsey saw that Pam spoke the truth. Many of her classmates were now secretly just a bit scared of her for this very reason.

Kathy added, "So all the more reasons to be nice to Lindsey." She worked hard to keep from giggling, however.

Lindsey decided to be helpful instead of a threat. "Say you four, have you worked out the most efficient order in which to cast all our spells on the test?" She explained what she meant. To her surprise and Pam's as well, this idea had never entered their minds! Peaches was planning to cast the ones she knew best first. Lilly and Janis were going to cast them in the order that they had learned them. Peggy had made an alphabetized listing to follow. Lindsey spent an hour with the four helping them to work out an efficient order of casting, keeping in mind to leave the ones with which they had the most trouble until the very end. All four were very pleased indeed and became very friendly with Lindsey as a result.

Peggy's comment, once her list was done, told all, "Now I am sure to pass, because I can get this whole bunch here off very quickly. Even if I can't get these, I will still pass! Terrific idea, Lindsey, thanks! I owe you one."

After supper, Emilio and several other boys had gotten permission to launch more of their rockets. While he was off having fun, the four girls went to their room to begin planning what they were wearing to the formal ball. After all, it was now only a week away. Emilio could not see why it took an entire week to figure out what to wear to the ball, however. Yet for most of the week, this occupied the four girls, whenever their schoolwork permitted it.

On Monday, Lindsey played guinea pig for many student's spells during their frantic spell casting session with Professor Janice. She was Warmed and Cooled, and Dirtied, and Cleaned, and much more many times over. Yet she didn't mind; she was helping her friends succeed. Whenever she could, she would offer a bit of advice such as "Calm down. Concentrate. You can do this." Emilio needed the most calming, however. Under pressure, he began to forget everything.

When the time was up, all thirty students looked at the giant chart to see how they did, as well as the others. Peaches could not help notice that all the boxes were checked by Lindsey's name. She had the free pass. Lindsey was pleased that her four friends had gotten every spell cast! Even more significantly, Peaches, Lilly, Peggy, and Janis had also gotten a perfect score, much to the surprise and shock of Professor Janice. All the others in the class missed at least one or more spells. However, Lindsey noticed that no one failed the test. Only Lyle missed the most. He could not get ten of them.

On their way to their next class, Lilly, Peggy, and Janis rushed up to Lindsey and thanked her again. "Because of you, I got a perfect score!" Peggy exclaimed, her red lips grinning boldly. "Thanks again!"

On Tuesday, they had their big geometry test. Three

students actually failed this one. Kathy was very pleased to obtain a C grade, while Emilio had somehow managed to bring his final grade up to a B. The other three had A's, naturally.

The last four days of science class were particularly fun for all them. Professor Jasper allowed them to "mess around" with anything that had interested them this past year. Most of the boys wanted to shoot rockets again. Amanda spent her time looking over the large rock collection, with Lindsey looking over her shoulder asking questions. Pam and Kathy played with the giant weather station, which gave weather predictions based on the input you fed into it.

In English class, Professor Mac Elroy allowed them to read any book in the Library that they desired, including the comic books, which many of the boys chose to read. Pam began reading about the spells she would be learning next year. The others read some novels suggested by Professor Elaine.

However, the next four days in Professor Janice's spell casting class were taken up with ballroom dancing lessons, much to the consternation of the boys. All the girls loved these four days, naturally. They were anxiously awaiting the formal ball.

This year the ball fell on a Friday night. All during the afternoon, Emilio tried to have the girls come outside and shoot rockets or do anything, since it was a perfect spring day. None did, complaining that they had to get ready for the big dance.

"How do I look?" asked Lindsey. She had slipped into her new silk, full-length gown that her mother had made for her Christmas present. The necklace that Kathy had given her adorned her bare neck, and she wore the bracelet of gold and turquoise that Emilio had given her.

"Wow, stunning. It's the latest style too. Your mother sure knows how to sew!" Pam complimented her.

"Yes, but those shoes just don't go with it," Kathy protested. "Black school shoes do not a prom dress match! Here, try on these of mine, they are a little darker blue, but that's better that those."

Lindsey switched her shoes; at least they fit her well

318

enough. "They do match much better," she replied.

"Yes, but you ought to have some nylons or hose not just bare legs," Kathy suggested. "What do you all think?"

Amanda came to her rescue, seeing the confused look on Lindsey's face. "They are not practical on a ranch. They rip and run if you look at them wrong. I don't have any either, not much use for them on the reservation."

Kathy showed them a pair of hers. "Mend comes in very handy with these. You need a darker pair to go with that dress. Let me see what I have in my bag. Soon, Lindsey was wearing her first pair of pantyhose. Next, for an hour the girls experimented with various arrangements of their hair, Lindsey finally just brushed hers out as normal, long brown hair down her back.

Kathy, with her short, curly brown hair, chose to wear a light brown prom style dress, which had just a hint of glitter in it. Amanda's dress was a light yellow, also full length with a wide walking slit, falling like a tube below her waist. Like Lindsey, she just let her long black hair lay down her back. Kathy loaned her a pair of darkish pantyhose that contrasted just right with her dress color. Pam's prom dress was a light shade of red, gleaming and silky looking, though not made of silk as Lindsey's was. Pam spent considerable time fiddling with her short black hair, trying to get it to look as good as possible. "Perhaps I should just let mine grow longer, like you two," she finally admitted.

"Mom says that I'm not old enough to wear any makeup," Kathy declared, looking at her image in the mirror. "I could sure use some."

"Why? I think you look beautiful as you are," Lindsey asked.

"Women are supposed to be attractive, to make men look at you and desire you and want you, silly. How else are you supposed to attract a husband?" Kathy replied. Lindsey thought about this one and had no answer.

"Well, I don't have to worry about that," Pam said quietly. "With my homely face and stupid front teeth, what I might attract I'm sure that I don't want!"

"You are still growing, Pam. Give yourself a few years. I

bet you will look just fine when you get a little older," Kathy tried to reassure her friend.

"Well, I don't want all that stuff on my face," Amanda replied, although she didn't know why she didn't, just that she didn't.

"Well, all the girls in Red Hall know all about makeup, the best ways to use it. How to hide or mask your not so good features, all that sort of thing," Kathy added. "I guess it wouldn't hurt us to have them give us some lessons one day, maybe this fall. By then, we'll all be teenagers, and mom said that's when I can finally use a little."

At last, it was time. First, everyone was to rendezvous in their commons, meeting up with their dates. Next, they would all dine together. Once the meal was finished, the dining hall would be turned into the grand ballroom. After a flurry of "How do I look," the four girls headed down the stairs to the commons.

As soon as they entered the commons, Jim spotted Lindsey and came up to her. "Lindsey, wow, do you ever look terrific! Here, I have a corsage for you." He pinned it to her shoulder. She noticed that he looked fabulous himself, a brown western suit, suede perhaps, with dark thread highlights and a string necktie. She'd never noticed before how handsome he looked.

Henry Waldorf, another first year, came up to Amanda. He looked like he was a perfect businessman, Lindsey thought, in his impeccable grey suit and black tie and highly polished black shoes. Henry was slightly taller than Amanda. "You look, well, incredible, Amanda!" She beamed and took his arm. Lindsey saw what she did and took Jim's arm.

"I've never been on a date before, Jim, so I don't really know what to do," she confessed to him.

"Please don't blab this, but I haven't either. If they knew, they'd make fun of me," Jim also confessed, putting both of them more at ease. "Tom told me to get you the flowers."

Lindsey looked around to see if Pam's date was here. She spotted them. It was Monique Blackburn from Red Hall. However, she was dressed like a very well dressed man, a tuxedo in fact. She wore her hair in a tight bun, but her red lipstick dispelled any notion that she was a man. Lindsey observed that Monique was taking on the role of the gentleman this evening, escorting Pam. Both were grinning, so Lindsey figured Pam knew what she was doing.

Jim escorted Lindsey to their table, held her chair for her to sit. While they chatted, Lindsey noticed that many of the older girls wore heels and nearly all wore hose. She was very thankful for Kathy's loan and aid. For once, she felt right at home among all the other girls. Her dress was every bit as fashionable as the others here were. Indeed, this was the night of the school year when all the girls felt special, and they looked it.

The professors and faculty entered equally elegantly dressed and Governor Alister gave a short welcome address and waved the food onto the tables with his wand. Monique and Pam sat next to Lindsey and Jim. "Isn't Pam just the greatest?" Monique went on chatting while they ate. Lindsey didn't quite know what to make of Monique, however. Clearly, she was at least infatuated with Pam. Pam also very much enjoyed the attention of Monique. Lindsey made a mental note to talk with Pam in private one day soon.

Before long, the delicious meal was finished. With a wave of his wand, after announcing that the chairs would be disappearing—three boys hastily got up from their seated positions from which they'd hoped to avoid the dance—all the tables and chairs vanished. Lindsey suspected that they were now in one of those hidden rooms off the underground tunnels that they had yet to explore.

She noticed a group of musicians setting up to play. They had come in while the students were eating, and she hadn't noticed them. Soon, the stately music began. With Jim leading her out into the middle of the hall, now decorated in candlelight with gold and silver fluttering reflecting ribbons, Lindsey hoped that she could remember the dance lessons! One-two-three, she concentrated and focused her mind. Yet, she need not have worried so. The music literally demanded that rhythm, and Jim was very adept and smooth with her. Soon, she forgot all about dance lessons and followed his lead.

Before long, it was intermission time. Pam insisted that Tom and Sandy use her cell phone to take a picture of the four couples. Grinning, all eight of them squeezed in, while Tom and then Sandy took several snaps. Only after Pam reviewed them, did she allow the group to move from their positions. She then took some of Tom and Sandy for them.

Once more the music began. Jim led Lindsey elegantly into the middle of the room once again. Before long, the lights were dimmed, and Alister's soft voice announced, "Last dance of the ball." So soon! How did it get to be ten p.m. so quickly, Lindsey wondered. Only a minute ago it was six.

Jim pulled her body close to his as they danced this last one. Before long the music ended. Jim leaned over, gave Lindsey a kiss on her lips, and said, "Thank you, Lindsey for a fabulous evening I will never forget."

She flushed, "I've never had so much fun. Can we do this again? I don't want it to end." Jim smiled and led her to the stairs. One by one, the four girls entered their room, all feeling as if they were floating.

"I've never had so much fun!" Lindsey exclaimed, still dancing to soundless music around their room.

"Me either. Henry is ten times a better dancer than I am. I think he likes me," Amanda replied. "I know that Jim is smitten with you, Lindsey."

"Emilio has got to be the most improved dancer in the lot," Kathy added. "During the practices, I thought what a klutz. Yet, after he got the hang of it, he did really well. How did the time fly so fast anyway?"

"Honestly, for the first time in my life, I felt pretty tonight," Pam spoke up. "Monique really does like me a whole lot, just as I am, buck teeth, homely face and all. Jeesh, she sure knows how to dance well!"

For another lengthy time, the four divided into partners and danced around their room. Around midnight, the four finally undressed and put away their formal dresses. Lindsey wished that she had many more opportunities to dress up like this, like once a week, maybe. It made her feel so utterly different. She didn't quite know how to describe the feelings she felt this evening, but certainly, they were extremely special.

The next morning even before breakfast, Pam had them all race to the commons. "Look there they are: our grades. It's a magical board. You find your name and read across for your classes and grades in those classes. Only you can see your grades, no one else."

Lindsey saw what she meant at once, as she glanced at Pam's line. While she could read Pam Betts, all the adjoining columns were blank. Lindsey looked down the list slightly and found Lindsey Barron. She scanned across the columns; she had received an A in all of her subjects!

Quickly, the four compared grades. Pam also had straight A's, while Amanda had all A's except for a B in science. Kathy had all A's except for a C in math and a B in science. Emilio soon joined them and proudly announced, "Hey, I didn't do so badly. I got an A in Spell Casting! Yes! All B's for boring in everything else." The four laughed.

Pam spoke authoritatively, "Well, let's not just stand here. We can go get our next year's course schedules and even pick up our textbooks, so that we can study over the summer. Emilio, I strongly advise you to study very hard during the summertime. You need to do better than B for Boring, you know." He groaned, saying something about losing all his playtime.

At the bookstore, a large sign announced that due to technical difficulties the course schedules for the next year were not ready, but that they would be sent to the students later in the summer. However, all five were able to purchase their next year's spell book, Grade 2 and 3 Spells. "I'm going to try to have as many of these learned as possible before school starts," Pam announced. "This year was just too hectic." Lindsey wondered if it was wise to do this on one's own.

Next, came packing. Since the bus would be leaving just after breakfast the next morning, everything had to be packed up today. Pam explained that you could get larger trunks or boxes or more duffle bags from the Bookstore. One simply put their Wizard Mark on them and left them out in the hall in the morning. They would be whisked down into your bus by the staff while the students were eating their breakfasts.

Lindsey was grateful for the advice. She discovered that she now had far too much to fit in her single duffle bag, which she brought with her when she first arrived here last fall. In fact, she needed three duffle bags to hold everything. Her schoolbooks alone filled one bag.

Near lunchtime, the four girls had everything all ready to go at last. As they marched down to lunch, Amanda said, "Lindsey, if there is any way you can, we all want you to come and visit us in Arapahoe this summer! It's only about forty miles from Plano. I'll email you about it. Somehow, I want you to see our place."

"Darn, Limon is nearly a hundred miles from you, Amanda. I'd like to have you all come and visit me too, but it's so far," Kathy lamented.

"Well, Pueblo is much farther," Emilio said sadly. He was going to miss his new friends this summer.

Pam lamented, "Well, if you think that's bad, I'm up in Sterling, in the northeast corner. It has to be at least a hundred fifty miles as the crow flies. Mostly state roads, widely spaced, head down your way. I studied a norm map of Colorado, once. Yet, I do wish there was some way we could get together over the summer. Ah well, when we get sixteen, maybe one of us can get a car and drive everyone."

"Heck by that time, we all will be able to teleport ourselves there and no need for a car," Emilio jested. They all chuckled.

Pam added, "I've heard that teleporting can be dangerous."

"Not as dangerous as driving one of the norm's cars," Emilio jested.

With nothing remaining to do, the five headed out for a last walk around the campus. Jim spied them and joined them, taking Lindsey's arm, which she found somewhat exciting, though she didn't know why. By the time that they got to the gardens, they met up with Tom and Sandy, who joined them.

It seemed a bit strange to Lindsey to be doing nothing but walking around the pretty campus. No thoughts of homework papers, spells to learn, math assignments to be completed by the morrow, just pure idle time. For the last nine months, it had been a frantic, day-to-day rush of schoolwork and studies. Yes, she had enjoyed it immensely; her life had been forever changed for the better. Still, it felt strange to be walking around without any cares or concerns about flunking a test or paper—even stranger to be walking arm in arm with Jim.

At last, it was time for the Awards Dinner Meeting. The dining hall was decked out with giant hall colored tapestries. Banners and ribbons hung from the ceilings. Between the rows of student dining tables and the long table for the professors and the Governor sat another table. The large third place track trophy stood prominently in its center for all to see. A banner hung above it that read Arthur Bradbury's School of Magic—Third Place—National Track Meet.

The six hundred students and their teachers filed into the dining room, gazing at the decorations and the trophy, chatting among themselves. One hundred students were graduating tonight. A large stack of diplomas lay in two neat piles on either side of the tall track cup. Around the Yellow Hall table, Bill Ferny was being congratulated by his friends and of course his track team.

"Well, done Bill," Tom said shaking his hand. "We will certainly miss you around here."

Jim and the rest of his winning team also shook hands with him, and he asked, "So who've you picked to be our captain next year?"

Amanda whispered to Lindsey, "Jim told me that the outgoing captain can choose who will be captain after him. However, if we don't like it, we all can veto it, if a majority of us so desire. It'll be Sally or Becky. They'll be sixth years this fall. Golly, we will really be second years, Lindsey!"

Bill looked at the two girls and smiled, he had already spoken with them about this. "Your new captain will be Becky Salinos." The team clapped and congratulated Becky.

Sally explained, "I'm not a leader type, and I sure don't want that kind of responsibility in my last year here. Sixth year is the hardest, and I was struggling this year, but I'll play, as long as Becky doesn't hold too darn many practice sessions, that is."

Becky's face grimaced, "But that's how we got beaten. We need to practice running at least twenty miles, not five." Everyone laughed, but Lindsey knew she was actually quite correct in her observation. While she could manage one five-mile race, she was not up to doing four of them in one day at the Nationals. Winning that cup would take a very different strategy. She made a resolution to try to run much longer distances during the summer, if she could.

Governor Alister clicked his cup with his spoon, getting their attention. All chatter stopped at once. "Here we are once again at the end of another fine year at Bradbury's, more eventful than most, if I do say so myself. Tonight we are gathered to celebrate our new graduates and present any that are due special awards. However, first, we must all eat, so let the final dinner of this school term begin." He waved his wand and the tables were covered with hundreds of steaming, hot dishes.

Now sitting on one side of Lindsey, Jim explained, "Final Banquet always has the very best food of the whole year! My Lady Lindsey, would you prefer the roast pheasant under glass or the duck with almonds? I recommend the duck personally." Everyone chuckled at his imitation of a waiter.

"Oh the duck please," Lindsey said coyly, as if she were some royalty being served. Jim gallantly filled her plate for her, and the group of friends chuckled. "I can't believe this year has gone so fast and Bill won't be here next year."

Tom said, "I heard him saying he was going to apply for a job with the Department of Defense."

Sandy added, "He's certainly got the stamina for it. Pass the shrimp cocktails please." The group ate the finest meal this entire year. Lindsey discovered that she did like the duck, though she'd never had such fine food before. Before long, everyone was stuffed, and the chocolate pies were a big hit at dessert time. Their tables were once more magically emptied for them, and Lindsey found numerous teapots sitting before them, along with fine china cups. She poured a cup for Jim and her.

"Now it is time for the awards presentations. As you all know, this year Yellow Hall track team went to the Nationals and brought us back this fine trophy. At this time, I would like the nine members who worked so hard to earn this trophy for our school to come up here and receive a special Bradbury award. Bill, would you bring your team up here. Let's give them a hearty welcome."

While the students clapped, the nine, led by Bill, walked up by their trophy. One by one, beginning with the oldest team members, Alister presented each with a sash and a ring, shaking each student's hand personally. Then, all the team members held the hand of the member next to them and raised their hands high in a victory celebration, while the students clapped loudly. Once they had returned to their seats, Alister began once more.

"Now it is time to hand out the diplomas. I'm very pleased to announce that this year all one hundred sixth year students have passed both the State of Colorado High School Exams and Bradbury's Magic Exams. I give you one hundred, full-fledged wizards and witches."

"While I am handing out the diplomas to these most deserving students, I want you who are graduating and leaving Bradbury's to think about this. You are now considered adults, but not ordinary adults, rather wizards and witches. You are special people, and as such, you now don a very special responsibility that is denied those of our world who do not possess magical abilities. You have great powers and skills. You have the obligation and responsibility to use them for good; use this power wisely and for the good of all mankind, not just for your own personal ends. I wish to remind you of your oath to obey these inviolate laws.

1. Thou shalt not use magic to injure or harm another unjustly.

2. Thou shalt not use magic to kill another unjustly.

3. Thou shalt not use magic to steal from another that which is not yours.

4. Thou shalt not use magic to force another to do something against their will unjustly."

"Now please withhold your applause until all one hundred have received their diplomas, otherwise we will be here all night long, and I will be forced to make the cooks work overtime to prepare yet another feast. That was a joke, by the way." Several chuckles echoed in the room.

"Addison, Jane." A tall Blue Hall girl rose and walked up to him. He shook her hand and handed her two diplomas. She bowed to him and returned to her seat, her friends hastily looking at her two papers. One by one, the one hundred names were called. Occasionally, some would forget and start clapping when a friend's name was called, but it quickly stopped. That happened when Ferny, Bill was called.

A half hour later, a thunderous round of applause was given to all these students. "Next—oh you thought I was done?" Alister teased the student body.

"It is with the greatest of pleasure that I announce that this year, Bradbury's is making some additional awards. As you all know by now, our school was twice attacked, broken into, and indeed robbed by Dominus Malefic. During these terrible times, four students displayed remarkable courage, valor, bravery, and wit. I daresay not many full-fledged wizards or witches would dare face off with Dominus Malefic. Yet these four first year students did so at great peril to their own lives. They acted not out of selfishness or some desire for great fame, but on behalf of all the people of the world. Had Dominus gained control of that ancient Rod of the Apocalypse, we would all be facing our doom tonight, not our awards banquet. It is with the greatest honor that I present these four the Bradbury's Distinguished Service Medallion."

"When I call your name, please step up here so that I may present to you your medallion. First, for extreme bravery, coming to the assistance of his friends who were facing Dominus, I present the Distinguished Service Medallion to Emilio Lopez." Looking rather embarrassed, he rose to a loud round of applause. Alister shook his hand and hung a golden medallion around his neck. "Please stay up here, just move over to the side a little," Alister whispered to him.

"Next, for perhaps the greatest sleuthing Bradbury's has ever seen, this young woman was the first to realize that Dominus had kidnaped Lindsey Barron, had used a Morph Self into Another to become as she says a not-Lindsey, and to alert us all in a timely manner to Dominus's attempt to steal

328

the rod, I am proud to present the Distinguished Service Medallion to Pam Betts." She also looked very ill at ease walking up in front of all the students. Pam never desired to be the center of attention. Monique cheered and yelled loudly, making her even more embarrassed. He shook her hand and placed the medallion around her neck. She stood next to Emilio.

"If your friend was taken prisoner by Dominus Malefic, would you risk all to follow him back to your friend and attempt to rescue him or her all by yourself? Yet that is precisely what Amanda Whitewater did. In fact, Amanda led the Department of Defense forces to the cabin where Lindsey was being held prisoner. It is with great pride that I present this Distinguished Service Medallion to Amanda Whitewater." As the Apache walked up, her brothers yelled and cheered; she flushed, but accepted her medallion with pride.

"You have undoubtedly heard all manner of fictitious reports on what happened in the news. I find that they seldom get their facts correct. Just how was Dominus able to break into our school? I must admit I overlooked this simple method. My enchantments allowed only students and staff to pass through our gates. Unfortunately, this forced Dominus to take another approach. While Lindsey was at the Nationals in Des Moines, he stunned her and used his Morph spell to change his body into one identical to hers, in effect becoming Lindsey Barron."

"For his spell to work, the real-Lindsey, to use Pam's nomenclature, had to remain alive at all costs. Yet, Dominus knew that she was a master of basic spells, well on her way to becoming a witch. If you tie up and gag a norm, that pretty well puts them completely under your control, but not a wizard or witch. A simple Untie useful spell and they are free. What could Dominus do to ensure that Lindsey remain a prisoner watched over by Rubius, while he stole the rod? As Professor Janice so fondly likes to teach the first years, your wand must activate properly, and that means proper hand motion as it is waved. His solution was indeed a simple one, if not wholly inhumane. He used a terrible spell to cut off her hands, while she stood there stunned, unable to even cry out from the horrible pain of the wounds."

"Still this was not enough, for she could yell for help as soon as the stun spell wore off and the pain subsided. She does have a shrill voice." Several giggled at that. "Dominus had to keep her silent at all times, what better way than to sew her mouth shut with a very nasty spell. Can you imagine being tied to a chair, your hands cut off, your mouth tied shut, held prisoner by the Death Stalker Rubius, and knowing when Dominus returns, he most certainly will kill you? That was what Lindsey faced, something so terrible that I would not wish that on my worst enemy."

"Then Dominus did return, bringing with him that awful relic. Now her only thoughts were somehow to get that rod away from him. She, a first year witch, did just that. No, Lindsey does not possess any spells that could possibly harm Dominus or even Rubius. Yet, she had to try. Few have ever shown such resourcefulness. Using only non-verbal, non-wand spell casting, in the space of a few minutes only, Lindsey cast every one of the spells in the Grade 0 and 1 book! Fog proved the most useful, along with Untie, of course. She correctly Identified the first rod command word and brought forth the First Horseman, whose task was to spread a great pestilence and famine across the entire world! She gave the rod to this horseman, effectively destroying the rod forever, saving us all from a most terrible fate indeed."

"Thus, with the greatest of honor I wish to present this final Distinguished Service Medallion to Miss Lindsey Barron, daughter of Samuel Rabnor, the great wizard, who captured Dominus over fourteen years ago." Lindsey hated being in the limelight. Only because Jim pushed her did she rise and begin to walk to Alister. The clapping was so loud she could barely hear him thanking her as he placed the heavy golden medallion over her chest.

"As you go forth into the summer vacation, you will hear all manner of wild rumors about what happened here. I wanted you all to know the truth from me. Use it as a yardstick to measure the rumors. Now let's give a final round of applause to our distinguished students." At last, the four were allowed to sit back down as the clapping and cheering died down.

"As the hour is getting late, I will stop my chatting. You all have a bus to catch first thing in the morning. I hope your summer vacation is a profitable and enjoyable one, and I anxiously await your return to Bradbury's in the fall. Good night." The professors all got up and left with Alister, while the students began filing out, heading to their rooms.

However, many of their friends crowded around the four, anxious to have a peek at their medallions. "It's pure gold!" exclaimed Emilio, quite surprised. By the time the four girls got to their room, it was nearly midnight. As Lindsey was getting into bed, a Message floated before her eyes.

I'll meet you for breakfast at eight tomorrow. A.

She smiled; tomorrow she would get to go to Denver and see what, if anything, was in her father's vault.

Chapter 19—The Vault

The five-some met for their last breakfast. Lindsey didn't want this school term to end. Finding these incredible new friends seemed like a miracle. Now they were leaving, splitting, going their separate ways, scattering to the corners of Colorado. She felt pangs of loss and yearned to be with all them during the summer, which was impossible, as none had any transportation. Perhaps the others were feeling pretty much the same, because all five talked nonstop, barely pausing to swallow. It was as if they had to say an entire summer's worth of conversation within these last few minutes.

Her emotions were a confused bundle. Jim, who gave her a farewell hug, only added to them. Thankfully, Governor Alister allowed her time to see her friends off to the bus. After a flurry of last-second goodbyes and hugs, Lindsey stood alone in the parking lot, as her bus with her friends vanished from sight. She sighed and walked slowly back to the dining hall, passing more students heading to the parking lot for the next bus to take them home.

It felt strange walking into the completely deserted dining hall. Gone was the constant background chatter of six hundred students. Only Alister now sat at the long table, sipping a cup of tea, waiting patiently for her. "Ah, the bus has left with your friends, I presume. Said your farewells, have you?" She nodded, afraid tears would show if she actually spoke.

"Good. That is as it should be. Yes, I must admit that I too feel sad every June 1. I do miss all you students. Yet, you do need some free time, time to play and just be a child growing up. Now, then, all packed?" She nodded. "Since the staff will be giving the dorms a thorough cleaning, let's move your things into my office shall we?" The two walked up the stairs to her room, where she had her duffle bags ready to go.

Only when the two entered her room did she realize that he had come up the girls'-only stairs. "How did you? I mean I thought?" she tried to ask.

332

"You forget. It was I that put that enchantment on the stairs. It certainly keeps the older ones from trying to sneak into their girl or boyfriend's rooms. Now then, Move: Bags to My Office!" His wand gave a little lifting motion and her bags vanished.

"Cool. Will I learn to do that soon?" she asked.

"Oh yes, I believe so. Now even I can't teleport from within the walls of Bradbury, so we'll have to go to the parking lot. Shall I open a door there or should we just walk?" he asked politely.

"It's such a nice day. Could we walk so I can take one last look at the school before I go?" she asked. He smiled, and the two walked down the stairs and out onto the grassy lawn. "It seems so deserted, so empty," she commented.

"Ah you notice that too," he said softly. "It's the students who bring life to the school. I miss them already. Yet, it is only three months, and we will once more be all together here." They walked on in silence, each with their own thoughts. As they passed the repaired gates, they saw the last bus leaving. It really was just the two of them, though Lindsey did not ask where the professors had gone.

"Now then, we are off to Denver. The bank also does not allow anyone to teleport inside it, security reasons, naturally. I will take us a block away so you can see the impressive building. Have you ever been to Denver?"

"No sir. I've only been to Plano. From the maps, Denver must be very big indeed."

"Yes, very. Hold my hand and here we go." He said their destination, some street location in Denver, but she didn't pay attention; she just held her breath. She blinked, and they were standing on a sidewalk. Many pedestrians walked past them, while Lindsey just stared at the huge, tall buildings, reaching towards the sky. She'd never seen such tall buildings before and was extremely impressed.

Satisfied that she was oriented in her new surroundings, Alister led her long the street. "Golly, I wouldn't want to be way up there at the top unless I had my Gentle Fall spell at the ready! It must take them ages to climb all those stairs to the top."

"They have elevators that take them up to the top in a matter of a minute or so. Here is our building." Lindsey saw a sign that read: Lloyd's Secure Vaults. This building was only perhaps six stories tall, far less impressive than those around it. Not many were entering this building, however. "The vaults are deep underground, heavily enchanted, and well-guarded, I might add." He opened the glass doors, and the two stepped inside.

At the reception desk, Alister said, "Miss Lindsey Barron to see Mr. Groggs, Vault Verification." While he was talking, Lindsey looked around. Several wizards were at the tellers making some deposits.

"Room 2, that way; you can't miss it," the bespectacled woman with somewhat overdone makeup pointed. She had long nails and red hair tied into a nice looking bun, very businesslike, Lindsey thought.

Mr. Groggs was in his late thirties, with an immaculately pressed grey business suit. His glasses sat on the edge of his nose so that his eyes looked over the top of them, as he looked up at the two who entered. He rose at once, "Ah, Mr. Broadwell, good to see you again. And this must be Miss Lindsey Barron Rabnor." He shook Lindsey's hand firmly and then Alister's. "Please have a seat. I know time is important, so we will make this as quick as possible. Now then, Samuel Rabnor has rented vault 716 for a period of one hundred years, paid in full. This means that, once you have been verified as the rightful inheritor, Lindsey, you have another eighty-one years of rent-free use of the vault. After that point in time, you may renew your lease for various durations. All that will be explained as the due date gets nearer. Now then, before we get ahead of ourselves, we must verify that you are the rightful inheritor. If you will open your mouth, I will take a swap for DNA checking. It doesn't hurt."

She opened her mouth, and he took a swipe with what appeared to be cotton ball on a stick. He inserted it into a device and pushed several buttons. He typed rapidly on his computer, while Lindsey wondered what he could possibly be typing, since she had not said anything. "There, I have Sam's file up for comparison. Yes, your birth certificate is in order and on file in Plano. Where is that town, by the way?" Lindsey did her best to describe its location far out on the high plains.

The machine beeped, and he looked at the screen and then pivoted it around so both could see it. "Here on the left is your father's DNA, and yours is on the right. Notice the red connecting lines between the two. Those makers are what you both have in common, proving conclusively that you are his biological daughter. Since no other birth records are on file in the State of Colorado, this makes you his only heir. Oh yes, we also have his death certificate on file. See, that was fast, simple, and totally secure. Next, I replace his DNA key with yours." He pressed another key.

"Done. Now then to business. When you wish to visit your vault, you come here and tell the receptionist that you wish access to your vault. She will direct you to the vault entrance room. From there, an assistant will take you by elevator and cart to your vault. When you push the open button, a cotton-tipped stick will appear, with which you simply swab inside your mouth. It then compares the DNA to what we've taken today. If they match precisely, the vault will open. Please note, due to security reasons, no other person can ever open your vault. We here, at Lloyd's Secure Vaults, pride ourselves on having the most secure vaults in the entire world, state of the art security."

"As an added convenience for our many customers, at any time you may make an automated deposit at one of the counters you passed as you entered. Usually, the deposits are monetary in nature. Tell the teller your vault number, 716, and the funds will be deposited there. However, because only you can actually open your vault, the funds actually go into a temporary holding vault. The next time you open your vault, the system automatically transfers all temporary deposits directly into your vault. If you are anticipating a large amount to be deposited in this fashion, I recommend that you wait a minute before entering. Some of our customers have been a bit hasty upon entering and got a pile of money dumped onto their heads. Harmless, but unnerving. If you have any questions, please ask. It has been a pleasure transferring this vault to you, Miss Barron, or do you prefer Miss Rabnor?"

"Barron, I think, for now, at least." Lindsey had never thought about which last name to use, so she stayed with what she had been given when she was born. They shook hands, and Alister led them to the vault entrance room.

"Good morning. Vault number?" the pleasant young man, equally immaculately dressed said. Lindsey replied 716. "Follow me, please." He rose and led them to an elevator. At the same time, another nearly identically dressed young man entered the room and sat down at the desk, awaiting another customer's arrival. They entered what appeared to be a normal elevator. However, Lindsey had never been in one before. It was a strange feeling, falling quickly down, while not actually "falling."

"First time to the vaults?" the man asked as they descended.

"Yes, sir," she replied, noticing that there appeared to be ten floors, all with negative numbers.

"Your vault is in the seventh layer below ground; hence, I pressed the −7 button. Ah, here we are. Please step into this cart. It is electrically driven, so it is silent." It looked rather like a golfing cart. Soon they were speeding down a long hallway. Lindsey spied the vault numbers on plaques as they passed. In short order, the cart stopped at 716.

"I will leave you now; your privacy is guaranteed. When you are ready to leave, pick up one of the white courtesy phones and tell us. Also, if your withdrawal is too large, bulky, or heavy, we have trailers that we can attach to the carts. Again, white courtesy phones. Finally, if your withdrawal requires top security, also call. We will provide a number of guards to guarantee your safety to the front doors. After that, it becomes your responsibility." He nodded and left.

Lindsey pushed the open button and swabbed her mouth with the stick that appeared. She inserted it back into the mechanism. Shortly, the vault made an enormous bunch of clicking noises and opened. Both stared inside as lights automatically turned on. His vault was twenty feet square, a rather large one.

"What is all this stuff?" Lindsey asked, dumbfounded. Opposite of empty, her vault contained quite a lot of items, including a fancy writing desk and chair. Piles of money sat neatly stacked in one corner, ten bars of gold lay beside them, along with a small pouch. Several large chests rested on one side of the room.

"My, my. It is indeed a pleasant surprise. It would seem that your father has left you quite a lot, Lindsey," Alister commented. From the surprised look on his face, Lindsey knew that he was very surprised to find this much in the vault.

Lindsey's eyes were drawn to the very nice desk. She had never had anything as fine as this. However, as she looked at the desktop, a letter was sitting squarely in the middle. Lindsey gasped. In clear, large script letters, it said: To Lindsey Barron.

"Well, it looks like old Sam knew what he was doing. I think that prudence dictates that you open and read that letter first, Lindsey. You do not need to show it to me, if you find it is too private."

Unable to hold back tears, she opened the letter as if it was the most valuable thing in the world. Indeed, to her at this moment, it was. She noticed the date at the top, he had written this when she was four years old.

My Dearest Lindsey,

If you are reading this, then many things have happened that I had foreseen. Well, I didn't, but my dear friend Mabel Pruit has. If you are reading this, I am no longer alive, and that is the one thing that I truly regret—not being able to explain my life and decisions in person, especially those concerning you. I hope you do not hate me after reading this. I will begin at the beginning and try to put this in context for you. Perhaps, some of this you already know by now.

Long before you were born a very evil and most powerful wizard, who went by the name Dominus Malefic, threatened the entire world with his madness. He murdered countless people, usually by magical spells. Eluding capture by the world's police forces, he built up a body of ardent supporters known as the Death Stalkers. They got that name because they stalked and murdered those whom their master, Dominus, wished slain.

At last, four of us could take this evil no longer; we formed a group dedicated to the capture of Dominus and his Death Stalkers. Others referred to us as the Rat Pack. Each of us brought a unique skill to the task. Mabel Pruit was our Diviner, who could foretell where they may likely strike next. Able Monument's task, as a Tracker, was to hunt them down, to follow them wherever they may go. Once we found them, my job as Dispeller was to nullify and render ineffectual the spells that they cast at us, murderous, evil spells. This then allowed Bill West, our Eliminator, to use his spells to capture them.

After a year of hunting, we were successful in capturing Dominus and ten of his Death Stalkers, of which three were killed during the capture. However, two things went wrong after that. One, the Court of Law refused to use Capital Punishment on these men, preferring to lock them in prison for the rest of their lives. Why was this wrong? Escape is inevitable; according to Mabel, eventually, it would happen. Then once more, they would be threatening our entire world. Second, we knew that we had not gotten all the Death Stalkers that day. No one knows how many of them there were; to me, ten seemed an awfully low number. That means many of these powerful wizards and witches are still on the loose, to say nothing of their underlings and hidden supporters, of which I believe many are in positions of power in our world.

While the magical and norm world celebrated the capture of these ruthless men and women, the Rat Pack knew retribution would be forth coming. Not long after Dominus was sent to prison, Mabel and her immediate family were hideously murdered in the night by those who remained anonymous and on the loose. We could not get the Department of Law or the Department of Defense to fund our continuing search to find these remaining ones. We never knew why that was, just that it was.

When Mabel was slain, the three of us decided that without the support of our leaders, we were sitting ducks, men with a price on our heads. Eventually, the Death Stalkers would find us and attack us. Able, Bill, and I decided simply to disappear from the world. Our long-range plan and bargain was to rejoin when the government finally came to its senses, publically apologized to us, and offered us double funding this time. In these past few years, I have had no word from Able or Bill, or they, from me.

I leased this vault for a century and put all my equipment and excess funds in here. I went undercover as a norm man, down on his luck. They would be looking for a powerful Dispeller, a powerful wizard, not a poor norm man. I headed out onto the desolate high plains, where I hoped to hide out until the government came to its senses. I chose remote Plano.

Lindsey, it was there that I met the most wonderful woman that I have ever known, your mother Lena. Strong willed, able, excellent rancher, no nonsense, loving, compassionate, kind, I just cannot find enough words to describe Lena. We married and those years became the happiest of my entire life. Then, when she became pregnant, the second greatest joy was to come into my life, you, my dear daughter.

Yet, when you were born without hands, I nearly died! Yes, the norms have their own brands of evil men. Some buried contaminated wastes instead of properly disposing of them. In my world of magic, the very day you were born, I could have taken you to one of our doctors and had hands grown at once. I have the funds many times over to pay for it. However, Lindsey, please, please forgive me. I could not do it. I dare not even mention that this was even possible to your mother. Why? When hands are re-grown, a DNA search is routinely done. Immediately, everyone would have known that you were my daughter; my hidden identity would be revealed to the world. Sam Barron was Sam Rabnor. From that moment onward, our very lives would be in dire jeopardy! The Death Stalkers would be seeking revenge on me, your mother, and you, my precious daughter. You two meant the world to me. I had to protect you from that.

Thus, I could not get your hands re-grown. Lindsey, I cried each night after I tucked you in and kissed your forehead. I was dooming you to a most horrible life. I had the power to change it, but dared not use that power. I have been in utter misery over this for the last four years. I beg of you, dearest Lindsey, please forgive your father for having allowed you to grow up in the most horrible of ways. If you are still without hands as you read this, I have attached a business card of a facility, which will re-grow your hands. There are more than enough funds to do so immediately.

When you turned four years old, I began to see that you, too, would be able to command the magical energies that we wizards and witches use. Finally, hope flooded into me. One day, you may well get the opportunity to attend a magical school. When that happens, you were sure to discover that I was your father, of that, I was certain, if only by having your hands re-grown. Thus, filled with miraculous hope for the future, I took a trip to Denver, to this vault, and am writing this letter of explanation to you. I also tidied up all my magical items, preparing them for you. By now, you probably know that each has unique command words that activate its magic. I have composed a complete listing of them to spare you the challenge of figuring them out on your own, with possible errors or incomplete identifications.

As soon as you have new hands, the Death Stalkers will know of it. Eventually, one or more of them will come after you. Therefore, I bequeath to you the tools of my trade. Three of the most critical items I made myself, they are unique in the magical world. I urge you to wear these three items on you at all times when you are outside of your magical school. Within the school's grounds, you should be fairly safe, though nothing is a sure thing in the world of magic.

The first item has saved my life on numerous occasions. I call it my Chameleon Robe. When you throw the hood over your head and say Robe: Hide, it will automatically blend your entire body into whatever the background looks like. Hence, you will be next to impossible to spot, unless you subsequently attack from hiding. If you wish to wear it instead of your magic school robes, it can automatically change its appearance to match all known school robes. Say Robe: Change to and then say the full name of the school of magic.

However, its major property has no need of a command word. When you are wearing it, it automatically nullifies all standard Grade 0 to 4 spells. None of those spells in those books will effect or harm you in any way. You see, when I am trying to capture a bunch of wizards at one time, spells are flying fast and furious. There just isn't enough time to counter all the spells that come flying your way. The robe handles all lower spells, so that I can concentrate on nullifying the higher level, vastly more dangerous, spells.

The second item that you should wear at all times is my Runner Pin. I apologize for its appearance not being so feminine looking. Yet, when you wear this pin, no one can ever summon you nor can they ever charm you and take over control of you.

The third item that you should also wear at all times is my Runner Ring. While you are wearing it, no one can scry on you. They cannot know your thoughts and intentions or plans. With these three items on you, you ought to be fairly safe.

In the corner is my Staff of Power. Again, I apologize for having made its command word so testosterone orientated. When you wish the staff to absorb a spell being cast, simply say Staff: Suck It, and point to the spell caster; it will absorb that spell. In school, you will learn more about such staff's operations. If not, ask one of your teachers. I gave her the name of Margarete, she will need to bond with you the first time you use her. Again, ask your teachers for help, if you do not already know all about such things.

There are many other useful items in this vault. I have catalogued them on the following pages, along with activation words. Use them wisely, as I know you will.

As far as the money goes, I have only one request. Please use some of it to help your mother live a better life. Be careful; she, like I, detest charity. We work for our pay, so be discrete in how you use it to help her out.

Finally, my dearest Lindsey, I wanted to tell you that in my entire life, I loved only two women with every fiber in my being, Lena and you. I have done everything I can think of to protect you two and keep you alive, free from my past deeds. I hope that you can forgive me for having allowed you to have lived so long without hands. There is nothing that I regret more in my whole life than this, but I could not see any way to avoid it. I am truly sorry that my past has caused you such a lifetime of grief, despair, and hardship beyond belief.

Your mother and you have taught me that love is the most important aspect of life. Remember always, I love you more than I can ever say.

Your father,

Samuel Rabnor

PS. If the world goes bad again, seek out Able and Bill. We all did the same with our names.

Bawling, Lindsey finished reading it, and said, "I forgive you dad. I always have. I love you too. I never blamed you." Alister put a comforting hand on her shoulder and said nothing for a time. At last, Lindsey handed the letter to Alister so he could read it as well.

A bit later, she heard him mutter, "So that's how you did it, you sly rascal. I always wondered about that." She looked at him questioningly.

"Oh, sorry. His Chameleon Robe, and to a lesser extent his Runner Pin and Ring. Clever man, your father. I think that you should follow his advice as much as possible from now on, though you may have to remove these when you are in spell casting class. I'm afraid the other students will not appreciate their spells not working when they finally get them right." She smiled as she grasped what he was implying.

"Now then, first, let's get the staff attuned to you. Margarete. Pick it up and concentrate on her name. Yes, that's the way. Now say to her, my father left you to me, and then tell her your name and ask her to accept you as her new owner."

Lindsey, holding the large staff taller than she was, said, "Margarete, my father Sam Rabnor has left you to me. I am Lindsey Barron. Please accept me as your new owner." After a pause, magical energies flashed from the staff and shot throughout her entire body. Her eyes opened wide, and she looked at Alister.

"She has accepted you. Now here is a vital detail about your staff. Please sit her over in the corner. Yes, there is fine. Now walk over by me. Good. Now say 'Margarete: Come' and hold out your hand."

She did as he asked. "Margarete: Come." She was not prepared for what happened. Instantly, the staff flew from the corner and landed vertically in her hand, ready for action. "Wow! Cool! Neat!"

Alister grinned, remembering the first time that he had summoned a staff, way back in his youth. "No matter where the staff is at on earth and no matter where you are, if you summon her, she will come. However, if she and you are separated by a thousand miles, it will take her a while to get to you." Lindsey giggled; this was the coolest thing!

"Now ask her 'Charges Please,' and she will tell you how much spell energy she is currently holding out of her total capacity. This is critical for her proper use. If she has absorbed all that she can, she will be unable to Suck It any further. You can discharge some of that accumulated energy by using her to cast your spells. Use her like you use your wand. Now ask her please."

Lindsey looked at her staff as if she was somehow alive. "Charges Please." In her mind, she heard "15 out of 30." She told Alister the numbers.

"Ah, excellent balance. Your father likes to keep his staff in balance. Wise practice. You see, she can absorb a good deal, and yet can activate a good deal, whichever is needed. If you are going into a battle where you know that you will need to absorb many spells, then shoot off a number of spells beforehand. On the other hand, if you know you are tired and need help shooting spells, cast spells into her to charge her up even further. Got the idea?" She nodded.

"Good. I suspect that you should also take your staff along with you as well. I will MagMail you a book on the proper care and use of your Staff of Power shortly. Your father is right; eventually, the Death Stalkers will likely come after you. However, let us hope that it is much later, so that you can learn all the spells you possibly can, Lindsey."

"Sir, with all this money here, I no longer need the full scholarship to Bradbury's. I can pay my way, I think, though I don't know the cost nor how much is here. This way, some other deserving poor student can have a chance of going to school," Lindsey explained.

Alister smiled. "Thank you for your generosity and for thinking of those less fortunate than you are. I accept your offer. You have a very large sum of money here. The cost of your remaining five years will hardly be noticed. He counted out some bills and said, "If I may take this with me, I will see that your fees are paid in full for your five remaining years and that another deserving student is given an opportunity to come to Bradbury's on a full scholarship. Thank you very much, Lindsey." She smiled.

He suggested, "We should take some of these funds and open up a mag bank account for you. Then, you will have the funds to purchase what you need as you need it."

"How much is in here, Governor Alister? Should we count it? What am I to do with all the rest of these things? Take them home with me? We don't really have room for all these things."

"I believe the wisest action is to leave those that you do not need at the moment here where they are safe. While you are at school, who's to watch over these? Some are very valuable. I recommend that you take the three items your father suggested and your staff. However, why don't you look over the rest of the items and see if there are additional things that you might wish to take with you. While you are doing that, I'll see if I can get a handle on the money tally. You are correct. You ought to know the exact amount that is here."

Lindsey liked this idea and began going down the list of cool magical items her father had left her. The magical stove and all the kitchenware, while really neat and efficient, Lindsey didn't need now, not for some years. After spending a half hour rummaging through the list and looking them over, she decided to take another ring with her, one that would make her invisible to others. That could be very useful indeed.

Alister used magic, of course, to count the stacks of norm monetary bills. Even after removing her donation for her schooling, she had $512,496 in bills of various denominations. The value of the ten gold ingots, the five of platinum, and the two of silver he could only estimate. He explained, "The last time I checked, gold was going for about eight hundred dollars an ounce, platinum, five thousand, and silver, two. They vary a little day by day. Probably you have another half million dollars' worth here. I believe he was planning to use this supply to create more magically enchanted items, where only the finest materials can be used. The small pouch contains an assortment of cut gemstones, diamonds, rubies, and emeralds, again, most likely for the construction of magical items. My suggestion is to open up a bank account with say one hundred thousand dollars. If you chose to use Lloyd's here as also your bank, there is an additional feature that you may opt to use. This chute here. You can place additional bills in there. If you use up the one hundred thousand, you can automatically draw upon the bills here in the chute."

"One hundred thousand dollars? Gosh, sir, how could I possibly spend all of that? I've never had more than a dollar to spend in Plano at the candy store. Yet, if you think this is the wise course to follow, let's do so. I don't know how I can ever get here again on my own."

"If you need to come again, I or one of your professors would be willing to bring you. Just don't make frequent trips," he teased. She giggled; she would love to spend days in the vault, if only because these things were her fathers. Somehow just being around them made her feel closer to him.

"I'll put another hundred thousand in the chute, and we'll take along another hundred thousand to open your account on our way out. Are you about finished?"

A sigh told him what he suspected, that she would spend all day in here if she could. "I guess I am ready." She stuffed the letter from her father into a pocket. She carried the Chameleon Robe in her arms, but put on the two rings and stuck the pin on her school robes. She picked up her staff and said that she was ready. Alister carried a large bundle of norm bills and the two left. He showed her how to shut the vault. The small cart was sitting just outside their vault awaiting them.

"Mind if I drive?" he said with a grin. "I've always wanted to drive one of these things." She giggled and watched him enjoy driving them the relatively short distance to the elevator. A few minutes later, they filled out the paperwork for her new mag bank account. He also insisted that she take one hundred dollars with her as summer spending money, but of course, she could easily withdraw more from her new account, if she needed more. Lindsey had no idea how she could possibly spend a whole hundred dollars though.

Around eleven o'clock, the two emerged from Lloyd's. "Now we should be getting you home to your mother. I promised her to have you back by noon." Lindsey held on to his hand and the next instant they arrived back at Bradbury's parking lot. A wand wave later, her bags arrived at her feet. Alister picked up two and she, the other. Another instant later, the two stood in the driveway leading to her front porch.

"Thank you ever so much, Governor Alister, for everything. Would you like to come inside and meet my mother?"

"Perhaps another day, Lindsey. I have some other important actions to take yet today. I will see you in just a few months. Goodbye for a little while." He was surprised; she leaned over and gave him a warm hug. "Oh my!" he said with a smile, and was gone, a magical ripple dispersed from where he was standing.

With two trips to the porch, she had her bags out of the sun. She opened the door and called out, "I'm home, mom."

"Oh, I didn't hear the bus. Let me see you," Lena exclaimed, gave her a long hug, and peppered her forehead with loving kisses. She helped carry her daughter's bags inside the small ranch house. From the kitchen, Lindsey smelled lunch cooking.

For the next few minutes, while Lena continued fixing lunch, the two chatted rapidly. Lindsey had so much to tell her. Still telling her mother about the spring, Lena rang the diner bell, as she sat the table for three. Lloyd Compton, the man from the Department of Defense, would be joining them. Indeed, shortly after the bell rang outside, Lloyd came inside, sweating from the morning's labors. "Hello, Lindsey, you are looking very well indeed."

"You two wash up. Lunch is ready," Lena ordered and the two obeyed. Lunch consisted of a hearty soup with homemade biscuits.

While they were eating, Lloyd asked Lena, "Have you

told her yet?" Lindsey looked at her mother, who flushed.

"Er, not yet, Lloyd," she said very softly.

"Okay, it really is my place to do this, Lena." He faced Lindsey across the table from him. "Lindsey, you have one incredibly fabulous mother here. She is quite a woman. We, er, I have, well, having been here for nearly a year now, we, er, well, we have fallen in love with each other." He paused to watch Lindsey's reaction thus far.

"Mom?" Lindsey turned to her side to look at her mother, questioningly. She was taken completely by surprise.

"Well, we have, dear. I never thought that I could again, I mean after your father died. It just happened, I guess."

"Cool, mom! That's great." Lindsey urged her mother on, but she didn't say anything more.

Lloyd did. "Last month, I proposed to Lena. She accepted with one condition, that you would accept her marrying me and having me as your stepfather. I know I can never fill Sam's shoes. I will not even try. I only hope you like me for myself. What do you think, Lindsey?"

Both adults faced her, she giggled, "Mom, this is so way cool! Wow. Great, I like Lloyd too. Does this mean you are going to be married and have a ceremony and all that?" Lindsey had no idea what weddings were like, never having been to one. "Now I won't feel so badly when I am gone to school for nine months, mom. You will have someone else around here."

Lloyd answered her question. "Normally, when two people get married, a big celebration is held, fancy dresses, dinners, all the trimmings. However, we both know your mom is a practical woman, who wants none of that. She is also a bit worried about the criminals who may be after you and her for revenge, to say nothing of the annoying reporters who keep coming around here. You heard that she ran one off with a shotgun blast, didn't you?"

Lindsey laughed, "Yes, I wish I could have seen that! I'm sorry mom, that these bad men are likely to threaten us. I didn't mean to have them find out about us and dad and all that."

"Well, dear, it could not be helped. The most important

thing is that you now have hands; that is worth the world to me. No matter what the cost, it was worth it," Lena explained.

"Lindsey, we've discussed this at length. We will get married and have a very private ceremony, just the three of us. That way, few people will know that Lena Barron is now Lean Compton. Perhaps that will help throw them off her trail," Lloyd suggested sounding hopeful.

"Fine by me. I like that idea."

Lena fiddled with her apron, "Lindsey, there is another thing I have to tell you. I hope this doesn't upset you. There is no easy way to say this."

"What mom?" curiosity swelling within Lindsey.

"I've sold our ranch."

"What?"

"Yes, the Blackstone Corporation who owns the surrounding land made me an offer I can't refuse. It seems we are smack dab in the middle of their operations here. They are giving me fifty thousand dollars for this small ranch. That's ten times the yearly profit I've been able to make out of it each year now."

"But where will we go? Where will we live?" Lindsey became a little upset. Her home was being pulled out from under her feet.

"This is the best part of it all, dear. I've just signed a mortgage on a new ranch. Old Haskell Breckenridge recently passed away and his ranch, twenty-five square miles, came up for sale. I bought it, dear, house, barn, wells, everything. I got it for one hundred thousand dollars. The land is significantly better than we have here. He has three, one-mile in diameter, irrigated crop circles! The yearly profit from those will be easily double what I have been making here, ignoring what else I can make from the remaining acreage. Our place here covered half of the cost, and the mortgage covers the remaining half."

"Mom, I don't know any Haskell Brecken-whatever," Lindsey said, unable to tell if she was happy or sad about this whole thing. "I thought the corporation owned nearly everything around here."

"They do, honey. He is not from around here. Our new

348

ranch is just to the northwest and abuts the Indian Reservation at Arapahoe, about forty miles east of here, near the Kansas line. I think you will like the house; it has seven rooms, not the three we have here. You will have your own private room now," Lena was trying desperately to say everything she could to convince Lindsey that this would be a good move for them. She was not expecting the reaction she got from Lindsey.

"Whoopee! Fantastic! The best news ever, mom!" Lindsey jumped up from the table and hugged her mother, unable to contain the flood of emotional excitement flowing through her.

Totally taken aback, Lena said, "I'm so sorry, Lindsey. I didn't know that you wanted your own private room so badly. If you had said something, perhaps we could have somehow made you a small room in this house."

"No, no, it's not that, mom. It's where! Arapahoe! Arapahoe! Some of my best friends live in Arapahoe! Now I can visit them! Whoopee, whoopee!"

Lena looked at Lloyd, both smiled at each other. He said, "See, Lena, you were all worried for nothing, though I didn't know she would be this excited about the move."

"Well, dear. Don't bother unpacking. We move tomorrow morning. This afternoon, we are going into Plano for our wedding ceremony. Nearly everything is already packed, just the last minute things," she explained.

As Lindsey sat there, the words from her father's letter came back into her mind. "Use some of it to help your mother live a better life." She had an idea how she could.

"Mom, dad left me an inheritance. That's why I came home a day late. Governor Alister took me into Denver to see what, if anything, dad left for me. He cautioned me that it may well be nothing, but it turned out that dad really did love you and me and left me some money. I think that both of you should read dad's letter to me. He left it there for me to find."

She took out her precious letter and passed it to her mother, less all the extra pages that outlined the numerous magical items. Lloyd came around to her side of the table and read it over her shoulder. Lindsey recalled how she had cried a whole lot as she read it. Lena did too. Even Lloyd was quite moved, and had to wipe a tear from his eye as well. When she had finished, tears streaming down her face, she hugged Lindsey and said repeatedly, "I never knew. I never knew."

"I know mom; I didn't either." After her mother regained her composure, Lindsey said, "Mom, I want to give you a wedding present and something to help support my new home. I am going to pay off the mortgage today. Then our house is our house, always. This way, mom, I can contribute for the first time in my life. You have always had to help me so much, now this is one small thing I can do to help around here. You must let me do this, mom."

"Lindsey! That is an enormous amount of money," Lena protested.

"Mom, that's a drop in the bucket. Dad left me a whole pile of money. If you ever need money, let me know. I've now got so much that I don't know what to do with it all. I paid Governor Alister for my next five years at Bradbury's too. This way, they can give the full scholarship to someone else who really needs it, like I used to need it. Please mom, let me help this time?"

"She has a point, Lena," Lloyd added.

"You are sure this will not drain you of your inheritance, Lindsey? Swear this to me? You know I can't live with myself if I find out you spent it all on the mortgage."

"I promise, mom. Governor Alister counted it for me, I think this is not even a tenth of what dad left for me," Lindsey explained. Lena and Lloyd gasped! To them, this was a staggering sum indeed.

Her mother agreed at last. Once lunch was done, Lena went to dress up for her wedding, and Lindsey went into their bedroom with her to assist. "I've still got my fancy wedding dress that I wore when I married your father. I hope it still fits me."

"If it doesn't mom, I can use some of my new useful spells on it." Indeed, it didn't fit; Lena had filled out a bit more in the intervening fifteen years. While her mother watched fascinated, Lindsey used a combination of Sew, Mend, and Alter spells on the lovely white gown, until it fit her perfectly.

"Gosh mom, I ought to wear my new dress too!" Lindsey retrieved one of her bags and got out her fancy silk dress that her mother had made for her ball a few days ago. Soon, the two women looked at themselves in the mirror and were satisfied. Hesitantly, like a schoolgirl, Lena walked out to meet Lloyd, who had already changed into his grey suit. His mouth fell open for a second.

"Oh my goodness, Lena, you look absolutely gorgeous! Lindsey, you are a knock out. Incredible women, you two are. Allow me," he extended an arm for each and led them out of the small ranch house. He had already hitched up their buggy, and he lifted each in turn into their seats. They took a short buggy ride into Plano and their local Justice of the Peace.

The wedding was simple and done in five minutes. Lindsey giggled when he said, "You may now kiss your bride." Not since she had been a little girl had she seen her mother so happy, her face so full of life. To Lindsey, now thirteen, this seemed a miracle of magnitude.

Lloyd took them to the Dairy Queen for an ice cream dish, which they ate as they rode back to the ranch, along the gravel road that Lindsey had run down so many times before. Seeing their happy faces, Lindsey wanted to do something special for them today. When they got home, she said, "You two sit out here on the porch. I'm going to fix you a wedding supper. How's that?"

"Have you learned how to cook? Well, I guess you've watched me so many times that you can do it. All right, we'll enjoy the afternoon. Holler if you need anything."

While the two embraced on the swing, thinking Lindsey couldn't see them (she peeked around the open door and stifled a giggle), she finally went into the kitchen. Most everything was already packed in boxes. She also realized that, although she had watched her mother cook many times, she had never done anything but make a pot of tea before. A minute later, she had her laptop up and running. A MagGoogle later, she began picking out an order. She decided on roast duck with almonds and added a small wedding cake to the order. Carefully, she entered her new bank account number and their location here on the ranch. The location was all point and click on maps, whose scale steadily increased until she could even click on their ranch house. Incredible what the norm's geo-satellites could do. Another click and the order was sent. Arrival time: 5 p.m.

"Need any help?" Lena called out several times. Lindsey yelled back no she didn't, and giggled.

Precisely on time, a package materialized in their dining room. "Cool!" she exclaimed and began undoing the package. The food was steaming hot still, and she set their table, adding a few spells without her wand. "Okay, you can come in now. Happy wedding day mom and dad." It felt strange calling him dad, but it felt even weirder calling him stepdad.

Arm in arm, the two entered and gasped. There were two red candles burning in the center of the table, which was covered with a fancy white linen cloth. White paper banners arced overhead. A small wedding cake sat in the middle of the table, and the large platter holding the duck was to its right, and several other bowls lay to the left of the candles and cake. Picture perfect, thought Lindsey, who had modeled this from a picture in a magazine she had once seen in school in Plano.

"You did all this?" Lena said flabbergasted.

She giggled, "Er, no, you were right, mom; there is more to cooking than just watching someone else do it. I ordered out. I hope you like it. They served this at Bradbury's Final Banquet. Jim—he's on our track team and Amanda's brother and who took me to the formal dance—he said I should try it. I liked it, so I hope you two do too. Besides, aren't you supposed to have a wedding cake?"

Lindsey got out her cell phone and took a number of wedding pictures, even one with the two trying to feed cake into the other's mouth. Her mother was incredibly happy with everything, which made Lindsey feel like a million. When they were finished, Lindsey suggested, "Why don't you two go for a walk, and I'll clean everything up?"

"But Lindsey, this is a mess. I should help."

"Mom, I can use my new helpful spells—only take me a jiffy. Besides, it's your wedding day." Somewhat reluctantly, she and Lloyd went outside to take a stroll around the ranch. "Clean," Lindsey commanded and soon had everything washed up and back in its place.

Then, she remembered her friends. Hastily, she got her laptop up once more and checked her email. Already she had several from her friends. Ignoring these which she'd read later, she began typing an email to Amanda.

A. You'll never, ever guess where I will be tomorrow, where my new ranch home will be!

A while later, she clicked Send and began reading the notes from Amanda, Pam, Kathy, Emilio. Even Jim had sent her one.

Sometime later, they returned from their walk. Lindsey realized that there was only one bedroom in this place. Lloyd had been sleeping in the tiny bunkhouse behind the main small cabin. This would never do, she thought. Her bed was on one wall of the room, while her mom's larger bed was against the opposite wall. Hastily, she cast several spells. "Create: Partition. Oops. Create: Door." Shortly, she had made a wall blocking her small bed from the rest of the room.

"Okay, I have the bedroom fixed up, mom. Come and see." Both the adults chuckled at her improvisation.

"Lindsey, Lloyd could just as easily stay in the bunkhouse for one night," Lena said.

"I know mom, but this is your wedding night. I think that you two are supposed to sleep together that night, but I'm not totally sure about that."

Lena smiled. "You are growing up way too fast, Lindsey. Okay, you win. You're making me feel like I was a queen or something today."

"You are," echoed Lindsey and Lloyd at the same time, then smiling at each other.

At dawn, Lindsey was awakened by her mother making breakfast for them. "Wake up, dear; movers will be here in an hour. We have to get the rest packed." Lloyd was outside handling the last minute chores. All their many animals were corralled, fed, and waiting transport to their new ranch, when Lloyd finally entered for breakfast.

No sooner had he sat down to eat than they heard the noise of a truck pulling up outside. "Hope you don't mind," the livestock truck driver said, when Lloyd and Lena went outside to see who had come. "Got here a bit early. Plano's only a mile away."

Lena left Lloyd to handle the loading of the livestock, while she returned to eat. "Don't' worry mom. I'll turn his breakfast into a takeout order."

"There is so much to do at the last minute!"

"I'll handle the table and the kitchen; you work on the rest. How's that?" Lindsey gulped her food down and began fixing Lloyd's into a sack lunch affair. Using her helpful spells, she had the rest of the kitchen gear packed within minutes. Her mom insisted that she lend Lloyd a hand, so she went outside in time to lead Betsy, her mare, into the livestock wagon.

No sooner had they finished loading the huge cattle semi, than the second semi arrived with three strong men, ready to move the household items. Considering that Lena had very little, only an hour was needed for everything to be loaded. The tractor had a large cabin space behind the driver's bench and the three climbed in here, while the men squeezed into the front. From the little window, Lindsey watched as her childhood home slowly vanished from sight. The pit of her stomach felt a little strange, however, as though she was losing something.

Out of Plano, they took a state road and then connected to US 40, heading east. About forty minutes later, she saw a sign that said Arapahoe ahead. About a mile before reaching the small town, the trucks turned onto a county road, going north and then shortly headed up a long gravel road. "Our ranch, Lindsey. That was the cattle barrier we crossed. See the three irrigated crop circles there and there?" her mother pointed out, very excited about their good fortune to have acquired this ranch.

A few minutes later, they pulled up at the ranch house. It was triple the size of their old home. Stately aspen trees dotted the homestead. The barn lay further to the north. However, Lindsey saw three Indians mounted on horses, standing beneath the trees. "Looks like we have visitors," Lloyd commented.

"Yahoo!" Lindsey exclaimed. It was Amanda, Jim, and

Tom! It seemed forever before she could scramble out of the back compartment to greet her friends. She and Amanda gave each other a big hug. They only had a short time for introductions, however, as the movers were ready to begin unloading.

Amanda said quickly, "Mom sent along some lunch for you to welcome you to our area. We can help you unload and unpack." Lena gave her a hug and said thanks. Soon, the boys were off helping with the livestock, while the girls joined Lena inside the new home. Boxes came in fast, and Lena could barely keep up with giving the workers directions on which room to put which into. Finally, the last box was unloaded and the semi left. Shortly after that, the livestock semi also left, and everyone piled into the kitchen to relax and chat.

"Lindsey, your room is the last on down that hall. Why don't you show your friends your room, and they can help you unpack," Lena suggested.

"Wholly cow! Jumping grasshoppers! That's a Staff of Power!" exclaimed Tom, as they entered her room. At once, all three had to examine it.

"Margarete is her name," Lindsey explained. "My dad left it to me. Alister got it attuned to me now. Watch this." She walked to the far side of her room and requested her staff come to her. All three were impressed as the staff shot across the room and into her hand.

"Whoa, now that *is* cool!" exclaimed Amanda.

"Gosh, Lindsey, no other student has their own Staff of Power!" Jim added.

Lindsey showed them the other items she had gotten from her father. "What, you mean if I shoot a fireball at you while you are wearing this robe, it will do absolutely nothing to you?" asked Tom, completely amazed.

"That's what dad's letter said, though I don't want to try just now, in case it doesn't," Lindsey admitted.

"Well, I didn't think your father would have just gotten rid of all his things, Lindsey." Jim added. Lindsey related all that had happened at the vault. The three were keenly interested in the details. None had ever been to such a place. Finally, they helped Lindsey unpack and make her bed. With four magic users, that took all of five minutes, as helpful spells flew rapidly. Soon, they wandered back into the kitchen at the other end of the house.

Even though it was not yet lunchtime, they were hungry. Their hasty breakfast was long gone. Lena had unpacked enough for the six to dine on what Amanda's mother sent over. It was a simple, hearty stew, easy to warm up, satisfying to eat, and filling. "Please thank your mother for her kindness. This hits the spot. We are going to be hours unpacking all this stuff, and I don't have that much. It must take others days to pack and unpack," Lena declared.

"We can help, mom."

"No, why don't you go outside and play. Lloyd and I need to figure out the best places for things."

"Say, could we take Lindsey to see our home?" Amanda spoke up. "We can show her the way. It's only about five miles by horseback. Then, she will know how to come visit us."

Lindsey was about to put on her most pleading look, but it was not needed. Lena said, "That's a great idea. Betsy needs some exercise too. Just have her back by suppertime and don't forget to tell your mother thanks for me. Lindsey, you make sure you thank her properly."

On their way to saddle up Betsy, Amanda said, "Lindsey, this is *so* cool! Never in a million years did I think that we would end up being neighbors!"

"And we are only five miles away. Now we can all practice our running together," Jim added.

"Golly, I feel lost, Amanda. I don't know where anything is. I've never seen this ranch before."

"We have. We used to work a bit for old Haskell, doing odd jobs around here," Jim explained. "Your ranch is a square, five miles on a side. There is an Osage orange fence post line all around it. Back that way is the arroyo. We go down it to the bottom, follow along it to the first fork to the right, and go up that fork and you eventually run smack into our home. You can't get lost."

"Don't say that, Jim. If she makes the wrong turn, she can go off for miles and miles and find nothing," Amanda protested his oversimplification.

Lindsey hopped into her saddle, while the three fetched their mounts. The four headed off to the east, passing over their new pastureland. Although still part of the high plains, the pasture here was substantially better than at her old ranch. In just under three miles, they came to the fence line. Near the start of the arroyo, there was a gate. Jim dismounted and opened it for the group and then closed it again. Now the fun part began, down the tree-lined slopes they rode until they reached the bottom. "Got to look out for rattlers around here," Jim warned.

Lindsey only saw one during the trip, sunning itself on a boulder off to their left. After about a mile, there was indeed a fork veering south, which they took. "We're on the reservation now," Jim explained. It's a small one, though, just ten miles to the north of US 40 and five to the south of it and about five miles wide, more like a strip, really. About five hundred of us live around here, most work in the casino and live in Arapahoe proper. We all get royalties a plenty from the casino, though, tribal thing. Our folks are traditionalists and believe in living in the open spaces, not in town. Our place is about two miles from town."

"Do you get lots of money in royalties from the casino?" Lindsey asked.

"Heck yes!" Tom replied. "Gamblers flock here from Kansas, especially on weekends. Most folks living in town have all the latest electronics, giant TVs and all that. However, our folks, well, they prefer making their own away in the world. Don't get me wrong; we have a TV, but a small one, nothing much on it, though. Dad dislikes Hugo and won't listen to MagNews. Mom does a little, though."

"You'll probably like mom and dad," Jim added. "They are an awful lot like your mom. You'll see." Now the bed began to rise, as they started climbing up out of the arroyo. Finally, they reached the top. Jim reigned in. Lindsey saw an old log sitting near the edge of the hilltop. "My log. This is my favorite spot. I come here and lookout over the land. See, Lindsey, you can see for miles and miles." She looked; the view was spectacular.

"Yes, but there is nothing out there, just dry plains,"

Amanda countered. "Pretty boring, if you ask me." Jim glared at her, and she giggled back at him. "Come on, Lindsey; there's our home up ahead.

They lived on this vast hilltop. Off to the left was a corral and several other horses whinnied to Betsy. To the right lay an adobe and earthen home, partially under the ground. Prairie grasses grew on its roof, which sloped back into hillside behind it. All manner of junk lay strewn around the premises, as if this were someone's junkyard.

As they rode up, Tom called out, "Hey, Sandy's here. That's her horse there tied to the corral. She wanted to come with us today, but had to work. She's probably inside with mom and Fern."

"My younger sister, she's going to be a first year Yellow Hall student this fall. We found out about it this morning. Sandy's probably telling her all about what to bring and all that," Amanda explained.

"Cool! Boy, there sure is a lot of old stuff around here," Lindsey said as they dismounted and tied up their horses. Betsy began snorting and sniffing at those in the corral.

"Dad's an inventor," Amanda explained. Tom had dashed off to find Sandy, while Jim and Amanda walked Lindsey towards their house. "This old weather vane here is his snow depth predictor. See these notches, the vane points to the expected snowfall depth. That old gas pump over there is actually an Alerter. It sounds a noise when unexpected people show up within a thousand yards of our place. It does work."

Jim added quickly, "Dad's made this house too, his energy efficient home. It doesn't look like much, but it really stays quite warm in the winter and surprisingly cool even in the dog days of August. We don't need an air conditioner like the one you have at your new house. The walls are three feet thick and sound proof as well. Dad had them enchanted to repel many spells that someone might attack us with."

"Most of this stuff out here actually is magically enchanted, believe it or not," Amanda finally broke in as they reached the front door. Lindsey was surprised to see that in place of a door, a wool, homespun Indian blanket hung down. One merely pushed it aside to enter. Two old, rusty cans sat on either side of the doorway. "Those keep all the vermin out. It actually works, but dad can't seem to sell others on buying them. I told him to use some really nice looking pots or cans and people might buy them."

Inside was incredibly different than outside. The home was very large and very filled with furniture and household items. "This is our front room and living room, you can tell I bet," Amanda said. Indeed, couches, stuffed chairs predominated. A TV was in one corner along with end tables piled with books; magazines and brochures lay scattered about. Sandy and Tom were in one corner, exchanging a welcome kiss, while a younger girl tried not to notice, staring hard at the papers in her hand.

As they entered, she jumped up and came dashing over to the three. She was tall and spindly, at least six inches taller than Lindsey was and as tall as Tom. Like Amanda, she had long black hair, bushy black eyebrows, and the same darker skin tones. Her eyes were bright and eager; her smile, infectious. "You must be Lindsey! I'm Fern. I'm going to be in Yellow Hall with you this fall! I'm so glad to meet you at long last!"

She timidly shook Lindsey's hand, while looking at them, as if they might fall off if she shook them too hard. "No, they don't hurt and are good and strong," Lindsey put her at ease. "That's great you are going to be with us this fall. Do you run too?" She was thinking about how they were going to replace Bill, who had graduated and would not be coming back this fall.

"Yes, but not like Amanda or Jim or Tom. I like to run shorter distances. It's too boring to run for very long. Did you really. . ." She did not get to finish her sentence. A tall older woman entered the room and interrupted her.

"Well, you must be our new neighbor—Lindsey Barron. You look fit. I was a bit worried about you when I heard all that you had been through this past term. I'm Lucinda Morning Dove Whitewater, but everyone just calls me Luci. Here, I'll take that pail. Did you like the stew?"

"Oh yes. Mom says to tell you thank you very much. We were starving and hadn't yet got the kitchen stuff unpacked."

Luci was around forty, but still had a very pretty face, with even longer black hair than her daughters had. Her eyes radiated kindness. She was the type of person around whom everyone felt instantly relaxed, as though she was their mother. She waved her wand, and the pail disappeared, probably into the kitchen Lindsey assumed.

"Have a seat, dear. Jim, move those books. You promised you'd move them before you left and now she's here and we've no place to sit except on your books." Jim reddened and hastily swished his book pile into another pile in the far corner of the room. "Would you like anything to drink, Lindsey? Tom, will you and Sandy please stop kissing. You are embarrassing your little sister. We have company, you know."

"No thanks. I'm still full from your stew. It really is quite cool inside here."

"Yes, R. B.'s invention. We save a bundle on heating and cooling, though why we need to save money is beyond me. We get so much from the casino revenues that we can't spend it all. Fern, stop staring at Lindsey. You are making her feel uncomfortable. You must forgive her. We've all heard of the awful time you have had with that evil Dominus Malefic. It must have been just horrible for you. I'm sure glad that Amanda had the good sense to track you so they could rescue you and just in time, the way she tells it."

"Tells what?" came a deep voice from a side room doorway. R. B. came walking into the room, his hands still fiddling with some new device. He was also around forty years old, with long black hair as well, though his ended at his shoulders, not the small of his back as did Luci's and Amanda's. He had strange blue eyes, but was keenly alert, giving one the impression of being slightly absentminded. His mind was usually on his next invention.

"Dear, this is Miss Lindsey Barron. She's come for a visit. We were talking about her horrible experience this term, with you know who," Luci said. Lindsey detected that Luci really wanted to hear all about it first hand, but was trying to be polite and only hint that it was okay for Lindsey to relate the tale.

Unexpectedly, R. B. said to Lindsey, "Knew Rabnor,

Sam Rabnor, I did. Made a few things for him, hum, yes I did." Lindsey's mouth opened wide in surprise as did everyone else's in the room.

"R. B. you never told me," Luci protested.

He ignored her interruption with his thoughts, "Let me see you up close." He walked to the stuffed chair in which Lindsey sat and looked her up and down. "By golly, see lots of Sam in you, Lindsey. You've his eyes and high cheekbones, oh, and his legs. He always was a good runner. I see you are wearing his ring and pin. Enchanted them for him, I did, been twenty some years since I've last seen these though. Recognize them anywhere."

"Wow, you did? You knew my dad?" Lindsey said keenly interested. Here was someone who knew him and was at least talking about him to her.

"Yes, my sister Monane Tumble—she was Monane Whitewater back then—and I went to Bradbury's with him. We were in the same class. Both of us were close friends with him. Afterwards, when he went into the Dispeller business, he made those two items and had me enchant them for him. Also made some other things for him. I wonder whatever became of that writing desk. Probably long gone now," he lamented.

"Wow, no, no, it's still there. It's in my vault in Denver. It the coolest desk, sir! Only I didn't bring it home with me because in our old house, there wasn't any room for it, and I didn't know we were moving. Can you tell me stories about my dad, sir? No one else will say much about him, though I don't know why?"

"R. B., dear, just R. B.—for Running Bear. No one seems to like long names any more, do they, Lucinda Morning Dove Whitewater? Always in a hurry, these younger folks are, cannot take time to say a beautiful name for a beautiful woman." She flushed.

"Well, I'll tell you stories about your father, if you'll tell us all about what happened at school with Dominus. Amanda has told us her side of the story, but Luci and I would really like to hear it firsthand, you know, not someone else's take on what you said. If it is too painful for you, that is perfectly fine. I certainly don't want to upset a pretty young girl."

"No, I don't mind, but it is pretty horrible though."

"Ah, drinks, Luci? Is it cokes that you kids want these days?" he asked. Fern nodded enthusiastically, and a carton of cold sodas appeared on an end table.

Jim opened the case and popped the top on one, handing it to Lindsey. "Dad's always doing that, bringing in refreshments without using a wand." He was teasing, of course.

Amanda could not help resist adding, "According to Professor Janice, you failed that spell, dad. Your wand failed to activate." Tom, Jim, and Amanda chuckled, and Lindsey giggled.

He looked shell-shocked. "What? We're supposed to use wands? Now why didn't someone ever tell me that?" Everyone roared with laughter. Evidently, this was his favorite jest to play on new guests.

Lindsey then began relating her tale, starting with opening the restroom door and suddenly coming face to face with herself. Fern gasped and held her hands across her mouth. As Lindsey described in detail what had happened, Fern's hands went white from the pressure she was exerting to keep from distracting Lindsey with her shock.

"And then Amanda was at my side helping me to stand up. She helped me all the way back to the Infirmary, where Doctor Caterwall fixed me up once more. Good as new," she waved her hands about.

"Hum, amazing, amazing. Oh," he looked up at Amanda, and another thought flashed through his mind, "Very good job daughter. You repeated the story most accurately. Matches what Lindsey says. Again, Amanda, very well done on protecting your friend here." Lindsey realized that he'd probably already said that to her many times before.

However, he looked at Lindsey once more. "Very like Sam you are. He operated that way, same as you, never says a word, just casts the spells, and likes improvisations. I remember the day that Monane, Sam, and I were taking our final exam in first year spells. Monane and I spent all weekend working out the best way to get through all the spells. Amanda says you two did this as well. Anyway, old Sam, he teased us, said, 'Wing it R. B. Be creative.' Come the day of the test, Monane and I, we followed our perfectly laid out plans, got them all, we did. Sam, he just starts shooting off the spells at random. First, he starts the fire but then puts a fog over it, and then he puts light into the mess. By the time he had all the spells piled up there, the whole class was laughing at it. Monane and I lost an entire minute of those forty-five laughing at his improvisation. However, he still needed his wand for the spells that first year, not like you, Lindsey."

"No, I reckon it was in our second year that he discovered he didn't need a wand anymore nor to say the command words. He was ornery; Sam was, after that. Oh, he'd go around playing tricks on other students, especially those in Black Hall. Hated one of them the most, though I never knew just why, though. He'd see Jimmy walking to class and Enlarge Jimmy's butt, without saying a thing, wand in his pocket. Caused a lot of laughs with his antics though."

Lindsey, who had previously only thought of her father as this incredibly kind and loving man, who somehow was a powerful Dispeller, capturing the most evil of criminals, now began to see a typical boy, using his skills to play childish pranks. She resolved not to do as her father had done—no childish pranks from her, though she began to see how she could make Deiter's life miserable, if he continued to harass her.

"Oh, before I forget it, Lindsey, we all know that Dominus and his nasty henchmen will likely be trying to come after you. So I made you a little invention of my own." He handed her a lucky rabbit's foot on a little chain.

"Dad, she doesn't need a lucky norm's charm. They don't work and you know it," Jim came to her rescue, believing that was what it was, nothing more.

R. B. ignored his son, "You are to wear this on your person at all times. It can be inside a pocket for instance. If ever someone approaches you with the intention to harm you, the rabbit's foot will begin to move around, attracting your attention. It's a little new invention of mine. I'm going to try to sell it at the next Wizard Inventor's Convention this fall. This way, Lindsey, you will have a little advance warning, though I realize that it might not have been enough to help you avoid that surprise in the restroom, but it would have been jumping around as you approached the restroom, so you could have decided not to go into the restroom you see."

"Wow! Cool. This is incredibly useful, sir, er R. B. Thank you so much!" She gave him a hug. He had that smug look on his inventor's face that said to the rest of his family, "So there!"

"Well, I had better get back to Mrs. Rainweather's rat eliminator. She wants it tomorrow; got many rats around her place, she says. Why don't you come around some evenings, and we can tell more stories? Bring your folks. I suspect they might like to meet us." Lindsey promised that she would. She could not resist! She'd learned more about her father in the last few minutes than she'd heard all year.

"Well, I've got cleaning to do. Why don't you show Lindsey around our house and your room, Amanda? I'm sure she would love to see your room."

As Amanda walked her around their house, Lindsey was continually amazed at the spaciousness, though each room was as cluttered as the next. As they approached Jim's room, he dashed inside and said, "Don't show her my room yet. I left it in a big mess!" Lindsey heard him hastily calling out, "Clean! Clean! Clean!"

In stark contrast to the other rooms, Amanda's room was as neat as their dorm room—everything was in its proper place. She had a large picture of their group hanging on the wall so she could look at her friends while lying in her bed. She had her own radio, TV, and computer station all in one well-made oak console, which also acted as a desk.

"Here, have a mom-made serape," Amanda gave her one of the Indian blankets that her mother had made for her. She'd woven the blanket and then put a head hole in its center and affixed a tying belt around the waist. "I've got a dozen of them now. Mom never knows when to quit making them for us. I suspect she will now start making them for you and your mom as well. They are warm, I will admit that."

"Come and see my room, now," Fern interrupted, greatly desiring to show off her room. Grinning, the two followed Fern into the next bedroom. Like Amanda's room, Fern's was also very neat. However, one thing really impressed Lindsey. Fern loved flowers. Her room had ten blooming plants, but the plants were growing from the walls!

"It's good dirt, I mean the walls. I cut niches in them and planted the seeds myself. I have a living room!" She was very proud of her accomplishment, and Lindsey complimented her on her inventiveness. "Honestly, I know our house looks very strange to most people when they first see it, but it is incredibly cool inside. No one else can have plants growing in their walls!"

Next, she showed Lindsey the boys' room. Tom's looked like a disaster had struck—books, dirty clothes, and clean ones lay scattered about the room. When they entered Jim's room, he was still frantically trying to clean his room up. Lindsey guessed that it had been as messy as Tom's. However, Amanda whispered to her, "Pretend you don't see your picture on the wall over there." She glanced there naturally. Jim had taken the photograph of the five friends, cropped everyone else out except Lindsey, and blown her picture up quite large. Lindsey flushed and pretended not to notice.

"Come on. I'll show you the kitchen next," Amanda whisked her out of Jim's room, leaving him to finish cleaning it up. "I think he has a crush on you, but don't tell him I said so. He's never cleaned his room like that before." A while later, they went outside to see their horses and barn. Amanda introduced her friend to their dog, whose name was Stinky.

"We call him that because as a puppy, he kept making very stinky messes. He doesn't seem to mind that name," Fern explained.

Shortly, after that, Jim came outside, joining them. He pointed out, "You see that second bend way down the arroyo there, beyond the turnoff to get to your place? Well, we run there and back and that is just about five miles. Of course, the last part is up hill, making it harder than in our competitions. We all should practice every other day. Tom's going to work out a schedule for us. I'd love to have you come and run with us. If Fern gets on the track team this year, we may have a better chance of winning than ever before."

"Yes, but we should be trying to go twenty miles, Jim, not five. I got horribly pooped and winded by the last race," Lindsey pointed out. Jim agreed with her.

Around four, Lindsey decided that she should head back home. Although she thought that she could easily find her way back alone, Jim would not let her. In fact, Fern and Sandy also rode back with the group, so they could see where Lindsey now lived. As she rode up to her new corral, she turned to wave goodbye to her friends. This promised to be the best summer ever! Lindsey watched her friends riding back the way they'd come. She felt so alive, so happy.

The End.

A Favor to Other Readers

How about helping other readers? Many readers rely on reviews to make the decision whether to buy a book. You can help them make their decision by leaving your opinions and viewpoint in a short review of the positive things of this book. Writing the review and expressing your opinion only takes a few minutes, and other readers will appreciate your efforts.

Click this link: Volume 1 The Rod of the Apocalypse scroll down to Customer Reviews; click on Write a Review, and enter your review. Thank you.

Author Information

Visit My Amazon.com Author Page
Vic Broquard Author Page

Follow My Blog
Vic Broquard's Blog

Follow Me on Social Media
Facebook
Google+
LinkedIn
YouTube

Other Books by Vic Broquard

Without Warning (fantasy)

The Trident Series: (fantasy)
>   Volume 1 The Trident and the Book
>   Volume 2 The Trident and the Scepter
>   Volume 3 The Trident and the Resurrection

The Adventures of Elizabeth Stanton Series: (science fiction)
>   Volume 1 The Evolution of the Path
>   Volume 2 The Great Messiah
>   Volume 3 Of Kings and Queens and Troubadours
>   Volume 4 Chaos in the Aftermath
>   Volume 5 Power Plays
>   Volume 6 Age of Exploration
>   Volume 7 Abducted
>   Volume 8 The Emperor and Empress
>   Volume 9 A Job Worth Doing
>   Volume 10 Degradation
>   Volume 11 The Second Crusade
>   Volume 12 When Worlds Collide
>   Volume 13 Dark Ages

The Lindsey Barron Series: (fantasy)
>   Volume 1 The Rod of the Apocalypse
>   Volume 2 The Board of Governors
>   Volume 3 The Crown of Moses
>   Volume 4 Dominus for President
>   Volume 5 The National Health Care Program
>   Volume 6 States Justice
>   Volume 7 Cross and Double-cross

Zoran Chronicles Series: (fantasy)
>   Volume 1 A Dragon in Our Town
>   Volume 2 Dragons, Power, Courts, and War

Planet of the Orange-red Sun Series: (science fiction)
Volume 1 When Kingdoms Fall
Volume 2 Dark Ages
Volume 3 Age of the Towers
Volume 4 Difficillis Exitus
Volume 5 Age of the Lords
Volume 6 The Renegade Tower
Volume 7 Rebellions
Volume 8 The Aliens Return
Volume 9 Power Struggles
Volume 10 Guilds, Genetics, and Gods
Volume 11 Magi, Witches, Swords, and Superstitions
Volume 12 The Voyage of the Eagle's Seed
Volume 13 Eagle's Seed and Origins
Volume 14 Justifications
Volume 15 Responsibilities

The Return of the Wizards: Twelve Companions – The Making of Wizards (fantasy)